Hearts of
The Dark Forest, B
Lisa Kumar

Cover Art: Trif Book Designs

Copyright © 2021 Lisa Kumar

This is a work of fiction, so any resemblance to persons, locales, or events is purely coincidental. The characters, locales, and events are products of the author's imagination or are used fictitiously.

The ebook format of this work may not be re-sold or copied. Except for brief quotations for book reviews, no part of this publication may be reproduced without the prior written permission of both the copyright owner and publisher of this book.

Table of Contents

Copyright Page 1

Hearts of Tar..7

Books by Lisa...8

Dedication 10

Into the Woods 11

The Earth Consumes from Below................................ 18

Getting His Creep On.. 22

The Ivy Ladder... 26

Danger Comes on Wings 29

The Paths We Trod 33

Mud Walls 37

The Dimming of Beauty.. 41

Cornering the Mouse... 45

From the Tree 49

People of the Darkness 53

Succor... 57

Burning 61

Unfulfilled.. 65

Vigil	69
Longing	73
Reticence	77
Sickness	82
Wicked Need	86
Cruel Awakening	92
The Dawning of Realization	97
The Bathing Chamber	101
Rude Interruption	105
Rash Decisions	109
Bittersweet Reunion	113
Hopeful Plans	117
Garden Rendezvous	121
Breathe You In	125
Frustration	130
Insubordination	136
Many Firsts	143
The Plan	153
Walking with a Monster	158

Sick Fear	166
Baby Blues	174
Chase	183
Giving in to the Heat	192
Foil	197
Secrets Leashed	206
Secrets Unleashed	214
Visiting We Shall Go	224
Unveiled	233
Advised	239
Panicked	246
Stumble	252
Forest on Fire	259
Mind Joining	266
Leafy Escapades	273
The Lighter Fae	280
The Spirit and Miri	286
Rousing Miri	294
The Question	306

Wedded..312

ABOUT THE AUTHOR..320

To learn more about Lisa and her books, visit https://linktr.ee/LisaKumar | Once there, you'll find links to Lisa's newsletter and Readers' Group. 321

Bound to the Elvin Prince | Mists of Eria, Book One...............322

Excerpt...323

Bound to the Dark Elf | Mists of Eria, Book Three..................326

Excerpt...327

The Fae Lord's Companion | The New Earth Chronicles, Book One 331

Hearts of Tar

She entered his woods. Now she can never leave.

When twenty-year-old Miri Summerland follows her younger sister into the Dark Woods, she thinks death is to be their fate. Instead, their lives are shaped into something so much more gloriously worse at the hands of the handsome but otherworldly fae leader, Eerin. He and his people have blackness flowing through their veins, but she wonders just how truly dark they are.

Compelled by magic and the Change, she embarks on an intimate relationship with the human-hating leader that leaves her awash in desire and confusion. Will something more come out of their mutual need, or will they lose their lives and people to a love that should've never existed?

Books by Lisa

Mists of Eria Series:
Bound to His Fate, Prequel
Bound to the Elvin Prince, Book One
Bound to the Elvin King, Book Two
Bound to the Dark Elf, Book Three
The New Earth Chronicles:
The Fae Lord's Companion, Part One
The Fae Lord's Companion, Part Two
The Fae Lord's Companion, Part Three
The Fae Lord's Companion, the Complete Edition
Love in Time Series (Time-travel Regency):
An Earl in Time
Saving Lord Avingdale
The Faerin:
Falling for the Driade, Book One (previously part of the anthology Crashing into You)
Falling for the Leonidas, Book Two (previously part of the anthology Like a Firework)
Other Titles:
Elven Lord for Christmas
To Claim a Dragon

Hearts of Tar
Copyright © 2021 Lisa Kumar
All rights reserved.
To learn more about Lisa and her books, visit https://linktr.ee/LisaKumar

On there, you'll find links to Lisa's newsletter and Readers' Group.

Dedication

Thanks to my family and friends for supporting me during all my writing craziness.

Into the Woods

"Catch me if you can!"

"Eve, come back here!" Faltering to a stop, Miri Summerland gave an exasperated smile as a small figure dressed in blue streaked away from her. With a sigh, she placed a hand on her aching side. Her little sister could run fast, but she was even quicker. A tiny stitch wouldn't stop her.

She gave chase again, and the distance they covered melted away under their feet. Eve's giggles drifted back to her. Exhilaration welled within Miri, and a merry laugh bubbled up her throat. This was the way to spend a glorious, sunny morning free from their father's scholarly lessons. The red of Eve's hair was easy to see as her sister bobbed and weaved over the hilly terrain.

Miri suddenly grimaced. Maybe she needed to stop giving Eve such a head start. Thank heavens, summer was fading away, taking the worst of the heat with it. Growling in annoyance, she swiped at a loose brown lock that kept tumbling into her eyes. Her cursed hair was forever tumbling loose of any confines she imposed on it.

The stitch in her side returned with a vengeance and urged her to slow. As she opened her mouth to call a halt to their race, the words turned to ash on her tongue. A dark forest loomed far ahead, a black blob marring the bright day. *The Dark Woods.* God, had they come so far without her knowing it? Fear, deep and gaping, arose before her and consumed her whole. Creatures, strange and ferocious, were said to live in there. Neither she nor her sister had a weapon. Not that it would matter if they did, because they didn't know how to wield one.

"Eve, stop! Don't go in there!"

Her sister kept hurtling toward the forest, apparently deaf to her voice or purposefully ignoring it.

Miri cursed and sped up until her legs were going faster than they ever had. "Eve, for heaven's sakes, stop!"

Brambles and low-hanging branches bit into her clothes and skin the closer she came to the oily-looking, black-trunked trees. The pain was easy to dismiss, though. All her attention was frantically centered on Eve, who had yet to slow. In fact, her sister seemed hell-bent on getting to that dastardly woods as quickly as she could. That, in itself, was telling. Eve had always had a healthy fear of that forbidden area, as did every sane person from Knocton, their town, and the surrounding countryside. In fact, probably everyone in the nation of Enpel had one.

Miri screamed at her sister yet again, panic weaving a tight net around her. Damn it all, why was Eve not listening?

The seven-year-old didn't look back at her once. Soon, the branches of the forest cast their long shadow over Eve. A scream of anger and fright welled from Miri's throat. If her sister went in, she'd never come out. That she knew with a surety that horrified her to the core.

But on Eve flew, and she could only stare helplessly as the dark woods swallowed her. Miri's feet were still eating up the distance, but there was no longer a hint of Eve to be seen. Still, she couldn't stop. How could she leave her sister to suffer whatever lurked in that forest? She'd never forgive herself if she did, and she doubted her father would, either. Though he loved them both, Eve would always be his favorite.

Miri sprinted onward until she came to the edge of the woods. Without thought, she skidded to a halt, sheer terror freezing her in place for a moment. The black-as-tar tree trunks leaned drunkenly, as if they could fall any moment. With a shaky breath, she marshaled her runaway feelings into submission and crept across the invisible line that seemed to delineate safe land from that of the dangerous.

Immediately, the temperature plummeted, and cold wrapped around her like a shroud. Dark. It was so dark, and she didn't know which way to go. Eve still wasn't in sight—nor was anyone else. She wasn't sure if that was a stroke of good luck or not. Those cursed trees blocked out most of the light, their leaves covering the sky as if with tar.

She glanced warily at the trees surrounding her. Were they now closer than they'd been before? God, she had to get her imagination under control. Still, the close-set, greasy-looking trucks made her shy away from brushing against them. In places she'd have to turn sideways to slip in-between them.

Though she hated to move one step farther, she couldn't stand here and let her sister face this horror of a place alone. If she couldn't find the way, she'd have to make one—somehow. Picking a course, she set out in that direction. Twigs cracked under her hard-soled slippers, and each time, the sound echoed eerily in the silent forest. Where were the birds and the other animals that usually made their home amongst the trees? Maybe they were just as scared of these woods as she was and avoided it at all costs. Not a heartening thought.

Tension and fright bit at her spine, an almost palpable presence that drove her onward. Some primal instinct told her not to stay in one area for long. Though she questioned the sanity of calling out for her sister because she could draw unwelcome attention, she did it anyway. "Eve. Eve, c-come back now." Her voice broke.

There was no response, nothing drifting on the air that told her where her sister might be. She spun around hopelessly in a circle, awash in a sea of black.

That was when she heard it—a burst of faint laughter. She froze and strained her ears. *Eve!* But when the sound came again, it chilled her soul. The sinister tone and voice weren't anything her sister could produce. Someone else was near. Did they have Eve? Cold sweat weaved down the small of her back.

Though everything warned her to run back the way she'd come, her conscience wouldn't allow that. Plus, the way out of the forest was likely lost to her now, anyway. There was no tell-tale sign of the outside world. It seemed this woods would be her grave—and Eve's.

Releasing a shaky breath, she crept in toward the malicious laughter. Her numb feet refused to work properly, and she stumbled over a root. She landed on the leaf-littered ground with a crash that knocked the wind out of her lungs. Small rocks and twigs cut into her palms. Gritting her teeth, she tried to ignore the pain. Aware she was in a very vulnerable position, she began to push herself up, only to abruptly stop when she saw a pair of small, pink hooves not more than a foot away from her.

Her gaze slid upward, and she gulped. A short creature stood before her. Though it had the legs of a pig, the brown, furry body and head were that of a cat. The creature seemed to glare at her the way only felines could.

Miri slowly backed up on her hands and knees. The animal hissed, revealing sharp, pointed teeth. That was all she needed to be off and running. Oh, God, oh God. What was that abominable thing, and was it capable of hurting her? As she crashed through the trees, she prayed the animal wasn't following her. Her heart was so busy trying to jump out of her throat that she doubted she'd hear the pig-cat creature if it trailed her. Where had that creepy laughter been coming from, though? She spared a glance back. No sign of the animal.

After a few minutes, she slowed. Her eyes had adjusted to the darkness, not that reassured her. The gnarled woods looked as terrifying now as they had when she first entered them, but other than that hissing creature and the odd laughter, she'd found no other hint of sentient life. Whether that boded well for her sister, she didn't know.

Worry prodded her to move again, but which way? Something crunched loudly under her foot. She squinted at the ground. A stick of white poked from a mass of black leaves and moss. Frowning, she felt as if she should be able to recognize what it was. The answer hovered around the edges of her mind until the realization slammed into her. She recoiled a step back. Was...was that a bone? She shivered. No, not even going to investigate further. Just find Eve and go.

As she started to glance up, a splash of black snagged her attention. She cringed at the tar-like substance that stained her light-blue dress. The trees had done that? Though something desperately urged her to take off the soiled garment, she wasn't about to remove the only protection her skin had against the elements.

With a resoluteness she didn't feel, she picked a direction and headed that way. If she stood and did nothing, she'd never locate her sister. If they were to die in this place, they'd die together. Absentmindedly, she rubbed her forearm. A stinging sensation flared over her palm and fingers. With a hiss of pain, she jerked her hand away. The skin was raw and red, and there were traces of black dotting her palm. Her gaze flew to the sleeve she'd been so thoughtlessly touching. Black was smeared over it. Well, she now knew what the trees produced was a poison of some type.

She carefully lifted a clean portion of her skirt and wiped her hand on it. The rough fabric grated against her sore hand, but letting it remain on her would surely be the worse alternative. That done, she continued plodding toward only God knew what.

Suddenly, an icy quiver stole down her spine, and the skin on the back of her neck prickled. She was being watched. A careful glance around, though, revealed nothing. Nothing but the same dreadful trees.

After untold minutes had seeped by, she huffed in frustration. Not only did she still have that feeling of being followed, but she might as well be going around in circles. Everything looked the same. Every creepy, forbidding, goddamned tree seemed to mock her. That was crazy, right? Trees weren't alive, at least not like humans and animals were. But it was almost as if she could hear their sniggering on the air. However, whenever she strained her ears, there was nothing but the sound of her own footsteps.

The feeling was enough to madden her and drive a bit of the fear away. Was someone toying with her, or had her own mind turned traitor? She didn't know, which only angered her further.

With a growl, she turned around in a slow circle, glaring at the boughs of the trees. "Who's there? Reveal yourself!"

She didn't care if her challenge led to her death. Why postpone the evitable? Whatever was out there stalking her was probably doing the same to Eve. Hopefully, there would be some justice in this world, and she and her sister could die together.

The laughter from earlier blazed to life, closer than ever. Miri froze, trying to pinpoint from where the sinister noise was coming. It built in volume until it encompassed her from all sides. Damn, damn, was it more than one voice? The ground reverberated with the sound until it rattled her bones. She held out her arms for balance, but that did little to help, and she tumbled to the ground.

She managed to get on all fours before the trembling threatened to knock her down again. Her weary body protested. Tears welled in her eyes and spilled down her cheeks. Too much, this day had been too much.

The laughter exploded into a pinnacle that nearly blew her eardrums out. She curled onto her side so she could cover her ears. But when she did, her gaze landed on the trees. Oh, God, the trees were now leaning down menacingly. Grotesque faces formed on their trucks, and she screamed. She couldn't move. Both fright and the shaking of the ground held her hostage. One tree in particular folded down so low that its massive branches were but inches from her face. It glared at her from a snarling face, but the silver of its eyes mesmerized her.

"Human, you will never leave this forest," the tree said, its voice deep and rumbling.

All the breath left her lungs. She couldn't have formed a word even if she'd wanted to. Then the ground was collapsing away from her, and she was falling, spinning, into darkness until her body hit warm, soft earth with a jarring thud.

The Earth Consumes from Below

Miri groaned, not even attempting to move for a few moments. God, had she just fallen through the ground? Every inch of her body ached, and her mouth felt gritty. Turning her head to the side, she spat out dirt and fought not to gag. An earthy yet slightly metallic taste remained in her mouth. She didn't want to open her eyes—she really didn't. Could this all be some horrible nightmare? Maybe she was safe at home, wrapped up in bed.

Her eyelids fluttered open, but instead of the white-washed walls of the bedroom she shared with her sister, she was surrounded by glittering darkness. No, not a nightmare, then. Something worse than one—reality. She gave a whimpering sigh before gathering the last reserves of her strength. Fear would only hinder her, wasting precious minutes that she and her sister might not have.

Had she broken anything during her fall? A flexing of her limbs promised sore muscles later that day. When she moved her right shoulder, it gave more than a twinge. Wonderful, it felt dislocated.

She needed to get up and regain her bearings. Too bad her body didn't want to obey. Her fingers dug into something soft—more dirt? Shuddering, she refused to think about what creepy crawlies might be down here. With a grunt, she pushed herself onto her haunches and took her first good look at her new accommodations. Black walls that housed thousands of glittering lights stared back at her. Were those jewels lit from within? But how? She rolled her eyes. Really, she was asking herself this after all that had happened?

Curiosity drove her to her feet and toward one of the walls. Her feet hit something that felt suspiciously like a body. She swallowed back the lump in her throat and carefully squatted down. Though nothing was readily visible at first, was that the faint sheen of red hair? She reached a hesitant hand toward what she hoped was a person's shoulder. A living person's shoulder, at that.

Her fingers touched material, and soft, warm skin could be felt beneath. With her breath coming quicker and her lungs threatening to explode, she squinted and ran her hand over the person's face. Hot air puffed against her palm. At this confirmation of life, tears sprang to her eyes. She ghosted her hands over the curve of a jaw and cheek. The features felt small and childish. Her sister. Her Eve! She'd know her from anywhere.

With a sob breaking loose from her chest, she collapsed onto her backside. Her sister was alive! Was she unharmed, though? Some of her joy abated as quickly as it'd come. Eve certainly wasn't safe. Neither of them was, and there wasn't a damn thing she could do about it.

Indecision gnawed at her. She wanted to hold her sister, but her gown was covered in that tar. But then, it wasn't soaking through to her skin, so it probably wouldn't hurt Eve. Anyway, surely, her sister had brushed up against the trees, too. It'd been impossible to not do so. Without further thought, she gathered Eve in her arms. Her sister didn't stir. Miri's eyes slowly adjusted to this new level of darkness until she could see the outline of Eve's body.

Maybe if she got them closer to those glowing, sparkling things set into the walls, she'd be able to make out something more? She scooted them closer, though her shoulder screamed with every move. Her sister didn't wake, which she didn't know was a blessing or a curse. Once they were a few feet away from one of the walls, she blinked and blinked again. Those were flowers, not jewels? Petals gleamed with multi-faceted, mica-like flakes. They were so beautiful, so at odds with the forest and this dirt hole in the ground.

Her fingers itched to touch the blooms for some unfathomable reason, though she knew that probably wasn't the wisest choice. Still, she found herself leaning toward the wall. As her hand neared, the flowers glowed brighter. Miri gasped and pulled back. Then she tried it again with the same results—increased radiance. Still, she hadn't actually touched one of the flowers. What would happen if she did? Could it possibly give them a way out? That sounded crazy, but this whole episode could be defined as insane.

As her fingers brushed over one of the flowers, the ground shook. She ripped her hand back. Awe and fear rolled through her veins. By Omera's grace, had she done that? With any luck, the tremors would stop on their own. But they continued until her brain felt as if it were turning to mush and dripping from her nose. Though her shoulders ached from the weight of holding Eve, she swiped at her nostrils. Her palm came back with a slick spot. Blood. Even in the earthy-smelling chamber, the scent was unmistakable.

She grimaced. What a wonderful time to get a nosebleed. They were going to die like dogs in the dirt. Literally in the dirt, surrounded by pretty, luminous dirt walls. A hysterical giggle bubbled out of her throat. Was that what their lives had come to? Dirt?

Suddenly, a deafening rumble roared through her ears, and a blinding light flashed through the dim chamber. Her beleaguered eyes screwed shut. Almost immediately, the tremors died away.

God, what now? Could she just sit there until she died, pretending nothing existed until it didn't? No, there was Eve. There was always Eve. Miri was the next best thing her sister had to a mother. She had to remember that and not fail in her duty to protect her, no matter how worthless her efforts turned out to be.

With that thought ringing through her mind, she opened her eyes, and the booted pair of feet that stood before her appeared with surprising clarity. Her heart dropped to the floor. Oh, great skies above, not again. But these immaculate, finely tooled boots didn't belong to a pig-cat creature. These were human-sized and the legs that belonged to them were clothed in leggings that displayed taut muscles. A man? Her gaze slowly slid up the form. Narrow hips and waist, broad shoulders.

She gulped down her dread and continued her perusal. Hazy light cascaded from the open chasm in the ground above her, and it shone on the long, silvery hair that framed a sculpted face. A scream welled in her throat. A ferocious expression covered the male's handsome face, but that wasn't what terrified her into a near faint. No, it was the veins of black running underneath his deathly pale skin that shoved her over the edge.

Getting His Creep On

Eerin glowered down at the human interlopers that tarnished his forest by their very presence. Everyone knew that race was an inherent threat. Yet he couldn't kill these creatures as he so wanted to. Crossing his arms, he tamped down the urge to wring their necks. Damn the Spirit of the Woods—and its crystallina flowers—that had spoken and said they weren't to be harmed. That didn't mean he couldn't terrify them a bit. And he had. How long would it take for a human to go mad?

He sent the older awake one a vicious smile, making sure to show her a flash of sharp, pointed teeth. The human shrank away. A shot of pleasure coursed through him. They were always so easy to petrify, their fright like an aphrodisiac. He knew he presented a fearsome sight to one who'd never seen a Taelin fae before.

For the first time, he took in the human's appearance. Long brown hair coming free of a bun tumbled in a tangled mess around her shoulders and down her back. He snorted to himself derisively. Her creamy skin might be beautiful to her people, but it wasn't to his taste. No human female could compare to the Taelin ideal of loveliness— black-streaked, white skin. The paler the white and the blacker the streaks, all the better. This female's only saving grace was the hint of paleness lurking under the slight suntan.

For some reason, his perusal of her only angered him further. Why did he care if she were male or female? She was human. That was all he needed to know. Nothing else was of importance.

After marshaling his emotions back into a small steel box, he spoke in a quiet, slow voice. "Well, well, what do we have here?" He nearly grimaced at the sensation of the human tongue on his lips.

Blue eyes widened, and her grip tightened around the younger girl. The scent of her fear was a wonderful thing. Still, she didn't reply. Was she too scared, or was she putting on a brave, foolhardy act? Either way, he'd have some fun with her, though she surely wouldn't term it as such.

"What is that human term? Cat got your tongue? Or more like Taelin got your tongue?" he asked lightly.

"Is...is that what you are?" Her pink tongue swept out to wet her lips.

That only annoyed him more, and he felt his sharp fingernails bite into his arms. She was afraid of him, of the woods, so why didn't she crack? "That is what we know ourselves as—Taelin fae. I know not what you call us, nor do I care."

"You're the strange people of the woods. We don't have a name for you, except—" She broke off, as if realizing she was speaking of something she shouldn't utter.

"Except?" he questioned in a voice that brooked no defiance. Even his own people couldn't ignore the power of that tone.

She blinked, her mouth opening and closing. But still she didn't talk. Irritation rose, quick and vengeful. Always, people had jumped to his bidding. What in the moon was wrong with her? Was she simple in the mind? That was the only explanation.

Could he take a nibble out of her? He and his people weren't cannibals. Well, not in the true sense of the word, but he might make an allowance for her.

"Except?" he asked again, a razor's edge to his voice that would demand any sane person start talking or more like babbling.

The infernal woman chewed on her bottom lip and glanced down at the smaller form in her arms. He stood taller, a looming shadow that commanded obedience.

She looked back up, a frown furrowing her brow. "You are the cursed people fae said to bleed black. Just like your tar forest."

His hands curled into fists so he didn't rip the skin off his own arms—or hers. She sought to tell who and what his people were? He bent from the waist and lowered his face until it was but inches from hers. She recoiled back, but it only took the barest spark of his fury away.

He hissed and let his eyes glow an unearthly shade of swirling gray. "You know nothing of us. A pathetic human mind couldn't even begin comprehending."

Her back was now against the wall, and a rumbling he'd know from anywhere roared to life. "Get away from that wall, stupid mortal rat."

Without waiting for her to comply, he grabbed her by one arm and dragged her away from it. She cried out, almost dropping the younger girl. The quaking of the ground only increased, the woods relaying its displeasure of his tactics to him in no uncertain terms.

Once she was in the middle of the chamber, he dropped her arm as if it were poisoned. To him, it was. Her human blood made it so, and nothing could wipe that taint away. Disgust turned his stomach. Why in Taelin's name would the forest want to save her and the worthless scrap in her lap?

Tears swam down her cheeks, and he admired the translucent streaks they left behind. Even in humans there could be beauty, and here it was. So sweet, so delicious. He was tempted to lick the salt off her skin. But he wouldn't so sully himself.

She stared at him with quivering lips that she pressed tightly together. The tremors decreased until they all but melted away. "W-what are you going to do with us?"

That *was* the question, wasn't it? What was he to do with them if he couldn't kill them? House them as treasured guests within the great forest city of Taerin? No, never. What choice did he have, though? One didn't ignore the Spirit of the Woods and not live to regret it.

He scowled down at the pathetic creatures on the floor. "That's for me to know."

With a snap of his fingers, a ladder of twisted ivy unfurled from the chasm above. It made a slight *thump* as it hit the ground at his feet.

He gestured to the young woman. "Get up and climb."

She gazed first at the rope and then at him. "No."

The Ivy Ladder

Miri stared at the tall being looming like a dark tree over her. Though fright played her nerves like a fine fiddle, he'd have to kill her before she would willingly leave Eve behind. "No."

He froze as if he'd never heard the word before, and his black lips parted. "What did you say?"

She shivered at the soft menace in his voice but knew she couldn't bulk now. "I can't climb while holding my sister. I don't know if I can do it at all." Her shoulder was throbbing, and her limbs felt like limp noodles.

He cocked his head to the side, never once removing his strange gaze from her. It only unsettled her all the more. Everything about him did.

Finally, he spoke in that accented voice of his. "If I have to carry you like a discarded bag of flour, I will."

"My sister?"

His nose scrunched in seeming disgust. "You're related to that thing?"

She bristled in spite of her fear. "She's a wonderful sister." The creature before her didn't appear to understand the comfort of family and friends. Or maybe he just hated them because they were human? That prospect chilled her heart further, but nothing would surprise her now. Not after this day.

He made a snorting noise. "If you care for her so much, then give her to me. Otherwise, let her rot down here."

She glanced down at her sister, who still hadn't stirred. Worry warred with relief. It might be better that she slept through this, but why was she not waking? What if she never stirred? Though she didn't want to give Eve over to Mr. Tall, Pale, and Creepy, she didn't have much choice. She didn't know if she'd even be able to haul herself up that ivy.

Blinking back yet more tears, she tightened her arms around Eve once more by way of a hug and then forced herself to turn her attention back to the fae before her. God, a fae. Until this day, she hadn't even believed they existed. It seemed this forest held a lot of unpleasant surprises. What would become of her and Eve? Their father would never know what happened to them. At the thought of him, her heart lurched. If the worst happened, maybe it would be better if he never knew their fate. The truth could be more upsetting than the unknown.

"I guess you wish to die down here?"

His snide voice cut into her thoughts. She jumped slightly and realized she'd been staring blankly at him. "I don't." Her next words threatened to lodge in her throat, but she forced them out. "Please take her."

He prowled toward her with a feline grace that both mesmerized and terrified. Why did she feel as if she were handing her sister over to a demon? Nothing about him was human except for the general shape of his body. His skin was oddly fascinating with its dark swirl of veins underneath, though the darkness of his lips made her shudder. In black tunic and leggings, he looked like death incarnate that breathed and walked on two legs. Would he bring theirs about?

All too soon, he was bending over them. His silvery hair slipped forward to reveal a pointed ear. She stared at it—more proof of how alien he was by nature. His arms reached out for her sister. She closed her eyes, not wanting to witness the exchange, and lifted Eve slightly.

Surprisingly warm hands brushed her own, and then the weight of her sister vanished. A shiver stole over her. She suddenly felt so cold. By the time her eyelids flickered open, he stood with Eve in his arms. She swallowed the soap-ball-sized lump in her throat. Her usually gregarious sister looked so small against him. So helpless.

He glared down at Miri. "Are you going to sit there all day?"

She sighed inwardly. Part of her couldn't understand why she was willingly following him, but what other choice did she have? None, not at all.

And they both knew it.

So she hoisted her stiff body up, wincing at the pain in her shoulder. Was it dislocated? She wasn't well-versed in medicine, but this felt more than just a twinge.

The fae man was already scaling the ivy ladder with a nimbleness that made her stare. He held onto Eve with one hand and used the other to grip the vines. Every step he took was confident, as if he knew the plant wouldn't let him fall. Maybe he did know that, but the ivy would probably do no such thing for her. If it was anything like the rest of the woods, it'd happily see her plummet to her death.

She eyed the distance up. It was a good nine feet. Well, she might not break her neck, merely a limb or two. Carefully, she placed her hand on one vine. Though she didn't know what she'd been expecting, nothing happened. It felt and acted just like ivy, which was strangely reassuring. Emboldened, she grabbed on with her other hand now.

Her left foot was next and found a hold fairly easily. Then came her right. Once she was completely off the ground, the gentle sway of the ladder turned into something much more violent. Surely, the tossing of the sea had nothing on this? Biting her lip, she made her slow way up the hellish green rope. The fae was nowhere in sight, so that meant he had to be waiting up above. With her sister. That thought spurred her on, and she gritted her teeth. She wouldn't let one stupid ladder defeat—

Ivy slithered around her hands and wrists. A scream skidded up her throat, but the vine wrapping around her waist yanked her up and stole it away. She was now hurtling toward the chasm with frightening speed. Oh God, this was going to hurt. She closed her eyes, waiting for the bone-breaking impact.

Danger Comes on Wings

Miri tensed, but the slam of the ground into her body never happened. Instead, the softness of grass cushioned her. She cracked open an eyelid. The black forest surrounded her. *Eve*! She searched frantically for her and found her unconscious form cradled against the shoulder of the fae creature.

"Are you waiting for night to come? There'll be plenty of animals on the prowl, ready to feed." His voice sounded pleased with the prospect of her becoming chow for some animal.

She sat up slowly, not sure how her body would react. Her right shoulder pained her, but that was no surprise. With a gliding slither, the vines of ivy slid off her wrists and waist, disappearing around a tree and out of sight. Gasping, she glanced down at her hands. Not a mark was left on her skin. She touched her wrist, scarcely able to believe it. Wha-what exactly had that been all about? If the ivy had wanted her dead, she had no doubt she'd be so. Maybe like everything else in the forest, it simply had wanted to terrify her.

"Get up. We don't have hours to dawdle in one place."

Her head shot up. The fae stood with impatience all but bleeding from his body. That, along with his words, got her up on her feet. He had Eve, so it wasn't as if she could protest.

Though she'd rather be near a rabid dog, she walked toward him and screwed up her courage. "What is wrong with her?"

He cocked a platinum brow. "How would I know? She is your sister, not mine."

"I mean why hasn't she awoken? This forest did something to her."

He shrugged. "Most likely she's merely forest struck."

A bolt of fear poked at her heart. "What's that? Is it something serious?"

"Maybe, maybe not." He started walking as if her world wasn't splintering apart before her eyes.

She hurried after him, suppressing the urge to shake the answer out of him. "What does that mean?"

"Exactly what I said. She'll either wake up on her own or when the forest decides she will."

Her hands fisted at her sides. "How would the woods wake her?"

He glanced at her before turning his head away. "It has its ways."

She'd get no more out of him, it seemed. They trudged onward. Well, she did. He strode with a grace that would make any woman envious. Just what was a fae?

The male didn't attempt to make conversation, which she was grateful for. She needed to find out where they were going. How to get that information from him? And once there, would they be killed, imprisoned? Somehow, it was impossible to imagine not seeing her father and town again. Her throat and chest ached at the mere thought. She may be many things, but unduly naïve wasn't one of them.

At least she didn't have to lug her sister through the forest. Miri stifled a groan as the various aches and pains afflicting her body worsened. Though she dreaded their arrival to wherever he was taking them, she'd rejoice in any respite they received.

After what had to be at least an hour of walking, the trees around them seemed to lighten, losing some of their blackness. These were more...gray. What did that signify, though? That they were less poisoned?

"The trees. They've changed."

"So they have."

She frowned. His noncommittal responses infuriated her, but she couldn't let it show. She wouldn't give him that power over her. He had enough as it was, and he seemed the megalomaniac kind to love every little bit he could scrounge up.

Though she was accustomed to speeding over the hills and valleys around Knocton, her body felt like a leaden weight that her legs had to carry. After about the tenth time, she stumbled over a root and nearly face-planted. The movement pulled at her sore shoulder, and she couldn't keep a gasp in.

As she righted herself, the male snorted. "Clumsy human."

Irritation itched at her, and the retort blasted out before she could stop it. "Well, sorry, but I've had a horrendous day, and it doesn't seem like it'll end anytime soon."

"You have a surprising amount of fire for one in your position."

His mild tone didn't fool her. Instead, it sent a series of chills speeding down her back. A bucket of ice would feel better. She knew better than to push him too far, but her mouth had a way of hijacking her brain. Silence was the wisest option for now.

The chirp of a bird snagged her attention. There were animals in the forest? He'd said there were ones that came out at night, but maybe those were the fearsome ones? She gazed around, trying to place where the sound had come from. There, in a tree to the left, a bird sat on one of the lower branches. It was clothed in feathers of red and orange and had a blue silky plume on its round head. She'd never seen such a colorful bird. It truly was a beautiful marvel in these less-than-lovely woods.

"Unless you want your eyes pecked out, don't stare at that bird overlong."

His voice sounded right to her ear, making her jump. He chuckled. "There are many things more dangerous than me in this forest."

She glared at him, not sure whether he was joking or not. It was clear, though, he took much enjoyment in her discomfort. She aimed a sour look at him. "Somehow I doubt that."

"It's your death, not mine, if you don't believe me."

So did that mean he wouldn't kill them? Then again, there were other things worse than death such as slavery or rape. She hoped they didn't become intimately acquainted with them.

Still, she snuck a glance at the bird. This time, it opened its brown beak in an awful ear-piercing squawk. Its wings unfurled like the sails of a ship, and the bird launched itself off the limb right toward them. She cowered, frozen in her spot. Its red eyes gleamed with a hellish light, and they were trained on her. She slammed her eyes shut as if that could protect them and belatedly flung herself to the ground with her hands over her head.

A harsh voice rang out, and the whoosh of wings stirred tendrils of hair into her face. She waited for the claw of talons that never came.

The Paths We Trod

Eerin rolled his eyes at the ridiculous human who refused to budge an inch. A good half-minute had passed since the aketon had tried to attack her, yet apparent fear still kept her glued to the ground.

He was tempted to just walk away and leave her. After a few more moments had seeped past, he made a noise of contempt. "Oh, get up, or are you planning on taking a nap?"

The girl shifted onto her side, and her eyelids flicked open. She stared at him for a few moments, shock appearing to hold her immobile. Really, he had saved *this*? He had important matters to attend to, and this wasn't it. But the Spirit of the Woods had spoken, damn its capriciousness. He marched over to the prone form. Did she expect him to carry her, too? He wasn't a beast of burden but the leader of the Taelin fae.

"Very well, I'll sling you over my other shoulder." And he would. He certainly had the strength to carry these two scraps of humanity. That they made him do it angered him to no end.

He took a threatening step toward her to punctuate his words. She gasped and threw herself upward. Before he could blink, she was on her knees. He suppressed a smirk. Her position was quite to his liking. If he were a different type of Taelin, he'd use it to his advantage. But even he didn't poach from damsels in distress. Besides, she was *human*. There were just some places where even he wouldn't go despite his healthy sex drive.

Once she stood before him, he lifted a brow. "So you require no carrying?"

Her mouth opened but nothing came out as she rubbed her right shoulder. Then she resolutely shook her head.

"Then start walking. And try not to gawk at everything unless you want a repeat performance of recent events. I might not save you next time."

Her brow scrunched up as she jogged to keep up with him. She glanced at him, uncertainty clear in her gaze. "Why did you, then?"

He scowled and readjusted his hold on the younger human. The brown-haired one just had to ask that question. "No particular reason other than I didn't feel in the mood for blood today."

She continued to stare at him as if she didn't know whether to believe him or not. "I'm glad for that." She paused as if thinking and asked hesitantly, "Are you often in the mood for blood, then?"

He sent her a sideways look. "It depends on the company and how much they annoy me."

"Oh."

After that, she didn't attempt to engage him in conversation for a few blessed minutes. The silence was soothing on his raging nerves. The trees were becoming lighter, freer of the darkness coursing through the outer edges of the forest. Animal sounds floated on the air. Though he loved the entirety of his woods, the dark portion brought out the feral in him that was always waiting to burst free. There was a peace in the inner reaches of the forest that settled him as little could. Except, now, he was bringing a human into that sanctuary.

His jaw clenched. He'd love to let the humans fend for themselves. Even though they were under the protection of the Spirit, the dangerous creatures of the forest were slow to follow its dictates. Nature was too strong of a pull to overcome instinct easily. That the humans would likely perish wasn't of concern to him. In fact, by their very existence, they deserved such a fate. And many of his people would agree with him but not all. It was that small population he worried about. They'd try to ensure that the humans were treated as honored guests, not the murderous vermin they were. He knew firsthand about human nature. Nothing could convince him they were nonviolent beings.

He cast a glance her way. She looked innocent and sweet, but he knew more than anyone how appearances could be deceiving. He had to stand strong against them and any wiles they may seek to use.

A bluish-black rabbit bounded out from behind a shrub and right into their path. The woman gasped. "A rabbit!"

"Your skills of observation astonish me."

She frowned at him. "There weren't any animals to be seen before the bird and now this rabbit. The trees...they're getting lighter in color, more brown than black."

The human thought to get answers from him? He wouldn't make it that easy. "Congratulations, your eyes are continuing to work."

She stared at the ground and sighed. "Where are you taking us?"

"Somewhere."

She crossed her arms. "That's obvious. Why won't you give me a straight answer?"

Her boldness nearly amused him in spite of himself. Still, he couldn't let that emotion take hold, let alone show. "Why did you trespass in the woods?"

With a hand outstretched, she turned toward him earnestly. "Not on purpose, I assure you. Something drew my sister toward the forest, and I couldn't stop her. It was as if she was possessed!"

That nearly stopped him short, but humans were notorious liars. Still, if there were a hint of truthfulness to her words... He didn't even want to consider what that meant. The forest ordering him to protect them was enough. "You expect me to believe that?"

"It's what happened. Ever since my sister saw these woods today, she hasn't been the same." The breath hitched in her throat, and her expression crumpled as if she fought off tears.

He bit back a groan. By the towering black trees, he hated tears! They were weapons to be used against unsuspecting males. He, however, wouldn't fall for that trick. "Don't cry," he said, his voice rough.

She sniffed. "I'm not. "

See? Humans lied. She was all but blubbering already. He wanted none of it. "If you cry, I'll leave you standing right here and take your sister."

She slammed to a halt. "You wouldn't!"

He planted his hands on his hips and leaned over her. "Try me."

Mud Walls

The urge to back away was so strong that Miri had to lock her knees and root her feet to the ground. Her looming tears dried up like a bone-dry desert. Why was the creature in front of her such a *bully*?

"You're not taking my sister anywhere without me," she said through gritted teeth.

He started in at a quick pace. "Then you better start moving."

She ran after him. Helplessness and annoyance swam in the pit of her stomach. At this rate, she wasn't going to survive these woods or the Taelin leading her to...wherever. Worse, he seemed to make everything a game designed to belittle and degrade her. If she and Eve could make it out of these woods alive, she'd gladly see the back of him and set out on her own. She snorted to herself. Yeah, right, as if he'd let them. They were no better than prisoners.

"Why are you so unpleasant?"

His shoulders stiffened just the slightest bit. "You're a human trespassing in our forest. But I'm not being unpleasant. You wouldn't be alive if I was."

He equated saving them with being genial? If she weren't so tired and afraid of prodding him further, she'd laugh. His words were cruel, so how did she respond to them? "Then I'm happy for your magnanimous disposition today."

"You should be."

She didn't protest. Why bother? Only by his grace were they still alive. Whether it stayed that way, she didn't know. However, she wasn't in a hurry to find out. Maybe, once Eve woke, they could escape and get back home. Though that sounded nearly impossible, she couldn't give up hope so easily.

Casting a glance at her sister, she bit her lip. What if Eve didn't wake up, or woke up but wasn't Eve anymore? All genuine worries, but ones that would only be solved in their own time.

Still… She looked at her captor, for that was what he was to her. Given the possible verbal slaughtering he might inflict, was it worthwhile asking questions that concerned Eve? Yes, yes, it was. The words hovered on the edge of her tongue but refused to slide off.

"Out with it," the male all but barked out, staring straight ahead.

Her mouth dropped open. How had he known she was about to ask something? Well, no matter. He'd told her to get on with it, and get on with it she would. "Is there anything you or your people can do if Eve doesn't wake up on her own?"

"If she's deserving of it."

His cold tone left her in no doubt he considered her sister unworthy of such assistance. How could anyone be so heartless? "She's but a child of seven!"

"For now. She'll grow into an adult who's capable of the destruction for which your race is well-known."

That made her stop and think. Sure, humans did fight and have wars, but her town? It was largely a peaceful one. The most disorderly conduct that they saw was drunkenness and some light thievery. "Maybe some are but, by no means, all."

He grunted and shifted Eve until her head lolled over his shoulder and halfway onto his upper back. She swallowed the remark that sprang to her lips. It wouldn't serve her well to anger him.

Right when she'd given up on a reply, he said, "I know the truth of your race. Nothing can convince me otherwise."

She stared at him with narrowed eyes. Great, she saw what she was up against. Bigotry and prejudice. He reminded her of some of the old townspeople who were so set in their ways that little could change their mindset. It was like arguing with a mud wall—one which had to either be walked around or smashed to pieces.

What had given him such a jaded view on humanity? Though he wasn't likely to tell her, she still asked. "Why do you say that?"

A muscle in his jaw ticked. "Experience. Vast experience."

She was onto something here. Maybe if she pressed a bit further. "What experience is that?"

He aimed a dark, venomous look her way. "Nothing I want to discuss."

His speed increased. Now, she found herself running outright to keep up. The ache in her shoulder increased. After a few minutes, she'd had enough. "Please, can you slow down?"

A sound of aggravation flew from his mouth. "Humans. So clumsy and slow."

"I've had a long, trying day, so forgive me if I'm now lagging behind." She tried to keep the sarcasm out of her voice but failed miserably.

"Let me guess...you're usually able to keep up with most anybody?"

"Well, yes," she said slowly, her mind whirring. How had he— Oh God, he wasn't a mind reader, was he? That was a possibility too terrible to contemplate.

Thankfully, he reined himself in. She took this time to focus on her surroundings, careful to not stare at any one place too long. Who knew what might be lurking behind tree and shadow? She now knew the danger of it and didn't want a repeat performance of the bird episode. Even now, the remembrance of its red eyes caused an icy fist to clench her heart.

That was when she noticed it. The forest was getting lighter, the trees a healthier brown color and the atmosphere considerably airier. A path of some kind of stone formed under their feet and wound through trees that stood ever straighter. That had to mean they were getting closer to civilization, whatever that encompassed.

The leaves of the trees, though... She couldn't stop her sharp intake of breath. They were shades of purple, red, and brown. Autumn might bring some of these colors, but as far as she knew, it was still spring. How was this possible? She shook her head in recrimination. This wasn't a normal forest, and the Taelin—what an odd name—were apparently the guardians of it. The one specimen she'd seen so far was just as strange as his forest.

She prayed that his people were a peaceful race. However, if the Taelin leading her was any indication, she'd sooner turn a lion into a vegetable eater than cure her captor of his bloodthirsty inclinations. He appeared as wild as his forest and just as ready to bite. If the rest of his people were like him, she and Eve would likely be dead by evening. But why bother to save them at all? His reasons were as unfathomable as the stars in the sky.

Which reminded her, she didn't know his name. It was getting tiresome thinking of him as "the Taelin," "the fae," or "her captor." No opportune moment had presented itself for her to enquire, though, so she'd likely have to make one.

She gave an internal sigh. So many questions and no answers. Well, as he said, she did have her eyes. She'd use them, along with her ears, to ferret out what she could.

Though it was probably futile, she started to ask, "Are we nearly there—"

They rounded a bend, and her gaze landed on a sight that froze her in midstep. Trees, massive and healthy, glowed with a luminescence that shouldn't be possible. Leaves of jewel colors glinted in the sunlight pouring through the canopy. Turquoise, purple, green, red, blue—there were so many variations in hue, she couldn't count them all. How could this exist in the middle of a shadowy forest?

The fae's dark, decadent voice sounded next to her ear. "Welcome to Taerin, the home of the Taelin. I hope you find it...amendable, for you will never leave it alive."

The Dimming of Beauty

All words evaporated, as did all hope. Never see her father again? Her friends? Even her dinky, little room that housed all her precious possessions and Eve's, too?

Only one word escaped, and it encompassed everything she felt. "Why?"

"Humans never leave this forest."

"That doesn't answer my question of why."

He slanted her an unimpressed glance. "For centuries, we've been left alone. If we let humans go, that'd quickly change. Even you know that."

His argument made sense, though she wouldn't admit to that. Instead, she focused on a possible bright point. "So there are other humans here?"

"No."

"But you just said..." As the implication speared through her, horror bathed her. "They're all dead?"

"Most never even saw the inner reaches of our home."

"So you killed them?" she asked, her voice rising.

"Some of them. The woods handled the others. Only a select few have ever been granted the right to live and die amongst us. They have all passed on, though."

Too stunned to speak for a few moments, she swallowed against the tightness growing in her throat. "Are we part of those select few?"

"That remains to be seen."

Miri walked along with him in silence. The sun-dappled forest no longer seemed so bright. The unknown loomed before her. Never before had her and Eve's futures been in such doubt. Though everyone lived with at least a bit of uncertainty, this was a mind-blogging amount that ate at the soul. Questions collided with each other until a headache started forming behind her eyes. Would her sister be fine once she woke? What kind of village would they find? Would the people and their culture be savage?

Even the buildings and other dwellings were sure to be foreign. Alien. If even they were spared death and weren't sentenced to a life of servitude, they'd never have a hope of fitting in.

"Why are you frowning so furiously, human?"

She sighed. He was so heartless he wouldn't understand. "It doesn't matter."

"Undoubtedly, but humor me. I have nothing else to amuse me at the moment."

So her suffering was entertainment? How nice to know. Something inside her snapped like a rope stretched too far. She rounded on him and jabbed a finger toward his face. "What do you think? I've been told I'll never see my family, my friends, ever again. What do you think is bothering me?"

He stared at her, and she stared back. With a calmness that chilled, he reached for her hand and lowered it. His expression revealed nothing, which made her breath rasp faster through parched lips. Her heart drummed so quickly she feared that it would thud out of her chest.

"It was your choices that brought you here. Never point your finger at me."

Some of her fear melted away, only to be replaced with anger. Her choices? Like she'd had a choice! Her sister had been bewitched into entering the woods. Suddenly, an idea hit, and she narrowed her eyes. What if he had arranged this whole thing? "Did you cause my sister to abandon all reason?"

He drew himself upright and lifted that fiendish eyebrow. "Me? Why would I do that?"

"I have no clue, but you would."

He rolled his eyes. "I would if I had actually done what you accuse me of. I loathe humans enough that I would never lure even one into the forest. I want nothing to do with creatures such as you. In fact, you're fortunate I don't drop your sister here and now."

By the time he'd finished, fire coated his tone. She slunk back involuntarily. His wrath terrified her as little had in her life, and she couldn't control her responses the way she usually could.

After one more killing look, he marched ahead, every line of his body stiff. She walked after him slowly, not wanting to get too close to that inferno. To think she'd been the angry one. How had they switched so quickly?

Miri sighed. She'd been doing an awful lot of that today but couldn't bring herself to care. How far was his village from here? Better to face her fate sooner than later. But nothing would be lived on her time, it seemed.

She contented herself by looking around for a bit. How many leaf colors could she spot? After counting fifteen, she gave up. There were too many shades, some only differing by a few degrees, to make counting easy.

Soon, her study of the nature around her palled. The sounds of animals made it to her ears, but she didn't see any sign of them. And while the trees were beautiful and otherworldly, they couldn't focus her attention for long. Not with all the worries constantly seeping through her mind.

Finally, she let the question slip out. "When will we arrive at your village?"

He kept walking and didn't answer. Her sister's head bounced slightly with each step he took, but whatever sleep she was in still claimed her. A growl worked its way up her throat. She wanted to pick up a stone and lob it at his back. With her luck, though, she'd miss and hit Eve instead.

"Did you just growl?" he asked, his voice floating back to her.

The amusement in his tone made her want to launch herself at him. But the thought of Eve, as always, stayed her. He held her sister and could do irreparable harm to her if he so chose.

She forced herself to speak in a remarkably controlled voice. "What of it?"

"You sound like a hissing, growling little kitten."

"What?" She sped up, a bit affronted.

"You heard me. Maybe having a human or two around won't be so terrible. The entertainment you'll provide promises to be great."

"But what about the annoyance?" she asked, her voice as sweet as possible. She caught up to him and aimed a victorious smile his way. "I know we engender that in you quite a bit."

He frowned. "Don't remind me." A shark-like smile curved his mouth. "For your own good. I have a way of making annoyances...disappear."

Icy chills poured down her back, but she wouldn't show how he affected her. "Your words threaten often enough that they lose their effectiveness."

He halted with a suddenness that would've made her slam into him if she'd been following directly behind. "Is that so?" he asked, slowly turning his head toward her.

Unease coiled about her like a sinuous snake. She'd pushed him too far this time.

A cold fire burned in his eyes. "Well, then I'll have to back them up, won't I?"

Cornering the Mouse

The human ingrate stumbled back a few steps, terror leaking off her in waves. Ah, how beautiful it was, so potent he could taste it on his tongue. If he could only bottle its aroma...

Eerin smiled, aware that a few of his people watched them from the treetops. None of them moved to interfere, not that he'd done anything yet to warrant intervention.

Oh, he wouldn't hurt the two little humans, but the wench before him didn't need to know that. Her mouth...well, she had to learn to mind it. Otherwise, sooner or later, someone would take exception to her saucy words, and put those pink lips to better use. If he didn't hate humans so much, he'd be tempted to try them out. But he wouldn't squander his time seducing someone who was so below him in every way.

Why was he even wasting time on such thoughts? She was looking at him as if she were a frightened rabbit and he the predator, which made it an opportune time to carry out her punishment. He glanced at the tree above them and melded his spirit to that within the core of the trunk. It accepted him willingly as long as he kept the darkness in his veins leashed. With a gentle push of his mind, he showed what he had in mind for the human woman and asked for the almira's participation.

The tree sighed gently. *We will not hurt her? The Spirit commands we don't.*

Eerin tamped down on his impatience and adjusted his hold on the smaller human. The lighter trees listened much more readily to the Spirit than the darker ones did, and he couldn't discount that. *We won't hurt her. This is merely a scare tactic and will teach her some respect. If she is to survive here, she needs to learn the natural order of things.*

The almira's jeweled-colored leaves shivered in agreement. *I will do as you ask, but I get to release her of my own accord.*

The human gasped, peering up at the tree canopy. He knew she hadn't heard the voice of the almira but rather the strong breeze that had rattled through heavy leaves. The tense lines of her body revealed that she fought the urge to run. However, her sister would keep her by his side—of this he was sure.

He glanced away, dismissing her, and responded to the tree. *Of course you can decide when to release her.* Unfortunately, he had no choice but to placate the almira.

I don't want this dragged out for too long.

He frowned, slightly displeased but made sure to bury that feeling deep where the tree couldn't sense it. *Naturally. Neither do I.*

A surge of doubt flowed from the tree. *If you say so.*

He ground his teeth. *With that in mind, can we please start before our human flees like a frightened mouse?*

In way of an answer, the breeze picked up. A creaking and rustling of leaf and branch sounded around them. The human woman quivered and appeared ready to bolt, sister or no.

Right when her feet sprang into motion, one large branch swept down. The smaller branches on the limb deftly grabbed her around the middle and up they hoisted her. A scream ripped from her throat, but the limb kept its upward trajectory. She struggled and kicked. But soon, all her appendages were held fast. After a minute or two, even her shrieks and demands to be put down faded away.

Eerin smiled. Such a beautiful sight. He might not be able to get rid of the humans, but he had this. He was as much master of these woods as anyone could be. But all wonderful things must come to an end, and the almira signaled it would soon set her down, safe and unharmed.

Deliberate footsteps stomped toward him. "Cousin, what do you think you're doing? Let her go this instant!"

He groaned at the strident voice he knew only too well and ripped his gaze away from the trussed-up human. Pasting a nonchalant smile on his face, he turned toward the blonde Taelin female stalking his way. "Innara, what has brought you here? Surely, you didn't come to spoil my fun?"

She halted before him and planted her hands on her hips, a frown slashing across her face. "Put that human down now."

He rolled his eyes. "She's not one of your strays. You can't adopt her."

Her gaze landed on the cargo slung over his shoulder. "And what did you do to that child?" she screeched.

"Nothing. She's been unconscious ever since I found her."

"*Hmmph.*"

The doubt in her voice did nothing to improve his mood. He cast a glance at the late afternoon sky as if it could offer him some guidance—or solace. Why Innara and why now? She was one of the few people who could speak her mind freely to him and not live to regret it. Unfortunately, she thought their familial connection gave her the right to unrepentantly boss him around. He might have to disabuse her of that notion.

"Help! Help!" came a faint voice from above them.

Eerin scowled. The human had found her voice again. *Almira, use your leaves to silence her.*

The tree sighed, and a leafy branch snaked over the girl's mouth.

"*Ahh*, silence." He turned back to his cousin with a satisfied smile.

Innara crossed her arms, appearing supremely unimpressed with his latest action. She opened her mouth, probably to demand the human's release, but the sound of creaking branches froze her tongue.

Eerin stared with narrowed eyes at the almira, who was already lowering the human chit, who was again struggling. Stupid human.

Didn't she know if she did manage to release herself, she'd plummet to the forest floor?

"At least the almira has the sense you don't," his cousin muttered.

He glared at her, which usually had the effect of quelling the most rebellious of his people. However, she just glowered back, stepping away from him with a flounce and toward the lowering branch.

A half-growl, half-moan rumbled in his chest. Wonderful, two impudent females to deal with. Not to mention that the littlest human hadn't even awoken, so who knew what to expect from her?

His mind spun calculatingly, and a smirk wiped away his frown. He had a solution for troublesome females. Innara could watch his newly acquired human nuisances, and they, in turn, could drive her to distraction.

After all, he did have a realm to run, and he couldn't expect to torment the humans forever.

From the Tree

With a lurch, the branch supporting Miri started to lower. She gasped, her struggles renewing. Hope and terror fizzled in her veins. Suddenly, the spindly limbs around her tightened. She whimpered in pain and bucked her body against the crushing restraints.

They immediately loosened. She slid precariously within their hold until she was hanging nearly vertical to the ground. The leaves over Miri's mouth muffled the scream flying from her throat. As if realizing she might plummet to her death, the branches yanked her up so she was sprawled sideways in their bony embrace.

Oh, God, were they going to drop her or strangle her? Though she was slowly getting closer to the ground, it looked so far away. She'd never been afraid of heights before, but then, she'd never been held hostage by a tree.

A whisper of something played in her mind, almost like a gentle touch of apology. She shook her head, trying to dislodge that crazy sensation. But she only managed to knock her temple into the surprisingly smooth bark of the limb.

Tears stung her eyes. This forest was driving her insane. Maybe it was a blessing her sister hadn't awoken—and maybe never would. If this were only some nightmarish dream that she could awake from...but this was too vivid, too real, to belong to the realm of sleep.

Finally, blessed ground loomed near. She'd never wanted to feel something beneath her feet more. With a snapping of branches, she dropped to the ground on all fours and barely felt the sting against her hands and knees. A sob burst from her lips. For a moment, she felt boneless with relief and couldn't have forced herself to move even if a flesh-eating creature came charging at her. That feeling soon faded as she remembered exactly where she was. The murderous tree, along with the equally murderous fae, lurked above her, just waiting to pounce.

She scrambled to her feet and away from them. However, trees surrounded her on all sides. Her gaze landed on a new sight, though. A fae woman who sported long, honey-blond hair stared back at her. Like her kin, black veins flowed under her pale skin. Miri shivered. It gave them such a morbid, otherworldly look, but somehow they were still beautiful in a way she couldn't define. Still, it was a beauty to which she was loath to get too close.

However, the expression on the fae lady's face was the opposite of what the male usually wore. A kind smile curved her black lips, and the skin around her startlingly blue eyes crinkled. "Come here, young one. I won't hurt you." Her gaze slanted to the male and darkened. "Unlike some others."

He growled. "Innara..."

The woman ignored him. "Come, let me treat your hurts."

Uncertainty tore at Miri. Could she be trusted? Maybe this was all some ruse to gain her trust and complacency. But what other choice did she have? And the fae lady's name was Innara? It seemed a fitting name for the exotic woman clothed in blue.

Miri's feet seemed to move of their own accord. Well, then, good or bad, her decision was made.

Once she stood within reaching distance of Innara, the woman gently latched onto her arm and pulled her near. "My cousin can be a brute, so please excuse him."

For some reason, Miri was still expecting their touch to be ice cold, but it was as warm as a human's. Then her words penetrated, and she jerked within her hold. "He's your cousin?"

Their demeanors were so different. Other than their eerie skin and sense of otherness, they didn't bear much familial resemblance, either.

The male barked something at his cousin in their fae language, who merely shrugged. Worry itched at Miri that she was causing discord amongst family members. She didn't want to further enrage the being holding her sister. Otherwise, she might find the situation slightly funny.

As if sensing her thoughts, the other woman squeezed her arm and spoke quietly. "I know how to handle him. Fear not."

Her cousin spouted off again, apparently hearing her despite the lowness of her voice. The fae woman paid him no mind and set them to walking. "We're still about twenty minutes from the city proper. Once there, you can seek rest and care."

Miri glanced back at Eve and the stalking figure carrying her. "My sister?"

"She will receive the same," Innara said.

In the face of this kindness, a lump formed in Miri's throat. "Thank you."

Innara shook her head. "Don't thank me so soon. Though I can offer you a measure of protection, you might never leave these woods."

Her words landed on Miri like a blow, and she recoiled.

Innara sighed. "It's not my intent to upset you but to merely be truthful."

"I know." Though she really didn't. But something in her trusted Innara, and she'd always judged herself a fair judge of character.

During their walk to the city, Innara was mostly quiet as if sensing the turmoil of Miri's thoughts. Still, the fae lady's presence was more of a balm than she would've expected. Innara walked so closely that the bottoms of their dresses swooshed against each other. Though Miri often didn't like her space infringed upon, now was not such an instance.

She did her best to take in her surroundings, not knowing if the remembrance of them would come in useful later. The beautiful trees were truly enchanting, but unfortunately, one looked much like the other. So no help there if escape was ever in the future.

In fact, given that the trees were sentient, they might impede her and Eve if they ever tried to flee. Still, their father had taught them that knowledge was power. She had the feeling that they could use any kind of power they could grab onto.

A rustling in one of the trees snagged her attention. A fae man leaped from a branch halfway up and landed like a cat in front of them. Miri gasped, backing away as much as she could from the crouching, black-haired creature.

People of the Darkness

She stumbled back until the firm hold Innara had on her arm stopped her. The newcomer who'd jumped to the ground was another fae male. His fearsome appearance was frightful, just as her captor's had been. And he appeared no more welcoming.

Her heart thudded in her throat. When would this insanity end?

He gestured from Miri to her sister, and a spate of words flew from his mouth.

Innara sighed. "Speak Taelin, Hunor."

He nodded. "These humans, my lady? They are under your protection?"

Hunor's slow, halting words took Miri a moment to process. He didn't sound so much hostile as curious, which was slightly heartening.

"They are, unfortunately," drawled her captor.

Miri whipped her head around at the platinum-haired grump of a fae who'd just spoken. He glowered at her as if she were the cause of all the world's problems. Why was he so hateful?

Innara stepped closer to him, dragging Miri with her. "Really? Why are they still under your protection, given your hostility toward humans?"

He turned his scowl on his cousin. "It's a hatred well-deserved."

"To you, it is. Still, why are they under your protection?"

A frown crossed his features, along with a hint of indecision. "The Spirit decreed it when it spoke to me through the trees' voices."

The spirit? What was that? And it wanted them protected?

Innara gasped, and Miri thought she heard Hunor do so, too. After a moment, Innara said in a slightly shaky voice, "Why? That's very...unorthodox."

Miri stared from one cousin to the other as confusion swam through her head. What was going on? Something of great importance, apparently.

"How would I know? It wasn't exactly forthcoming."

Innara wagged a finger at him. "Were you rude to the Spirit?"

"I was pleasant enough."

Innara sighed. "Which means you were rude."

"You forget who is leader. Now isn't the time for *your* disrespect."

Her lips tightened. "As you wish, Lord Eerin."

His voice was so cutting Miri winced in sympathy for her newfound friend. Then her thoughts froze. Eerin? Leader? She finally had his name but... Dread unfurled in her belly. He was the Taelin leader? If so, she could forget about asking for mercy from a higher power. He was the higher power.

Lord Eerin strode past them. "Come, let us get our newest...*residents* settled."

Every word of his leaked out with a sneer. If she and Eve weren't in such dire straits she'd find it amusing. Lord Eerin was arrogance personified. It oozed from him, drowning any softer emotion he could possibly express. To be held captive to it, however, was something else entirely.

Hunor bowed to the cousins but made no move to join them. Innara pulled her past him so they could trail after Lord Eerin. Something urged her to glance back. She did, only to see the male fae leap and grab onto a branch. He swung himself up with an ease that astonished. The strength and muscle coordination that would take was impressive.

Were these people acrobats or merely physically inclined to feats of superhuman ability? She snorted to herself. There was no "mere" about it. She ripped her gaze away because she really didn't fancy falling on her face. Even if Innara was as physically able as her brethren, she couldn't count on somebody else to save her from a spill.

The rest of the walk toward the city was blessedly trouble-free. Still, she didn't hold out much hope for their reception once inside Taerin proper. The city hid behind beautifully etched, solid gold walls that stretched as far as her eye could see. The sight ripped the breath right from her. Who would've guessed this awaited them in the middle of a cursed forest? The sweeping lines and knotwork patterns of the gates grabbed one's attention. The perfection displayed mesmerized her. Motifs of animals and nature scenes splayed across the golden surface of the walls. If this was what the outside looked like, what wonders hid inside?

Soldiers in golden plate armor guarded the gate and were strategically placed both on the ground and on walkways on top of the walls. She frowned. There'd be no easy escape from the town.

Innara gently squeezed her arm. "I hope you like your new home."

Miri gave her a wan smile, nerves stretched to the breaking point. Innara sounded so sincere that she couldn't bring herself to say anything petty, though.

"Give it time."

If she and Eve were stuck here forever, they'd have nothing but time. But how would they spend it? Surely, they'd be put to work doing some labor. She stared down at one of her hands. It was soft, unused to anything harsher than dishwashing. The unknown yawned before her, completely, terrifyingly blinding. But maybe it was better not knowing. While there was uncertainty that way, there was also hope.

Lord Eerin jerked his head toward the nearest guard, who signaled to another soldier on the wall. The gates parted without a sound and revealed the waiting town within. Miri stumbled to a halt, but Innara patiently propelled her along.

A sense of surrealism engulfed her. If she'd thought the walls gorgeous, it was nothing in comparison to the beauty she gawked at now. This was to be her prison? Well, at least it was a beautiful one, though otherworldly.

Silver and gold buildings sprawled across the ground and on different levels in the trees. She'd heard of treehouses, but this was something entirely different. How did such large structures stay aloft? But then, this was no normal forest. Magic was likely the answer.

But the most disconcerting sight was the townsfolk. Each one was utterly foreign, so different from her people. Just as with the fae she'd already met, pale skin streaked with black covered all visible portions of their bodies. Groups of Taelin slowly gathered and stared, some on the startlingly green grass and some cradled in the jewel-leafed trees. Not one word was uttered among them that she could hear. The quietness burned through her, singeing her already taxed nerves.

How could these people of seeming darkness live in such a place of light? But then, the kind Innara didn't live up to the name of a lovely but deadly monster. As a whole, were these people goodness personified or evil incarnate? Maybe like humans, they ranged somewhere in-between, with each person belonging on their own sliding scale.

Only time and experience would give her that answer.

Succor

Eerin glowered down at the small human in his arms, studiously ignoring the gobsmacked one ahead of him, and nodded his head toward the nearest Taelin. The black-haired fae male froze for an instant before walking toward them. Could Galin be any more hesitant? Eerin held a girl, not a rabid animal. Then, again, those two weren't mutually exclusive and could be quite similar.

"She's unconscious," he said, not bothering to hide the impatience in his voice. "So she can't attack."

A slight smile flitted over the other Taelin's face as he took the girl. "Such a small thing could do very little damage."

Eerin snorted. "Don't be fooled by their size. They're treacherous creatures by nature."

Galin frowned. "Some are, but this one is naught but a child."

Eerin laughed humorlessly. "They grow into adults. Never forget that. Now off with you."

As Galin set off with his armful of cargo, Eerin rolled his shoulders in an attempt to alleviate the soreness there. Now what to do about—

"Where is he taking my sister?"

Eerin winced at the shrill voice assaulting his ears. The older human had stumbled to a stop and stared after Galin and his baggage. Every taut line of her body screamed that she wanted to run after them. Somehow, she stayed herself, which was an impressive feat for a human. Who knew they had the self-control?

Innara opened her mouth, but Eerin cut her off. "To the healers, where else?"

If possible, she stiffened even more and took a step in the direction of the swiftly disappearing Galin. Innara, still holding onto her arm, followed her.

"I need to go with them," the human said, urgency coating her tone.

He planted his hands on his hips and found himself saying, "You will do no such thing."

"Why not, cousin?"

Innara's soft voice cut through him, and he glared at her. "Then take her. I care not."

With that, he spun on his heel and stalked away from them. His people scattered away from him, likely sensing his poor mood. Let Innara deal with the humans. After all, that was what he'd planned. The less he had to see them, the better. Just the thought of them in his realm made him twitchy. Humans willingly accepted into the heart of Taelin land. What was his world coming to?

He couldn't kill them, couldn't banish them, but he could ignore them. They'd have their protector in Innara, not to mention in the Spirit. He'd done his duty, and they had no further use of him nor did he of them.

Satisfied he had all settled, he strode toward his administration chambers. He'd traipsed in the woods for long enough. Time to get some work done.

***

Miri watched Lord Eerin cut through a slowly dispersing crowd of people. Though she knew she should hold her tongue, the question popped out. "What is your cousin's issue?"

Innara guided her in the direction that her sister had been carried. "He has a problem with humans. It's an old, long story that you needn't worry about right now. Though his manner is grudging, he understands his responsibility to you and your sister."

Curiosity and worry battled within Miri. The fae male who had her sister was out of sight. But since Innara seemed to be taking them to the healers, she tamped down on her fear for Eve. "But why does he have a responsibility to us? It's clear he hates the very sight of me and Eve."

"Eve? That's your sister's name?"

Since it'd already slipped out, she didn't see the benefit in denial. "Yes."

"It's pretty. Which reminds me, I don't know what to call you. I'm at a distinct disadvantage as you already know my name."

"Miri."

Innara lifted a blond brow. "It is the tradition of your people to have more than one name, isn't it?"

"Miri Summerland."

"Well, Miri Summerland, I am pleased to meet your acquaintance, even though the circumstances surrounding our meeting were less than fortunate."

Miri grimaced. "I can't say it's been enjoyable. I just want to go home."

Innara squeezed her arm. "I don't know if that will ever be possible, but we'll see what we can do."

"Lord Eerin won't let us leave. He was very adamant about it."

"My cousin is one thing, but the Spirit is another."

There was that mention of the spirit again. "What is that?"

The other female frowned thoughtfully. "That's not easy to explain unless you've grown up surrounded by it. The Spirit is...the soul of the woods."

Miri stared at the fae woman, but she couldn't detect a hint of humor. "Its soul?"

Innara nodded with a bright smile. "It's a guardian of the forest, so we help it as it helps us."

Miri blinked, wondering how this day had turned out to be so...so crazy. But then, why not? There were black, poisoned trees and fae people and animals, so why not a spirit?

"Hopefully, this spirit doesn't hate humans as Lord Eerin does."

"It offers you protection, so it's doubtful it harbors any such prejudices."

"Why would it do that?"

Innara shrugs. "No one knows. It divulges information only when it wants, not when we desire it."

It sounded sort of arrogant, like Lord Eerin did. Maybe that was where he got it from. Still, it wanted to protect them while he most certainly did not. Was it the only thing standing between them and death? But why let its forest attack them so?

Nothing made sense and probably wouldn't for a long time, if ever.

Innara's voice ripped her back to the moment. "We're nearing the healing chambers. After a brief visit to see your sister and have any of your ills attended to, I'll show you to your home. There, you can bathe, eat, and rest."

Miri's chest tightened at the mention of a new home. *One day at a time, Miri.* That was the only way she could handle this and possibly stay sane. Anyway, she was about to collapse from exhaustion. Her muscles protested with each step she took. Everything felt like one big bruise. So a bath, along with food, would be a welcome sight before she rolled into bed and stayed there forever. At least until someone—or worry for Eve—dragged her out into the light.

Burning

Eerin stared down at the parchment scattered across his desk, idly toying with the quill in his hand. Hours had passed, and the pile still seemed insurmountable. Though he'd never loved paperwork, this all-out avoidance and disinterest was troubling. And it was all the humans' *fault*. How could he possibly rest easy with them under the boughs of his forest?

Their very presence was an affront that was hard to stomach. Even now, his gut churned at the idea. If only he could—

Eerin lurched out of his chair. No, such thoughts were fruitless. Restless energy coursed through his muscles, forcing him to pace the confines of his office.

He couldn't kill or banish the humans. Not since the blasted Spirit ordered that he protect them. Though he was a law unto himself in many ways, even he wouldn't lightly go against its decrees. After all, the Spirit was as much a guardian of the woods as his people were. In some ways, it was much more since it was the sentient soul of the forest.

So that only left one option—avoidance. Innara could be an interfering nag at the best of times, so let her deal with them. It'd keep her busy and out of his affairs. And she was soft-hearted enough to protect the two humans, so he'd be doing his duty by them. Other than that, he had no use for them. With their short lives, they'd pass soon enough. Time was his friend in this regard.

Eerin scowled. Why didn't that feel like a feasible plan? He fisted his hands until a splintering sound, along with a burning sensation on some of his fingers, ripped his focus away. Slowly unclenching his hands, he saw the remains of the quill against his black-stained skin. He'd drawn blood. A growl rumbled from his throat. All because of the humans.

Everything in his life always came back to them. Everything bad and dark. He wanted to crush them like the ants they were.

A rap on the door drew his gaze. Though even he couldn't see through the wood, he could sense it was one of his people and that the person was worried.

Ignoring a surge of irritation over the interruption, he stalked the few feet to the door and wrenched it open. The city guard stood frozen with his hand poised to knock again.

"What is it?" Eerin snapped.

The surprise fled from Cian's face, and a neutral expression replaced it. He held out a missive. "A message from Lady Innara. She says it's most urgent."

With a huff of annoyance, Eerin snatched it from the guard. The other fae made no move to leave, so Eerin glowered. "You may go."

A worried gleam formed in Cian's brown eyes. "Lady Innara said—"

"I don't care what she said." The fae soldier flinched, and Eerin sighed to himself. He didn't have to be such a monster to his own people. "If it's anything important, I'll go there myself."

That seemed to satisfy Cian. He nodded, bowed, and left.

Eerin stared down at the missive in his hand. Whatever Innara had to say about the humans, he wanted no part of it. With a snarl, he crumpled up the parchment.

As far as he was concerned, it could wait forever.

***

Miri sighed and leaned more comfortably against the fluffy pillows of the bed. She was clean and now had a lap tray of food spread before her. Though she didn't understand why she had to stay in the healing chambers, she couldn't complain. The airy room soothed her senses. Its wood paneling was painted an ivory that seemed to capture the waning sunlight. In some places, engravings and carvings strategically drew the eye. All in all, it was a beautiful place.

Best of all, Eve was in the next bed. The healers assured her she would awake soon, so all was well for now. Still, there had been a funny expression on their faces during their examination of both her and Eve, which she couldn't quite dismiss. Surely, it was nothing, though. Shrugging away that worry, she took a hearty bite of a delicious stew. The warmth of it filtered all the way down to her toes. She'd been so cold after the adrenaline left her body. The bath had helped, as did the blankets piled on the bed. This stew, though, was something else. It seemed a wonder food.

Her hand froze, halfway to her mouth. Wait, was the stew enchanted? *Could* it even be enchanted? Her stomach rumbled, reminding her that it certainly didn't care if it was. But the rest of her was another matter... After a few minutes of wrestling with herself, hunger won out. After all, she'd already tasted much of what was on the tray. So the harm, if any, had been done.

"Where is Lord Eerin?" Lady Innara quietly asked a nearby guard stationed in the healing chambers.

Miri frowned, just able to make out the question. Lady Innara seemed quite concerned that he come. Why? He was hateful, and she much preferred if he stayed away. In fact, if she never saw him, that would be wonderful. Even now, the thought of him sent shivers down her spine. Intimidation leaked from him like a potent toxin. He was scary in a way she couldn't even define, in a way the rest of his people weren't.

Yet he lurked in her mind like a phantom, haunting her when she least expected it. Suddenly, her hunger died. She pushed away the tray. An itch on her arm caused her to scratch idly at it. The healers had put a salve on all her various bumps and bruises. It had tingled, though the sensation was starting to fade.

Suddenly, the itch turned to a stinging burn that made her gasp. She hadn't been rubbing that hard, had she? When she glanced down, she froze. The scratch on her skin was red and raised. But that wasn't what frightened her. No, it was the black radiating from the center of the wound and out across her skin for a few centimeters. The air in her lungs turned to lead.

"Lady Innara"—she called out shakily—"something strange is happening."

Unfulfilled

Eerin closed his office door and warded it, a smile coming to his lips. Though he hadn't gotten the work done that he'd wanted, he planned to work off some of his pent-up energy in the arms of Selina. If anyone could take his mind off his troubles, it was her. She gave wild and willing a new meaning, but so did he when he was in this kind of mood.

As he turned around, a groan slipped loose. In the fading light, Innara was bearing down on him with all the attitude of an invading army. She had the worst timing and never cared what she interrupted.

"What do you want? Already bored with your human waifs?"

She clutched at his arm. "Eerin, come with me now."

He lifted a brow. "I'm off to see Selina."

"Your mistress can wait!"

He smirked. "You try telling her that. She's quite...*ah*, demanding."

She gave him a disbelieving stare and slapped him on the arm. "You have her at your beck and call."

"Well, *I* can't wait." And he couldn't. Right now, he felt as if he'd explode if he didn't achieve some kind of release.

She scrunched up her nose. "*Eww*, I didn't need that visual."

"You don't live an unchaste life."

"I've been with the same male for three hundred years," she said, sending him an unimpressed look.

"But you're not bound to him."

"Stop it. You know we're betrothed." She ground her teeth. "This isn't what I've come to talk about."

"Then what?" *Ah*, how he loved to rile her so. It was payback for her interfering ways.

"It's about Miri and Eve. They—"

"Miri and Eve?"

"The humans. They're—"

He held up a hand to forestall her. "I don't want to know."

She jabbed a finger at him. "You're our leader. Act like it."

He cast a poisonous look at her. What did she think he'd been doing in his ground office all afternoon? "I am."

"They're your charges. You're ultimately responsible for their welfare, not me, not the healers."

"You're saying you and the healers can't care for two simple humans, one of whom happens to be unconscious?"

"There's been an unforeseen consequence of them being in the dark portion of the woods."

Why him? Why now? "And only I can handle it? What is it?"

She shifted from one foot to the other, unease clear in her actions. "I don't know if there's anything you can do, but—"

"Then why bother me?"

"Are you going to do your duty or not?"

He heaved out a frustrated sigh. "Fine. Lead me to them."

She latched onto his arm and started to pull him down a sloping walkway. "There's not a minute to waste."

He rolled his eyes at her haste. Underneath it all, though, a seed of concern began to grow—along with a sinking suspicion.

***

Miri gritted her teeth against the fire scorching through her body. "What is happening to me?" She'd asked that question many times, but no answer had been forthcoming. This time would probably be no different. Anger swelled along with the pain. The Taelin knew what was ailing them but would say nothing of it.

Were they dying? She bit back a scream as agony rolled through her. Sweat poured down her face. Right now, death would be a welcome reprieve from this pain.

A hoarse cry caused her to whip her head to the side. Eve, who still seemed unconscious or at least in some sort of delirium, thrashed around on the bed. Hopelessness coiled about Miri. She couldn't even make it to her sister's side. Even when the fire ebbed, it left her as wrung out as soggy laundry. Each time, too, an unfulfilled sensation grew in her breast. She felt empty and in need of something but what?

Healers hurried to their sides, and hands placed cold compresses to overheated skin. Her body greedily accepted every drop until the cloth felt bone dry. Sometimes, her mind drifted away, and only a scant awareness remained. But she fought that loss as much as she could, though she suspected it was a battle she wouldn't win. Innara had disappeared a while ago, not that she'd offered any explanation beyond the vague.

Why, oh why, had she ever taken Eve out for a run? Their father barely approved of their excursions. If they'd just remained in Knocton, none of this would've happened. But when viewing the past in hindsight, it was easy to come to such conclusions. If they survived, she couldn't incorporate those "if, but, and when" words into their life.

Suddenly, Innara stood by her side. Miri wasn't sure if minutes had passed or hours. Every minute could be an hour and every hour a minute. She opened her mouth to say something, anything, though the hoarseness of her voice made her cringe. All words died, though, when she noticed the glow of platinum hair. From there, it took only a second for her to ascertain who stood by Innara.

She wanted to cry, to moan. Him? She'd brought him? She wanted to die in relative peace, not be tormented by him. He watched her with inscrutable eyes until she wished she had the energy to squirm. All she could do was stare back at him with watering eyes. That was the only part of her body that seemed to have any moisture at all anymore.

Though it was fruitless, she tried to wet her parched lips with her sandpapery tongue. "Why have you brought him here? To have him mock me while I die?"

He cocked his head to the side. "You might be lucky and live."

His attitude still grated, no matter that a wagon mowing her over would've felt better than whatever was currently racking her muscles and nerves. A toddler playing with an adult's guitar would have a gentler touch than the illness plaguing her. Thank God, Eve seemed largely unaware of what was occurring. She couldn't bear to witness her sister's pain, especially when she, herself, was dealing with more than she'd ever felt.

She glared at him, though a wave of fire took most of the bite away. "I'll live just to spite you."

He shrugged. "It matters not to me. Regardless, you're undergoing the Change, something that only fae people have survived. Let's see if you and your sister are the first humans to live through it."

Vigil

Eerin shifted position in the stiff-backed chair located between the two humans' beds. Why was he still there hours later?

They'd either live or die. Healers came and went, tending to the sick humans. His presence here wouldn't affect the outcome. Innara, though, had repeatedly reminded him of *his* duty. That, along with some morbid curiosity, had won out. Or maybe he'd finally slipped into madness, as his people half-feared him to do.

For whatever reason, he found that he couldn't turn away. Something about the older human especially gripped him.

He shouldn't care. In fact, he should be overjoyed. This was a process no human had ever survived, and they'd inflicted it on a few in the beginning just to see if humans could become like them—carriers of the darkness. Other fae races scorned them for what they were, but his people wouldn't change that facet of themselves for anything.

Would these two be the first? If pure will could determine an outcome, he'd say Miri stood a good chance. Miri. The name fit her. It was cute, girlish, and so human.

He stared from his hand to hers. The black was streaking through her veins quickly, but it hadn't reached her face yet. Her flushed cheeks offered up the only color on her face. How would the black veins of the Taelin look on her? If she lived, he'd find out. He shied away from that trail of thought, finding it more interesting than it should be.

When would she become restless again? After fifteen or so minutes of thrashing, she'd finally quieted. Her sister was much less animated and fitful. He didn't know if that boded well for her recovery or not. Neither did the healers. This was unchartered territory for them all. Time alone would reveal the outcome.

But for now, his bed called to him. Sleep had been a scarce commodity lately, so it probably was a good thing his evening with Selina had been canceled.

So why was he still sitting in this blasted chair? There was nothing to hold him there. He'd done his duty, and as long as the Spirit couldn't hold him accountable for the humans' likely deaths, he should be satisfied.

As he leaned forward in preparation to stand, the older human moaned. Her limbs moved weakly, and she shook her head as if denying something. Some insane urge gripped him, and he nearly reached to comfort her before reining in the impulse. What was he doing? She wasn't his problem, no matter what the Spirit said. He pushed himself out of the chair and retreated a few steps.

Instantly, her flailing increased until he thought she might tumble from the mattress. He frowned. The healers had mentioned the possibility of strapping her down if her fits continued to escalate, and it appeared they might have to.

Well, he'd tell them this latest development so they could tend to her. He turned on his heel, but from the corner of his eye, he saw her back arch off the bed and her limbs kick out. Suddenly, the edge of the bed hovered near her left side. Without thought, he sprang toward her and grabbed her shoulders.

The touch of her clammy skin against his hands caused him to gasp. Heat, more heat than skin could ever possibly hold, tore through him. He ripped his hands from her, disbelief holding him immobile by her bedside. How could she produce so much warmth and still be alive?

Though she no longer bucked, her legs and arms still moved restlessly. He stood motionless by her bedside, nearly forgetting how to breathe. What kept him captive here, he didn't know. All he knew was that he couldn't pull himself away.

As the minutes ticked by, her thrashing grew. Calling himself all kinds of a fool, he bent to place a hand against her forehead. Again, her skin seared his. It wasn't exactly a painful feeling, but it was...disconcerting. Sparks sped up his arm, and he gritted his teeth. As he made to yank his hand from hers, her agitated movements quieted. Her head turned toward him. He frowned and removed his hand. Was a vestige of normal color returning to her face?

Suddenly, she moaned, but it wasn't one of pain. The sound struck fear into him as an answering lust shot to his groin area. Abhorrence and fascination warred in the pit of his stomach. When one was undergoing the Change, was it possible to feel physical desire? His people had transformed so long ago that none of the original now lived. Every one of the present Taelin had been born into the darkness.

She gasped, and her hands clenched on the bedding. The sheets covering her had long been knocked aside. A thin nightgown clung to her body, highlighting all the curves that would fit so nicely in his hands. The material had ridden up to her hips and revealed long, toned legs. And her arms...the feminine shape of them, with their new hint of shadowy veins, were a work of art.

He gritted his teeth, some inner voice screaming at him to leave. What was he thinking? She was not only human but deathly ill. To desire someone at such a time was shameful and beneath him.

Her chest thrust up into the air, the areolas and nipples prominent. Eerin found he couldn't tear his gaze away from the sight. Desire flowed southward again. What would they feel like in his — He stumbled back from the bed, shaking his head. These thoughts—they were insanity.

He closed his eyes and took a few deep breaths. Then a growl rumbled in his throat. There were better things to do than watching two humans die. He'd not waste a moment more on it. From now on, they would solely be under Innara's care.

Still, as he walked toward the door and past startled healers that he hadn't noticed before, something compelled him to glance back. Miri's body was slowly seeping into a restiveness not of the erotic kind. Stiffening his resolve, he marched out of the room. Nothing would ever draw him back there if he had any say.

Longing

Miri moaned as agony seared every particle of her body. Her fevered mind blurred time until all she knew was pain. But worse, oh, so much worse, was the yearning. It was a lustful blaze that seemed to underlie it all. Oh, God, she burned, burned for something she couldn't grasp onto. It was fleeting and always moved away. This something—maybe a presence—dulled the searing agony. And when it touched her, she burned with a different kind of flame. It always left too soon, though, leaving her adrift in a black sea of fire.

Many times, gentle hands soothed her. Though they offered an amount of comfort, they didn't give her the relief she craved—no, needed. She moved restlessly. Her body demanded movement, though her muscles protested.

God, stop, stop this torture. She ground her teeth until the metallic taste of blood filled her mouth.

That presence…she needed it back. She'd do anything to abate the curse tearing through her. Somehow, she knew it held the key. The key to everything.

***

Eerin strode through some of the side paths of the city, craving some sense of movement. He'd been cooped up in his office for too long, stuck with reports and meetings. So after lunch, he was enjoying the beauty and splendor that was Taerin. Every so often, one of his people called out a greeting, but otherwise, he was left unhindered.

The bright, sunny day soothed the blackness in his veins. As the leader of his people, the dark portion of the woods called to him the most strongly. It was both a bane and a blessing, one he'd accept many times over for the benefit of his people.

His thoughts turned sour. All would be well if he could just dispose of the humans. Their kind only brought problems. Too long had he protected the Taelin's borders against the creatures. Several hundred years had passed since the humans' last attack on them. Though his occasional cloaked scout, not to mention the rumblings of the darker part of the forest, reported nothing suspicious, he was wary of a long-lasting peace.

Humanity was never content with their own lands and resources. They invariably sought to expand their towns and kingdoms through war and pillaging. Though the fierce reputation of the Taelin kept them away for now, he knew that respite wouldn't continue forever.

Now, with these humans here... He didn't know where the whole situation would lead but doubted it would have a good end. Combine that with the older girl being much too fascinating for her own good—or his—and nothing but trouble awaited him.

"My lord Eerin, how fare you?"

At the sound of the familiar voice, Eerin blinked, coming to a stop. As his troublesome thoughts drifted away, he slowly smiled and turned around. A tall, brown-haired fae was striding toward him, an answering smile pasted on his face. Though Eerin hadn't longed for company, Kavin was one of his dearest friends, so it was a welcome intrusion.

"Quite well. And you, my friend?" Eerin leaned against a silver fence, making himself more comfortable.

Kavin halted a foot or two away from him. "Just visiting my lovely wife over lunch. Alas, I must get back to the smithy."

Eerin nodded and crossed his arms. "My respite was short, too."

"At least I don't have a mound of paperwork waiting for me," Kavin said jollily, clapping a hand on Eerin's shoulder and mirroring his stance against the fence.

Eerin shot him a sideways glance. "No, just the inferno that is your forges."

His friend chuckled. "True, but I also produce the fine weapons that outfit our soldiers."

"There are none better, but I'd like to see you wield one."

"I'm not a warrior. Your basic training was enough for me and all I need to know if called upon to protect home and family."

"If you say so." His friend had the physique of a warrior, thanks to his work, but not the disposition to be one. *Ah,* well, not everyone could be a fighter.

Kavin changed the topic. "Will you be at our gathering tonight? Liana would be overjoyed if you came."

Eerin frowned and stared at the neat row of buildings set into a copse of trees. "Maybe." He didn't know if he was up to a crowd of people, even if they were *his* people. An evening spent alone sounded as good as anything right now.

"Is it those humans?" Kavin asked, though there was no censure in his voice.

"By the Dark Woods, don't even mention them."

Kavin lifted a brow. "That bad?"

"You don't want to know." He swore that just the thought of Miri caused a headache to explode behind his eyes.

His friend shrugged. "What trouble could two girls cause, especially when they're unconscious?"

Eerin ground his teeth. "They have their way, the older one particularly."

"That sounds like it might hold a story. Come tonight and tell it to me."

"We'll see."

"*Ahh.*" Kavin snorted. "The fine art of the non-committal answer."

"Of course, did you expect anything less?"

"No, you learned from the best, after all," Kavin said, smirking.

"Your father?"

Kavin reared back with an expression of profound affrontment. "Me!"

After a few more minutes of inane chatter, they both drifted in opposite directions. He headed back to his office, feeling lighter than before. Some of the tension that had been plaguing him had lifted. Running into his friend was just what he'd—

His line of thought died a brutal death as he caught the sight of Innara marching toward him. As if sensing her mood, the people around her scattered. Eerin stifled a groan. That, along with her brisk pace and determined expression, left no doubt that she was coming to harangue him about her favorite topic of late. The sick humans.

Bah, would they just die? Somehow, that notion didn't bring him the joy it should, and that only made him angrier. Those humans had no hold on him, so why was he having these maudlin feelings?

Innara halted in front of him, pinning him with a glare. "They worsen, especially Miri. You must come."

Reticence

"I must?" Eerin crossed his arms, even as something in his chest jolted. Not his heart, surely. That organ was as shriveled as it could become.

Innara grabbed onto his arm and pulled him in-between two stores. "The healers noticed something interesting."

"What?" Truly, must Innara waylay him everywhere he went? He brushed off her hand. She took much liberty with their familial tie, and it needed to stop.

"Miri...her condition was stable in your presence yesterday. Now, she's deteriorating quickly."

Innara's words yanked his train of thought around, sending them flashing back to his visit with the girl.

How she would first become restless in his presence only to quiet at his touch.

The remembrance of her fevered skin and the sensations it had unleashed in him hammered at his mind. Unease exploded through his veins, but he forced himself to ignore it. "What problem is that of mine?"

A low growl of frustration rumbled from Innara's throat. "Need I remind you of the Spirit and its decree to you?"

"My memory is quite sharp. I have no need of your reminders."

"Stop this!" she said, slashing her hand through the air in a downward motion. "She's dying under your negligent care, and your only response is a flippant one? If you don't care for the humans' sake, then do so for the sake of your people. Angering the Spirit is never wise."

He knew all this. That she was right fanned his ire to a new height. "The Spirit doesn't know what it asks!"

"I loved your father, sister, and Anneth, but they're gone, and hating humans won't bring them back."

Even now, their names could still bring pain. "No, but revenging their deaths is something I'll always pursue."

Innara sighed and rubbed her temples as if to ward off a headache. "Those humans are already dead—killed hundreds of years ago by your hand. These innocent girls have nothing to do with them. Nothing."

"They all have the same evilness in their veins."

"Do they? Some would argue that we have that in abundance in our own veins. After all, we carry the black taint."

"The non-Taelin fae may call us that, but they know nothing about us. They bask in their supposed brilliance, yet ignorance is what they truly wallow in."

"And you don't think you are with this silly hate against humanity?"

The urge to yell, to scream, at her nearly overcame him. He shoved it back, though. They'd had this conversation more than once over the years, and their shouting matches were legendary. He had an afternoon to get on with, so he might as well not prolong the inevitable.

"Let's go see your precious humans."

Her mouth opened as if she was about to say something, but she merely nodded.

Up and down a few winding paths they went. All too soon, they arrived at the last place he wanted to be—the healing halls. His day couldn't progress until this visit was done, though. Innara would nag him until he capitulated. He scowled at how much power she had over him. It was the unforeseen consequence of her being his last remaining family member.

She pushed open the ivory-colored doors guarding the entrance to the halls. The scent of medicinal plants and herbs hit his nose. The smell turned his stomach as it had for centuries, and he swallowed against the bitterness rising in his throat. It wasn't a bad aroma, but too many of his people, some family and friends, had lain in these halls and died. It would always be a place he preferred to avoid when he could. His position as leader made that largely impractical, if not impossible, though.

The airy, pastel green hallway did nothing to improve his mood. Innara kept up a brisk pace, so they'd reach their destination that much faster. He didn't know whether to be appreciative of that or not. After they rounded a corner, she stopped in front of a beige door inset with plant motifs.

Innara knocked once before entering. With a sigh, he followed her. His gaze swung across the room, barely taking in the healers who milled around the perimeter of the room. When he caught sight of one of the beds, he froze. The human...Miri...what he saw nearly made him recoil. An air of complete stillness lay about her. Her complexion held no color except for the blackness creeping through her veins up to her neck and jawline. He stared at the other bed. Her sister seemed to fair little better. The veins in her face stood black against the paleness of her skin.

"We can do no more for her or her sister."

The voice of one of the healers ripped his attention from the human to the fae in question. "So you just give up?" he asked, an edge to his voice.

The male—a defeated-looking, brown-haired Taelin that Eerin couldn't remember the name of and didn't want to—took an uneasy step back. "We've tried all we know. Making her comfortable is all that is left to us unless..." He trailed off, reluctance clear on his face.

Eerin glowered. "Unless what?"

When no answer was forthcoming, he glared at the group of exhausted healers. One of them had been his lover many years ago. She'd been a pretty, black-haired lady then, and she remained that. The haggard expression on her face spoke for itself, though. She didn't glance at him once with a come-hither look. Instead, she looked nearly as hopeless as the head healer had.

Suddenly, she squared her shoulders and moved forward, her hands clasped solemnly before her. "My lord, there is one thing."

Her voice contained the slightest waiver, so he knew she was putting on a brave façade. Whatever she was about to say, he was sure not to like.

"What is that, Anha?" he asked, his voice losing some of its hardness.

She inclined her head respectfully. "If you will, please stand by Lady Miri's bed."

As he stared at her, Innara's words pulsed back to him. Did they think he could revive the human somehow? His first inclination was to say that was preposterous, but something stayed him. As if his feet had a mind of their own, he drifted toward Miri. An inexplicable urge propelled him to sweep back her blanket.

Her body resembled her complexion—lifeless. She was so pale and still. So unnatural. If not for the subtle rise and fall of her chest, he'd believe her dead. For some reason, that thought was more upsetting than it should be.

"She's so far gone that you'll have to touch her," Anha murmured from behind.

Eerin stiffened. "What?"

"Anha, let me handle this," Innara said, strolling farther into the room. "Everyone is dismissed for the time being. We'd like some privacy."

The head healer, the defeated-looking male from before, opened his mouth to protest. Innara held up a hand. "The humans will be fine enough under our care. Do not forget I have medical training. Besides, I know where you are if we have need of you."

As the healers filed out, Innara walked over to him and placed a hand on his arm. He stared at the offending appendage without uttering a word.

With blinding clarity that sunk into him like a leaden rock, Eerin knew he wasn't merely going to dislike what she had to say, he was going to absolutely *loathe* it.

Sickness

"Go on," Eerin snapped, wanting to get whatever bad news that awaited him out of the way.

Innara squeezed his arm as if to impart a measure of comfort. "Her body is trying to fight off the darkness, and it's losing. The battle is taking too much from her and leaving her with no reserve of strength or energy."

Her words and actions did everything but reassure him. He ripped his arm away from her. "What does that have to do with me?"

Innara pointed to the bed. "Look. Even without a touch, you're reviving her."

He glanced at Miri's still form and blinked, then blinked again. Pink, tinged with a gray flush, had seeped back into her cheeks, lending her a fevered look that had been missing. "What insanity is this?"

"You calm the darkness in some ways, but you also call out to it."

"So I have to cuddle with her?" He adopted an expression of disgust, something of which he wished he felt more.

Innara shook her head. "That would help but wouldn't be enough for long."

"Well, there's nothing further I can do, then." His heart lurched, but he ignored it. He couldn't allow himself to care about what happened to a mere human. No one of that species was deserving of his concern.

Something that looked suspiciously like pity flashed across her face. "Yes, there is."

"What?"

She didn't speak right away, and impatience tugged at him. "I don't have time for this." As he pivoted on his heel, she uttered words that stopped him cold.

"Join your body to hers."

Had Innara gone insane? He turned toward her slowly and glared. "What?"

"You heard me perfectly."

By the Spirit, how he wished he hadn't. "Why would I sleep with her?"

"To save her life."

"What makes you think that me doing *that* would make a difference?"

"For the reasons I've told you. You're the only person to which she responds. The healers and I..." She shook her head. "And when I communed with the Spirit, it did not confirm nor reject my hypothesis. It merely said to do what feels right." With a passionate gesture, she flung her hand out toward the bed. "Look, even now, she stirs. It's due to your presence! This feels right!"

"Right? How could this ever be right?" As much as he wanted to deny it—oh, did he ever—he recalled the effect that his presence had on the human the last time he'd visited. It all made some kind of cruel, abhorrent sense.

Even if he'd desired to do as Innara wished, he couldn't. "I don't rape women, even human ones."

"In this case it wouldn't be force. It's clear she wants you."

"Because of that damn change. It's an artificial desire. She's not even aware of what she's doing!"

She folded her hands before her. "It's what she needs to survive."

"Why doesn't the younger one feel that way, then?" He motioned angrily toward the human in question.

"The Spirit is guiding this whole series of events. Eve seems to be pulling energy from her sister."

"So the Spirit wants me to mate with the older human? In Taelin's name, why?" He ran a hand agitatedly through his hair.

Something flashed through her eyes before it disappeared. "I don't know. Only the Spirit could answer that."

"I won't do it." He shook his fist toward the ceiling, glaring around the room. "Do you hear me, Spirit?"

"Then she'll die and likely her sister, too."

He set his mouth into a thin line. Damn them all, he'd not be manipulated into something so against his beliefs. "So be it. I'll not impugn my honor so."

"You worry more about your perception of yourself than two innocent lives."

"They're humans. They'll die soon enough due to their short lifespans."

She crossed her arms and sent him a disbelieving look. "Have you no heart?"

He smiled thinly. "It died with our family."

***

Eerin scowled at the door to the humans' room. They'd medicated her and her sister to keep them comfortable but said there was nothing more they could do. Why was he here again? He'd vowed to leave them to their fate.

With a sigh of annoyance, he shoved open the door and stalked over the threshold of the dim room. This would be the last time he'd see them—see Miri. He had to weed this weakness out of his blood one way or another. Time was on his side in this. They'd be dead within a few days at most.

No healers remained, as they'd sedated the humans for the night. They said there was no more they could do but make them comfortable. He snapped his fingers to activate a lamp, though he could see well enough without it.

He stood by the wall, an unfamiliar hesitance pinning him in place. As he clenched his hands, he scoffed at himself. What had happened to his courage? One lone human would not scare him away.

As he marched over to the beds, he couldn't stop his gaze from zeroing in on the young woman who lay so still and waxen. She should be dead. Why wasn't she? No human should be able to weather this, especially with her sister siphoning energy from her.

After coming to a halt, he stared at her. If she passed, everything would go back to normal. Life would be so much easier. His thoughts—and conscience—wouldn't be haunted by imaginings he should never have. But it seemed she wouldn't die when it was convenient for him. That he could restore life to her wasn't a thought worth exploring, so why was it never far from his mind since Innara had spoken of it earlier that day?

Suddenly, the seemingly lifeless woman moved. So much for the healers' sedation. As before when he'd visited her alone, her movements were restless. Soon, her body moved in a way that spoke of need, of pain. His breath came faster. He wanted to run from the sight, run from the room. Instead, he was held captive.

The real torture commenced when her moans started. He gritted his teeth. His hands itched to reach for her and do...what? Strangle her? Kiss her?

He'd do neither. Marshaling his failing control, he stepped away from her.

"*Eerin.*"

The sound of his name on her lips poured cold-hot chills down his spine and froze his feet to the floor.

Wicked Need

"Eerin."

By the darkness, how could she put so much feeling—so much need—in the mere utterance of his name? He wanted so badly to bolt from the chamber, but something kept him cemented to the floor.

Pink color, with a slightly grayish cast, leaked back into her face, and her eyelids fluttered. Sweat popped up on skin that had been bone-dry.

He bit the inside of his cheek, forcing back a cry. Or was it a moan? If he'd wanted to deny Innara's words, he could no longer. Here was irrefutable proof that she reacted to him—only him. Horror cascaded through him at that knowledge. Worse, a lustful excitement coursed right along with it.

Shuddering, he pressed a hand to his eyes. Why did she draw him so? Was it the altered blood flowing through her veins? Innara had said Miri's darkness cried out to his. He was the strongest of his people, so maybe that was why. Even before that, though—

"Eerin." This time it came out as nearly a pure moan. Her lips parted, and a light-lavender-colored tongue darted out. That sight almost undid him. To see something so familiar yet different on her, unlike the black or gray tongues of his people.

Her hips undulated, and her back arched off the mattress. In her restlessness, she kicked off the blankets covering her. Perspiration coated her skin, making her light nightgown stick to her body as if plastered on. His mouth turned as dry as a torrid summer day. The all-but-see-through material revealed the darkness snaking over her body, enflaming him even more.

He fisted his hands until the bite of his nails sunk into his skin. By all that was sacred, those moans... He couldn't take them anymore. Each one acted like a shot of lust through his veins.

The human's eyes shot open and tracked straight to him. Her hand lifted slowly as if beckoning him. "I need this—I need you," she rasped. "Please, make the burn go away."

His resolve cracked and splintered beyond repair. His body moved toward her as if pulled by invisible strings. Her eyes were half open and hazy, yet she watched every move he made. Some distant voice in his head screamed at him to resist, but he was powerless to heed that cry.

He didn't stop until his knees hit the bed. His gaze soaked in her form, starting from her tousled hair to the curling toes of her feet. But what mesmerized him so was her full breasts with their erect nipples and dusky rose areolas. He itched to rip the material away so he could feast on them.

"*Please.*"

That word broke something within him, though some distant part of himself knew he'd be damned in the morning. They both would. His legs buckled, and he slid into a slumped sitting position on the mattress. Her entreating eyes were fixed unblinkingly on him. He gulped, finding it hard to get air.

She reached a hand out and laid it heavily against his cheek. That simple touch burned through every fiber of his body and ripped away any last coherent thought of human versus fae.

He slowly climbed onto the bed on all fours until he hovered over her. Dropping his head, he let it fall into the curve of her neck. He breathed in the medicinal scent that coated her, but underneath, there was a scent all her own. Innocent, sweet, yet smoky. Decadent. All Miri.

Breathing became hard for a minute. Miri? Was that her name? It suited the siren before him.

Biting back a groan, he nuzzled at her throat with lips and nose. She gasped, tilting her neck to the side so he could get a better angle. He lowered himself over her. The blood pulsing through her veins…it rushed so temptingly, singing a potent song. That life force always called out to his people during amorous times, due to the darkness in their veins. But no one's blood had ever lured him as hers was doing. But biting her wasn't an option, though he could barely remember why. His tongue raked over his sharp teeth in frustrated annoyance until he tasted the tang of blood. Somehow, he forced his mouth to travel up to her chin, away from that vulnerable neck.

His mind grew increasingly hazy, but somewhere in the back of his mind echoed warnings he'd learned long ago. *Most Taelin only partook with those they loved or wanted a long-term relationship with. Exchange of blood created a bond of sorts, at least for a time.* That was something he wanted with no one, least of all her. But why not? She was intoxicating, like a drug. What other reasons he'd had for his reticence slipped away like sand through his fingers.

But no...he *couldn't*. With a growl, he caught her lips in a hard kiss. She responded with equal fervor. He lowered himself to one side until he was only partially on her, making sure not to break their contact. His hand drifted to a round breast, and he cupped the globe. It filled his hand as if it'd been made for it. His fingers ghosted over her nipple, which stiffened after a few swipes. She moaned into his mouth, and that sent a jolt of lust through him. He ripped his mouth from hers and lowered his lips to the areola crying out to him. The thin material of her nightgown was a poor substitute for her flesh.

With impatient fingers, he undid the laces holding the front of the gown together. It parted easily, and her breasts spilled out in all their naked glory. He lost no time rolling a nipple between his fingertips, watching as it grew stiffer, harder.

Bending his head, he captured a tip between his lips and flicked his tongue over and around the sensitive bud.

Hands threaded through his hair and pushed his face harder against her chest.

"*Eerin.*"

His name sounded like a prayer. He sucked on her breast harder and then used his teeth to scrape across the areola before switching to the other one. Her hips were moving, and the side of her leg was pressing into his erection. With each undulation, he grew a bit harder until he thought he'd explode. By the Spirit, he needed her—needed to be in her.

His mouth wandered down her abdomen as he yanked the fabric down her body. In his haste, the rending of material filled his ears. She lifted her hips and helped to remove the useless item. He kicked it off the bed in disgust, wanting nothing between his skin and hers.

As he sat back on his haunches, she licked her lips, staring at him with desire-filled eyes. For a second, he blinked, and things swam back into focus. But as quickly as it came, it all grew hazy again.

He ripped off his overtunic and shirt in one motion. The temptress rolled onto her side. One hand reached for the ties on his leggings, and he sucked in a sharp breath at the sensation of her soft touch against him. As she pulled the ribbon loose, she gave him fleeting caresses and even cupped him a time or two. He twitched each time she did so.

Finally, he sprang free, and she fisted a hand around him. Up and down her palm went, fingers gently exploring. He gritted his teeth as he watched her. She had to stop, or he'd come in her hand like a young, inexperienced Taelin.

He grabbed her hand and lowered it back to the bed. After removing his leggings fully, he glided up her body on hands and knees. Lowering himself somewhat carefully, he settled over her. His knee parted her legs, and she opened them wide to cradle him. The head of his erection prodded her opening. He reached down to check if she was ready. His fingers slipped into her easily. Her gasp flew through his veins like a shot of magic.

Her wetness increased as he stroked her walls and trailed a finger over and around her nub. Her hands clenched around his arms, her nails biting deep into the skin. The pleasure-pain of it nearly caused him to roar.

Then he inserted one finger deeper, then two. In and out. In and out, he thrust them. Her hips followed the movement as if she were afraid the digits would be stolen away. A low moan was tugged from his lips. After a few strokes, he knew she was as prepared as she could be.

Positioning himself at her entrance, he stared down into her eyes. Her breath was coming erratically, and her cheeks were flushed pinkish-gray. Pinkish-gray? That wasn't— He shook his head as if to clear it but lost his thought. By the darkness, it didn't matter, anyway. Only getting buried in her did.

With one thrust, he entered her. A cry of pain and need escaped her and lingered in the air. He froze for a second. The squeeze of her channel was so tight, he almost forgot what to do with himself until nature reasserted himself. His hips took up a rhythm as ancient as the forest around them. They stared into each other's eyes as she met him thrust for thrust. The slap of skin against skin was an erotic sound that ratcheted his lust up another scorching notch.

Her hands gripped his rear-end, ever seeking to get him deeper, faster. Little noises escaped from her throat. By the Spirit, he'd never been that horny before! That overcome. He bent down and snagged a nipple between his teeth, nipping and licking at it. Candy hadn't ever tasted so sweet.

Sweat wove down his back and face. It created a slippery glide between their bodies that heightened the already overwhelming tactile experience flooding his senses.

Pleasure gripped him so strongly he closed his eyes. Oh, by the Dark Woods, he'd never felt anything that incredible. Her breaths came in gasps, and her body strained against his. Their pace sped up, his sweat mingling with hers. He was moving so quickly now that his member was pistoning in and out, only the tip remaining within her tight clutches.

Suddenly, she spasmed around him. That tight-glove feeling sent him careening over the precipice. The first rolling wave of his orgasm jerked through his body, and he buried his face in her neck. As his hips frantically rolled against hers, his sharp canines poked against his lips, and he hissed. Before he could think, he sunk his teeth into her throat. Warm, sweet liquid filled his mouth. A high-pitched, feminine scream, one of pleasure and pain, pierced the silence of the room. *Miri!* The name rushed through his overloaded brain like a shot of alcohol. His release pumped through him, ricocheting around every corner of his body until he was utterly spent.

With a gasp, he collapsed against her, still buried within her warm heat. Weak arms wrapped around him and smoothed over his back. His lids closed. Though he'd never felt so replete, he had no energy to keep them open and saw no reason to try. The most wonderful taste coated his mouth, relieving a terrible thirst he'd never known he had. All was well in his world for the first time in what felt like forever. With that, the welcoming blackness of sleep enveloped him.

Cruel Awakening

Eerin stirred and immediately regretted the action. Every muscle in his body protested. What had he been doing last night? Drinking the entire city dry?

Light pricked at his eyelids. *Ugh*, morning. Time to get up and be a leader to his people.

His body didn't want to listen, though. He groaned. Had a horse run him over? No, that would be a kinder fate than what he was feeling.

With more effort than he cared to admit, he forced his eyes open and immediately slammed them shut. By the Dark Woods, he wasn't in his bedchamber. In fact, the room had looked suspiciously like one in the healing wards. An inkling of just where he might be bludgeoned into him. A sick feeling twisted his gut. Surely, he hadn't been so lost to reason? But last evening was hazy as though veiled behind a wall of fog.

Though it pained him both mentally and physically, he forced himself to glance to his side. He stifled the curses that wanted to fly from his mouth. The human woman lay beside him, asleep and naked from the waist up. A blanket covered her lower half. By the blackness' balls, he'd slept with her. How? Why?

He glanced around the room. Thank the Dark Woods, there was no one else here right now. However, someone would have monitored the patients at some point during the night. Though the thought made him cringe, he could only hope that Innara or Eamandian had been the one to check on them.

Though all healers took an oath not to discuss their patients with family and friends, such juicy gossip might nearly be impossible for some of his people to resist relaying to others.

Even if no one but Innara or Eamandian had seen them, it didn't change the fact that some of the healers *did* know about the supposed cure. Once they learned that Miri and Eve would survive, they would all but know what had happened in this room during the dark of night.

Gods, he'd have to ensure no one talked. A strong warning would have to do. After all, not even he could stomach killing a host of healers.

He rubbed a hand over his face as he stared at her. Her color appeared completely normal, if one could call a grayish-pink normal in a human. The rise and fall of her chest wasn't labored, so she breathed easily for the first time he'd seen since she'd started changing.

The realization that she lived and was likely to keep living kicked him in the stomach. And it was all due to him. Because he slept with her. Anger kindled within him. He was furious at her, yes, but mostly at himself.

Why in Taelin's name had he done it? He gritted his teeth, wanting to tear into something. As if in answer, the remembrance of breathy moans filled with need and agony wafted back. That was no excuse, though. He'd been weak to succumb. Why was last evening so blurry, though? What he did recall was puzzling. He'd been resolved to leave, and then, it was as if his body mutinied against him. And...the rest just wasn't there, at least not in a clear manner.

He glanced around the room, his gaze landing on the younger sister. Dear brightness, they'd had sex while her sister was in the room.

The walls of the chamber seemed to shrink around him until only he, Miri, and the bed remained. He sucked in a deep breath and knew he had to get out of that room now. The smell of their night activities lingered in the air. Somehow, that made it all the worse, an even greater betrayal of everything he stood for. Everything he believed in.

Anger made it easy to ignore the pained tiredness of his body. He slowly got up, careful not to disturb her. Suddenly feeling naked, he glanced down and grimaced. With an inaudible sigh, he tucked himself back into his pants.

For a minute, he stood by the bed, something keeping him pinned there. Would she remember? Damn, he hardly remembered. Only jumbled bits and pieces leaked back. If he had any luck at all, she wouldn't. He'd worry about that later, though.

As he made to turn around, something at the base of her throat grabbed his attention. He narrowed his eyes, hoping they were fooling him. All that did was bring into clearer sight something he'd never wanted to see.

Puncture marks.

Disbelief pummeled him like a brutal fist. Damn it. He hadn't! The proof, however, was staring him right in the face.

His eyes closed in despair. What had he done? For him to experience such a loss of control...it didn't happen. Not until now. He had to piece the events of last night together. He'd go mad, otherwise. Only one glass of alcohol had passed his lips, and it took much more than that to even get him tipsy.

He needed to leave before she woke up, so this line of thought wasn't doing him any favors. If need be, he'd clear his schedule so he could think.

How to handle Miri, though? He scowled. She didn't have to know. Only he would feel the repercussions, as she hadn't tasted his blood. And what were a human's emotions to him? For a short while, at most a few weeks, he'd feel hers to a degree, but that was a trifling matter. Humans were shallow creatures, after all. Her emotions shouldn't give him much, if any, hardship. Given that he didn't sense anything from her right now, she must be in a dreamless sleep. Once he put some distance between them, he shouldn't be able to feel anything, either, even if her emotions flared wildly.

That decided, he spun on his heel before some other terrible discovery could hold him captive. The mere thought had him stalking quickly out of the healing house. If the human did live, he was definitely not going near her again, even if he had to banish her to the farthest reaches of Taelin land.

***

Miri slowly swam to consciousness and hated every minute of it. Every portion of her body ached from her head to her toes. For a few minutes, she was too tired to think, and only disjointed thoughts flowed through her mind.

When some of the bleariness burned off, she allowed herself to ponder what had brought this calamity about. Had she picked up some illness that left her thinking she'd gone twenty rounds with the best boxer in town?

Light filtered through her lids, so that ruled out the night. Where were her father and Eve? If she was ill, one of them usually sat by her side reading or doing some other busy work. It was a tradition in their family. Though she'd found it a bothersome one at times, she found herself missing it sorely for some reason now.

She shifted slightly in bed and winced as multiple stiff muscles screamed in protest. At least the soft bed was heavenly against her skin, which she swore felt raw.

Frowning, she focused on one word. Bed? Hers was never this comfortable. Maybe she'd been so sick that even a rock would feel good. Somehow, she didn't believe that, and some premonition told her she wouldn't like the truth. Dread worse than anything she'd experienced in years flooded her. Though she wanted to keep her eyes closed forever, she had to face whatever stood like a phantom before her.

At first, her lids didn't respond. When they did, they refused to move as if they were stuck with glue. She raised her hand to rub at them. Once the crust was removed, her lids fluttered open. The foreign sight of a room not her own bombarded her.

Where...where was she? This wasn't home or anywhere that she knew of in the village. Memories poked at the edges of her mind, floating away when she tried to grasp them.

She glanced around the room, hoping something would jar her recollection of what had occurred. Her gaze glided over the room, finding nothing of note, until it landed on her sister. The breath froze solid in her lungs at what she saw.

The Dawning of Realization

Miri stared in horror at the streaks of black running underneath her sister's skin, at the blackness running through her veins.

Dark like the Taelin. Those words echoed through her mind out of nowhere.

But that was enough for memories to crash through any barriers holding them back. Memories of being captured by Lord Eerin and being taken to their town.

Oh, damn. Damn, damn, damn. Somehow, the Taelin had turned Eve into one of *them*.

Miri pushed herself upright, only to collapse onto her back again. Her muscles had all the strength of dough. She stared hopelessly at her sister. Eve needed her, and she could do nothing to help. Not even be by her sister's side.

Anger, fear, and helplessness all swirled around in her gut. She had to do something—get to her sister and demand a cure. But even the thought of trying to stand made her head swim. She gritted her teeth, determined not to abandon Eve so easily.

With a grunt of effort, she shifted to her side. Her gaze fell to her arms, and she shrieked. Ribbons of black ran under her own skin. Oh God, they'd corrupted them both. She followed the dark branching lines up to her shoulder and down to her chest. Her naked chest. Why was she naked?

Why did she even care about that fact right now? She and Eve had turned into some kind of monsters. Were they even human anymore? So many questions swirled around her head until her mind became one big, tangled mess of uncertainty. First, though, she had to get to her sister. They seemed to be in some kind of healing ward, which made sense because anything that could make her feel so worn out had surely made her ill. The same had to hold true for Eve, too.

After slowly forcing herself up with both arms, she slouched forward into a seated position. Her muscles shook like jelly, and she hadn't even stood up. At this point, she didn't think she could. Her heart thudded painfully, and she couldn't catch her breath. She'd likely end up a crumpled mess on the floor.

Grunting, she scooted herself toward the edge of the bed one torturous inch at a time. If she couldn't stand, she'd crawl. Sweat popped up on her forehead, but she didn't have the extra energy to brush it away. The sight of her pale skin mottled with black streaks sickened her, so she did her best to keep her gaze from it. That was no easy task when that same sight seemed to hold some sort of morbid fascination over her.

Oh, God, was her skin flushing a pinkish-gray from exertion? She shuddered, hovering at the edge of the bed. If this was her fate, maybe death would've been better. For both her and Eve. However, she hadn't gotten to choose. The one thing she did know was that if there wasn't a cure, they could never go home. Never.

Feeling her thoughts spiraling downward, she forced herself instead to concentrate on the task at hand. *One, two, three.* She lowered her legs to the floor, and the rest of her followed with a crash. Pain jarred her body, and the air rushed out of her lungs in a groan. For a minute she couldn't have moved even if she'd wanted to. Had she injured anything? The big ache that was her body gave no concrete answer.

She took stock of herself. Nothing seemed to be broken, probably only bruised. Still, the direness of her predicament struck her. She was naked, lying helpless on the floor. Never a good position to be in.

How had she and Even even gotten into this state? The answer seemed to lurk at the fringes of her mind. What was the last thing she remembered? She frowned, fingers curling against the cool wood floor. Had the Taelin really done something to them? Why would they, though? Most would not welcome the idea of a human turning into something similar to a Taelin.

The door banged open, and Innara came rushing in. "I thought I heard a crash."

Miri ignored her concern. "What happened to us?"

The sound of her gravelly voice pierced the quietness of the room. Innara visibly wilted. Then the fae woman gathered herself and bustled over to Miri. With gentle hands, she helped her back onto the bed and spread a blanket over her.

Though exhaustion still hounded Miri, her mind wouldn't rest. "Tell me what happened."

Innara sighed and sat on the mattress beside her. "You and your sister both received scratches from the Taelin tree. Unfortunately, the toxin coating the tree entered your bloodstream, and you were infected. We didn't know if you'd live through the Change, but praise the skies above, you both did."

Miri stared at Innara. The story sounded plausible. It even *felt* right. Still, she couldn't remember anything from that time clearly.

A frown formed between Innara's brows. "Do you not remember any of this?"

"Not really. Some of it's there, but it's all mixed up and out of order."

"The high fever you had would do it. By all rights you should be dead."

A chill stole over Miri's heart. "Then why am I not?"

The fae woman grabbed one of Miri's hands and squeezed it. "By good grace alone." She paused, clearly hesitating. "And Eerin."

Miri frowned. "What did he have to do with my recovery?" She couldn't see him willingly lifting one finger to save her. He'd be the type to take joy in her death. At the very least, he would've been relieved to have her and her sister permanently off his hands.

"He calmed the darkness running rampant through your veins. Without him, you and your sister would have perished."

That response only raised more questions than it answered. "How did he do that?"

"With his presence. As our leader, he's quite powerful. The forest respects him. Connects to him more so than with any other."

Miri swallowed the lump forming in her throat. Such mystical talk still wasn't easy to deal with. "So all that was required was his presence at our bedside?"

Innara stared down at their hands, her pale lashes fanned out against even paler cheeks. "For the most part." She stood up and cheerfully clapped her hands. "Let me arrange a bath for you. That should help ease any lingering aches and pains. After that, a bite to eat wouldn't be amiss, either."

Miri frowned but didn't press her further. Why did she feel as if she were missing something, though? Something important?

The Bathing Chamber

As soon as Innara let go, Miri collapsed onto a bench near the hot springs that served as the healing chambers' bathing area. She hugged the sheet that was wrapped around her tighter as she took in her surroundings. Though there seemed to be a larger communal bathing area, thankfully, this section was partitioned into smaller yet still generous-sized baths. The last thing she wanted was to be the object of anyone else's attention. She didn't even want to look at herself. To have others do it... A shiver racked her body.

Innara bustled around the steamy room, gathering towels and bottles of toiletries. "You'll feel much better after you're fresh and clean. I know I always do."

Miri doubted there was anything that could truly make her smile right now—or maybe ever. She was a monster. Nothing could change that. "How long was I unconscious? When will Eve awaken? She will, won't she?"

Innara froze for a moment but then flashed her a reassuring smile. "Your sister should rouse at any moment. We have no fears on that account."

Relief poured over Miri's ragged nerves like a soothing balm, but when a horrible realization struck, that sensation immediately died.

Eve would soon have to face what they'd become.

Miri nervously swiped at her dry lips with her tongue. "How long was I out?"

The other female glanced down at the bottles in her hands. "It's the morning of the eleventh day."

Miri felt her face go slack in surprise. "That long?"

"In some ways, it seemed so much longer." Innara gave a forced smile. "But it's done and over."

Miri couldn't stop the words pouring from her mouth. "No, it's not over. It'll never be."

Innara sighed, sitting down her load of crystal bottles, and glided over to her. "You mean your Change?"

"Of course I mean it." Her voice reeked of anger as she glared at the other female, but she didn't care. That she found herself and Eve changed was due in large part to the Taelin. It was *their* trees, *their* forest, that had done it. In fact, they were responsible for everything that had happened since they'd entered these cursed woods.

"That will take some time to get used to."

Miri crossed her arms. "I don't want to get used to it."

"I understand you don't," Innara said, her tone kind. "But you have no choice in the long run. To fight yourself on this will just lead to further heartache."

"How can I fight myself when I don't even know what I am?"

"What do you think you are?"

There was no hesitation. "A monster."

Innara's smooth brow furrowed, and her black lips tilted downward. "Do you think that's what I am?"

Miri's mind hit a stone wall. Put that way... "No."

"The Taelin in general?"

That wasn't so easy to answer. Lord Eerin seemed pretty monstrous, and he was Innara's cousin and the Taelin leader. What did that say for them as a group? But then again, humans weren't any better in this regard much of the time. "I don't know most of your people well."

"So you do believe us to be monsters? Well, that's problematic, indeed. We'll have to work on that perception. As to what you are, I'm not sure."

Miri's heart plummeted at her words. "So I'm doubly cursed? And Eve, too."

Innara shook her head and sat down beside her. "Never that. You're merely the first of your kind to ever successfully go through the Change. As such, we have nothing to measure that against. So we'll learn along the way." She patted Miri's shoulder. "You're not alone in this. In fact, I take full responsibility for what happens to you."

Miri pursed her lips, not sure why Innara would take on such a thing willingly.

Apparently seeing the question on Miri's face, Innara gave a dry laugh. "My cousin told me since I'm so fond of you and your sister that you're both my problem."

"That sounds like him," Miri muttered. For some reason, the notion of him pawning them off on Innara grated a bit. However, it wasn't a feeling she wanted to explore.

"Don't worry. He'll do right by both of you, even if I have to drag him kicking and cursing."

Miri lifted a brow. "Do right?"

Innara blinked, and her face went blank for a second. "Accept both of you as members of Taelin society."

There was something more there, but Miri didn't know what. She'd put that suspicion aside for now, though, and revisit it later.

Innara took her arm gently and pulled her up. "Come, let's get you in the springs."

Miri leaned against Innara and allowed her to all but haul her there. The fae woman was abnormally strong, but that was probably due to her being fae. In some ways, those of that race seemed blessed in comparison to humans. She swallowed thickly as a thought rammed into her. Would she pick up any other Taelin traits? Though she didn't want to find any good in such a possibility, the more rational part of her whispered not all changes were bad.

Suddenly, a peculiar sensation in her nether regions intruded. Not was she only a bit sore down there, but there was a slickness between her thighs. Just what had she been dreaming about? She might be a virgin, but she wasn't naïve. Erotic dreams weren't a stranger to her, but this one must've really been something in her delirium.

Once at the mouth of the springs, Innara whipped the sheet off her before she could protest and pushed her down gently onto the first step. "Scoot down to the inbuilt ledge, and I'll help bathe you."

The hot water lapped at Miri's chest, and her train of thought evaporated into the steam swirling around her. She groaned, forgetting to be self-conscious as the heat created a painfully pleasant sensation throughout her body. When had she last felt anything so wonderful?

"Lean your head back."

With a sigh, Miri did as Innara bid. The fae woman poured water over her head and applied some sort of cleansing oil to her hair. Gentle fingers massaged her scalp. The rhythmic motion lulled her eyelids into a nearly closed state.

"Sleepy, dear Miri?"

"*Mmm,*" said Miri, nodding slowly as if in a trance.

"Then let's hurry and get you back into bed."

That sounded like a delightful plan. Her body was crying out for more sleep, and nothing could pierce that misty veil obscuring her mind.

"I see the human is awake and living," a cold male voice said, startling Miri out of her stupor and yanking her eyes open.

Rude Interruption

Lord Eerin loomed like a bad dream just inside the door to the bathing chamber. Embarrassment and outrage caused Miri to sink down until water came up to her neck. Could he see anything through the steam?

Any notion of sleep had vacated her. Instead, her breath rasped in her throat, and her heart rate sped away from her grasp. What was he doing, barging in here like this?

Innara stood up and planted her hands on her hips. "Really, Eerin? Give the girl some privacy."

A sneer sprang to his lips. "It's nothing I haven't seen before."

The pompous pig. Miri found her voice. "Well, you haven't seen mine."

A strange look flashed across his features before he glowered at her. "Who says I haven't?"

Horror drenched her. He'd seen her naked while she'd been unconscious? "Get out! You have no right."

He crossed his arms. "I have every right. I'm the lord of the Taelin. Right now, everything you do falls under my purview, including observing what you've become."

Innara growled and pushed him toward the door. "Go. Now is not the time for this."

He raised a brow coolly. "This? Whatever are you talking about?"

"Whatever you're trying to prove to yourself can wait. She just woke up, thanks in part to *your* special attentions."

Miri stared at them. What on earth was going on? And "special attention"? His presence at her bedside hardly seemed to qualify as that. To him, maybe it did, though. He was an arrogant ass, after all. Any crumbs he gave, he surely saw as magnanimous gifts.

He brushed off Innara's hands, which had left wet spots on his navy tunic. "Don't bring that up! You're the one that implanted the idea into my head. That she lives and breathes is due to your interference."

Miri bit her lip. She had to be missing some crucial information. Nothing they said was making any sense.

Innara shook her head and opened the door in clear invitation for Lord Eerin to leave. "We both had our parts to play. Did you ever think the Spirit called on us to do so?"

He stiffened. "I won't be a pawn in anyone's game, not even to the heart of the forest."

"While the Spirit may call to us, it's up to us if we choose to listen."

A bitter expression played over his face. "I wouldn't be so sure of that."

His gaze catching Miri's, he cast her such a hateful yet penetrating look that she involuntarily shrank back. What had she done to direct so much venom her way? Somehow, this seemed to go far beyond his whole "hating humans" thing.

Breaking their eye contact, he spun on his heel and stormed over the threshold.

Miri sucked in a gust of much-need air. She hadn't even been aware that she'd forgotten how to breathe until now. His intensity...it had threatened to consume everything she was. Even now, the invisible scorch marks it left behind branded her. She felt shaky, and tiredness seeped into her veins.

"Well, he's certainly got a bee poking him somewhere in his briar patch," Innara said, walking back toward the pool.

Miri choked on her own saliva. Had Innara just said what Miri thought she had? Her cheeks burned at the thought of his...*umm*, privates. She shifted on the stone seat, heat spreading over her body.

God, these Taelin mortified her like none other. "I really don't need that visual right now, Lady Innara."

"*Pshaw,* I grew up with him and saw him as a naked little boy." Innara knelt by the edge and scooped up a cloth, handing it to her before she continued on. "I forget others don't view him in such a light, though objectively I know he's handsome enough."

Why was Innara even discussing such things with her? Miri wanted to curl up and pretend this conversation had never happened. Instead, she settled for squeezing the washcloth in a death grip. To consider Lord Eerin as a sexual being was dangerous. He was dangerous. Surely, Innara, of all people, realized that? "Can we talk of something else? It feels...wrong to discuss your cousin in such a way."

Innara cocked her head to the side. "Why? He's living, breathing flesh like the rest of us."

"He's a little—no, make that a lot—intimidating and always seems to unleash that side around me."

"*Ah,* you get used to that. His growl is much worse than his nip."

Miri scrubbed at her arm slowly, careful not to look at the black-laced skin. "I'd much rather not hear or feel either of them." If only she could avoid him...forever.

"Give him time. Though it's not my story to tell, he has reason, at least in his mind, to hate humans."

"I don't know if that makes the situation any better." Miri sighed, hating that her life was completely ruled by the unknown. If only she could go back in time a few weeks ago, she'd never complain again. To be back, safe and unchanged, with her father and Eve in Knocton...she'd give nearly anything for that.

Innara touched her shoulder. "Let me wash your back. Your eyes are getting heavy, and you need to eat and then sleep. Once you're refreshed, we can discuss a course of plan for you and your sister."

Miri blinked, feeling more wrung out by the second. "Fine."

Her body and heart ached, and depression clouded her mind. At this moment, she didn't want to think about the future. The only thing she desired was the sweet embrace of sleep. Maybe there, she could forget her dismal life for a short time.

Or would it haunt her dreams, too?

Rash Decisions

Eerin fumed as he stalked away from the healing quarters and into the warm spring sunshine. What madness had driven him there? He'd promised himself just that morning that he wouldn't go back.

Damn him and his libido. Even now, the smell of her lingered in his nostrils and the sight of her was emblazoned on his mind. He felt as if anyone who saw him could somehow see the invisible marks she left on him, marks seared into his skin.

Thankfully, only a few of his people raised their hand in greeting, but none attempted anything further. His fierce expression alone should keep most from waylaying him, but his tongue would do the rest if any should be so bold as to approach.

Still, his mood was one he had to shake, if not for himself then for his people. He had an office full of work, not to mention a training ground full of incoming guards to pass final inspection on. Instead, what had he been doing? Sniffing after a human abomination, one that *he* had helped save. Some part of him whispered that saving someone had never been more pleasurable. He snorted to himself. If the human ever remembered their night together, he doubted she'd call it that.

Deciding to head to the training grounds first, he veered off to the right. One of his captains, Callon, soon joined him.

The captain inclined his head. "My lord, how are you on this fine day?"

Eerin bit back a grimace and locked away his bad mood. "Well enough. The new recruits are still shaping up well?"

"For the most part. A few will require extra training to officially earn their guard rank." Callon waved a dismissive hand. "But you will see this for yourself. I, however, come bearing other news."

"And what is that?"

"Though it's probably nothing of concern, humans have been sighted right outside the forest."

Aggravation lit a fiery ember in his chest. His two resident humans were likely to blame for their arrival. Were they friends or family of Miri and Eve? Not that it mattered. Annoyance turned his tone sour. "You thought to just tell me of this?"

Callon cocked his head to the side, his brown warrior's braids holding the rest of his hair back from his face. "Today was the first time they were spotted."

Eerin sighed. Callon didn't deserve a verbal lashing, no matter how he longed to give one. "They come looking for the two humans?'

"That would be my guess. A group of ten or so are present at the moment. So far, they haven't ventured into the forest."

"But you think it's only a matter of time before they do?" Eerin asked, his voice grim.

"If they build up their courage, it seems likely. They nose around the border and stare into the woods. If they enter the woods, what do you wish to be done?"

"Kill them." He'd have no more humans in his forest, disrupting his life.

Callon's brows drew together. "Should we first not give them a warning shot with our arrows to turn them back?"

"My order stands. Kill them. Or let the forest have them. It's the same in the end."

The captain's lips thinned, but he merely nodded. "Your command shall be done."

***

Miri slowly swam to awareness. *Ugh*, what time was it? After a few minutes, she managed to open her eyes. A glance at the nearest window revealed that it was likely getting close to sunset.

She scowled, her mood sour. Though her sleep had been peaceful, everything had come back to her immediately upon waking. She blinked the sleep from her eyes and glanced around.

Her gaze landed on Innara, who stood behind a small table on the other side of the room. She appeared to be tinkering with some herbs and sent Miri a grin. "Have a nice nap?"

"I feel more rested." As she said it, Miri realized it was the truth. The edge of her exhaustion had been taken off.

"Wonderful." A mischievous smile curved her lips. "Notice anything different?"

Miri frowned and sat up, her eyes searching over the room even as she spoke. "I don't think—" Her vocal cords seized up. Eve wasn't in her bed. "Where's Eve? Is she okay?"

Innara gave her a brilliant smile. "She's awake and getting a bath."

Happiness warred with disappointment. She'd missed her sister's return to consciousness. But her sister was finally awake! "How is she?"

The question was a loaded one. Not only did Miri worry about her physical health but also about her mental. Eve had been unconscious or near to it ever since entering the forest. What did she remember, if anything, of their time there so far?

Innara laughed softly and walked around the table. "She thinks her new coloring is fantastic and readily accepts where she is."

"Well, that's a relief." Maybe one crisis could be avoided, at least for today.

"She has the resilience of the young, so I'm not overly surprised."

The innocence of a child. "There is that," Miri said, her voice quiet. How she wished she could call upon that coveted quality right now.

Innara came to her bedside. "You think you won't adjust so well?"

"I don't want to adjust. That's the problem."

"Time may change that." Innara touched her shoulder. "Don't despair yet on that account."

"I'll try not to." That was all she could promise. "Can I see Eve?"

"As soon as she comes back."

Though Miri wanted to demand to visit her right now, she doubted she could walk there on her own yet. Yes, she felt more refreshed than before, but her muscles still ached. "Well then, I hope they come back soon."

Innara gave a merry laugh. "Would a minute or two suit you? I believe I hear them coming down the hall."

Miri strained to hear something—anything—that would reveal the coming presence of her beloved sister. *Nothing.* However, after a few seconds elapsed, the patter of soft feet floated to her ears. She cocked her head to the side, frowning. The sound seemed quite far away. How could she possibly be hearing them if they were a minute away?

She turned to Innara. "Are those soft footfalls theirs?"

Innara stared at the door for a second. "Yes, they're the only ones walking the halls at the moment."

All words deserted Miri. An inkling about her Change sunk in. Was the transformation more than skin deep?

After a few moments, she shook her head as if in denial and blurted out, "How in the world can I be hearing them?"

Bittersweet Reunion

Innara's brows flew skyward. "Can you not always hear them at such a distance?"

"No, I don't think most humans can."

The fae woman hummed. "You're not fully human anymore."

"What am I?"

"Something more, though what that 'something more' encompasses, I don't know."

Miri's heart dropped. Not fully human. She'd known that, but to have another piece of evidence so clearly presented in front of her... It was too much, too soon, might always be too soon.

"Are there any other changes you've noticed?"

Miri shook her head. "I don't know. I guess not, besides the obvious alteration of my skin and veins. But I've been sort of preoccupied, to say the least."

"Indeed, you have. Time will tell if there are other changes." Innara frowned as if a troubling thought had struck her.

"What is it?"

"Nothing to worry about now. *Ah,* they're here."

Miri started. She hadn't been concentrating on listening to the actual steps any longer. Her gaze swung to the door right as it opened. She drank in the sight of her sister, who was being assisted by a red-headed fae lady in a plain, white gown. A smile broke out on Eve's face when she saw Miri.

"You look like me, Miri!" She lunged toward Miri, but her attendant quickly stayed the motion.

A laugh unwillingly tore from Miri's throat. Her sister had a way of making everything seem simple. "I do. You like the new look?"

A more subdued Eve was led to Miri's bed by the redhead, but her sister still wore a sunny smile. "Yeah, it's pretty neat."

Miri hoped her sister kept thinking that. "That's good to hear." She patted the bed, and Eve all but tumbled into her. Miri closed her eyes, hugging the young girl to her. She had this, at least, to be thankful for. With a contented sigh, Eve snuggled against her side.

Miri took a moment to examine her sister. She had changed so much, but in some ways, she was exactly the same. For some reason, her sister's appearance didn't seem as upsetting as her own. Eve was her little sister and would always need her love and reassurance, no matter what. A pinprick of hope leaked in. If she could accept Eve as she was without qualm, maybe she could come to accept her own changed form.

The familiar weight of Eve in her arms caused a measure of peace to settle about her. Her sister's eyes closed, and red lashes swept over skin stained a lavender color. Poor thing was tired.

Aware of their audience, Miri turned her head to the new fae woman, fighting down her self-consciousness. She had to face people sooner or later. It might as well be sooner. "Thank you for helping my sister. What is your name?"

Steadfast eyes gazed back at her. "Calieth, my lady."

Miri shook her head. "None of that. Just call me Miri."

Calieth looked at Innara, who nodded in apparent permission. A small smile came to the attendant's pale, black-veined face for the first time. "I am a junior healer in the wards here."

Relieved and a little more than heartened, Miri grinned back. Calieth seemed to accept her as she was, though, admittedly, a healer would hopefully be more compassionate than most in that way.

Calieth leaned down and touched Eve on the shoulder. "Do you want to get back in your own bed, young one?"

Eve drowsily shook her head. "Stay with my Miri."

The healer gave a soft peal of laughter. "The little princess has spoken."

A smile twitched at Miri's lips. "If she hears you say that when she's more than half-conscious, she'll demand that you call her that forevermore."

"I think it's too late for that if I know Calieth at all. She adores children. That's why I assigned her to Eve."

Calieth dipped her head in Innara's direction. "You know me too well, my lady."

Miri sucked her bottom lip between her teeth, staring from the junior healer to Innara. "I have yet another thing to thank you for, Lady Innara."

She waved away her observation. "I would do this for any good-hearted person that needs aid."

Miri gently ran her fingers through Eve's nearly dry locks. "Still, you treat us with a kindness that many would not show." Lord Eerin, for one.

Innara sighed. "I find it's easier to show a little kindness and get it in return. Sadly, not everyone believes this way, not even amongst my own people."

"If only everyone would be like you."

Innara shrugged lightly. "Well, I guess there'd be no variety in the world, then."

"If you don't mind, I'll leave the little one where she is," Calieth said, gazing expectantly at Miri. "I think you could both use a nice rest together in the comfort of each other's presence."

Miri nodded. "Please." Right now, it seemed she was in more desperate need of that comfort than Eve.

Innara *tsked*. "Your own eyes are getting heavy. Unless you're hungry, rest until tomorrow, and then we'll talk more about your future."

Anxiety welled in Miri's chest. Innara apparently saw some tell-tale sign of it because she laid a hand on her shoulder and said, "Don't worry. Nothing will be decided in a day or during one discussion. I'd rather get a feel for what you want and ease you into your new life over time."

Miri took in a deep, shuddering breath and stared down at the top of Eve's head before glancing up again. "Okay. I can handle that." *I think.* It wasn't as if she had a true choice. For better or worse, this was their new home. "I'm not hungry, though. Thank you." The little she'd eaten after her bath had made her queasy, so she didn't want to chance anything right now.

After one gentle squeeze, Innara removed her hand. "Sleep and feel refreshed. Everything is always clearer afterward."

Part of Miri wanted to protest that all she'd been doing was sleeping and she still was no closer to clarity than before. However, she bit her tongue and merely nodded. Innara had been so sweet to them that being snarky felt wrong.

Both Innara and Calieth smiled, saying in unison, "Have a peaceful night of dreams."

Miri held back a frown. She'd rather not dream at all, either in false hope or in remembrance.

Hopeful Plans

Miri groaned and turned weakly onto her side, being careful not to disturb Eve. The sheets under her were drenched in sweat, as was her body. Those dreams... Her breath was finally returning to normal, and her rapid heart rate slowed. Still, dear God, her dreams last night... They'd make a prostitute blush.

Her skin tingled with the aftermath of desire. Though she'd just woken up to a life-shattering orgasm, the euphoria had quickly died. Now, there was a yawning void left in its place. She'd never felt so *unfulfilled*.

She moaned. Was this part of the Change? She peeled one eyelid open and stared at Eve's slumbering form. If so, why did her sister sleep so peacefully? Not that she wanted her sister to suffer from such erotic dreams. Eve was just a child and shouldn't even know of such things.

Miri let her eyes close in defeat. Her body still throbbed, and she needed a bath. Only that could wash away the evidence of the night. She wanted the dreams and sensations erased from her skin and mind before anyone else could view them. They felt like dirty beacons upon her that would draw every gaze.

And the person featuring in the nightscapes...he'd never morphed once into someone else. That was small comfort, though, because she couldn't quite place who he was. The answer was there on the edge of her consciousness, teasing and taunting her.

She frowned and flung a hand over her eyes. They were just dreams. Why did they haunt her so? Somehow, she knew they were more, though. Their vividness had wound around her, and their tendrils still held her mind and soul captive. Maybe they were just the byproduct of her previous delirium, but surely the effects of the fever would have faded by now?

A soft knock sounded at the door, and Innara glided into the room, followed by Calieth. As soon as Innara's gaze landed on Miri, she smiled. "You're awake."

Miri nodded and spoke quietly. "Eve's still sleeping, though." Calieth came to the bedside and stared down at Eve. "I daresay she will wake soon."

"In the meantime, can I get a bath?" Miri asked, addressing no one in particular.

Innara folded her hands before her. "Of course."

Calieth leaned in over Miri. "You look a bit flushed. You are well?"

Mortification washed over Miri. "I'm fine."

The healer straightened and shared a look with her lady. Miri stared, feeling as if something passed between them. Something Miri didn't know, something that concerned her. All in all, it was a disconcerting sensation.

In a few minutes, they had her soaking in one of the private baths. She leaned back against the stone back of the ledge and sighed as the hot water stole away the dried sweat on her body. That empty-canyon feeling, however, remained settled firmly in her chest, in her soul.

With a mental shake at herself, she attempted to turn her mind from it. Who knew what temporary effects the Change had wrought? She had to believe they were temporary because she couldn't imagine living with this sensation of incompleteness indefinitely.

Calieth tilted Miri's head back and gently wet her hair with a wide-lipped pitcher. "You seem preoccupied. Is there something troubling you that I can help you with?"

Besides the obvious? She held back that response, barely. "Just my new circumstances."

Innara spoke from where she sat on a nearby bench. "That's something we can start talking about if you're of a clear enough mind."

Miri swallowed the lump popping up in her throat. Discussing the future made it feel real. As much as she'd rather delay the inevitable, she knew it was fruitless. "Okay. Now is as good a time as any."

"I know this is hard, but have you given any thought to what you'd like to do?"

"Do?" She frowned. Even Calieth's soothing massage of her shoulders couldn't relax her.

"Yes, a vocation? Something with which to pass your days?"

Oh, she'd have to earn her keep—both she and, at some point, Eve. It was a thought that'd barely pierced her mind before now. After a few seconds, she answered, "I like learning and know a decent amount about the various herbs and plants my town...my old town...uses for ailments and illness."

Innara clapped her hands as she seemed wont to do if she was excited or pleased. "Perfect. Once you feel up to it, you can apprentice to a healer and see if it's something you'd like to learn in-depth."

That vocation appealed to Miri more than any other. If she had something to focus on, maybe she could do this—handle what life had given her. Having a calling could ground a person solidly to the present. Right now, that was what she needed. Something to immerse herself in. Until Eve was of age, Miri would also have a way of supporting them both.

Though so much remained unknown, just having this tentative decision made cast a more positive light on the future.

***

Eerin groaned as he settled into his bed. Alone. He'd thought about visiting Selina. The thought hadn't appealed, however, so he'd dismissed it quickly. In fact, the notion had downright turned his stomach.

Damn that witch! What had the human done to him? Lust still gripped his body, but no release sounded palatable unless it was in her and only her. That was an upsetting notion at any time, but when it concerned a human? Doubly so.

Even sleep wouldn't erase her memory. No, she haunted him there, too. She was a nightmare wrapped in sensual dreams. Tiredness, however, forced him into bed.

The day had been intolerably long. Even the inspection of the junior guard hadn't gone as planned. A few of them had sorely tried his patience, bumbling their way through their exercises. At least the humans hadn't breached their borders, though with the mood he was in, he almost longed for blood. Still, if the humans were villagers of Miri's, killing them would probably cause her upset. Not that it would stop him, but he hated crying females. Much easier not to have to deal with it at all.

He sighed and shifted slightly. No, still not comfortable. His normally comfortable bed felt like a rock. The smell of his sheets was all wrong, too. They didn't carry her scent. Disgust welled within, and he punched his pillow. What was wrong with him? These feelings...they needed to be eradicated. The mere presence of them made him a traitor to his people, to his beliefs.

A plan was what he needed. Whatever was driving him toward her—the Spirit or some other bewitchment—he had to be able to combat it. He'd slept with her once to save her life and her sister's. He hadn't agreed to anything further. In truth, he hadn't even planned on saving her. Only insanity had seen to that.

And that was what desiring her in any shape or form was. Insanity.

Garden Rendezvous

Miri meandered through one of the city's many gardens, lost in thought. Her hand trailed over a stone ledge. As her fingers ghosted over the surface, tender young branches reached out and glided their leaves against her skin. When she'd first encountered the moving, living plant life in Taerin, they'd spooked and awed her. Still did to some degree. There were certain plants she'd learned to avoid. Though Innara told her the truly vicious ones lived outside Taerin, a few species seemed to delight in taunting her with rough touches that too often wound about her as a snake would.

She liked this garden because every tree, shrub, and flower only exuded a gentle kindness. Her life had been uprooted enough that she'd take solace wherever she could. On this particular spring afternoon, the warm air and bright sunshine soothed her ruffled spirits.

Two weeks had passed since she and Eve had woken. Her sister was as irrepressible as ever and seemed to be adapting well, though she missed their father. Miri didn't think the full repercussions of their situation had sunk into Eve's young psyche yet. Given her age, they probably wouldn't for some time.

Miri, too, was healing nicely, at least physically. Her state of mind was another thing. Realizing her old life was gone and accepting it were two different things. Though it did no good to mourn for what couldn't be, it never stopped the grief from tearing at her soul. She was wise enough to know that only time could address that wound.

And those erotic dreams...they hadn't stopped. No, in fact, they'd gotten worse. All consuming. Even during the day, the memory of them haunted her.

Worse, she felt as if she were missing something, something important. It hovered on the edges of her mind, kind of like the man of her sensual dreams did. The sensation was maddening, frustrating, but there didn't seem to be anything she could do to make it abate. Or remember what she may have forgotten. Somehow, it all tied back to when she'd been unconscious.

She sighed and leaned a hip against one of the fountains that dotted the area. This restlessness that was gripping her was most disconcerting. Her Change likely played a large part in it. Most people would probably say it encompassed all of her emotions, but somehow, she knew it wasn't just the Change in and of itself. Something else weighed on her but what?

Knowing she was no closer to the answer before, she stared down at her watery reflection. Even now, it was hard not to shudder at the sight she presented. Though the image rippled, her black-streaked, pale skin was the thing of nightmares, at least to her. She couldn't very well confide in any of the healers—or any Taelin, for that matter—because they all bore a similar ashy complexion and black veins. To them, it was normal and beautiful.

Frowning, she started to push herself away from the fountain when a voice intruded on her solitude. "Well, look who's up and about."

She froze and closed her eyes for a second. That voice...she'd know it from anywhere. Why him of all people? Did he purposefully enjoy destroying any equilibrium she could find? But she couldn't very well tell him to leave, not when he was the Taelin's lord. However, she didn't have to enjoy his company. Not at all.

Turning slowly toward him, she bowed her head. "Excuse me, my lord, but I'm just going."

A wicked glint gleamed in his eyes as he strode toward her, stopping a few good feet away. "Don't leave on my account."

That look caused apprehension to zip through her. Why did he appear to be a cat to her mouse? "I wouldn't dream of it. I have somewhere to be, though." *Away from you—that's where.*

"My cousin said you had no obligations." He lifted a brow. "Unless you have a secret assignation?"

Her unease spiked. Innara had mentioned her plans to Eerin? Miri had to think rationally, though. He was the leader of this city and had a right, not to mention duty, to know how all inhabitants kept themselves occupied. But why seek her out here? Unless he'd run into her by accident and not design.

Aware she had yet to reply, she shrugged. "I was just going to meet my sister."

A knife-sharp grin curved his lips. "Who is receiving her daily exercise with the healers, just as you do. Think of another excuse."

It took all her willpower not to gape at him. Did he know everything? Better yet, why was he even here? "Surely you have other things to do than worry about me."

"Not worried." He started a slow prowl around the fountain.

Miri did her best not to follow his path with her gaze, but it was nearly impossible not to know where he was at all times. He always made her feel cornered and defenseless. A mouse indeed.

He sighed dramatically. "I merely had a lull in my schedule and wanted to see how my newest resident fared. After all, you were at death's door a mere week ago."

"Sorry to disappoint you with my survival."

He halted in front of her abruptly and glared at her as if she was the most hateful thing in the world. "Disappointed? When I was the one who ensured you lived?"

Alarm slammed her heart against her ribcage. "What?"

His face blanked. "Naturally, I ordered the best healers to attend to you. Lady Innara, who is greatly skilled in medicine, was also by your bedside much of the time."

"*Uh*, okay." He seemed to be leaving something out. Why she thought that, she wasn't sure. Really, she was surprised he hadn't left her and her sister to die. He'd always seemed more inclined to happily watch them rot. Most likely Innara had stood up for them and insisted they receive the best care.

He stepped closer until only inches separated them. "What? No thank you?"

She stumbled back until her backside hit the fountain. "I do thank you for the care you provided my sister and me with."

His head lowered until his nose nearly touched hers. God, what was he doing? Shock held her completely still.

Breathe You In

Eerin breathed in deeply, savoring the aroma that was uniquely Miri's. By the great Spirit, he still wanted her. His need burned through him, scorching and maddening. It wouldn't be hard to seduce her. Though she was startled, he knew she wasn't averse to him. She had never been. Even now, her raspy breath and dilated pupils attested to that.

He was so close, could swoop down for a kiss, for a— With a growl, he pushed himself away and stared at her lovely face and wide, alarmed eyes. He'd not succumb and disgrace himself again. But some part of him whispered that the damage had already been done, so why not revel in it? Why not take what he wanted and enjoy it in every way he could. Oh, there were *so many* ways. And he could make her take pleasure in each and every one of them.

"What are you doing?" she whispered, a mixture of confusion, fear, and desire written across her face.

Combating his temporary insanity, but he wouldn't tell her that. "Just testing something."

Her brow furrowed. "Testing?"

"It proved what I'd believed."

"Which was?"

He smiled cruelly, aiming to wound her with words. Anything to push her away. "That you're nothing." *Liar.*

Hurt flashed across her face. "You tracked me down to tell me this?"

He shrugged. "I happened across you and wanted to see for myself how you've changed. Though you're a bit prettier now, the taint of humanity still lingers about you."

She crossed her arms as a bitter sigh left her lips. "I'm not Taelin enough for your people, but I'd never be regarded as human amongst my own people anymore. I belong nowhere. Neither Eve nor I do," she added quietly, as if it was an afterthought.

"Eve has more hope than you do. She's young and adaptable. My people see her as a child. You, on the other hand..." He trailed off, leaving her to draw her own conclusions.

"Everyone regards me as an anomaly, a freak, strange occurrence."

Her tired voice struck a chord of pity within him, one which he squelched immediately. He shouldn't feel anything but scorn and contempt for her. "That's what you are."

She slipped past him, her body stiff. "With all due respect, I don't need this right now, my lord. I came out here for some peace and comfort, not to have my face shoved into the mess that is now my life."

"Running away?" He sneered. "How like a human."

She rounded on him. "That's unfair, and you know it." She pointed an accusing finger at him. "Your life hasn't been uprooted. You haven't been changed into something that haunts you when you stare into a mirror."

Her words bit into him with sharp, jagged teeth. *Oh, but I have transformed into something I can't fathom.* He didn't recognize himself any longer, and that metamorphosis had been going on since the day she'd come into his forest. He hated that fact, loathed it. Loathed her. But he didn't seem to be able to do a damn thing about it. To make matters worse, she stood there and lectured him?

He knocked her finger away. "You don't know anything about me."

"Nor do I wish to."

"Then we're of an accord. You stay out of my way, and I'll remain out of yours." That was the most reasonable solution. The town was large enough, so surely it wouldn't be too hard.

She glared at him. "Fine. It's not as if I seek you out, anyway."

Maybe not now, but she had sought him before. Her breathy cries for him during her Change crashed back over him, dousing him with heat. That only fueled his anger. He didn't want to desire her in any shape or form.

He stared down his nose at her. "See it remains that way."

"Gladly. No problem there, my lord. Good day." With a flounce, she whirled on her heel and proceeded to get her foot caught in her long dress. She fell toward him. Though he could've stepped away and let her hit the ground, he instinctively caught her.

Her soft body pressed against his much harder one. Immediately, blood rushed southward. He held back a moan. By the Dark Woods, he was a fool to be so easily tempted. The feel of her should disgust him. Though she'd been altered, her human heritage was still clear to his eyes. That was a taint that could never be erased, no matter how he wished it could. He froze. Did he wish that? No, that was crazy thinking.

Miri's closed eyes slowly fluttered open. "I guess I should thank you for not letting me fall flat on my face. I'm sure you wanted to."

Unease seeped into Eerin that she seemed to understand him so well. She was no mind reader, so her powers of observation appeared great.

She cleared her throat. "You can let me go now."

That would be wise, but he found himself making no move to do so. "Why should I do that?"

Her eyes contained a dazed look. "Because we agreed to avoid each other?"

Another good point. Still, he didn't release her. The sensation of her full breasts against his chest was doing funny things to his resolve, to his mind. "We did."

"Then why aren't you letting me go?"

He astonished himself by uttering the truth. "I don't know." True insanity must be gripping him, but he barely cared at the moment.

Her tongue swiped across her grayish-pink lips. "This isn't a good idea."

"It isn't," he agreed as he lowered his head.

Her breath hitched in her throat. "It's crazy."

"Yes. Completely insane."

His mouth landed on hers, and it was the most satisfying experience he'd had since his body found release in hers. She gasped against his lips but made no effort to push herself away. Blood sang a pounding rhythm in his veins. He wanted to consume her and be consumed in return. Could they crawl into each other and never surface? To live in the haze of heady desire...he could think of worse things.

Her mouth opened under his, and his tongue swept in, exploring. Soon, hers danced forth to meet his. By the great Spirit, he wanted her. Now.

After pushing her to the nearest bench, he sat down and pulled her down on him. Her legs straddled his hips, and he held her in place with an arm around her waist. His other hand cupped a breast. She groaned, the sound sending another bolt of lust to his member. His fingers played with her nipple. She squirmed against him and pressed harder into his hand.

"Like that, do you?" he murmured, lifting his lips from hers slightly.

She stared at him with dark, passion-filled eyes. "Your touch...what is it doing to me?"

"The same thing yours is doing to me—driving me mad." Whatever was addling his mind loosened his tongue. "You're a dirty human. How can I desire you so?"

The hazy expression on her face started to lift, and her face hardened as she pulled back slightly. "If you hate me so much, why are you doing this?"

Some of his control flowed back, and he grasped onto the lifeline like a man being swept away by a raging current. "Why are we doing this, you mean? I'm not the only one who was responding."

She heaved out a long-suffering sigh. "Fine, why are we doing this?"

He slid her off his lap and stood, needing to put some space between them. She remained where she was and made no attempt to be near him. Thank the Green Forest for small favors.

For a few seconds—or maybe it was minutes—he didn't answer. When he did, it was wholly inadequate. "I don't know."

His vague response frustrated him, but it was all he had to offer either of them.

Frustration

"I don't know." Eerin's words echoed in Miri's mind as she watched him start a slow pace in front of her.

Agitation shone through every movement he made. She wasn't faring any better, though. Confusion badgered her. Why had he kissed her and more—and why had she responded so wantonly? A haze had seemed to cloak her, shrouding her in pleasure until only he existed—and the sensations he aroused. Though she knew the mechanics of sex, she was a virgin who didn't have much experience beyond a kiss or two. Nothing made sense. His behavior and hers. It was all unfathomable.

At times, he seemed to be hinting at things she had no recollection of. But that was insane. Though she'd been unconscious for over ten days, what could've happened in that time? It wasn't as if she could've done more than ramble on in her delirium.

She didn't know what to say, what to do. It would probably be wise to leave the garden, but somehow, rising didn't seem wise. So she remained glued to the bench, watching him warily. He was like a wild animal she hated to disturb, beautiful but dangerous.

He made no effort to talk, but every so often, that glittering gaze of his would pierce her with all the gentleness of a skewer. A shiver coursed through her. He upset her equilibrium. His touch…it'd felt so familiar. Why? This was the first time he'd kissed her or touched her so intimately.

Memory of her dreams hammered back. An icy-hot chill stole over her, and she rubbed at her arms. Was he the man in them, that faceless figure who played her body like a fine-tuned instrument? But why would she have those fantasies of him? She didn't even like him. Sure, he was handsome in a creepy, otherworldly way. However, it took more than an attractive face to draw and hold her attention.

His personality was abhorrent, and that was enough to keep her away from him.

Finally, she couldn't stay silent. "I'm sure we both have things to do."

He whipped around and glowered at her. "Go, then."

She resisted the urge to shrink back. "I think I will."

Miri stood up with as much dignity as she could. Making sure to give him a wide berth, she hurried around him. The sooner she left, the better. She didn't need anything else strange happening, which he seemed to be a harbinger of.

"You can run but can you forget?"

She froze, already halfway to the nearest exit. What did that mean? She didn't turn around, afraid she'd be caught up in...whatever this was again. "Forget what? A kiss, a fondling, that shouldn't have happened? It's behind me already." Too bad she didn't believe that, and probably neither did he.

He didn't answer, so she all but ran out before he could call her back.

***

"Miri, where are you going in such a hurry?"

The sound of Innara's voice halted Miri's mad dash. She attempted to gain control of her heaving breath. The Change had taken a lot out of her, sometimes more than she thought she could bear.

Innara stood a few feet away, watching her with an inquisitive expression. Miri licked her dry lips. What was it with these Taelin and them disconcerting her so? "Oh, I...to see Eve. She should be about done with her exercises." Hopefully, that excuse was believable, and it was indeed about time for her sister to be finished.

Innara cocked her head to the side. "You're flushed more so than usual. Are you sure nothing happened?"

"No!" She spoke more loudly than intended and inwardly winced. Softening her voice, she said, "What could've possibly happened?"

Innara clasped her hands before her. "I don't know, but my cousin seemed to find news of your whereabouts most interesting."

Miri's pulse sped. "He did? I doubt that."

"Well, not in so many words. He's not the type to come out and say such things."

"He was probably just interested in seeing how the interlopers were doing."

The Taelin lady shrugged and stepped closer to her. "Maybe so, but he's been apprised of your progress daily."

Miri's cheeks warmed. Why was Innara pursuing this? Everyone was acting crazy today. "He likely wanted to check out said progress in person. Even if he hates us, we're still his duty."

"True enough, but he gave your care and wellbeing over to me."

Miri latched onto another possibility with desperate tenaciousness. "Mere curiosity, then."

"Well, whatever it is, I think he found you, did he not?"

Did he ever. "He happened across me."

"I hope you had a pleasant conversation."

She wouldn't term it that. "We didn't kill each other."

Sympathy flashed through the quirking of lips that Innara gave her. "He can be a bit prickly."

What an understatement. "A porcupine has less bite."

"He might grow on you one day," Innara said, wiggling her brows suggestively.

Miri groaned and put a hand to her forehead. This duo of cousins was going to give her a migraine or a heart attack. Or maybe both. "You're seriously not trying to play matchmaker, are you?" Lord Eerin thought her some kind of human mongrel, and he was a pompous ass. Definitely not an ideal match. Apparently, common sense was sadly lacking today for more than one person.

"I would never." The twinkle in her eyes belied her words. "I merely think you two could teach each other much."

Miri screwed her face up. "What could I possibly teach him? He seems to think he knows it all."

"*Ah*, that comes from being our lord. Besides, he's always been self-assured. Has been that way for all his two thousand years."

Miri felt her face go slack. She wanted to collapse onto the ground. "Two thousand years?" She'd heard mention of centuries before but thousands of years?

Innara touched her arm. "Did no one ever tell you that we're nearly immortal in comparison to humans and that you and Eve might have some of our longevity now due to the Change?"

"No, no one ever told me those tidbits," Miri said faintly. Her ears buzzed, and her head swam. "When you say nearly immortal, how long do you typically live?"

Innara grabbed her around the waist. "Oh dear, we better have you sit down. Too much, too soon, I guess."

Miri didn't know if she meant too much physical activity or too much information. Maybe both. She let Innara guide her to a bench and slumped down onto it. "Sorry."

"Don't apologize, and there's no need to worry. We truly don't know how much the Change will affect your lifespan. We can live for tens of thousands of years before we seek release from life."

Ha! No need to worry? Easy for her to say! In fact, not knowing if she was practically immortal felt worse than *knowing* she would live for ten thousand years, if not more.

Innara sat beside her and rubbed her back soothingly. "Take a few deep breaths. That might help. You've really had quite the time of it since arriving here."

Miri swallowed the bile rising in her throat. "I like how you say 'arriving.' As if I had a choice."

"Don't think of that right now. Take those deep breaths."

Miri sighed and did as told. Once some of her dizziness had abated, she slowly straightened from her slouch.

"Feeling better?"

"A bit."

"I think you need something to occupy your time now. Are you ready to start your healer apprenticeship?"

Miri mulled that over. Though her stamina still wasn't what it was before, she did find herself staring into space a lot. Too much rumination was good for no one. If she had something to keep her mind and hands busy, it would likely be a boon to her mentally. "I think that's a great idea."

Innara clapped her hands together. "Fantastic. I'll let the master healer know to expect you tomorrow. In the beginning, you'll do a lot of listening and observing, but trust me, you'll be learning."

"O-okay." Starting so soon? Well, why not? Anyway, it should keep her out of the path of Eerin, which was a definite plus. An idea hit, and she frowned. What if he visited the wounded and sick a lot? Then he'd be underfoot much too often. But given he was the leader of the Taelin, he was probably hard to avoid completely.

"I'm in and out of the wards a lot, too. So some days, I'll be your teacher. The master healer, Eamandian, is strict but fair and runs his place as such," Innara said, a fond smile on her face.

A moment of confusion blindsided Miri. "I thought you were a master healer."

"Oh, no. Well, I'm more of a head healer and can do as I please for the most part. But even I follow Master Eamandian's instructions when he gives them." She shivered. "He's not one to ignore lightly, especially if you have to live with him. You think Eerin is scary, but one glower from that male is enough to make most quake in their slippers."

Miri shifted uncomfortably, not so sure about this anymore. "You're not putting me at ease."

"You'll be fine," Innara said with a giggle.

Insubordination

Eerin reclined in his office chair and pinned the two fae men with his stare. "Are the humans still nosing around the border of the forest?" He almost hoped the answer was yes. More than ever, he was thirsting for a good fight and some blood. Damn that human changeling for inflaming him so. He had to get her out of his system one way or another.

Alegion, the commander of the Taelin army and his close friend, shook his blond head and came to stand in front of Eerin's desk. "Not at this moment. They come and go, still hesitant to enter the forest."

Callon frowned, joining his commander. "But it's only a matter of time before they screw up the courage to do so. We must be prepared."

A derisive noise escaped Eerin's throat. As if the humans could be a true threat. Some part of him whispered that humans could decimate as well as the fae could, but he shoved that voice aside. "We are prepared. We're ready to mete out their deaths."

Callon chewed on his lower lip, a habit that spoke of nerves. "What if they bring their women and children?"

"Do you think they'd be so stupid as to bring them?" Eerin asked. "They're not exceedingly bright creatures, but even they have some intelligence."

The captain shook his head. "I'd never call them stupid but wily. They might use women and children to enter the forest safely."

"Then we kill them all."

Alegion gasped. "My lord, surely you don't mean that? Not women and children."

Eerin waved an irritable hand. His commander and captain were too soft-hearted at times. "It probably won't even come down to that, but if it does, spare the women and children. Does that make you feel better?"

The commander's brows drew together. "Even you don't usually talk so lightly of life, any life."

"Well, this is human life. With them, it's often kill or be killed."

"We've had no battle with them for centuries," Alegion said, his voice reasonable.

That only irked Eerin. "So it's about time they're yearning for another one. That's the nature of humanity. We've both seen it."

"For some, it is, but not all. Our people aren't so different. Look at the lighter fae. We've had our troubles with them, too. It's part of why we retreated to this forest and isolated ourselves."

Eerin growled low in his throat. "The lighter fae are only so in name." That they referred to themselves as so was a sore point of contention with him. The "lighter" fae might not have black in their veins, but their actions were no purer than those of the Taelin fae, the hypocrites.

Alegion crossed his arms and gave him a flat look. "My point exactly."

"Next you'll be saying we should let humans overrun the woods."

The commander rolled his eyes, and Eerin sent him a glower. At least, Callon remained silent. Unlike some, *he* knew his place.

"I suggest no such thing," Alegion said. "Anyways, the woods has its own means to protect itself. I'm not sure how much we would actually have to do." He paused. "By the black blood flowing in our veins, you're in a foul mood. Well, a fouler mood than normal. Why not go visit Selina to take the edge off?"

The suggestion, one he would've taken if he could, only enraged him. He stood abruptly. "You forget who you speak to."

Alegion snorted. "I talk to you this way all the time—and in front of Callon, too," he said, gesturing toward his captain.

Eerin threw himself back into his chair, realizing the spectacle he was making of himself. "You're lucky you still have your tongue."

The commander shrugged. "It's yet firmly attached, so I'm not too worried."

Callon cleared his throat. "I have to get back to my post and oversee the soldiers there."

Eerin flicked a hand in his direction. "You're dismissed and may go." He aimed a steely look at the captain. "No word is to be shared of your commander's insubordination."

Callon bowed shallowly. "Discretion is my forte, as always."

Eerin knew it was but preferred to take no chances. "Good."

As soon as the door closed, Alegion slid into a chair that was positioned in front of the desk. "So what's eating at you?"

Eerin inwardly cursed. His friend and his perceptive eyes missed little, especially if it pertained to Eerin's own private matters. "Nothing." He picked up a pen and made a show of examining the nib.

Alegion lifted a brow in clear doubt. "Really? The gray areas under your eyes tell a different tale."

"Taelin business keeps me up at night. A leader has many responsibilities."

"But rarely do they ever make you this short-tempered and volatile."

Eerin clenched the pen before throwing it down. "Must I account to you my every step now?"

"No, dear friend. I merely worry about you. There's been a change in your demeanor." Alegion hesitated for a moment. "Ever since the two humans came to the forest."

Eerin slammed a hand down on his desk, the wood shuddering under his assault. By the black blood, he wanted to rail against his friend and order him out of the office. Doing so, however, would only further convince them both of the validity of his words.

Instead, he slumped forward and rested his forehead on his upraised hand. "Everything's a mess. I'm a mess."

His friend leaned over the desk. "How so?"

Eerin stared at Alegion. How much could he tell him? All of it? None of it? His stomach twisted. The sensations that gripped him were slowly killing him, driving him mad. If he couldn't trust his dearest friend, who could he trust? Innara was so firmly in support of the two humans, he wouldn't get a sympathetic ear. She already knew the full extent of his perfidy with Miri, though he'd sworn her to silence and ordered her to quell any rumors amongst the healers.

He wanted the whole situation with her done and over with. It seemed she might have to be burned out of his veins. He feared that meant giving in to his lust and sleeping with her again. She was attracted to him, so it'd be easy enough to seduce her with a few well-placed touches. He'd nearly had her in the garden until they'd come to their senses.

Sighing, he picked up the much-maligned pen again. "It's not a pretty story."

Alegion regarded him with a solemn expression. "I didn't think it would be. Whatever the matter is, it weighs heavily on you. Besides, you don't do anything by half measures. If it was an easy, simple problem, I'd be astonished."

"This one is more convoluted than anything I could think up."

"Then tell me and share your burden." Alegion glanced at the clock on the desk. "I have an hour before my next meeting."

***

Nearly twenty minutes later, Eerin's words crashed to a halt. He was wrung out, emotionally and physically. He felt as if he'd gone ten rounds with Alegion, one of the only people who could match him in a fight. Gods, he hated talking about his feelings, unless they concerned hate and anger. Oh, those he had, but a confusing mixture of other emotions had been in there, too.

Alegion stared at him, not offering up one word, and drummed his fingers on the top of the desk. That noise, along with the otherwise utter silence of the room, made Eerin shift uncomfortably. Was Alegion judging him and finding him lacking? If so, Eerin couldn't truly blame him. He was sorely disappointed and confused by his own actions.

"Well?" he asked, his tone impatient. Best to get this over with so he could move on and try to put this behind him. After all, he had plenty of experience of shutting the past out, even if he wasn't always as successful in keeping it there as he would like.

Alegion still regarded him with a blank look. "You slept with the human to save her life?"

"Yes."

"And you feel drawn to her still?"

Eerin gave a long-suffering sigh. "Yes."

"That angers you?"

He glowered. Was his friend turning into an idiot who couldn't understand what he'd been told? "Yes, of course. She's human!"

"Not anymore. She's something...else."

"She might have changed, but she'll always remain partially human." No transformation could completely wipe out who she had been from birth. Even with the Taelin, it'd only altered them, not morphed them into something completely new.

"You mean to you she will always be human."

Eerin didn't deny it. "I have good reason to hate and mistrust humans. This won't change just because I slept with one."

Alegion propped his elbow on the arm of the chair and rested his chin on his fisted hand. "Yet you saved her."

"My cousin wouldn't stop badgering me until I did. She's fond of the two little humans." Though he wanted to say he couldn't see the allure, that would be patently false. He didn't know why Miri had any kind of hold over him, but it didn't change the fact that she did.

Alegion gave a fond smile. "*Ah*, Innara can be very persuasive."

"If that's what you want to call her nagging."

"You better not let her hear you saying that."

"I'm not one of those who lives in fear of her wrath," he said, his voice dry.

"Well, I'm not you. I'd like to avoid her tongue lashings if possible."

Eerin sent his friend an icy look. "My cousin is not the topic of this conversation. What do you think…of my situation?"

"That you're attracted to your little human and that you hate both yourself and her for it."

Eerin rolled his eyes. "Thank you for that startling commentary, Commander Obvious."

"In all seriousness, it does sound as if there's some magic compelling you two together. Neither of you sounds as if you're in full control of your faculties when you're around each other."

"But why would the Spirit do this?"

Alegion shrugged. "Your guess is as good as mine. But you were commanded to see to their wellbeing and not harm them. There's something afoot, but I don't know what."

"What I told you goes no farther than this room."

"That goes without saying. I'm not stupid, after all."

Eerin opened his mouth to give a snippy reply, but his friend held up a hand. "Don't say it. I walked right into that one."

"You did." Eerin hated asking for anyone's opinion on personal matters, so his next words stuck in his throat. "What do you think I should do?"

A flicker of surprise etched itself across Alegion's face before it quickly faded away. "Sleep with her as long as it's consensual but still have a care with her."

Eerin scowled. "I'm not a rapist!"

"Never said you were, but she's fragile and experiencing a new way of life. She doesn't remember your time together. It might be easy to seduce her, but do you really want to break her in the process?"

"When did you become a human lover?"

Alegion shrugged. "Never hated them as you do. As I see it, she's an innocent woman caught up in some game that neither of you understands."

"So we're both pawns." His words shot bitterly out of his mouth.

"And neither of you is wholly responsible for what you're doing to the other right now."

"That makes it sound so much better," said Eerin, his tone dripping with sarcasm.

Alegion sat back in his chair and grinned. "Glad I could be of help."

Many Firsts

Miri trailed behind Master Eamandian as he gave her a brisk tour of the healing wards. He was an imposing figure—a handsome yet daunting one. His red hair was braided back from a sculpted face that held green, piercing eyes. Like many of the Taelin, he was tall and lithe.

His light-blue robes swished behind him as he swept down the hall. She tried her best to keep up without puffing like a smoking chimney.

They finally returned to where they had started. "Well, girl, do you have any questions?"

It took her a moment to find her voice. "No, not right now."

"Speak up if you do," he said, his tone just as brisk as his stride had been.

She nodded obediently. "Yes, Master Eamandian."

"You're not scaring my poor Miri, are you?"

Miri whirled around at the sound of Innara's voice. "Lady Innara, you've come to join us?" She tried not to look more hopeful than what was considered polite, but just seeing her friend helped to put her at ease.

"For a bit. I wanted to see how your first day was going." She flashed a smile at both of them. "Has this brute been treating you well? I threatened that he better, or he won't get dinner tonight."

Dinner?

Eamandian rolled his eyes. "Innara, now isn't the—"

Innara cut him off and slapped him on the chest. "He's my intended."

Miri stared at the two, not having imagined anything like what she was seeing. She hadn't even known Innara was involved with anyone. "You two are engaged?"

To her surprise, Eamandian spoke up and grabbed Innara's hand before she could poke him. "We would have been married centuries ago if she would've been agreeable to it."

There went that mention of centuries again. Just how long did the Taelin live? Would any of their longevity be conferred on her and Eve?

Innara smirked, which was an expression Miri didn't often see on her friend's face. "What he's saying is, I was very disagreeable."

He crossed his arms, and a fire danced in his eyes. "Just to me. Always to me."

"And you love it."

He sighed. "Must you come and lower me off the teacher pedestal before I've even truly begun?"

Innara looped her arm through Miri's. "She is my friend, first and foremost. Though I won't interfere with your teachings, I want you to treat her as family."

Miri froze. Family? Did Innara really feel that strongly about her and Eve?

Eamandian stared at Innara. "I wasn't being cruel to her."

"No, but you were doing your usual cool, brisk routine."

He glanced around as if afraid that someone might overhear. "I have a reputation to uphold and protect."

"And you can protect it all you want. Just treat Miri with some kindness, at least in private."

His mouth twisted into a wry smile, the first one that Miri had seen grace his face. "Fine."

Innara clapped her hands excitedly, jostling Miri's arm in the process. "Wonderful. It's about lunchtime, so I've arranged for a meal for us and Eerin."

Eamandian groaned. "Him? I need a stomach of steel to put up with his arrogance."

Miri swallowed the ball of nerves forming in her throat. She quite agreed with Eamandian's assessment. Why, oh, why did Innara have to invite Eerin of all people? Sure, he was her cousin, but she knew they loathed each other.

Innara jabbed a finger into Eamandian's chest. "Hush, you two are too much alike for your own good. That's why you pretend to dislike each other so but are secretly fond of one another."

He glared at Innara. "You'll be eating alone tonight if you're not careful."

She turned to Miri. "See? I told you his glower was worse than Eerin's."

Miri gave her a thin smile. Her stomach was revolting, and she felt ill. That he could tie her up into such knots over the prospect of sharing a meal... She didn't know whether to laugh or cry. Or both.

***

Miri carefully avoided looking at a frowning Eerin, which was kind of hard to do, given he sat across from her at the makeshift table in Eamandian's office. Still, she was giving it her best shot. The plate in front of her was piled with food, food that didn't seem the slightest bit tempting now. There wasn't anything wrong with it, but Eerin killed her appetite just like a stomach bug would.

"Doesn't the family cook provide divine meals, Miri?" asked Innara, who sat beside her.

"It looks delicious, but I fear my appetite hasn't fully returned." That was sort of the truth, at least. If it was just Innara and her, she'd be enjoying the food a lot more, though.

"It will come in time." Innara brightened. "We should have these lunches weekly."

Horror spilled through Miri. More of them? This meal...oh God, this meal alone was bad enough. She didn't think she'd ever forget the trauma of it. Well, she might be exaggerating a bit but not by much.

Innara did most of the talking, with Eamandian bringing up the conversation when he could. Eerin sat there, resembling a stiff thundercloud. And Miri, well, she was barely hanging onto her nerves or her sanity. Now Innara had the audacity to suggest more of these debacles? The lady was either clueless, cruel, or up to something. Given that she knew how Miri felt, it couldn't be the first. Or the second. Innara was too kind to be this mean.

"What? No one is answering me." A pout formed on Innara's lips. "I thought it was a brilliant idea."

Eamandian cleared his throat after casting a wary glance at Miri and Eerin. "I don't know if that would be wise."

Miri's hand tightened around her glass. Great. Just wonderful. So he was catching onto the tension sizzling between them? Since he wasn't blind nor dumb, it wasn't surprising.

Innara waved away his objection. "Nonsense. We all could use a nice, relaxing lunch break once in a while."

Incredulity speared Miri. Had Innara lost her mind? It'd be more relaxing to swim in alligator-infested waters. The lady was definitely planning something. Not more matchmaking? God, she hoped not, but what else could it be?

Whatever it was, it was bad, and she wanted no part in it. But how could she extricate herself safely? Trying to scrounge up a reasonable excuse, she said, "I don't know. I'm sure I'll be busy learning and studying, but please go on ahead and plan without me."

"I'm sure Eamandian can spare you and tear himself away from work for one noon hour a week."

"Beloved, I—"

"Who says I have time for this foolery weekly?" Eerin all but snarled as he set his fork and knife down with a clank.

He was such a nasty ray of sunshine. Apparently, Innara thought the same thing because her eyes narrowed, and she pinned him with a glare. "You can't spare your dear cousin an hour a week?"

He crossed his arms. "No, I can't."

Eamandian sighed and wore an expression that seemed to ask how he got involved in all this. "Don't badger, my love. If Eerin can't, he can't."

Innara turned her frown on her affianced. "I don't think I'm being unreasonable."

Yes, yes, you are. However much Miri wanted to scream that, she kept her mouth shut.

Eamandian answered her with a snort and a muttered "of course not."

Innara calmly set her fork down. "We'll all talk about this later."

"Meaning you'll keep harping until we all come around to your line of thinking?" Eerin said.

He appeared to ignore Innara's sputter and instead glanced at Eamandian, the latter of whom raised his brows and said, "You know my affianced too well."

Miri watched their banter. Apparently, the two males had found something to bond over: Innara.

"She's been my cousin much longer than she's been your betrothed."

"True, but I best say no more. I have to share a bed with her."

"Not tonight you aren't," Innara said, her voice sickly sweet.

Miri fought the smile that wanted to break onto her lips. The interplay between the three was sort of adorable, and it cut through some of the tension that'd been between her and Eerin.

Maybe this meal wouldn't end so badly after all.

"Miri, I need a word with you after we're done here. Eamandian, I'll return her to your tutelage as soon as possible."

Her heart dropped at Eerin's words. There went the possibility of a nice ending. What could he possibly want? They'd all but agreed to avoid each other, despite that kiss.

"Okay," she heard herself saying evenly.

The inquisitive gazes of Innara and Eamandian traced from Eerin to her as the master healer advised Eerin not to keep her for too long. Inwardly, she groaned. Why did she capitulate so easily? Well, he was lord of the Taelin. It wasn't as if she could say no in front of Innara and Eamandian without eliciting even more curiosity. After all, it was his right to ask to speak with her. No one but she and Eerin knew exactly what had happened during their last conversation. She preferred to keep it that way, too.

After that, time seemed to fly by much too quickly yet creep on in a most maddening fashion. She pushed her food around on the plate, only taking a bite now and then. Her leg bounced under the table, a nervous habit of hers. She tried to keep all apprehension from her face, but she suspected she wasn't succeeding too well.

Finally, they were all finished eating. Miri offered to help with cleanup, but Innara shooed her away. With a small sigh of defeat, Miri pushed herself away from the table and stood. Eerin mirrored her action.

He strode around the table and offered her his arm. She stared at it. Was this some trick or joke? A glance at his face showed he wore a neutral expression, not a mocking or cruel one.

After a hesitation, she placed her hand on his arm. A zap shot through her as if she'd been hit by a mini bolt of lightning. The muscles under her palm and fingers jumped, making her think he felt it, too.

His voice gave nothing away when he spoke. "Come, we'll walk in one of the gardens. I know you like them."

She nodded and shoved away the worst of her apprehension. This was just a talk. Nothing serious. Then why was her heart beating like the hooves of a runaway horse?

After a quick goodbye to Innara and Eamandian, they were off.

The overcast day mimicked her mood perfectly. A few Taelin called out greetings to Eerin and even her. So this was definitely no secret meeting. Anyone who was out and about could see them strolling toward the gardens.

Once they arrived at one of the entrances to her favorite garden—the one he'd seen her in yesterday—he motioned to the ivy-covered gate. It swung open before them. Miri jumped a little. She'd known the fae had a magic of sorts, but seeing it in play was entirely an entirely different matter.

He quirked a brow at her, and she shrugged, saying, "Not used to that yet."

"I guess I take it for granted. It's the norm for me."

He was talking to her like a decent human...well, being would. What was wrong?

When they reached the center of the garden where the fountain was, he guided her to a bench. "Please sit."

She stared at him before she did as asked. Okay, now she was getting really disturbed. He was acting the gentleman, which was a new experience for her. It begged the question of why.

After she darted her tongue over her dry lips, she mustered up the courage of broaching why they were here. "What did you want to discuss?"

"Us."

"Us?" she echoed.

He nodded and sat beside her. "I feel we got off to the wrong start."

Was this his form of an apology? If it was, it was coming a little too late. "Really? When was that? When you scared me to death? When you hauled Eve and me back here?"

His mouth tightened, but when he replied, he spoke in a mild voice. "She would've died if I hadn't. You would've, too."

Given what she'd seen in that dark part of the forest—or even what she'd experienced in the city with the Change—she couldn't deny that. With a sigh, she nodded. "Point taken."

"However, I was much more hostile than need be. I let my hate of humans cloud my...behavior." His face twisted as if getting the words out was painful. For a prideful being like him, it probably was.

"I..." She didn't know what to say. He confused her, and she didn't like the feeling one bit. "Why are you making amends now?" If that was indeed what he was doing.

One side of his mouth tilted up. "I guess you could say I've seen the errors of my way."

That really didn't tell her anything. He often spoke cryptically, saying nothing at all and saying everything. "You truly mean this?"

"Of course I mean it," he snapped.

And he was back. The change didn't last long.

He inhaled sharply. "I shouldn't have spoken so sharply."

He apologized without actually saying he was sorry and instead just implied it. Typical male. Still, it was something. "So you want to try again? Be cordial?"

Angling himself toward her, he nodded. "Yes, if that's agreeable to you."

He was actually asking her for permission? "I guess we could try." She doubted they'd be very successful. They seemed to rub each other the wrong way. Besides, she didn't fully trust his change of heart.

"That's all I ask." He grabbed her hand, which had been resting on her thigh. The brush of his fingers sent pleasurable chills shooting through her leg and hand. She nearly gasped in surprise.

He pressed a kiss to her knuckles, and disbelief speared her. What was he doing, and why did she like it so much? After lowering their hands, he settled them on his right thigh.

She bit her bottom lip. "What are we doing?"

He arched a platinum brow. "Sitting in the garden. What do you think we're doing?"

"I don't know."

"Who says we can't get to know each other better?"

She narrowed her eyes at him. "I can understand being cordial, but you propose a friendship now?"

He ran a thumb over the back of her hand, drawing little circles over the skin. "Can I not change my mind?"

"You can, but I wonder why you did. This turnabout is very sudden...and drastic."

"You believe it's false?"

She tried to ignore what that simple touch was doing to her. "I don't know. Maybe."

"You're slow to trust?"

"On the contrary, I'm usually too quick. Or at least too quick to forgive."

He stared at her as if he were peering into her soul. "That's not a bad quality to have."

"It isn't? It's more useful to the person who has committed the wrongdoing than to me."

"At least you don't let grudges fester." His eyes took on a faraway expression as he spoke.

Was he speaking from experience? "I don't, and that would be more toxic than forgiving too easily in most cases, I believe."

He grunted, not sounding entirely pleased. Since he didn't offer up anything more, she let the subject drop. Though it was unexpectedly pleasant sitting there, she couldn't grow too complacent.

Besides, she had a commitment to Master Eamandian. "I think I should be getting back."

"I also have matters to attend to, though sitting here with you is much more pleasing."

Was he flirting with her? After that kiss and interlude they'd shared, she couldn't say that he didn't harbor some kind of desire for her. If she were being truthful, she'd always found him attractive but foreboding. This version seemed much tamer. Safer.

"But responsibility awaits us," she said softly.

He squeezed her hand lightly. "That it does. I'll see you back to Eamandian."

"Okay." She found herself absurdly happy at that prospect and really didn't want to examine why. Nothing made sense, but for now, she'd willingly go with it.

The Plan

As he escorted Miri through the garden, Eerin could scarcely believe his own audacity. He was so convincing he should be an actor. Jubilation flowed through him like an invigorating liquor. He had her right where he wanted her. Keeping the grin off his face sorely tried him, but he would manage.

All he had to do was act caring, and she'd be in his bed in no time. Though it pained him to be so sappy, his actions had a good purpose. He'd work her out of his system and reap a little pleasure in the process.

A pleasant quietness had fallen between them, one he savored. Unlike some females, she didn't seem to feel the need to fill the silence with idle chatter. He breathed in her scent. Instantly, arousal jolted through him. He needed her sooner rather than later. That meant moving his plan along quickly. Gaining her trust was paramount.

As they neared the healing wards, he cast about for some reason to see her soon. "Would you join me for dinner tomorrow night?"

She blinked up at him, frowning. For a second, a flicker of panic hit. What if she said no?

"Okay."

Her quiet acceptance should've been hard to hear, but to him, it was louder than any shout. "Wonderful. I'll come by your quarters at seven to escort you to my home."

She nodded. "Do I need to bring anything?"

"Just yourself." Ready and willing to get naked. "I'll take care of everything else."

"We've arrived now."

Her soft voice ripped him back to the present. Indeed, the healing halls lay before them. "Would you like me to walk you inside?"

She executed a jerky shrug. "I'm fine."

A strange reticence at leaving her consumed him, but he couldn't give into it. He did have some pride, after all. "I'll see you tomorrow evening then."

"Yes."

Their arms had been linked on the way back. When she withdrew hers, the acute loss of her warmth slammed into him. He frowned, knowing that boded nothing good.

She stood before him, seeming hesitant to leave. "Well, goodbye."

"Until tomorrow." He surprised himself by leaning down and kissing her forehead.

A small sigh escaped her. It wasn't a downcast-sounding one but rather one of contentment, dreaminess even. What a positive sign for his campaign of seduction.

After one lingering look, he spun on his heel and didn't glance back. Doing so was harder than he ever would've thought. That told him more than he wanted to know. He'd be in dire trouble if he wasn't careful.

***

Miri stood before the main entrance of the healing halls, watching Eerin stride away with purposeful steps. Oh lord, what had she agreed to? She took in a shaky breath, but it did nothing to ease the trembling of her body.

Marshaling a bit of self-control, she squared her shoulders. She didn't have the time for this right now. Master Eamandian was expecting her. She could panic later about her impending dinner with Eerin.

A hand touched her arm, and she jumped. She spun slightly, nearly losing her balance. Innara grabbed onto her.

"You're trembling like a leaf caught in the wind. Are you feeling well?"

Miri nodded, though she did feel a little nauseated. Too much excitement, too soon. Her body and mind were paying for it. "I'm fine."

Some of the concern faded away from Innara's expression. "How did your talk with Eerin go?"

"It was...surprising."

Innara lifted a brow and guided her inside the cool halls. "How so?"

"He wanted to establish a truce of some kind." She was leery of telling her the whole truth when she didn't even know it or understand it herself. Besides, Innara was his cousin and would be unduly invested in the situation. Even though their dinner probably wouldn't remain secret for long, she needed a bit more time to process everything.

"Ah, my cousin's way of apologizing," Innara said.

That yanked a bit of a smile from Miri. "That's what I thought, too. Some human men aren't so different in that respect."

Innara gave a soft chuckle. "The male species is unfathomable. They're strange and wondrous creatures."

"Even your master healer?"

"Especially my master healer."

"What are you saying about me, my dear?"

Innara and Miri both jumped at the sound of Eamandian's voice. For a second, guilt slid over Innara's face until an innocent mien covered it. "Nothing."

"Why don't I believe you?"

She cocked a brow. "Because you're a suspicious person?"

"Because I know you so well," he said, coming to stand before his affianced.

"That could well be."

He tapped her on the nose. "You're not going to admit to maligning me."

"Not at all. I was merely stating a truth."

He shrugged. "No matter. I know how gossiping females are."

Miri forced back a smile. Really, these two were too cute.

Innara opened her mouth, no doubt to counter his assessment. Eamandian had other plans, apparently, and headed her off. "As enlightening as this is, we all have to get back to our various responsibilities."

Innara sighed. "Duty awaits."

He leaned in and gave her a peck on the cheek. "Go, I'll see you this evening."

Miri watched the two, something akin to envy and loss spouting in her chest. Would she ever have that? When she'd been a normal human, it'd seemed a possibility somewhere in the distant future. Now it felt all but impossible. Whatever Eerin was up to, there could be no future between them. She wasn't that naïve.

Innara turned to her. "I'll try to see you later in the day, Miri. I think I'll make a quick stop in to see how your sister is faring."

"Knowing Eve, she's chattering away," she said, a fond smile coming to her face at the thought of her favorite person.

"She's a dear child. So sunny and inquisitive."

"Yes, and very active." Sometimes too active. Eve seemed to regain her stamina much more quickly than Miri had. Every night, Miri fell into an exhausted sleep in the adjoining guest chambers she and Eve had been given. Eve practically bounced around until she crashed into bed.

"She does seem to have boundless energy. We have to make sure she has sufficient outlets for it."

Miri nodded. "She tends to make her own if she doesn't, which can lead to disaster more often than not."

"Well, she should've had her lunch by now. I'll make sure one of the tutors keeps her occupied not only with studies but physical play."

"Fantastic." Innara's words lifted a weight Miri didn't know she'd been carrying. Knowing that Eve was in good hands made all the difference.

"I see Master Eamandian glowering down the hall at us, likely muttering something about mindless chitchat. You better go before I land myself in trouble and take you with me."

Miri nodded. "Thank you for all that you're doing. I'll talk to you later. Say hi to Eve for me."

Innara gave her a quick hug, which discomfited Miri for a second. Then she tentatively hugged her back. Innara was becoming a dear friend already.

"I'll tell her," Innara said.

With a smile, Miri trod down the hall where Master Eamandian awaited her. Today suddenly seemed brighter.

Walking with a Monster

In her bedchamber, Miri checked her reflection in the smooth glass mirror the Taelin had somehow produced. Her nerves warred with her distaste for her new visage. Until coming to Taerin, she'd never seen such a clear image of herself. While it was a marvel, it was one she couldn't truly appreciate. The alien-looking person staring back at her shouldn't be her, yet it was. This was her new reality, so she'd resolved to not avoid her reflection, though it always caused a pang whenever she came across it.

Still, she looked as good as possible. A new gown hugged the modest curves of her body. Innara and Calieth had stopped by to help her arrange her hair. They'd somehow found out about her dinner with Eerin that evening, probably from the source himself.

She flushed as she remembered their innuendos and her protest that this wasn't a date. But what if it was? What did Eerin expect of her?

Eve burst into the room. As Miri turned toward her, the girl threw her arms around her. "Have fun this evening!"

Miri hugged her. "I will." Or at least she'd try. "Be good for Calieth." The junior healer had offered to watch Eve, so that was one less worry.

"I will. She said she'll do some painting with me."

"That's nice. Try not to make a huge mess, though."

Her sister sighed, rolling her eyes. "Yes, I know." A mischievous smile tugged the corners of her lips upward. "And if I do, I'll help to clean it up."

Miri chuckled, shaking her head in amused exasperation. "I guess I taught you something."

"You teach me a lot."

"Glad to hear that."

A knock sounded on the door. Miri's stomach jolted. Was it Eerin? Eve hurried over and yanked the door open, all the while obscuring her view. "Calieth! Oh, you're not her."

Eerin's solemn voice floated to her. "No, I am not."

"It's still nice to see you, Lord Eerin."

"You also, child."

Miri drifted closer. Eerin's large form filled the entryway. His gaze caught hers and drilled into her with an intensity that left aftershocks.

She swallowed, trying to get some moisture back into her parched mouth. "Good evening, Lord Eerin."

"Yes, it is a good one so far."

A flush warmed her cheeks at the implied compliment. "I hope it continues to be so."

His eyes glittered with a light she couldn't describe. "I have high hopes."

"I see Calieth coming!"

Eve ripped her back to the moment, and she blinked to clear away the cotton filling her mind. As she glanced over Eerin's shoulder, Calieth's smiling face came into view.

"Here I am, and not a minute too soon." Calieth nodded to Eerin. "Good evening, my lord."

Miri motioned for Eve to move aside. Once she did, Eerin stepped over the threshold, allowing the healer to enter.

Calieth stared at Miri, and her grin widened. "You look lovely, Miri. But I knew you would."

Miri touched her coiffured hair self-consciously. "If I am, it's due to your handiwork and Lady Innara's."

"My sister is so pretty, isn't she?" Eve piped up, looking up at Eerin.

The innocent question hung in the air until he nodded. "That she is."

Miri didn't detect a hint of guile, but that wasn't saying much. Calieth settled a hand on Eve's shoulder and glanced from Miri to Eerin. "I'll let you get on with your evening. Come, Eve, let's go to my home. You can meet my younger brothers and sisters if you haven't already."

The little girl nodded. "Okay, bye, Miri, Lord Eerin."

When the door closed behind them, an awkward silence stretched between her and Eerin. Finally, he closed the distance between them and grasped her hand. After he placed a gentle kiss on the back of it, he asked, "Are you ready to go?"

She tried not to quiver at the touch of his mouth. "Yes." It was a warm evening, so she didn't even need a shawl.

Holding her hand firmly, he guided her to the door. "I've had my cook create what I hope is a delicious dinner that almost anyone would love."

Those hot chills she so often felt at his close presence spread throughout her body, leaving her tingling in her most intimate places. "You didn't have to go to all that trouble or ask him to."

"The head cook, Nestar, is always happy to oblige and usually provides me with more than I can possibly ever eat."

She forced herself to speak nonchalantly, not wanting to make a spectacle. "Well, I hope we can make a dent in his food, then. If he's like most cooks, he equates an empty plate with your appreciation of his food."

Eerin gave a chuckle—a rich, warm sound that sunk right into her bones—as they stepped out into the hallway. "You've got him pegged, but I won't tell him."

"I would hope not. I don't want to fall into a cook's bad graces. Who knows what I'd be served, then?" She pretended to shudder, all the while wondering what had gotten into both of them. This cordial, lighthearted conversation was still so unusual for them that a moment of surrealism struck her. Not that she was actually complaining. No, not at all.

They strolled down the guest corridor, which was in one wing of the great house Innara and Eerin called home. The architecture was unlike anything she'd seen in the human world, echoing the rest of Taerin. The closest term she could come up with to describe their home was a manor. But the rambling building incorporated nature in a manner most humans hadn't thought possible. Tightly woven roots formed some of the walls and ceilings, and light entered each room and space in dramatic and strategic ways. All in all, the manor held a fairytale quality that most of the townspeople back home would envy. She had to live in these surroundings every day, though, and at times she felt as if she were a stranger from another world. Which really wasn't that far off.

"How do you like my home?" he asked.

She jumped a bit. Was he reading her mind, or was she that transparent? Or maybe he was just striking up some chitchat. "It's very lovely, quite different from anything I'd ever seen before."

"I'm glad it meets your approval because such a place will always be your home." His voice softened, and he spoke far more kindly than he ever had. "There's no going back for you, now more than ever."

She ignored the lump sticking in her throat. "I know." Knowing, though, was different than truly accepting.

He squeezed her hand. "Enough of sad matters. This was to be an enjoyable evening, not a sad one."

"You're right." She gave him a slight smile even as confusion burrowed deeper within her. Was he interested, or was there something else at play? Why would the leader of the Taelin seek her, of all people, out? She would be thought a monster amongst humans and was probably viewed as little better by the Taelin. She hated to be so suspicious, but then, she had reason to be.

They entered the main public wing. Suddenly, there were fae servants and lords alike in the corridors, and they all seemed to be staring at her. Well, at her and Eerin. What a strange sight they must've presented. The Changed human and their human-hating leader.

She'd always hated being the object of scrutiny, but now it was a thousand times worse. What they thought of her shouldn't have mattered, but it did.

"You've paled. Are you feeling well?" Eerin asked next to her ear, startling her in the process.

She frowned. When he said "paled," it was a nice way of saying that her face was gray. "I'm fine. There's just a lot of people."

"*Ah*." He inflected that word with a wealth of meaning. "We'll soon be to my private suite of rooms."

"Can't be too soon for my comfort."

"I'd forgotten that Innara said you don't like to be out in public unless you have no other choice."

Miri shrugged. "I'll have to get used to it."

"Maybe so, but it won't happen overnight."

His observation was reasonable and so unlike him. Was he usually like this unless the person in question was human? According to Innara, he was grumpy at the best of times, so probably not. That meant he was putting on an act. She'd have to be careful and observe him closely.

Thankfully, their foray into the public wing lasted only a few minutes. She breathed a silent sigh of relief. A large wooden door, engraved with motifs of nature, stood sentry over the private family wing. The portal swung open before them. Neither of the guards on either side moved, so fae magic was at work. The hallway she found herself in was sunny and spacious, just like the rest of the manor. But here there was an understated elegance that seemed a bit homier and not so alien.

"I believe this is your first visit to the family wing?"

"Yes. It's quite lovely but has a warm, comforting vibe."

"Kind of like you."

That made her stumble to a halt. She stared at him, sure her ears had misheard. "What?"

His lips curved into a sexy smile. "You heard me perfectly well."

Oh, God, she'd heard him correctly. How did she answer? "Thank you, I think."

"I'm being honest. Take it as you will."

"With my Change, I just find it hard to believe anyone would find me attractive."

"For a human, you were pretty before, but now you're positively lovely," he said, his voice a silky purr. "Seeing my people's markings upon your skin, the darkness within your veins, is a sight that is most tempting." A strange expression crossed his face as he finished speaking, but it vanished as quickly as it came.

"I..." God, his declaration stole all coherent thoughts and words.

A glitter of something in his eyes caused a flutter of unease and excitement to roll through her. He licked his lips slowly, his gaze never leaving her face. When he lowered his head, she made no move to escape or push him away.

His lips captured hers in a gentle, tender kiss. But that soon melted away into a passionate dueling of their tongues. Heat flowed through her body as she pressed herself against him. He moaned, his fingers sliding down to grip her hips. His erection pressed into her belly, leaving no doubt as to how aroused he was.

Suddenly, she wanted nothing more than to have him driving into her. To feel each stroke and thrust. To savor how he shook when he came and how— She frowned against his lips, her head clearing a bit. Then horror drenched her. For a few long moments, she forgot how to breathe. These thoughts and feelings—where were they coming from? Why did they feel so real? Even the dreams hadn't been this convincing. Everything with him...it was all too much. She didn't know him, and she *never* acted this way. With very little persuasion, he could've had her in this very hall.

With desperate determination, she pushed him away. "Stop."

He pulled back slowly, his eyes still burning with that peculiar light. "Yes?"

She crossed her trembling arms, and a second passed before she could get her breath under control. "I don't know what's going on here, but something's not right."

His brow creased. "How so?"

"Everything! You, me, my Change. You name it, and it's all a mess."

"You wanted that kiss as much as I did."

"That's precisely the point. My actions with you aren't normal. They rarely are."

Frustration flitted across his face before he replaced it with a concerned expression. "So what do you want to do?"

"I don't know. However, I feel it'd be better to avoid each other for a while until things settle down." Until she settled down. Her emotions were going in every direction.

"This evening's dinner—"

She shook her head. "I think that's unwise." If she wanted to remain a virgin, she couldn't be around him. If she knew nothing else, she knew this. She wasn't about to give herself to someone who'd hated her only days ago—and who she'd hated just as much.

He closed his eyes as if her words pained him. Physically, they probably did as he came down from the desire clouding him. That she could even have such insight into him rocked her and made her all the more certain she had to leave.

"Fine," he said, his tone tight. His eyes opened, and his mouth pressed into a thin line. "I'll escort you back to your chamber."

She shook her head. "Thank you, but I just want to be alone for a bit. I was being honest when I said I think we should avoid each other for the time being."

He stared at her until her nerves stretched to breaking. "I will endeavor to abide by your wish." After one particularly dark look, he turned and stalked away.

Only once he was out of sight did she release the breath she'd been holding and sink against the nearest wall. All the strength in her body had vanished, leaving her quivering and nauseous.

Sick Fear

Three and a half weeks later, Miri rushed to the nearest bathroom in the healing halls, bile rising in her throat. She slammed the door open and made it just in time to spew out the contents of her stomach.

As she clutched the edge of the box-like toilet, she groaned. What kind of infernal stomach bug had she picked up? The Taelin rarely fell ill, having heartier constitutions than humans. So where had she picked this up? Unless she'd eaten something spoiled? But no, she'd been feeling this way for the past couple of days. It was an all-day nausea that came and went.

Ugh, she didn't need this. The erotic dreams were enough of a disturbance, intruding even during her waking hours.

A knock came at the open door. She turned her head and saw it was Eamandian. He wore a concerned expression as he stood there silently. She shakily stood and grabbed a soft cloth. Wiping her mouth, she ambled over to him.

"This is the second time you've been ill today. I think you should let me examine you." She opened her mouth to protest, but he cut her off, saying, "In fact, that's an order. Whatever this is, it needs to be taken care of."

"Fine." He was probably right. Why be miserable when she didn't need to be?

He strode swiftly into an examination room while she trailed behind, not wanting to tempt her queasy stomach. After opening up a drawer, he withdrew a loose robe-like gown and threw it on the high-perched cot. "Put that on, and I'll be back in a minute. I need to retrieve someone."

She bit her lip as a foreboding sensation chilled her overheated body. Grab someone? Why would he need to do that? Did he suspect something serious? Wonderful, just wonderful. Just what she needed in her life right now.

After sighing in resignation, she undressed and slipped into the gown robe. She hefted herself up onto the cot and sat on the edge, swinging her legs slightly. Worry built within her. What if something horrible was wrong with her? What would happen to Eve if she couldn't take care of her or, worse, died?

Miri, stop this. Don't look for trouble where none may exist. Easier said than done, though. Her mind spun with all sorts of terrifying possibilities. Eamandian entered with Innara at his side. Miri didn't know what to make of that. Most likely, he thought she'd need the moral support. That realization seeped in, and an icy hand clutched at her heart. Innara being here had to be a bad sign.

"Miri, please lie back, and Eamandian will examine you."

"Okay." Miri hesitated. "Why are you here?"

A sad smile came to Innara's lips. "To offer support if need be."

Any hope of this not being a serious matter died a brutal demise. "Support?"

Eamandian smiled encouragingly, which was quite out of the norm for him. "Maybe it's nothing. Please lie down."

Her body quivered as she complied. What could be wrong with her? Did she have a wasting disease?

He washed his hands in a bowl of water. "This shouldn't hurt."

"Okay." What else could she say?

With brisk, efficient hands, he undid the ties of the robe down to her waist. He used an instrument she'd seen a few times and listened to her heart.

"Your heart rate is rapid, but I suspect it's usually lower, especially now," he murmured. "The faster rate is due to nervousness, which is to be expected."

She didn't reply as he took her blood pressure. This was all part of the intake routine she'd seen the healers do. A glance at Innara revealed her to be silently communicating with Eamandian. It was a trait that affianced or wedded fae couples supposedly shared, though particularly gifted fae could do it with almost anyone. That Innara and Eamandian felt the need to do so sent a spear of new fear into her chest.

He set the device down. "Blood pressure is slightly low. Let me check one other thing." With gentle hands, he palpitated her stomach. "Does that hurt?"

"No, but my stomach's acting up again."

He stopped immediately and pulled up a chair. "I'm positive I know what afflicts you. Have you felt tired lately? Or had any other symptoms besides the vomiting and nausea?"

Miri frowned. "I thought the tiredness was due to lingering effects from my Change. My stomach has felt crampy, too, but I thought it was just my period getting ready to make an appearance."

His gaze sharpened. "Have you had your flow lately?"

She bit her lip, thinking back. "No, I had it about a week before arriving in Taerin."

Eamandian and Innara traded another secret look that Miri guessed didn't mean anything good. "Why do you ask?"

"You're late by about four weeks," Innara said gently.

Miri stared at her, not seeing an issue with that. "Probably because of my

Change."

Innara took her hand in hers. "Do you remember anything from during your Change?"

"Bits and pieces, but even those are fuzzy."

"Do you remember anything you might have thought a dream?"

Miri licked her dry lips. Dreams? Ever since the Change, she'd been having those steamy ones. She glanced at Eamandian, embarrassed at having to say so in front of him. "I have been having erotic dreams since the Change."

"Even during it?"

"Yes, I think so." Why was this important, though?

Innara sat on the bed and squeezed her hand. "Miri, what if I told you those dreams were based on an actual experience?"

Miri could only stare at her friend, her brain refusing to comprehend. What?

"How about if I said you had a sexual encounter during the last evening of your Change?"

Horror sizzled through her mind. "You mean someone forced themself on me?"

Sympathy coated Innara's face. "No, it was as consensual as it could be, given neither of you had full control of your faculties. I believe your dreams mimic what happened in real life. Was there any rape or coercion in them?"

Miri shook her head, dazed. "No, but why would this even happen?"

Innara glanced at Eamandian, who gave her a slight nod. "Lives were at stake, yours and Eve's. There was also some magical compelling going on, likely by the Spirit, which, if you recollect, is a guardian of the forest."

"But...I..." She'd lost her innocence and didn't even remember? Or maybe it hadn't been full-blown intercourse. Who had been the male? A sinking suspicion about his identity took root. First, though, she had to find out something. "Am I still a virgin?"

Innara closed her eyes. "You are not."

Numbness hit Miri. She'd had sex with a man? And not with just any male but with Eerin? If it was anyone, it had to be him. In fact, everything he'd said and did now made perfect, frightening sense.

Miri stared at Innara. "Oh, God, I slept with Eerin, didn't I?"

Innara blew out a breath and nodded. "You did, and it saved your life but with repercussions."

Miri groaned and threw a hand over her eyes. She didn't want to know, yet she had to. "What repercussions?"

"You still desire him, as he desires you. It seems as if what the Spirit has in store for you isn't completed. But I'm afraid there's more."

More? What more could there be? A hysterical giggle welled in her throat. The magical desire thing sounded bad enough. "Are you saying we're tied together by some magical kind of lust?"

"Yes, and while the Spirit is undoubtedly behind it, there's another complication that adds to it and amplifies that desire."

Nausea clawed at her tummy, but tiredness kept her pinned to the bed. The only thing she could manage was to remove her hand from over her eyes and glare at Innara. "Just tell me."

Might as well get it all in the open. She didn't know how it could get any worse.

Innara remained silent, appearing to be picking her words carefully. "Miri, you haven't had your period, and you engaged in intercourse since your last one. What do you think that could mean?"

Miri wasn't a complete innocent. A chill froze the blood in her veins. Oh God, no. She shook her head. "I can't be!"

Innara stroked her hand. "You are. Eamandian confirmed it, and I've never seen him diagnose a pregnancy wrongly."

Eamandian spoke up. "You're nearly six weeks along, give or take a few days. I know this isn't what you wanted to hear, hence Innara's presence here."

Terror gripped her. "I can't be pregnant. I'm not married. I don't like the father! We're not even talking at the moment!" Dear Lord, the father. Eerin was the father. *Damn, damn, damn.* Her breathing increased until she was panting.

Innara laid a hand on her cheek. "You must calm down, or you'll make yourself ill."

Miri wanted to snap that she couldn't calm down, but she recognized the wisdom in Innara's words. Later...she'd break down in private.

After a few deep, steady breaths, she reigned in her panic enough to be coherent. "Does he know or suspect?"

"No. Only Eamandian and I suspected."

"And you didn't think to tell me?" Anger roiled through her.

Innara's shoulders slumped. "I was hoping there would be no consequences and that the truth would come out in its own time. You were—and are—having enough issues with becoming acclimated to Taerin and your Change. I see now that might have been a poor choice on my part."

Right now, being angry at Innara solved nothing. "I...I can't tell Eerin."

"We don't have many abortions," Eamandian said. "However, it's early enough that we can arrange for one if you wish."

Miri gasped and stabbed him with a glare. "I didn't say I wanted one. I just meant I needed some time to wrap my head around this."

"Do you want me to tell him? After all, I feel partially responsible. I noticed the effect he had on you and your possible recovery." Innara stared down at their hands. "I advised him to do it." She glanced up, and tears glittered in her eyes. "I didn't want you and your sister to die."

Miri blinked, a bit shocked. "And I wouldn't have wanted us to die, especially not Eve."

Innara squeezed her hand. "Take the time you desire, and I'll be there to help you with whatever you need."

"You really would tell Eerin for me?"

A rueful smile tilted her lips in a lopsided grin. "It's not as if we can hide your condition forever. And I know my cousin. The longer we keep it from him, the angrier and bitterer he'll be."

Miri couldn't fault that logic. Innara knew Eerin much better than she did. "He has a right to know." What surprised her was that she meant what she said. "But I need a few days to process it."

Innara nodded. "Fair enough."

"Can I sit up?" Miri asked, glancing at Eamandian for confirmation.

"Yes, just slowly."

She chuckled wearily and lugged herself into a sitting position with a hand from Innara. "Don't worry. I always get up slowly since I've been hit by this morning sickness, which ironically lasts all day."

He stood up as she settled against the pillows. "With some women, it tends to. Now that we know, I can give you a tonic to control the worst of it and give you some energy. It won't hurt the baby, no matter the human or fae blood, so don't worry."

"Okay." She'd be a fool to turn down feeling better.

He strode over to a cabinet and removed a glass bottle. After pouring a bit of the contents into a small glass, he glided back to the bed and handed it to her. "Drink, and you'll feel better in a few minutes."

She raised a brow. "That quick?"

"Absolutely. The wonder of herbs combined with fae magic."

The orange-colored tonic had a tantalizing smell. She was used to medicine smelling nasty. She took a tentative sip. Even the taste was delicious. In a few short sips, the liquid was gone. Was it her imagination, or was her nausea abating already?

With a smile, she handed the glass back to him. "It's quite the miracle. I'm positive I feel better already."

"What remains of your human physiology probably makes it work a bit faster."

Concern nudged her to ask, "What will that mean for me and the baby?"

"Truthfully, I'm not sure. I would like to watch you closely."

At her alarmed expression, he chuckled. "Not so much for potential problems, though that's an issue, but to observe and learn about your unique physiology."

"A*h*, okay."

Innara snorted. "Always count on Master Eamandian to use every opportunity for study and learning."

He drew himself up tall and stared down at Innara. "Do I have to send you back to the schoolroom?"

"If I'm naughty, what are you going to do?" she asked, a wicked smile on her lips.

He answered her with a smirk. "I'll tell you in private, but I promise you it won't be a punishment you forget."

Innara snickered. "Promises, promises, but we have Miri to attend to." Then her cheeks flushed gray, and she turned contrite eyes on Miri. "I'm sorry. I didn't mean to downplay your issues."

Miri smiled and waved a dismissive hand. "Think nothing of it. Your lightheartedness eased my concerns for a bit." Now that her nerves had settled somewhat, she found she wanted the full story behind her Change. "Could you explain to me a bit more why it was necessary for E-Eerin"—she stumbled over his name—"to sleep with me so I and Eve could survive?"

Baby Blues

The question seemed to startle Innara, but she readily nodded. "Of course. Where should I start?"

"How about at the beginning?" asked Eamandian from across the room where he was rinsing out some glasses.

"That's as good a place as any." Innara smiled fondly at him before looking back at Miri. "When you fell ill during the Change and we couldn't do anything for you, I demanded Eerin come and see for himself. Once he arrived, your health improved and you settled almost instantly. Only he seemed to bring you relief of any kind from the pain. When he left, you always invariably relapsed into pain and terrors. But after his first visit, you also started to call for him and seemed to experience lustful urges only you wanted him to satisfy."

Miri felt the blood drain from her face. "I did?" She couldn't imagine being so wanton, but then, she hadn't been in control of herself. At least according to Innara, she hadn't. "So every healer knows what happened?"

Innara shook her head. "Some of them suspect what led to your recovery, but none can talk about it to others. They all take an oath not to discuss things that happen within the wards. And they've been commanded by me, Eamandian, and even Eerin not to divulge anything about your stay in the healing halls."

Panic chewed on Miri's insides. "Oaths are broken all the time."

"Not these. These are held in place by strong magic. They couldn't talk about this even if they wanted to."

Relief rolled over her. "That's fortunate." She couldn't bear for everyone to know, however unlikely that had been. If it *had been* common knowledge, Eerin would already know that he was to be a father. "I'm not ready to share the news yet."

Innara smoothed Miri's blankets. "People will come to know, but not before you choose to tell Eerin."

"To clarify, Eerin thinks that I don't remember the night...the night we..." God, she couldn't even say it.

"Though he knows you could remember at some point, he's operating on the assumption that you won't."

Miri scoffed. "Wishful thinking. I would've never thought him the type." Then she sighed. "How angry is he going to be? I can't imagine he'll have a good reaction." What she knew of his general personality and demeanor pretty much told he'd have a hissy fit.

"I won't lie. It's sure not to be pretty. He's not very good at handling his own emotions."

A snort sounded from across the room. "That's an understatement."

Innara *tsked*. "Don't you have work to do? Anyway, I say you could be Eerin's mood twin at times."

He straightened up to his full height. "Excuse me, I'm much more in touch with my feelings." He glared at Innara. "You forced me to be."

"Exactly, so it's possible to soften Eerin. It only takes the right influence, the right person, to do it."

Miri held up a staying hand. "*Whoa!* He hates me and is sure to hate me all the more after I tell him about the baby." Part of her couldn't believe the words coming out of her mouth. Baby? It still felt surreal, but she knew Eamandian and her morning sickness weren't wrong.

Innara patted her knee. "You're carrying his child. Trust me, that will count for something."

Miri chewed on her bottom lip. God, this was a nightmare. A baby she hadn't asked for, and the father loathed her very existence. She could barely comprehend any of it. A breakdown was probably awaiting her once she was alone and could actually start to process everything she'd been told.

One thing was clear, though. "He'll probably want nothing to do with me or the baby."

"Eerin could well spout that off at the beginning, but once he regains his senses, he'll be there for you. Family is very important to him and all Taelin."

"But the baby will have human blood." Miri frowned. "I think." Who knew how these things worked when she wasn't quite human anymore.

Innara glanced at Eamandian. He shrugged, saying, "Who knows? There's never been a case such as this." He gave Miri a slight smile. "You'll go down in our historical scrolls."

"I'm not sure I want that dubious honor."

Innara scowled at her fiancé. "You're supposed to be a reassuring force." With a frown, she paused. "Well, this is you after all, so silence is probably better."

"I'm just pointing out the positives." He dried his hands. "I need to devise a regimen for the pregnancy. The first thing I'll add is the tonic for your morning sickness."

"Regimen?" Miri echoed, not sure if she liked the sound of that.

"Expectant mothers receive a certain level of care." He raised a brow. "I assume this is so for humans? Though I'm well aware that your physiology is likely different now. In fact, that's something I've been meaning to discuss with you."

Innara groaned. "Can't this wait?"

"Wait for what? It's been a few weeks now."

"And you could wait for a few more."

Miri cocked her head to the side and stared first at Innara and then Eamandian. "What is it?" She'd already received the ultimate surprise, so what was one more?

"I'd like to take some vials of your blood so I can compare it to Taelin and human samples."

That sounded easy enough, but how would he draw the blood? "What would you use, and will it hurt?"

"A syringe with a needle. The experience isn't exactly comfortable, but it's truly not that bad."

"I guess it'd be fine," she said slowly. If it would help her pregnancy, she had no good reason not to agree. Already, a strangely protective feeling had taken root for the little one growing in her. She'd always wanted children, though this was certainly not the way she'd planned to get one.

Eamandian rubbed his hands together. "Wonderful."

Innara snorted. "Ever the researcher."

"Well, if it sheds some light on my condition or pregnancy, that's a good thing."

Eamandian cast her an approving look. "If everyone had that attitude, it'd make my job so much easier."

"You normally subdue your patients with the ferocity of your growl," Innara said, chuckling.

"I'm not quite that beastly, but thank you." He focused back on Miri. "Let me take that blood. Then you can rest while I work on your regimen."

Miri gave a weak chuckle. "Wonderful."

***

Eerin prowled around the training grounds, watching his warriors train. He'd taken several to task already, so everyone was giving him a wide berth when possible. Even Alegion was sending him wary glances.

How much more time would Miri need? It'd been four weeks, for the great Spirit's sake. He saw her in passing most days, but she barely acknowledged him. It was hard to ignore her in return, but he managed it somehow. He didn't know how much longer he could avoid going to her. Avoid touching her, caressing her, having sex, tasting her blood—

He inhaled deeply in an effort to subdue his thudding heart. The dreams were bad, but now, even his days were being dogged relentlessly by Miri. The taste of her blood still lingered in his mouth. No matter how he cleaned his mouth or what he drank, the dratted sweetness remained.

And the ghost of their night together followed him around, slipping through his mind like a thief when he least expected it. Too many times had he been left disconcerted and in painful need of relief.

It was a thirst, a hunger, he couldn't quench elsewhere. And that enraged him, made him quiver from the intensity of it. Every time he thought about another female, his stomach would knot and twist. Worse, she didn't even remember their night of mutual need. Given her condition at that time, it was doubtful she ever would.

At first, he'd been satisfied at that realization. Now, however, was another thing. He almost wished that she would regain those memories, just so he could get a reaction from her, one that encompassed something other than avoidance.

He growled out a command to a warrior-in-training to hold his sword correctly. Imbeciles, the lot of them. As soon as that was done, his mind snapped back to Miri, damn her.

Why didn't she seek him out? He needed her. She'd set his body and mind on fire. She had to be experiencing the same sensations, so where was she? He *felt* her desire for him, so that wasn't in question.

Though the one-sided bond he'd formed with her through the tasting of her blood had to be gone, at times he swore he still sensed certain emotions, sensations, from her. Sometimes, there was discomfort, even nausea from her. Other times, sadness and confusion, along with quite a bit of happiness or joy. Given her recent Change, even he couldn't fault her for feeling those things.

Besides, it wasn't a constant deluge and was quite muted much of the time. Underneath all he sensed from her, though, was a deep, unquenchable desire. For him.

He'd toyed with the idea she remembered their night together. Surely, though, the spitfire would rage and accuse him of taking her virginity. It was something she'd kept and would likely mourn the loss of, especially since he'd been the one to divest her of it.

Somehow, she'd bewitched him, and yet she didn't have an iota of magic.

At least she hadn't as a human. She and her sister had been checked upon their arrival. Even now, Innara and Eamandian were observing them for such changes. So far, nothing had been noted in that regard.

A snarl worked its way up his throat, but he bit it back in time. He had patience, but even it had its end. This damnable longing, the anger associated with it... He wasn't the leader of the Taelin for naught. He had much restraint, but once it was lost, it was horrifically lost. His people feared his possible actions for a reason.

Alegion strode over, breaking him from his dark musings, and stared at Eerin consideringly. "If glowers could kill, we would all be dead."

"When, then, it was a good thing I wasn't asking you."

"Something's bothering you. The dark circles under your eyes speak to that. Care to engage in a little sparring to work the problem out of your system?"

Eerin gave him a dark grin. "Are you prepared to lose?" Alegion was one of the few Taelin he didn't have to worry about seriously hurting because his friend was as skilled as he. Eerin wouldn't mind drawing a little bit of blood today, though.

"Mighty confident, aren't you?"

Eerin grunted. "Are you going to natter at me all day, or are we going to have a match?"

"The nattering does annoy you more," said Alegion, a smirk coming to his face.

"I'll enjoy wiping that look from your face."

"Promises, promises." Alegion grabbed a sword from a nearby warrior and handed it to Eerin. With a flourish, he unsheathed his own. "Let's see if you can live up to them."

They found a clear spot in the training yards. After a brief stretch, he advanced first and took the first swing. Alegion met the blow easily. As they settled into the match, warriors quit their practice and drifted over to watch them.

The satisfying clang of their weapons was the finest thing he'd heard since Miri's moans of ecstasy.

No!

He would not think of her. There were some places she could not intrude. He desperately lunged at Alegion, nearly nicking his shoulder. His friend slashed back, the blade aiming for his neck. Eerin dropped to his knees, rolling out of the way.

His friend was no longer playing. Suddenly, he found his mind consumed by something other than Miri.

What a balm it was!

He grinned in delight. This dance, this moving of the mind and body, sated the ever-present longing and rage. Oh, they would come back. They always did, but he'd take this reprieve for now.

Thrust and parry. Feint and spin. He and Alegion knew each other's style well. Soon, sweat dripped down his back. His respiration had increased dramatically, but so had Alegion's. They both scored minor hits on each other, a cut here or there.

He whirled around and slammed his blade against his friend's. The force reverberated up his arm. Then, sliding his sword upward, he forced Alegion's weapon back before kicking it out of his grasp.

Alegion dropped the sword and shook out his arm. "Well played, my— "

Suddenly, a gasp from off to the side ripped through his consciousness. He and Alegion turned toward the source.

Miri stood outside the patchy circle of soldiers surrounding them. The stark paleness of her face brought back uncomfortable memories of the days when she hovered near death. She was staring straight at him. He took a step forward, but she spun around and bolted away.

He watched her until she had nearly faded from sight before he shook himself. His people were now looking at him with a curiosity that he didn't want to feed.

With an inward sigh, he forced himself to look away and gather his composure. To think he'd almost succeeded in forgetting about her for a blessed hour, only for her to stumble across him. By the great Spirit, fate must really dislike him right now. Why had she run, though? Surely, he wasn't that much of a scary sight?

He slowly faced his friend again and took stock of his appearance. A few rips and tears dotted Alegion's sweat-soaked and dirt-encrusted tunic. He was sure his own shirt was in no better shape. Both he and Alegion also bore several superficial wounds. Still, they weren't frightful.

Alegion's brow rose, and he leaned in close. "The reason for your dark mood just fled from us. I believe you should seek her out. Isn't she apprenticing with Eamandian? If so, have her tender hands administer to your wounds."

Eerin wanted to snap that was the most ridiculous suggestion ever but couldn't. Not when that was exactly what he wanted to do. Instead, he straightened his shoulders and raised his chin. "I'll see you later. Clean yourself up, for darkness's sake."

As Eerin strode away, Alegion chortled. "You're one to talk. You smell pretty fresh yourself."

Eerin didn't bother to turn around or respond. He grabbed a proffered washcloth and then set out on his mission.

A mission to capture himself a human changeling named Miri. And once he had her, he knew *exactly* what to do with her.

Chase

Miri didn't know why she was running like a ninny. She didn't miss the curious glances and stares thrown her way. All she knew was that she was heading toward her favorite place—that secluded spot in the garden near the guest wing where she and Eve stayed.

And she wanted to be there right now.

Her aching feet and the stitch in her side forced her to slow to a brisk walk. Plus, she was starting to sweat. She slowed even more and clutched at her side. The garden was just a minute or two away. Not long.

Besides, there was no reason to run anymore. There'd been no reason to flee in the first place. So she'd seen Eerin? That didn't mean she'd had to flee from him like there was fire lapping at her feet. Yes, she could do with more exercise, but this wasn't the way to get it. Unlike with Eve, the Change hadn't given her more energy, at least that she could tell.

However, being pregnant was another thing entirely. She was dead-tired all the time. Innara said it was normal, as did Eamandian. Huh, what did they know? They'd never been with child. So what if they were both healers?

Okay, she was being a bit unreasonable. She was allowed to be, though. She'd just found out about the baby two days ago. Only one meltdown later, she was slowly wrapping her head around bearing Eerin's child, or so she'd thought.

She snorted. Yeah, that was why she turned tail and ran when she saw him. Maybe she wasn't so ready.

Certainly not ready to tell him. The mere thought of that ripped a shudder from her. Well, Innara had offered, so if she was too cowardly, that was an—

"Miri," a voice said from right behind her.

She jumped, startled, and then closed her eyes. That voice.

Eerin.

He'd followed her, which she hadn't even given possibility to. Why hadn't she *thought* and been more aware of her surroundings?

She inhaled sharply before facing him. "Yes?"

Despite the disheveled state of his clothes, he looked as frustratingly handsome and alien as ever. Well, not so alien anymore. She, herself, was stuck somewhere between resembling a human and a Taelin.

He stepped closer. "Why did you run?"

"I fancied a good sprint?" Yeah, that excuse was as weak as her voice.

The doubtful cant of his brows told her all she needed to know. He didn't believe her in the slightest. Not that she was surprised. He was too smart for that.

"You were fleeing from me," he said. It wasn't a question but a statement of truth.

She sighed. "Maybe." After all, she did have some pride left.

"What have I done to so upset you? I've respected your wishes and have given you time."

What a loaded question, and he didn't even know the half of it. "I thank you for that. I've just...my mind has been busy trying to wrap itself around many truths."

He placed a gentle hand on her arm. "Your Change and the fact you can never return to your previous home has to weigh on you heavily."

Oh, if it were only that. Still, she grabbed onto those reasons without hesitation. "And Eve. It's not just my life that is being affected. She'll never see our town again, our father."

At the mention of her dad, her throat tightened. She supposed that never seeing him again would always pain her to some degree. She and Eve were all the family he had. Sure, he had friends and acquaintances, but Anthony, her father, had existed for them since her mother had died.

If only she had been more careful and not let Eve run into the forest...

Eerin pulled her closer until their bodies were almost touching. "Your father and the rest of Knocton can never know you're here. If they did, they would likely seek you." He paused. "And what would they find?"

"Eve and I altered. They'd fear us, as they fear you."

"Your lives would be in danger." His voice grew softer, more pained. "I know the danger of fearful humans all too well."

Her gaze shot up to his as a shiver iced its way down her spine. His eyes appeared to be seeing something locked far away in the recesses of his mind. Innara's words about him having cause to hate humans also echoed back. Suddenly, she wanted him back here, with her, in the present moment.

She placed a gentle hand on his cheek, marveling she had the gumption to do so. A month ago, she would've never dreamed of it. But so much had changed since then. Sometimes, she didn't even fully believe it herself.

His eyes slid closed, and he leaned into her palm. His aspiration seemed to slow, and some of the tension in his shoulders drained. Was he so lacking in comforting touch that he found succor in a freely given one? Or was it just hers? Though the first possibility upset her more than it should have, the latter one made her heart race.

Miri, focus on the present. On him. Not flights of fancy.

He felt so strong, sturdy, and *real* under her hand. So like her dreams and yet not. His skin was slightly clammy, probably from the exertion of his sword fighting. She didn't find it distasteful. In fact, his very presence sent a small shot of desire southward. Interestingly enough, his smell was one thing that didn't turn her stomach, either.

However, this moment wasn't about her.

"And you find yourself haunted by the past," she said, her tone soft.

He blinked as if coming out of a trance. A dark expression flashed across his face. "What do you—" He broke off, apparently gathering his composure and a sense of civility.

She breathed easier and let her hand drop. He was so much more pleasant to talk to when he was being kind or, at least, not hostile. "You seemed far away in thought, and given your words, I thought it might have to do with painful memories."

"I..." He cleared his throat. "They are not good ones, no."

She glanced around, aware of how compromising their proximity to each other might appear. Though once knowledge got out about her pregnancy and who the father was, that would be the least of her worries. No one was in sight at the moment, but with them being so near to the manor, there was bound to be a stray servant or two wandering about.

He seemed to read her mind. "Come, the gardens are just ahead. We can have the privacy we seek there."

Her pulse rate felt as if it increased tenfold. Privacy? God, that sounded too good right now. Her insides jittered with anticipation and excitement—and no little dread.

Doubtful.

She wanted to kiss him, to touch him, but the truth also lurked on the edge of her tongue. Or, at least, it should.

Since she couldn't find adequate words, she merely nodded.

A small smile curved his lips upward. He laced his arm through hers. "I believe our time shall be quite enlightening."

Her tummy did flips at his husky tone. Enlightening? It certainly could be, but maybe not in the way he expected. What did he have planned? And would she say no?

***

Eerin bit back a smile as they strolled into the garden. He'd chased her down, and now she walked by his side. Right where he wanted her. He frowned. Well, he didn't actually want her by his side permanently. More like under him temporarily.

And these gardens were the perfect place to seduce her.

Few came to these particular gardens other than the landscape workers. It was known to be the haunt of the ruling family. His people understood their need for privacy, as they had little of it outside of their house and gardens.

Now, he'd use that privacy to his utter satisfaction—and hers. Never let it be said that he left a female unfulfilled. He pulled her deeper into the garden, to the center where a small maze awaited them. The heart of the maze was what he sought.

"I love this garden," she murmured. "But I don't think I've ever ventured in so far. It's far larger than I thought."

"It's known as the family gardens, though it's not officially closed off from the public. However, to get in, one has to go through a security station of sorts, so most people seek out the public gardens elsewhere in the city."

She gave him a sideways glance. "So we'll be alone?"

"As alone as you want to be?" He shot her a charming smile that he knew melted a woman's reserve faster than a hot day did ice.

For some reason, a contemplative expression crossed her face. Not the feeling he'd been hoping to evoke. However, he still had plenty of time. He didn't plan to leave the garden without having her or, at least, arranging for an assignation later.

Miri halted, gasping. "A maze! I've never seen a hedge one before. In the autumn, Knocton and some of the neighboring ones have corn mazes in celebration of the harvest."

She whirled toward him eagerly. "Is this a large one?" Suddenly, she stopped and slapped a hand to her head. "*Whoa, the world is spinning.*" As if to prove her words correct, she swayed precariously.

His heart skipped a beat. He grabbed her before she could fall. Her eyes slid closed, and she groaned. Her skin was grayer than normal, its pink disappearing almost totally.

"Are you unwell?" he asked urgently. He didn't know what to do with sick females.

"I've been better, but I'll be fine in a moment. Could we sit down for a little?"

"Of course." He hurried her over to a nearby bench near the entrance of the maze. By the Dark Woods, was she going to vomit? Give him guts and blood, not ladies vomiting.

Feeling uncharacteristically uncertain, he hovered over her as she took in deep, slow breaths, her eyes closed. "Should I summon a healer?"

"*Lord, no.*"

He reared back at the vehemence in her tone. "Is there anything you need? Water?" A bucket?

"No, I'll be fine." Her eyes fluttered open, and she gestured to the spot beside her. "Please sit."

With a gingerness that made him grimace, he folded down beside her. Why did he feel so off-center around her? He didn't like the feeling one bit and would much rather be beating Alanon on the training fields. Was she ill or still adjusting to her Change?

She continued with her deep breathing. After a few minutes, she shifted on the bench. "I'm okay now. What did you want to talk about?"

"What was that episode you just had?" he asked. The question lingered heavily on his mind.

She licked her lips nervously and glanced away from him. Interesting.

"Nothing to concern yourself about at the moment," she said. "If you don't mind telling me, what do you want?"

So she didn't want to talk about whatever had brought about her episode. Fine with him. He could now launch his plan.

"You."

A pink-gray flush spread over her cheeks. He wanted to follow its progress with his tongue but knew it would be too soon.

"What do you mean?" she stammered.

"As I've said before, I want to get to know you better." He paused deliberately. "In every way."

Her brow furrowed before clearing slightly. "Why?"

Why must she be so suspicious? *Maybe because you've given her cause to be.* He ignored that little voice in the back of his mind. Nothing could interfere with his plans. Not even his conscience, as rusty as it was.

He pasted a smile on his face and let some carefully controlled truths spill. "There is a pull between us. I think—no, I know—you feel it. I'd like to explore it."

Her pupils dilated, a sign of attraction. "What would that encompass?"

He scooted closer on the bench until their legs were touching. Her gaze tracked his every movement, but she made no attempt to inch away. Definite victory on his part.

"It'd encompass anything and everything you want it to," he said, his voice husky. His words, heavy with a decadent promise, hung between them like a caress.

The scent of her arousal drifted to him. Since her Change, she smelled slightly different to him, a hint of smoke that hadn't been there before. Oddly enough, even when she'd been fully human, her aroma had been sweet yet rich, a scent he had unconsciously inhaled deeply in search of. Now, he would partake of her scent until he was drunk on it.

She looked down at her clasped hands. "You want a sexual relationship."

He didn't bother to deny it. "Yes. Right now, there is no one else I want."

"Right now," she echoed.

He back-pedaled a bit. "I can't predict the future, but it's been some time since I've been...so taken by a female." Not since Anneth, and that had been several lifetimes ago, it seemed. He waited for the age-old hurt to arise, but only a bittersweet fondness drifted up from the depths.

"I'm not experienced."

"I know." He knew that quite intimately, but her passion, her fire, was all he needed. Would their next time be like their first? He looked forward to finding out.

However, a clear hesitation existed on her part. Why, though? She desired him. He knew this like he knew all the scars on his body. "We will go at your pace," he cajoled. *With a lot of help from me.*

She sighed and stared at a nearby flowering tree. "That's what I'm afraid of."

He frowned. "What do you mean?"

She faced him, her face solemn. "I'm not great at making good decisions when it comes to you."

He swallowed the lump forming in his throat. Did she remember their night, or was she referring to something else? A foreign bout of nerves caused words to spew out of his mouth. "Sometimes, I feel the same, which, I admit, is not optimal for the leader of a people."

She blinked. "Truly?"

He gritted his teeth behind a wry smile. Why had he let that slip? "I have no reason to lie to you."

Hating being caught off-guard, he abruptly changed the subject. He had to know. "What do you remember of your Change?" If she remembered their night, it would change his plan somewhat.

The small grin forming on her lips froze. "Bits and pieces." She paused before adding hesitantly, "Why?"

"I visited you one evening, and we had a very interesting night."

Her face blanched to a grayish-white. "You mean the night we slept together."

Giving in to the Heat

Miri stared at him, her rear end firmly rooted to the bench. In fact, she was dimly aware she'd forgotten to breathe. She inhaled sharply to give her deprived lungs some sustenance. He'd truly done it. He'd raised the topic of the night together in a roundabout way.

Eerin gazed back at her, his own eyes wide as if he were astonished by his audacity or by her admittance.

She clutched her shaking hands in her lap. Too bad the rest of her was quivering like a blade of grass in a storm.

Of all the things she thought might happen, this hadn't been one she'd ever seriously considered. Given what Innara had said, and by his actions over the last weeks, he'd seemed loath to admit it to anyone, let alone her.

She was somewhat surprised by her forthrightness, but since he'd asked, she'd seen no reason to deny her knowledge. Especially since that night had borne fruit. Is this where she told him that truth?

Part of her wanted to, so desperately wanted to, but her mouth refused to form the words.

"You remember?" he asked, his voice thick.

Before she could answer, a fast, faint beating filtered to her ears. She strained to place the sound with her new, improved hearing.

A heartbeat.

Eerin's. Though her own drummed just as quickly.

But it told her something she'd failed to realize. Eerin could be nervous, unsure.

And he was that right now.

In fact, when she'd been dizzy and nearly vomited in front of him, he'd acted like a typical young man from her town. Clueless and flustered. She'd just been too preoccupied at the time to notice it.

Suddenly, he was more relatable than he'd ever been. Truthfully, it was an adorable look, one far removed from the arrogant alpha male she'd seen alternatively strutting and stomping around.

She smiled at him slowly, a spark of playfulness hitting her. "Yes, I've had many, as you would say, interesting dreams. It took me a while"—falling pregnant—"to figure it out."

A dark flush coursed over his face, even coloring the tips of his ears. "So you know we've already had sexual relations."

"I have for some time."

"That's why you've been avoiding me."

If he only knew... She glanced at him through her lashes, hoping he couldn't sense her hesitation. "It is a large part of why, yes."

"And the other reasons?"

"My Change and the way you treated me and Eve are not reason enough?" she hedged.

"Why not tell me sooner?" he asked, deflecting her question.

She raised a brow, her manner cool. "You didn't bring it up before, either."

"Truly, I never expected you to remember."

What she had suspected. She leaned away from him slightly. "And you think that paints you in a better light?"

He crossed his arms. "It's not as if I had planned all this. Curse the day you entered the Dark Forest!"

She stood abruptly. "Well, if you feel that way, I'll leave you to your own devices."

He grabbed her arm. "I spoke hastily. Harshly. Don't go."

As she stared at him impassively, he added, "Please."

The sincerity of the grudging plea bit at her heart. That was a word she knew he didn't use often or even lightly.

She sighed but didn't sit down. "Okay, but I want our conversation to remain cordial."

Good luck there. She might as well ask that the sun turn purple. In fact, she might have better luck with that.

He yanked her down into his lap. She squealed, her heart pounding. His arms closed about her firmly, keeping her sideways in his lap.

"Got you right where I want you," he whispered in her ear.

She turned her head to stare at him, all the while attempting to calm her heart. "I thought we were going to talk." She tried to sound stern but failed miserably.

"Oh, we still can." He flashed her a wicked grin. "I just find this seating arrangement preferable to any others."

"How about asking me next time?" she asked dryly.

"Because you'd probably tell me no," he admitted with a good-to-honest pout.

A chortle welled up in her throat. "You're pouting. If only your people could see you now!"

A fierce scowl chased away his sulky expression. "I do not pout, and they'd never believe you."

God, when had he become this endearing? Was it her hormones speaking? Right now, she didn't care about its origin. "I beg to differ. You do pout."

His eyes gleamed. "You beg? I like the sound of that."

Heat flooded her cheeks. "I didn't mean it that way."

"Challenge accepted."

"What?" she asked, her brow furrowing.

"I'll make you beg."

"I asked you to do no such thing." He was trying to fluster her. It was working.

He pulled her against his chest. "You don't have to. It's something I believe we'll both enjoy immeasurably."

"I—"

He leaned down and stole her words with a kiss. Curse him, it was a fabulous one, too. The press of his mouth was addicting, the swipe of his tongue against hers even more so. She moaned, warmth kindling low in her belly. Heady desire and the need to consume him in her passion roared to life within her.

A crick in her neck pinched at her. She rolled her shoulders. He picked up on her discomfort immediately and shifted her until she straddled his lap. It was impressive he did all that without breaking their kiss.

In the position she was in now, she could feel the evidence of his desire. His erection poked against her stomach. If she angled herself a bit higher and got a little closer, it'd be poking somewhere else a bit lower.

She should be shocked at the lewdness of her idea and, what was more, at her actions. But right now she didn't care. She just wanted to touch and be touched.

By Eerin. Everywhere.

That could be arranged. And this time she'd remember every delicious moment of it.

As if reading her mind, he slid his hands to her hips and scooted her closer while also hefting her higher. Her mound settled over his erection, and Eerin made a hissing sound of lust as he broke away from her mouth.

His lips settled over the rapid pulse in her neck, where he sucked and licked. As he did so, she found that her hips swayed against his. With one hand, he roughly tore the front of her plain gown open. Her bare breasts sprang free. They had been painful and achy lately, so she hadn't bound them.

He palmed a globe, playing with the tip before taking it into his mouth. Soon, the nipple was hard and distended. She gasped at the pleasurable pain shooting through her.

With one last lick over the areola, he lifted his head. A dark flush had settled over his cheeks, and he grinned darkly at her. "Are you ready for me to take you? Here and now?"

Heat flowed southward. All she could think of was him. Him making love to her.

"Say it," he commanded.

The words came unbidden. "Take me. Please."

And he did. Right on that bench, first with his fingers and then with his cock. It was just like she'd remembered from her fleeting snatches of memories and dreams. But it was also so much more. This time, she stared into his eyes as they thrust against each other. She caught every facial expression that flickered over his surprisingly naked face, each sound that flowed past his lips. Call her crazy, but she thought he was doing the same thing. All the while, they strained to reach their completion but never forgot about one another.

When they collapsed upright against each other, her still seated on him and his head buried in the hollow of her neck, a closeness linked them that had been missing.

A pang speared her, and she stared at the bright garden with unseeing eyes. During their round of lovemaking, she'd forgotten about the pregnancy. She had to tell him. Somehow.

Foil

"Wake up, Miss Sleepy," a deep male voice whispered in Miri's ear. She snuggled into the sheets. Haze clouded her mind and drew her back into the snug darkness.

Something soft tickled her nose. Mumbling, she ripped her hand out of the blanket and batted at the nuisance.

A soft chuckle drifted through her consciousness. The cadence was so familiar that she should know who that was, but her mind refused to supply the answer.

Suddenly, the blanket disappeared. Warm air hit her naked skin. That forced her eyes open. Above her was a grinning Eerin who actually appeared happy in the early morning light. She blinked as the last two and a half weeks rushed back to her. She and Eerin, having meals together, taking walks, talking. Making love. Her heart threatened to explode from all the fullness it held—and the fear.

She still hadn't told him. But she would. Today, even. Maybe.

She snatched at the blanket he was holding. "Give that back. I'm trying to sleep." He'd stayed the night with her and was a disgustingly early riser. Thank the heavens for Eamandian's tonic. Her stomach wasn't rebelling. It was probably just as shocked as she was about the hour.

"Oh no." He shook a finger at her. "It's time for you to get up."

"Shake that finger near my face, and I'll bite it."

A gleam formed in his eyes. "Is that a promise?"

She mock-scowled at him. "Just for that, there'll be no biting at all." He was a biter during their more amorous moments. To her surprise, she liked it. He took care not to break the skin so as not to hurt her. She even reciprocated occasionally, which he loved. He was always...*um*, very vocal and demonstrative in his appreciation.

"Now, that's not fair," he protested, reaching for her and hauling her upright against his clothed form.

Normally, a swell of desire would hit her at such antics. However, all that came over her right now was a roiling stomach that hated the sudden switch in positions. She managed to swallow back the bile rising in her throat just in time.

He peered at her face, placing the back of his hand on her forehead. "You look a little pale. I've seen you have several of these spells in the past week."

The deep inhale she'd taken froze in her lungs. Trepidation settled on her chest like a physical weight, making her feel all shaky. Here was the perfect lead-in, if only she'd grab onto it.

She had to tell Eerin the news *now* because no time ever seemed right. Their relationship was going so smoothly—well, as smoothly as it could with someone as intense as Eerin—but it wasn't built on the full truth. She hated to destroy this newfound peace, but her pregnancy would only be more devastating on their relationship, or whatever they had, if she kept it a prolonged secret. As for their relationship, she couldn't say that he loved her or that she loved him. It was too soon, but she believed she could love him.

Already, he engendered feelings within her that she'd never experienced before. Warm, tender sensations mixed with passionate, possessive feelings and left her breathless. Whether he could ever return her affections would have to be seen. However, whether by lust or something more, he wasn't left unaffected by her.

She licked at her dry lips. "Eerin, I have—"

A loud knock cut off her words. A sob of frustration and relief caught in her throat. Who was bothering them at this hour?

He scowled and covered her quickly with the blanket. "Stay here. I'll see who it is. If it's any one of the male persuasion, I don't want them to see you unclothed."

A smile tugged at her mouth. As if anyone could see her when they were in the bedroom with the door closed and locked. She'd warned Eerin that Eve would bounce into the room whenever she felt like it. The one time they'd forgotten to lock the door... She cringed. That had taken a lot of explanation. Eve still asked her questions.

As Eerin shut the door behind him, Miri reclined on the bed, determined to get a bit more rest. She didn't have to go into the healing halls today. That was a rare treat, as her apprenticeship kept her busy. Though Eamandian made allowances for her condition, she still averaged thirty hours per week, and that didn't count the time she spent with the textbooks he'd given her. Those studies consumed an extra ten to twelve hours a week on average.

Eve and, now, Eerin had been taking up all her spare time, not that she begrudged it to either of them. Eerin was starting to accept Eve, though he still could be somewhat petty and petulant if he was feeling slighted. They were both so much like children at times, except Eve actually *was* a child. She didn't know what Eerin's excuse was, except he must've never learned to share well. Especially not a lady's attention.

Eve, for her part, loved Eerin and found him *hilarious*. She broke into giggles each time he called her *child*. Even Miri found it funny. She snorted. It was like a comedy show to put those two together. They were the perfect foil for each other.

The murmuring of voices snagged her attention. Did she detect three voices? Her hearing was much improved, but she still couldn't make out what was being said—or by who.

She shrugged her curiosity off. Most likely it didn't concern her, though it was interesting that the person outside knew where to find Eerin. Not that they were trying to keep their relationship a secret. Eerin had been surprisingly open and ardent in his...she wasn't sure what to call it. His courtship? Was he courting her, though?

As for her, she saw little reason to be secretive. After she had told Eerin about the baby, everyone would come to know about her pregnancy sooner or later. In the meantime, she was trying to get to know the father of her baby.

A flush heated her face as she thought about how well she'd gotten to know him lately. She slapped her palms to her cheeks, trying to calm the warmth flooding them. Worse, the fire was spreading to other parts of her body, making her shift restlessly. Suddenly, she wished Eerin was back with her in bed. He was turning into an addiction, one she feared she'd never tire of.

The sound of the bedroom door opening caused her to glance up. Eerin all but stomped into the chamber. *Uh-oh, must've not been good news.* She certainly would've hated to be the bearer of whatever bad news he'd received.

She sat up slowly, letting the blanket fall down to her waist, and fixed a sympathetic smile onto her face. Maybe she could cheer him up. She'd already seen how an eyeful could turn his mood around. "You don't look too happy."

He huffed as he strolled over to the bed, his gaze drifting down to her chest all the while. "What gave it away?"

"Your glower. It's more fearsome than usual."

"For good reason. Though I much prefer the sight you offer, I have matters that need my attention."

"You need to leave right now?"

He bent down and startled her with a searing kiss. "Unfortunately."

Her lips tingled pleasantly after he righted himself. She blinked a few times to clear her mind of the lustful cloud hazing it. "Is this issue anything that I should know of?" She wasn't sure why that question crossed her lips, but it just felt right.

A strange expression flitted across his face. "Not at this time."

"What do you mean?"

He shook his head. "Nothing."

The ways of males—or at least *this* male—would never make sense to her. However, she resolved not to worry about it. She had much better things to do.

Miri grabbed the cover, dragging it back over her shoulders. "Guess I can go back to sleep, then."

His mouth hung open for a second, and then his eyes narrowed in apparent outrage. "You are surprisingly cruel when you want to be."

She smirked at him before lying down. "I'm learning from the best."

***

As soon as Eerin slammed into his study, he found Alegion and Callon waiting for him as he'd commanded. He lost no time beginning his interrogation. "You said there were humans in the forest."

Alegion nodded grimly. "A group of eight human men entered the forest but stayed within the fringes. The eastern border control managed to catch one while the others fled."

"One?" Eerin's voice came out sharp. "Why were any of them able to escape?"

Callon stepped forward. "Most of the border patrol were deeper within the woods. Only two of our scouts were in that area. They did manage to wound two of the other men, but the human men helped the injured out of the forest."

Eerin pinned a glare on his captain. "And the two did not give chase?"

Callon's expression, to his credit, barely moved an inch. "They had orders not to leave the forest unless given the command by either me or Commander Alegion."

Alegion snorted, apparently not appreciating Eerin's manner at that moment. "Leave the forest? Most of our people would never set foot outside our woods, even if they're allowed to. Anyway, those scouts could've walked into an ambush. You know that's why we command them as we do. You're the one who instituted the order in the first place!"

Alegion had him at that, but Eerin was fuming and needed to take it out on someone. He knew just who.

He bared his teeth in a vicious smile. "Take me to the human."

Alegion and Callon traded a glance before the former answered him. "He's in one of the holding cells."

A moment later, Eerin stalked toward the holding cells, his two companions close on his heels. He ground his teeth. Not only had humans ventured into his forest, but they'd also interrupted his morning with Miri. Though he had a full day of duties ahead, he'd planned to spend another hour in her arms. Now, that pleasant idea was all ash in the wind. The man in their custody would pay. Oh, yes, he'd pay.

Then an unwelcome truth speared into his mind. These humans had likely come in search of Miri and Eve. He couldn't forget that. Was one of these men friends or acquaintances of the two sisters? From what he knew, Miri and Eve only had their father and a few distant relatives left in Knocton.

So no killing. At least until he'd ascertained who the young human was to the sisters.

Within a few minutes, they neared the building that housed the holding cells. Right before they stepped through the guarded entrance, Alegion sent Callon ahead and drew Eerin off to the side.

"Are you sure you want to see the prisoner right now?" he whispered.

Eerin glowered. "Why wouldn't I? I'm the one who asked."

"Your temper...it seems quite roused."

Another spike of anger pierced Eerin, but he pushed it aside. Alegion, although possessed of an interfering disposition, meant well. "I'm in a perfect frame of mind to see the prisoner."

Alegion eyed him doubtfully. "If you say so. I just don't want you to kill him. We haven't even interrogated him yet. Plus, Lady Miri and her sister might not approve."

"I'll rein myself in. Never fear." Truthfully, he still wanted to smash something or someone. However, he was a leader and had an example to set.

A good leader didn't kill wantonly.

He had to remember that. Plus, he didn't need Miri angry at him because he killed an acquaintance of hers.

Eerin strolled inside, Alegion trailing after him. A set of stairs off to one side took them down to the cells. Soon, darkness enveloped them, which was only broken by sparsely placed hanging lamps.

Callon stood by one cell, his hands folded before him. He must've dismissed the two guards that were usually assigned to that section.

Eerin ghosted forward and saw a pitiful form huddled in one corner of the small enclosure. Besides its new occupant, the area only held a beat-up, old mattress with a threadbare blanket, along with a chamberpot and a tin bowl of water. "This is the prisoner?"

Callon nodded.

The young human stiffened before raising his head from his knees and glaring at the three of them. Messy brown hair fell into his eyes. He appeared no older than Miri, but Eerin had never been good at estimating a human's age. He'd never cared enough to learn.

"Let me out," the young man demanded. "You have no right to hold me! I only came looking for two people missing from Knocton, our town."

Rage, hot and spikey, roared through his veins. This...this vermin *had* come for Miri and Eve. His Miri and the sister she so treasured.

His hands curled into fists as the urge to pummel the man hit him. Only the bars between them stopped him from moving.

He calmed his ire. He couldn't let rage rule him at the moment. Besides, the being before him wasn't an impressive specimen of malehood. He had no reason to worry.

With a smirk, Eerin tapped the fingers of one hand against his arm. "You'll be going nowhere, except to an early grave."

Eerin felt Alegion's disapproving stare on his back. *Bah*, his friend was much too tender-hearted at times. It was a wonder he could function at all as the commander of Taerin's forces.

The man slowly stood up, his shoulders straight and a determined glint in his eyes. Still, it couldn't hide the slight shake of the man's limbs. He stunk of fear. Eerin would enjoy ratcheting it up another level.

"Is that a threat?" the male asked, his voice steady.

Eerin lifted his chin higher and stared down his nose at the prisoner. The human was brave but foolish. No one that came onto Taelin land ever left. And they didn't accept outsiders, so that only left one possibility. Some part of him whispered about Miri and Eve. However, they were the exception, more Taelin than human now.

However, they'd always been special.

"Not a threat. It's a vow," he said, his tone as chilly as a snow-shrouded day.

A sharp intake of breath sounded behind him. Either Alegion or Callon—or both—were shocked at his words. Vows weren't undertaken lightly, as such words contained a capricious power that could just as easily turn on him. However, in this case, he'd quite happily bear the consequences. No one touched what was his.

Miri was his.

Some part of him, no matter how small, should be upset at such a realization, but only cold rage and possessiveness filled him. No one would ever take her away. Certainly not this weak human.

The human's eyes narrowed on him. "You won't get away with this. We know the Summerland sisters are here."

"Oh, do you?"

"Miri and Eve were seen near the forest. It's simple deduction."

Eerin clapped. "Fascinating. I didn't know humans were capable of that kind of intelligence." He paused and pierced the man with a cold stare, causing the human's chin to quiver minutely. "Now, tell me when the other interlopers will be back."

The man crossed his arms, vainly attempting to hide his shivers. "What will you give me in return?"

"Your head still attached to your shoulders?"

"You'll guarantee that and the whereabouts of Miri and her sister."

Miri and her sister? Not the Summerland sisters or even Miri and Eve? It was easy to tell which sister was more important, more precious, to the man. How did Miri know this man? "You will tell me what I want to know. Else your nails won't remain on your hands and feet. Need I relay to you how painful that is?"

The man blanched. "I harmed no one! Neither did any of my companions."

"And anyone with even an iota of sense knows that these woods are not to be trifled with. It is the haunt of the Taelin and only the Taelin. None other shall pass."

"Then why are the sisters here?"

Why wouldn't he drop the subject of Miri and her sister? Eerin slammed his hands against the bars. The sound reverberated around the otherwise silent room. "They are none of your business."

The man jumped but then lifted his chin. "They are. Miri is to be my wife."

Secrets Leashed

Eerin bared his teeth, and a growl rumbled deep in his chest. A red haze filled his vision, starting at the sides and creeping inward. His Miri this whelp's wife? Over his dead body. Miri had mentioned *nothing* of a suitor she might be missing or even thinking about.

A hand touched his arm, ripping him out of his fog of rage. He blinked before spinning around to confront Alegion. "What?" he snapped.

"We still have to...talk to him."

Eerin realized the warning in his friend's words—*don't kill him*. He blew out a breath. "I know."

However, his body didn't seem to understand that. He wanted to whirl around and part the human's head from his neck. He counted backward from fifteen and then faced the cell.

The man watched them with wide eyes. Eerin cursed his own stupidity. By overreacting, he'd given the human a show. Oh, he still wasn't happy about the man claiming Miri as his future wife, but he had his murderous anger under control.

"You'll be marrying no one from a cell, boy." And never Miri.

The young man's lips thinned. "I want to see Miri. I demand you bring her."

A bark of laughter left Eerin's lips. The audacity of this human. "You *demand*?" he asked softly.

"Yes, I'm Henry. My father is mayor of our town. I'm not without some influence."

"That influence means *nothing* here." Inwardly, Eerin cursed. The whelp would have to be the son of one of the most important men in Miri's village. Not only would the townsfolk probably be stupid enough to come looking for their missing "heir," but the man's position in Miri's village gave him pause. Had this human boy truly been courting her? Worse, had Miri held him in affection?

He allowed a feral smile to curve his lips. Well, if the human had been courting her, he certainly hadn't tasted her charms. Miri had saved those for him.

They were all his. Would always be his and his alone.

The human stared at him, seemingly at a loss for words at last. How enjoyable the silence—

"Are Miri and Eve housed down here?"

By the Dark Forest's damnation, did the whelp ever shut up? He knew of many great ways to rob him of his ability to speak. Cutting out his tongue was the one that hovered at the front of his mind.

A subtle pulse of calming magic—Alegion's—hit Eerin, pulsed through his skin, and sunk deep into the muscle. He squashed the urge to roll his eyes at his commander. However, his thundering heart rate had declined, so Alegion had been somewhat useful. Instead, he grinned maniacally at the young man. "Who says they're on Taelin land or, for that matter, even alive?"

"Y-you didn't deny that they were here earlier," the boy stuttered.

"Nor did I confirm it." Damn it, some of his words *had* backed up the whelp's opinion, though.

The arrogant boy gazed challengingly at him. "If they weren't here, I think you would've said so."

Eerin ground his teeth. The insolent pup was perceptive, too much so. He'd have to die and die painfully.

Alegion stepped to his side. "Lord Eerin, may we interrogate him now?" The commander's voice was pointed and broke into the encroaching red haze.

This time, Eerin did roll his eyes as he turned to his friend. "Of course. Interrogate away. Never mind me."

Alegion nodded his good-naturedly as if he hadn't picked up on his sarcasm in the least. "Callon and I shall do the honors."

Eerin raised a brow, considering that. Callon and Alegion wouldn't have been his first two choices. Though both males were more than proficient at their role, neither had a penchant for the ruthless methods that were sometimes needed. Taregon and others of his ilk were better suited to the job.

However, until he knew if Miri held the boy in esteem, it might be wise to use a gentler touch, no matter how that grated on him. Eerin certainly could try to keep the prisoner secret, but Miri had a way of slipping past his defenses. Besides, all it would take was one person who would let something slip to Miri about the human.

Alegion leaned forward and whispered, "I'm sure your lady is waiting for you. Why don't you pay her a little visit before you start the rest of your duties?"

"What a fine idea." He sent a triumphant glance at the caged human. "Don't be too gentle on him."

***

Eerin lay snuggled against Miri. She'd fallen asleep after another round of lovemaking. He marveled at her easy ability to do so. Was this a part of her humanity? At the thought of humans, his mood darkened again, and he took stock of his morning so far.

Contentment coursed through his sated body. However, his mind was another matter. Though he had duty awaiting him, he found himself loath to leave her side. The human boy had upset his equilibrium more than he'd like to admit.

Words to tell her of the boy's finding had formed on his lips, only to die again and again. He found himself strangely hesitant to tell her of the young man. He wasn't sure what to call his relationship with Miri. However one defined it, though, there was no doubt that it was going well. The whelp was certain to put a strain on it.

At best, he was a fellow villager. At worst, he was a beau. Miri would never countenance putting him to death.

Which made Eerin doubt he could.

But he was leader of the Taelin. If he wouldn't protect his people, who would? Not only that but he also needed to find out the name of his rival. No, the whelp was merely a boy. He could never be a true opponent and was inferior in every way. Still, it was an oversight on Eerin's part not to learn the human's name.

He let loose a huge sigh. This feeling of being conflicted... He hated it.

It made him vulnerable, and vulnerability was too often deadly. Ever since Miri had crashed into his woods, he'd felt this way.

If he were wiser, he'd dig her out of his life. An invisible band around his chest tightened at that idea. She was his. He was selfish and couldn't bear the thought of letting her go. His mind shied away from what that might mean.

Miri stirred beside him. A smile tugged at his lips as he watched her roll onto her back and stretch. The blanket slid down to her waist. Heat jolted southward. By the Dark Forest's damnation, would he ever get enough of her?

He cupped one of her cheeks. The feel of her skin against his sent a frisson of pleasure through his fingertips and palm.

Her lids fluttered open. A slow smile came to her lips. "Hey, you're still here."

"Indeed, I am."

She cocked an eyebrow lazily. "I thought you had a busy day ahead of you."

He leaned over her, raking one hand through her unbound tresses. "I do. I need to leave soon." Except he could stay and do this all day. He pressed a kiss on her mouth, meaning to rise then.

She grabbed the back of his head and deepened the pressure of her lips against his. "Don't let me keep you," she murmured into his mouth.

After untold seconds, he untangled himself from her. "Minx, I know what you're doing, and it's working. But I have to get ready now. It's past nine already. If we want to spend the evening together, I have to see to my duties now. I'm already late for one meeting."

As he stood, she settled back against the pillows with a sigh. "Go and do your job. I'll see you later. In the meanwhile, I'm going to laze in bed." Her gaze ghosted over his naked form. "Maybe you can join me for a quick...lunch?"

His mouth watered but not for the want of food, and he licked his lips. "I might be able to ink in your delectable charms on my schedule."

***

The next evening, Miri smiled as she walked through the heart of Taerin by Eerin's side, his arm through hers. The bustling city, with its multi-level buildings guided by nature, always held so many sights, sounds, and smells that were simply amazing. Would she ever grow bored of it?

The scent of now-familiar spices tickled her nose. A flute played a foreign melody in the distance, and a voice joined in with stunning harmony. Where once she would've strained to hear the words, they came easily to her now. The lyrical Taelin language was a hard one to master, but she could already pick out a few words in the tune, thanks to the lessons she and Eve were taking.

She jiggled Eerin's arm. "So where are we dining?"

"That's a surprise, as I've told you twice already." A huff of amusement left his lips. "You're very impatient."

She gave a pretend pout. "I'm not terribly good at surprises."

Except for one. You've kept that one under wraps easily enough.

He gave a good-humored snort that she almost missed because of her distraction. "I'd never have guessed."

Tonight. She'd tell him tonight after she enjoyed one last evening with him.

He'd get angry, probably fearfully so. In a few days, however, he'd cool enough to talk with her. Even Innara said the same. If anyone knew Eerin well, it'd be his cousin.

That decided, she pushed it to the back of her mind as her arm tightened around his. She had an evening to enjoy and would fully immerse herself in the experience.

She took in her surroundings and opened her senses. The muggy evening air clung to her skin. It was July, after all. Even at night, the temperature didn't abate by much. The sun was sinking lower into the horizon, streaking the sky that was visible through the leaf cover in shades of pink and rose.

His people nodded or called out their greetings to them. What had surprised her was the Taelin's easy acceptance of her and Eve. Oh, there were some people who never deigned to talk to her. She was sure some individuals weren't pleased with their presence, even altered as she and Eve were. It'd also become clear that people talked about them as soon as they were out of earshot. Innara had also warned her that she and Eerin were a popular topic, with some approving of their liaison and others not. By and large, however, she and her sister felt quite welcomed.

Which was good, great even, as this was their new home. She'd finally made some peace with the fact she'd never see Knocton again. Even her appearance wasn't so upsetting anymore. It seemed true that one could adapt to almost anything, and her life could be worse by far.

She had almost everything she could ask for—a promising career, her sister, a baby on the way, and a male that made her blood sing. Now, if she only knew how those last two things would fit together.

"You're quiet this evening," Eerin said quietly by her ear, startling her a bit.

She blinked several times. "Oh, just thinking."

"About what?"

His expectant stare weighed on her. "About all the scrolls and books I have to study for my apprenticeship." Which wasn't a huge lie. She often did think about all the challenging subjects she was learning or would be. In fact, Eerin sometimes teased her about how bookish she was.

"You mean you're dreaming of your old, dusty scrolls when you should have your focus on something more pleasurable? For instance, me?"

"Who says you're my only indulgence?" she teased as they both waved at various acquaintances.

The lofty look on his face morphed into a scowl, which made her want to giggle. His ferocious expressions could no longer cow her the way they used to. She refused to let them. Anyway, she was coming to see what he hid under that harsh exterior. He was truly a case where his buzz was worse than his sting. At least with her. From experience and rumor, she knew he could be a fearsome opponent.

She cocked her head coyly to the side and gazed at him through her lashes. "You're my favorite main indulgence, never fear."

He tugged her closer until their hips bumped. "I better be your only sexual indulgence."

She shivered in delight at his low, growly voice. When he spoke like this, it always slid along her synapses like oiled honey. Then she gave a sputtered laugh. "You think I have time for anyone else? You're with me nearly every night and leave me tired out."

He straightened, a satisfied, smug mien about him now. "Good. If I don't leave you wrung-out with pleasure, I haven't done my job."

Heat flowed to the area between her thighs. Aware they may be overheard if they kept on this course, she said a bit breathlessly, "Tonight, you'll have to show me in-depth what you're talking about."

"It'll be *my* complete pleasure to bring you to yours," he whispered wickedly in her ear.

A flush scalded her cheeks. Oh God, his voice should be outlawed when he said such things. She quickened her stride, pulling on his arm because she was suddenly eager to get their meal over and done with.

He chuckled and followed behind her sedately for several strides. Then he was in step with her, his side brushing hers.

"Wicked tease," she hissed at him.

"I'm learning from the best," he said, stealing her words to him from earlier that day.

Secrets Unleashed

Eerin knew he and Miri needed to leave the eatery soon. She moaned in delight as the dessert hit her tongue. The front of his pants pressed painfully against his erection. If he didn't want to embarrass himself by losing all control, she needed to finish soon.

She flashed him a blissful grin. "This is so delicious." Lifting another forkful of the moist loaf, she held it out to him.

He didn't particularly like almond cake. At that moment, however, he found he couldn't deny her. As his mouth closed around the tines, sweetness hit his taste receptors like a magical bomb. For once, the flavor of almond didn't make him grimace. He chewed slowly, automatically as he watched her take another bite.

By the great Spirit teats, he'd never realized how arousing it could be to ogle someone while they were eating. He'd have to be sure to do it with some regularity.

Still, maybe ordering Miri cake had been a poor choice. No, not a poor one. He shook his head at that blasphemous thought. The location was merely wrong. He should've asked for the sweet to be packed so they could've taken it home. His mouth watered as he imagined what they could've done with that cake.

She licked her lips, wiping away some of the smeared frosting that had been coating them. Then she lifted a brow. "Why are you staring at me like that?"

He blinked as if coming out of a trance. Maybe he was. "I find watching you eat to be very erotic."

"Really?" Her tone held a note of incredulity.

He nodded curtly. "Unfortunately, this isn't the time or place...to desire other activities." His lips twitched. "I have a reputation to uphold. My people would be quite shocked to see me ravage you right here on the table."

She shifted in her seat and set down her fork. "Let's have the rest of this packed up."

He motioned for a waiter and requested a paper box. As Eerin deposited the dessert into the receptacle, one of his off-duty city guards approached them. Eerin frowned, but Nelin, the oblivious dolt, didn't pick up on his displeasure.

Normally, Eerin would be more vocal in his ire, but he was very aware of Miri by his side. She'd been coming to see him as something other than a brute, a monster. He sighed inwardly. Sometimes, it was so hard to reign in his tendencies. Well, as long as Nalin didn't mention Henry, which happened to be the whelp's name, he could push through this unfortunate interruption.

"My lord, good evening." His gaze slid to Miri, where it lingered far longer than Eerin thought appropriate or acceptable. Nalin inclined his head. "My lady."

Miri nodded more graciously than he would have in her position. At least she didn't seem to notice the guard's undue attention.

Nalin opened his mouth again, and useless nattering poured forth. "A pleasure to see you here, enjoying..."

Eerin tuned him out and instead focused on regulating his heart rate. His pulse was thundering in his ears, which usually heralded a loss of his temper. Next, he quashed the urge to pinch the bridge of his nose. No, what he truly wanted was to smash Nalin's nose.

Miri's gasp ripped him out of his increasingly violent thoughts. "Oh, your parents own this establishment?" she asked the guard with an eagerness that made Eerin scowl. Why was she being so cheerful and *nice*?

Nalin beamed, which was a horrible look on the young Taelin. It made him appear puppy-like. Eerin's foot twitched. If the fool stepped over a few more inches, he could easily land a kick to his shin. That would wipe that expression off his face. "They've run this eatery for centuries."

Her ready smile faltered. The idiot! Didn't he know that Miri was still sensitive to the lifespan discrepancy between humans and Taelin? From their discussions, he knew that she'd been shaken to realize the Taelin could live up to ten thousand years and that she might inherit some of their lifespan.

Eerin felt a blistering retort on the tip of his tongue, but before he could let it loose, Miri recovered her composure and spoke. "Give your parents my compliments. Everything was delicious."

Nalin preened like a huge, gaudy bird. Maybe he'd squawk like one, too, if he trussed him up. It'd be easy to stash him in some faraway place for a day or two...

Miri was still talking. "Do you help run the place?"

The guard shook his head. "Not anymore. I'm a city guard. Right now, I'm assigned to the cells."

"Cell?" asked Miri, her brow creasing.

Alarm bells blared through Eerin's mind. He glared at Nalin who, blast the darkness, wasn't even looking at him.

"For prisoners," said Nalin oh-so helpfully. The dolt.

Eerin placed his hands down on the table a bit forcefully. Both sets of gazes now rested on him. "I hate to cut short our pleasant little talk, but we must truly be going, Nalin."

The guard's eyes widened in a surprised, yet disappointed expression. "Of course." He brightened. "Oh, my lord, the human prisoner is demanding to see you and Lady Miri."

Eerin cursed silently. Miri's stare was suddenly on him, and its weight was practically burning a hole through his skin. He gritted his teeth and then addressed Nalin with cutting ice in his voice. "This is not the place for such discussions. We will talk about all of this on the morrow."

Nalin blinked, his face slackening in shock. His throat bobbed as he swallowed thickly. "Of course. Apologies, my lord." He sketched a quick bow and all but ran away.

He and Miri both turned to watch Nalin's retreat until he ducked into a back room, the door carelessly slamming behind him. A sadistic satisfaction twisted through Eerin. It served the dolt right. Now, Miri knew.

Damnation, now she *knew*.

As soon as he faced her, he realized how bad it was. She leaned across the table and said quietly, her voice hard like steel, "Which person do you have from my town? Tell me now."

With effort, he ripped his gaze from hers, aware they were drawing attention. "Not here. There's no privacy."

She seemed to deflate for a second before straightening. "So you don't deny it. As for privacy, you've had *a lot* of that with me lately, and still you never mentioned holding one of my people captive. Do you make a practice of it?"

"What?" He shook his head when he realized what she was implying. "No!" he said lowly. "This is not the same as you and your sister."

"Then what is it?"

"Not here."

She glanced up and froze for a second. "Fine." Pushing away from the table, she grabbed the box and started for the door without him. Whispers followed her.

For a second, he sat there, rooted to the seat. Then he lurched up, scowling, and dropped a few coins on the table. How undignified he must appear, chasing after a woman.

He caught up just as the door was about to close on him. He stuck his foot in the opening, kicking the door open, and stepped out into the warm night air. He canvassed the area until he spotted a familiar form. It was Miri, but she was already disappearing into the distance.

For a second, he admired her speed. When had she gotten so fast? Then he shook the random thought away and set out in pursuit. The dratted woman refused to slow down, so he had to increase his stride to a jog.

As he weaved through his people, much of his indignation died as he remembered how much explaining he likely would have to do. He ignored the called-out greetings and instead let loose a huff of annoyance that masked his growing dread. Why didn't she slow down? She seemed to be headed to her set of rooms. Where then, he'd run her to ground there. It'd be so much easier if she would be rational and just listen to him.

Not that he truly had anything to worry about. Still, what a nuisance. There went all his plans for a pleasurable evening.

However, he was sure that within a few hours he could make her see reason about him not informing her of that development right away. *If at all.* He pushed that last part away.

An extra dose of guilt wouldn't help him at the moment. All he knew was that he had to get through to her. The thought of her not being in his life produced a sharp pain in his chest. It made him want to gasp. He didn't like the sensation in the least.

***

Miri paced around her room, knowing Eerin was but a minute or two behind. Eve would be back within half an hour. She was tempted to lock the door but knew Eerin would just produce a magical key or something. That or knock it down. He definitely had his ways. Many ways.

She crossed her arms around her middle protectively, as if that would block the shock of the evening. Why hadn't he told her about holding one of the people from her town prisoner?

An insidious thought crept deep into her heart and mind. He'd always told her that humans weren't welcome in the forest, that they never left alive. Since she hadn't seen or even heard talk of other humans living in Taerin, that likely meant one thing: that those unfortunate or misguided enough to venture into the woods were killed. It'd been monstrous when he'd told her. It still was.

That was why he hadn't told her.

He knew she'd never countenance killing a person who, in all likelihood, had been on a search mission for her and Eve.

Her stomach heaved and churned the food she'd just eaten. Taking in a few deep breaths, she concentrated on settling her rattled nerves. She didn't need to add vomiting to the growing list of things that were going wrong tonight. Her nausea abated enough so she could once again think.

What was she going to do about Eerin? She was involved with a human-hating leader. Even though she was Changed, she was still partly human. She could feel that truth in her bones. She would never completely abandon her humanity. It'd been an integral part of her for too long. Did he understand that?

Yes, maybe that was another reason why he hadn't told her.

She scrubbed her hands over her face, feeling the skin on her cheeks stretched under the pressure. God, what a mess. She couldn't just walk away from him, though. Not only because of the baby. For some insane reason, he made her happy, at least most of the time. The pull she felt was undeniable.

Still, how could she be with someone who would kill an innocent person? Yes, Eerin was the leader of his people, with a duty to protect them. But she knew all her townspeople well. Most weren't warriors. They were simple farmers and tradesmen. People like Henry, her first kiss. He was a merchant, just like his mayor father. They owned the fabric and feed stores.

God, she hoped it wasn't him they had. Though she'd once been infatuated with him, that had worn off over a year ago, right when he'd gotten pushy for more than kisses. At one time, she thought she might marry him in the distant future. Now, that future couldn't exist even if she wanted it to. Still, even without his humanity being a death penalty, this would be the worst place for him. Eerin had a possessive streak that spanned a mile. Even poor Nalin had felt the bite of it.

She had to get Henry out of Taerin. To do that would mean facing him in her altered state. Her tummy rolled at that thought.

The door thudded open without warning, causing her to jump. Eerin didn't look happy, not that she'd expected him to. However, there was no fury on his face. Good, at least he had some sense. If anyone was getting angry here, it was her.

He warded the door behind him with a slashing motion. She narrowed her eyes and recrossed her arms as he fully faced her. "Well?"

"Why did you run?"

Dense male. "Do you really need to ask that?"

"You're angry," he said.

"Your perceptiveness astonishes me."

"Please don't run from me again. I don't like it."

She blinked at his quiet admission and his use of *please*. "Then don't hide things from me. If you have one of my townspeople, I should be the first to know!"

His mouth tightened. "It was a poor choice on my part. I meant to tell you sometime."

"Yeah, *sometime*. Who do you have in that cell?"

"A young man called Henry. I think you know him," he said, his voice taut.

She closed her eyes in defeat. God, one of the worst possibilities. Well, at least Henry was still alive since he was asking to speak with her and Eerin. She needed to see him, see that he was fine. Eerin wouldn't deny her this. "When are you letting him go?"

"You know I can't do that. No one human who enters this forest leaves it alive."

She flicked her eyes open. "It's a stupid, outdated rule. Change it."

He shook his head. "I cannot just for you."

"Not for me but because it's the right thing to do."

"I have my people to protect."

Frustration pulled her to stand but a foot from him. "Henry's a tradesman. He doesn't even know how to properly wield a sword."

"If we let anyone who dared to trespass go, humanity would soon overrun this woods."

She poked him in the chest. "Oh, please. I've seen your cursed woods. The Taelin don't even need to do anything. Your forest could kick them out easily enough."

He gripped her fingers gently yet firmly, refusing to let go. "The forest would kill them if they entered its boughs too deeply."

"You control the forest." She huffed, still trying to free her fingers.

"I don't." He paused. "Stop, you're not getting loose right now."

She stilled her efforts. "What do you mean that you don't?"

"Exactly that. Though I have some power over the forest, I only have what it grants me. The darkness running through our veins allows us to live here, unharmed. But those without it..."

"You've talked about a Spirit of the Forest before."

He snorted. "No one controls the Spirit."

"It controls the woods, though?" she asked, partly in exasperation and partly out of curiosity.

"To an extent but not completely."

"But *it is* the woods? The Spirit of it?" She still struggled with the idea of a sentient forest and an even more sentient Spirit that arose from it.

"It's part of the woods but separate."

She furrowed her brow at him. "That doesn't make sense."

"To most humans, it wouldn't. Not when you haven't been raised within it."

"I want to see him."

His hand tightened around hers. "You are concerned about your beau?"

What? "He's not my beau."

He raised a brow. "Really? He said he was your future husband."

Henry didn't. The idiot. "He's not my future anything."

His eyes flashed with ire. "That's correct. He's not."

His little jealous fit would be endearing if the topic wasn't so serious. "No, I meant I'm not engaged to him."

"So he didn't court you?"

"A year or two ago, yes. However, I ended it."

"Why?"

"He wanted more from me than I was willing to give," she said quietly, meeting his eyes with an earnest stare. "Instead, you were the one to receive it."

His rigid stance relaxed. She could feel the tension all but flow out of the hand that held hers.

"Why do you want to see him, then?"

"Can't I be interested in a follow townsperson? I may not care for him romantically, but I've known him all my life."

A sigh gusted out of him. "I can't let him go."

Though she wanted to demand that he could, she knew it'd be one step at a time with him. Nothing, especially a policy that was likely centuries old, would change in a few minutes. "I'm just asking to visit him."

"For now," he said, apparently picking up on what she'd left unsaid.

"I do want to see him free, but right now, I'm more concerned that he's alive and well." She could compromise with the best of them while still chipping away at this policy he held.

His hands slid up her arms, making goosebumps break out over her skin. "We can see him in the morning. Your sister will be back soon. After she's in bed, I plan to give you that night I'd promised."

The rich darkness in his voice sent lustful shivers up her spine. She gave him her best seductive smile. "You've got a deal."

Visiting We Shall Go

Miri wrung her hands as she and Eerin transversed the stairwell to the cells. The lower floors weren't dirty or dank, but they weren't exactly welcoming, either. There were no windows to let the light in, so to say it was dim was an understatement.

What would she find once they reached their destination? Hopefully, Henry would be no worse for the wear. But what would he make of her appearance? That was, if she revealed herself. She adjusted the lightweight cloak around her face. Underneath it, though, sweat wove down her back. She didn't think it was due to the already sweltering morning. No, nerves were the cause of most of her perspiration.

Once they reached the bottom of the stairs, Eerin placed a hand on her arm. "You're nervous."

"A bit."

"I promise he's in one piece."

"Well, that's something." She pulled the cloak's edges tighter around herself.

"You're completely covered." He paused before pointing out once again, "The whelp will wonder why you're hiding."

She scowled, both because she didn't like the reminder and because she also didn't like him calling Henry the whelp. "I know. I'll make some excuse."

He tugged on the front of the cloak. "Or you could reveal yourself. Your home is here, after all."

A well of tears sprang to her eyes. That was the first time he'd called Taerin her home. Damn her hormones. Still, her heart felt too full. Now wasn't the right time for that sensation. Not when Henry was here.

She finally confessed what she feared. "I'll look like a monster to him."

"Do I look like one to you?"

"At first, you did. A handsome one, admittedly, but one nonetheless."

He grew still. "And now?"

She touched the high collar of his tunic. "You're just Eerin. The big, fearsome leader of the Taelin."

He smirked. "How nice to know how you view me."

"Don't let it go to your head." She sighed, letting her hand fall back to her side and into the darkness of the cloak.

He merely nodded and grasped her elbow. She walked by his side, heart valiantly trying to somersault into her throat.

Through one set of guarded doors they went. A row of cells flanked both sides of the hallway. If possible, it was even darker in this section. She squinted, but her eyes were slow to adjust. Though her sight was better than it'd been, her hearing was the sense that was vastly improved by the Change. She strained her ears. There. The sound of another person breathing.

As if pulled by a magical force, she drifted forward toward the left. The breathing became louder. She halted before one of the cells. A slumped figure sat on the bed. She touched the bars, careful to keep the cloak over her fingers. As her eyes focused, the familiar form of Henry came into view.

His drooping shoulders showed his mood. His brown tunic bore dark traces of something, maybe dirt. She couldn't make out his face, but he appeared unharmed.

Unharmed but depressed.

Well, who would be happy down here, away from a home one might never see again? That comparison hit a little too close. She blinked at the tears that never seemed far away as she took in his surroundings.

Besides a bed, there was only a chamber pot in one corner, along with a tin pitcher of what was probably water. She swung her gaze back to him. A barely touched meal of oatmeal and a hunk of bread sat before him. He was staring down at his lap, seemingly in deep thought. So deep he hadn't heard her. Odd. Maybe it wasn't only her hearing that had improved. She now had stealth unlooked for.

Eerin's presence was suddenly at her back. It flowed like a warming current through her chilled veins. Still, Henry didn't look up.

She called out his name quietly. He jerked upright, whipping his head to stare at the bars of his enclosure. "Miri?"

His wavering voice was like a blow to the stomach. She may not be in love with him, but he was someone she cared about. To hear him sound so uncertain, so frightened...she didn't like it in the least.

"Yes, it's me. I came as soon as I could." The lie stuck in her throat, for it was a lie, wasn't it?

She could've insisted on coming last night, but she'd wanted another night in Eerin's arms. So selfish when Henry was down here, alone and suffering. Oh, he didn't look to have been abused. However, this was a place designed to be its own torture with barely any light for human eyes.

"M...Miri." He stumbled from the bed and lurched to the bars. His hand landed on her cloth-covered one. The sound of Eerin's breath catching penetrated her consciousness. However, she didn't remove her hand from under Henry's. If he needed a person's touch, then he would have it. Eerin would have to get over his paranoid jealousy. What better time to start than now?

He pressed on her hand and seemed to try to peer into the cover of her hood. "You are unharmed?"

"Yes, I am well." Well, it depended on how one defined "well."

"And Eve?"

"She is also unharmed."

His eyes shifted to behind her, and a wary expression grew on his face. "They don't keep you locked up? Why are you covered like that?"

She wanted to shift uncomfortably. Already, two hard questions. Her mind worked furiously to choose the right words. She slipped her hand free of his, somehow afraid he would be able to sense her deception through cloth and bone. "No, we're free to roam the public areas."

"I'm glad for it, but why? Because you are both ladies?"

"How are you, Henry?" she asked, switching the topic off of her and Eve. "Are you in good health?"

His brow puckered but then cleared. "I've been better, though I've suffered no real harm. Just a lot of threatening questioning."

So they had interrogated him. Though she wasn't surprised, she didn't like the idea of it. "Nothing more...forceful was used?"

His gaze shifted behind her once again. "No, not as of yet."

"And it won't happen in the future." Her voice was firm.

Turning around enough to stare at Eerin, she raised a challenging brow. "Will it?"

His voice was smooth when he spoke. "That all depends on the good Henry here."

"Let us go," Henry said, his tone hardening. "You are the leader of the Taelin, are you not? You have no reason to keep us."

Eerin came to stand at her side. "No human who ever enters the forest can leave it."

The smirk in his voice grated on her ears. She squashed the urge to elbow him. He could be an ass at the best of times, and now he held a special dislike toward her old beau. Which was quite silly. She didn't love Henry. For heaven's sake, they hadn't even gotten much past kissing. When he'd asked to see her bare breasts so he could kiss them, she'd ended their relationship. Now, she marveled at what an innocent she'd been. Eerin had stripped her of any vestiges.

"I'm only here for Miri and her sister." Henry shook his head as if confused. "Since they're unharmed and walking around free, I can't see why you won't let us go."

Miri took one automatic step back, the thudding of her heart ringing in her ears. Neither of the men noticed, so focused on each other as they were. Why hadn't she considered all the questions Henry would ask? Of course, he'd demand that she and Eve be set free with him. What could she say in reply? That she and Eve looked like monsters now, and there could be no home for them but in Taerin? That she was pregnant and the Taelin standing by her was the father?

No.

She wasn't ready for this. Oh, she'd known she would have to face her past someday, but she never thought it'd be so soon.

Eerin sighed as if he were addressing a simpleton. "As you've already been repeatedly told, no one leaves this forest alive. I believe every human village within several hundred miles knows that and has for centuries. We aren't so keen to change our ways for one spoiled human youngling."

Henry's pale cheeks flushed and glared at Eerin through grimy, disheveled brown locks. "The town's mayor is my father, and he won't stand for this."

"His so-called position means nothing here." Eerin lifted his hand and glanced down his nails as if examining them. "Actually, less than nothing."

Henry slammed his hands against the bars. The sound left Miri's head spinning most unpleasantly. *God, please don't get sick right now.* She reached up and pressed a hand to her mouth, resisting the urge to heave.

Eerin's hands were on her shoulders immediately, turning her toward him. "You need to see a healer, Miri."

She sagged against him for a moment before straightening. "I'll be all right."

"You keep—"

An enraged shout reverberated around the enclosed space. "Take your hands off her."

Miri winced again and shut her eyes.

Wrapping a protective arm around her and anchoring her firmly to his side, Eerin slowly turned to face Henry. "Silence, you fool. She is ill. Besides, she doesn't mind me having my hands on her."

She didn't have to look to see the smugness on his face. His tone said it all. She gave a quiet groan of misery and opened her eyes. "Not now, Eerin."

Henry deflated and leaned heavily against his bars. "*What?*" His gaze zeroed in on the hand Eerin had wrapped around the curve of her waist. Shock and devastation lined his face. "Miri, you and he... You are *with* him?"

She grimaced. *Eerin, why?* Oh, she knew why, the possessive idiot, but it didn't make this situation any easier. "We are in a relationship."

"You've only been here for two and a half months." He frowned and then scowled, his hands curling tightly around the bars. "Is that why you're dressed the way you are? He's forced you to be his mistress but doesn't want anyone else to see you?"

She opened her mouth to respond, but Eerin beat her to it and snorted. "Please, you try telling her how to dress."

"Miri, is he forcing you?" he said, pinning her with a stare that demanded the truth.

She shook her head. "Not at all."

Eerin, apparently, not content to be forgotten, sneered at him. "If I were, what would you do about it? You seem to be quite stuck."

"Eerin," she hissed, glaring at him. "Stop it."

"I'm merely pointing out the holes in his logic, love."

Love? Searing heat rushed through her chest and up to her cheeks. He probably meant nothing by the term, but oh, how she wished he did. She forced herself to speak levelly. "Be that as it may, you're not helping right now."

He merely lifted a brow. "We have to leave soon. Do finish your talk."

She frowned at him, not pleased with his antics. When she turned back to Henry, he was watching them with disbelief staining his face.

"Miri, he's holding us captive. I don't understand..." He shook his head. "If your lover cares for you at all, he'll open negotiations for our release. My father and his business associates can pay handsomely."

Eerin's arm tightened against her waist. "You think your paltry human treasures have meaning here? You have nothing I want."

Miri stared at Henry. His father was the wealthiest man in town but all his funds and property combined would be a pittance to Eerin and his people. Though most of the Taelin lived modestly, none were poor from what she could tell. Everyone had a home, food on their table, and lovely clothes in their closet. Some of the jewelry the women wore was a work of art and would cost an exorbitant amount in the human world. Eerin had said there were other Taelin settlements in the forest, but as this was the capital, Taerin was the largest and grandest city.

"There must be something you want," Henry pressed.

A small smile played around Eerin's lips. "I have all I want." He paused and then tapped one finger against his chin. "Well, there is one thing. I desire that humanity leave us in peace and stop seeking entrance into our woods periodically."

"My townsmen would be happy to agree. Just let us leave."

"Even if I could let you leave, Miri and Eve would have to remain here. Indefinitely."

Rage burned bright in Henry's eyes. "Why? You'll tire of your human pets soon enough. And for heaven's sake, take that cloak off her. I know what she looks like." A smirk formed on his mouth. "In fact, I've seen her in far less."

Eerin's form stiffened until he nearly quivered against her side. *Damn it, Henry.* Neither of them was making this easy for her. Sensing possible violence toward Henry, she worked to diffuse the situation. "You left out an important part, Henry. You only saw me in my undergarments when we went swimming with five other friends. Eve was even there."

Eerin made a choking sound, his quaking increasing until he shook against her. Then suddenly, his guffaws filled the breadth of the room. "Oh, so scandalous. I'm sure you both corrupted Eve."

Miri elbowed him in the side this time. He didn't let her go. After giving an aggravated huff, she crossed her arms. Both of these males...they were impossible. "There was no corrupting going on whatsoever. All our parts were more than sufficiently covered."

A cherry-red flush spread over Henry's face, and he pressed his lips together tightly. However, he kept his mouth shut. A wise move if she was to keep him alive. By this point, Eerin was probably tempted to kill him for nearly any reason.

Eerin might be tempted to kill her, too, after what she planned to say. She studiously kept her gaze on Henry. "I can't secure your release, Henry, but I'll try to better your...accommodations."

Her old beau flashed her a grateful look. "If that could be arranged, I'd be very appreciative." He glanced at Eerin and then at her. "Only if it causes you no undue hardship, though."

A swell of affection for the man roared to the surface. Henry feared any concession granted to him would come out of her own hide or wellbeing. She may not be in love with him, but he'd always been a good friend. Even now, he managed to show her a remarkable amount of concern.

She chanced a glance at Eerin. As expected, he appeared none too thrilled, but he kept his tongue silent. Thank goodness for small mercies.

Eerin leaned down. As he spoke quietly in her ear, his breath puffed hot and moist against her skin, teasing a shiver from her. "We have to leave now. Say your farewell."

She nodded, suppressing a sigh. There would be a battle ahead to secure Henry a little more comfort, so she might as well prepare for engagement.

Fixing a smile on her face that Henry couldn't see but she hoped he could hear, she touched the bar beside one of his hands. "I'll come back and see you as soon as I can. Stay strong. I'll do what I can." She dared not say anything more with Eerin loitering beside her.

Henry gave her a weak grin. "I know you'll do what you can. I'll be fine. I'm not going anywhere at the moment."

Eerin made a noise of disgust. Miri read the barely disguised command in the sound. Time had run out. "Bye, Henry."

As she and Eerin turned away, Henry called out, "Wait, Miri."

She froze and then spun around, Eerin's arm loosening about her. Suddenly, there was a tug on the side of her cloak. She fumbled to grab the material securely around her, but another powerful yank stole that opportunity from her. The hood tumbled off her head, and the cloak slid off one shoulder.

She gaped at the fallen material and followed the graceful drape of it upward, where it was held in a shaking grasp.

In *Henry's* shaking grasp.

Her gaze met his. Horror coated his face as he stared at her.

Unveiled

Miri closed her eyes, unable to face the disgust and judgment on Henry's face.

"What have they done to you?" he breathed.

She couldn't find the words to reply. Eerin's side brushed against hers, alerting her to his presence. Trembling, she sank against him, needing the comfort only he could provide.

Eerin growled low in his throat and pulled the fabric from Henry's grasp. "We have done nothing to her, whelp. She has undergone the Change but not at our hands."

The bars rattled forcefully. "Then whose?"

Miri inhaled deeply, calming her heart rate. After several deep breaths, she opened her eyes. She draped the cloak over her shoulders, leaving the hood down.

"The forest brought about her Change," said Eerin.

Henry scoffed. "You expect me to believe that?"

"Do you not remember the greeting you and your kinsmen received when you entered the forest?"

"A hallucination caused by your people or some trick of your magic caused the forest to appear...alive." He blanched as if remembering something unpleasant, but Miri heard his doubt loud and clear.

She straightened so she wasn't leaning so heavily on Eerin and shook her head. "The forest does as it pleases. I'm new here, and that much I know."

He sent her a reproachful look. "He's swayed you so much that you're willing to lie for him?"

She planted one hand on her hip. "I'm not lying."

His gaze traveled over her exposed skin. "It's paint."

"What?" she said as Eerin snorted in derision.

Henry pointed a triumphant finger at her. "They painted you to look like them."

I stared at him, bewildered. "Why would they do that?"

Henry shrugged sharply. "I don't know why, but that has to be it."

"Whatever you have to tell yourself," Eerin said. "Miri doesn't owe you any further explanation."

"Why are you doing this to her?" Henry hissed, his eyes narrowing.

"I haven't done any—"

"Stop this, Henry. He didn't cause my Change." At least not directly, though my fate seemed tied to his somehow.

Henry's heated gaze swung in her direction. "You're infatuated with him, so you'll say anything to dislodge his blame."

Ugh, Henry was going to persist with this irrationality. She could only think of one way to stop it. Eerin kept a small knife in a sheath at his waist. Before she could rethink her course of action, she grabbed the blade, sliding it free. His hand shot out, but she danced out of reach.

Before he could halt her, she drew the knife over the palm of her hand. A hiss escaped her lips as the sharp edge sliced into her tender flesh. Still, she watched in satisfaction as black blood welled through the thin cut.

Holding out her hand, she stared defiantly at Henry. "Is this proof enough?"

***

Henry gaped open-mouthed at Miri as Eerin clenched his hands into fists. He wanted to rip that blade from her grasp. The blade that had dared to mar her beautiful skin.

He gripped her arm firmly. "Point proven. It's time to go."

She didn't protest as he firmly led her away from the holding cell.

As soon as they were out of view on the ground floor, Eerin pulled her aside, took the knife from her, and grabbed her injured hand. What had she been thinking by taking his blade like that? His heart had threatened to stop. What that meant exactly, he didn't want to think about.

"Why did you do that?" His voice contained a snappish quality that highlighted his displeasure.

"It was the thing to do. He needed to be convinced. That was the surest way. Though I hate that it came to that, I saw no other way to clear up his skepticism quickly."

"You could have let him stew in his skepticism and doubt. What you did was foolish." He ran gentle fingers over the shallow cut.

Miri grimaced at his prodding touch. He had a way to relieve her pain for a bit. A tingling sensation itched over his fingers, but he knew it would chase away the burn of her wound.

She gaped at him slightly and then gave him a shaky smile. "You know some fancy healing techniques."

"All leaders and warriors should."

She remembered his skilled yet forceful sparring. There was no doubt he'd been a warrior—and still was.

"You need to get this tended to," he said gruffly. "I've numbed the pain, but that won't last. We also need to guard against infection."

Her stiff shoulders relaxed. Did she even realize how tense she'd been? Her hand was chilled, and the rest of her probably felt the same. Facing Henry had left her drained. "It's just a little cut. Not deep at all."

"In these woods, even little cuts can become infected, and sepsis can set in."

She sighed. "Eamandian had warned me of that during one of my first lessons. To tell the truth, it isn't so different than being in my old town, where little injuries could become big ones if left unattended for too long. Let's go to the healing halls. I can treat it there."

"No need. I have all that we need in my chamber."

She raised a brow. "*Oh*, really? And you have no ulterior motive?"

He gave her a sharp smile. She owed him a little soothing after her stunt with his knife. "I always have one when taking you anywhere that's private."

After tending to her wound and indulging in a most satisfying round of lovemaking, Miri lay cushioned on his chest. Eerin groaned into her hair, not wanting to move or leave the comfort of her embrace. "Time to arise. I believe we both have places to be."

She lifted her head and gave him a lazy grin. "Speak for yourself. I don't have to go into the healing halls until one in the afternoon."

He whacked her on her backside lightly. "Spoilt girl."

The humor faded from her expression. "Eerin, can you stay a few minutes longer?"

He had a meeting with several of his advisors in twenty minutes. If he left soon, he could still make it. He gently lifted her off him and sat up. "Can this wait until tonight?"

Indecision and disappointment skittered across her face. "I guess, though this is important."

"The lighter fae are sending a messenger who is due to arrive today. I have to discuss the possible consequences of this to our people."

Her cheeks darkened attractively as she pulled herself into a sitting position. "Do you consider me one of your people?"

He froze at that question. At one time, that answer would've been an equivocal no. Now... "You and your sister are adapting well to life here among the Taelin. Even if you wanted to return to your town, as you've seen with Henry, it wouldn't be possible."

Hurt creased her face as she gathered the sheet around her. "What kind of response is that? That we are mere burdens to you?"

He wanted to roll his eyes but not at her. Having to deal with softer emotions wasn't his forte. "I explained that poorly. You are members of this society now. I'm all but publicly courting you. Have I not made that clear to you?"

The truth of his words struck him. He was courting her, spending all his free time with her, and for the most part, enjoying every minute of it. At some point, this had stopped being about trying to get her out of his system. Instead, the fascination he'd felt toward her had grown into more.

Her tongue darted out to nervously lick at her lips. "It felt that way, but we never spoke of what we...are or of any expectations."

He raked his fingers through disheveled hair as he stood to gather his clothes. "I'm not good at these discussions, but if you want to talk about this at length, we can tonight."

Determination straightened her shoulders. "I would. What I have to talk to you about ties directly into our relationship, and I've been trying to tell you about...it for some time."

A thread of worry caused him to pause in cleansing himself with a rag from a nearby pitcher. What could be so important that she hadn't been able to bring herself to tell him about it right away? "I will postpone my meeting until after lunch."

She shook her head. "No, it's probably better that you finish your day. Waiting until tonight will be fine."

Now, he didn't want to leave, not until he knew what she kept secret. However, the meeting was an important one, and he and Miri *would* talk tonight.

He frowned as he pulled on his undertunic. "Against my better judgment am I leaving."

She smiled, but it seemed forced. "Go, do your duty, and we'll meet in my chambers tonight."

Suddenly, he didn't like the idea of *her* chambers or *his*. Why not *theirs*? Another issue to tackle this evening.

Advised

Eerin frowned at his advisors from his chair. He disliked all of them right now, even though one was his mangy cur of a best friend. Alegion, as the commander of his army, was in possession of an advisor seat. Worse, he was smirking at him right now, his arms crossed as if he were watching something highly diverting. The ass knew he wanted to escape—and to whom.

As for the rest of the group... He didn't hate them all equally. Some were much more of a nuisance than others. Given that they were well-known scholars, strategists, or other high-ranking officials that made up the Taelin government, though, he had to pretend to at least listen to them. That was their appointed duty, after all—to be meddlesome and advise on everything far and wide.

The seven, four males and three females, never agreed on much. Now was no different. A headache was forming behind his eyes, and he squeezed the bridge of his nose as he rested one elbow on the arm of his chair.

Alitha, the minister of the treasury, shook her head in disgust at Surregeon's suggestion and stood from her seat. "We can't do that, you imbecile. To turn away the messenger without even hearing his tidings is very ill-mannered and likely to start a diplomatic incident or, worse, war."

Surregeon, the import and export minister, scowled at the tall, buxom woman but wisely said nothing. Nor did he move to arise. Many people, including a majority of his other advisors, were hesitant to take on the lady verbally. Eerin couldn't blame them. He didn't particularly like going against her and hadn't called her a shrew to her face in several years. However, in this case, he did agree with her. The messenger would have to be heard out. He was no admirer of the lighter fae and didn't trust them, but they had their uses as trade partners. Very distant trade partners.

As Alitha prattled on, he studied her idly. He had nothing better to do, after all. Miri's sweet face suddenly popped up before his eyes in his mind. He'd much rather be hearing her talk. He found nearly everything about her engaging. Right now, his advisors were all disagreeable, especially Alitha. Frowning, he cataloged all the reasons why she might be that way.

The treasurer had a surprisingly pinched face that could scare away even the hardiest of Taelin. Her face had likely frozen into that position due to a few centuries' worth of sour expressions. His moods might be just as unpleasant at times, but he took care his face wouldn't turn into *that*. He thanked the Dark Forest he'd never sampled her charms.

If he could only get back to Miri...

Miri, who with her lovely smile and that one dimple in her cheek, had turned his life inside out. However, he didn't begrudge her that fact. To tell the truth, his heart pounded quicker as he realized the fate she might have saved him from. He'd been turning into a person as sour as Alitha. He nearly shuddered at that thought.

Miri had wrought some change in him but what? He couldn't quite pin it down, but he would. Oh, he would.

Menillan, the steward who helped him oversee the daily administration of the land and its laws, cleared his throat. "Lady Alitha, I think you've proven your point."

Eerin nodded. "Indeed, you have." *More than once and quite forcefully at that.* The sooner this farce was over with, the sooner he could get back to Miri. "The messenger will be welcomed with all due hospitality, even though it might grate on our nerves. Now, I have to prepare myself for that duty. I suggest you all do the same if you're on the welcoming retinue."

He stood. There was no better way to signify the closing of a meeting than with his leavetaking. "We're not the uncouth animals that they like to whisper about behind cupped hands, so I expect everyone here to be on their best behavior." Unfortunately, that included himself.

With those words, he spun on his heel and marched toward the exit.

"My lord," Alitha protested. "Our meeting isn't—"

He paused but didn't bother to turn around. "We are done here." Alitha, thank the Dark Woods, wasn't on the welcome committee.

As he grasped the door handle, it was ripped from his hold as the door flew inward. He jumped back before the hard wood could smack him in the face and scowled. The idiot could've broken his nose. He opened his mouth to deliver a blistering reprimand, but his words froze on his tongue when he saw who stood on the threshold.

Hunor, one of his top city guards, glanced around the room, his eyes frenzied. Eerin stepped around the partial cover of the door. "Hunor, what is it?" He wouldn't be here if it wasn't serious.

The guard jumped a bit, a testament to how shaken the male was. "My lord, a large group of humans have nearly reached the inner sanctum of the Dark Forest."

Sharp inhalations sounded from behind him, even as rage exploded within him. "How?" The woods should've stopped any interlopers that his warriors couldn't.

Hunor's throat bobbed, and Eerin knew the guard carried even more disastrous news.

"The lighter fae...we were awaiting their messenger, as you know." Hunor's words sped up. "Instead, it appears the messenger and his small group met up with the humans outside the forest. We don't know if the lighter fae planned this meeting or not. All we know is that they assisted the humans through the forest, keeping them safe."

Eerin's hands clenched. "So there are lighter fae running loose in the forest?"

How *dare* they!

These were his woods, his people's woods. The lighter fae had no business here behind sending one lone messenger. Worse, they'd joined forces with the humans. They had to be plotting against him and his people. He needed the interlopers out of the woods. *Now*. If he had to take some lives to do it, well, he was more than up to the task. It wouldn't be the first time, and it certainly wouldn't be the last.

An intensely serious Alegion was suddenly by Eerin's side. "What is the current status report?"

"Captain Callon managed to send a runner who reported that our warriors are trying to keep them from venturing farther, but they're besieged between the humans and their weapons and the lighter fae's magic."

Alegion and Eerin shared a look. Before either of them could reply, Alitha stomped over, hands on her hips. "The Taelin army must be growing lax if they can't fight off a few lighter fae and a group of humans."

Red spread over Alegion's face, and the commander seemed to struggle for words. Eerin found a few easily enough and swung around to face her. "You know nothing, heartless shrew."

Alitha gasped in surprised outrage while a few pleased murmurs floated to Eerin's ears. He narrowed his eyes at her. "Now is not the time for your cutting attitude. Go back to your accounting books. *We* have a threat to see to."

He had to get out to those woods. As leader, he had a special bond with the Spirit of the Forest and most of its creatures, both plant and animal. He smiled viciously. With the forest's assistance and that of its denizens, he'd crush the lighter fae and humans. First, however, he had to see to the protection of the city.

***

The healing halls were silent, and Miri was bored. Eamandian was off somewhere doing healer-ly things, and the other healer on duty was locked in their office. Her lesson would have to wait until later. She'd completed all her assigned tasks. Freshly made cots lined the walls. No dust touched any surface within reach. The supplies and medicines had all been sorted and placed neatly away.

Miri sighed and sat on one of the beds. Master Eamandian wouldn't mind her taking a rest. She'd discovered, to his embarrassment, that the crusty healer had a huge soft spot for pregnant ladies. Not that he would ever admit that. She and Innara, mostly Innara, had tried to tease the truth out of him. A smile snuck onto her lips. He reminded her of Eerin so much at times.

Glancing at the clock on a nearby wall, she sighed again. She had three more hours to go before she was free to leave. Free to see Eerin. Hopefully, his meeting had gone well and his schedule hadn't clogged itself up with duties that would take him away from her this evening.

Her hand slid to her stomach. She wasn't showing yet, but she could imagine the little being growing within her. The baby was deeply loved already. But would Eerin be as welcoming?

Well, no matter what happened, she couldn't keep this from him anymore.

After another twenty minutes of sitting and then standing to wander around the room, she decided to ask if she could leave early. She was doing no one any good right now.

Suddenly, a guard burst through the double doors. She jumped a few good inches into the air, her heart thudding. However, he didn't stop. Instead, he raced past her as if she wasn't there.

She frowned, narrowing her eyes. Wasn't that Hunor? Worry gnawed at her insides. That he was in such a hurry couldn't mean anything good. Was someone seriously hurt and couldn't be moved?

Hunor had crashed through another set of doors, these ones leading to the healers' offices. *What in the world?* She stared after him, chewing on her bottom lip. Though she might regret it later, she set in pursuit of him.

He was far enough ahead of her that she couldn't see him. As she saw no open doors or heard any telltale voices, though, she headed down another hallway. Eamandian's office was down this way. Another short turn, and she froze.

Eamandian's office was open, and voices floated out of the room through the partially open door. Apparently, the healer had returned. She crept forward, feeling as if she might be intruding but unable to stop herself.

She raised her hand to knock but stopped as the words from within the office became clearer. That was Hunor speaking.

"Expect an influx of injured patients. The attack has wounded many of our warriors."

Attack? What attack? The urge to glance around the edge of the door was strong, but she didn't dare.

"I'll call in all available healers and apprentices," Eamandian said briskly. "Where is Lord Eerin at the moment?"

"Still in the city, overseeing the effort to protect Taerin and remove the humans and lighter fae from the forest. He is…"

The rest of Hunor's words faded away. *Humans?* Even the part about the lighter fae barely penetrated her consciousness. Why would there be humans in—Ice shivered up her spine as the answer socked her in the gut.

They were here for her and Eve.

Worry and fear bit at her insides. Was her father among those in the woods?

She shook herself slightly. It wouldn't do her any good to assume. Maybe the humans in the forest weren't *her* humans.

Though she was shaking, she turned her attention back to what Hunor was saying. "Why? Do you need to speak with Lord Eerin? I assure you now is not—"

Eamandian snorted. "I have no such need. Both myself and our lord have more than enough to attend to at the moment." His tone grew dry. "I was...merely asking on the behalf of someone who might be most concerned about his whereabouts."

Miri flinched. Shit. Nothing for it now. Anyways, she needed to know who those humans were.

Feeling like a puppet on a string, she opened the door wider and stepped through. The two fae stared at her, and an icy-hot blush spread through her. "I didn't mean to eavesdrop. I was coming to see if I could be of service after seeing Hunor's haste."

Eamandian eyes her critically. "If you're hale enough, you can assist the healers and replenish supplies."

She straightened her shoulders. "I'm fine." She hesitated for a moment, glancing from Eamandian to Hunor and back. "Do you know who the humans in the woods are?"

Sympathy streaked across Eamandian's face. Her stomach plummeted. "I think you know," he said.

Miri nodded mechanically, words deserting her. Oh God, this was her worst nightmare. Considering what had happened to her and Eve these last few months, that was indeed saying something.

Full-blown panic rooted in her belly. She had to find out if her father was out there, injured or worse.

But how?

Panicked

As the light faded into dusk, Eerin stalked toward the healing halls, intent on seeing Miri before he headed out into the forest. Fortunately, no one waylaid him, every person going about their own duty right now.

He didn't know what drove him to seek her out, but it wouldn't be denied. Given all the injured that had been streaming into the halls, he knew she'd be there. He would just see her and then leave. Whatever was pushing at him then *should* ease. The tension further tightening his shoulders didn't relent, hinting that he was sorely wrong on that account.

At least he finally had the preparations for the city's protection ironed out. As commander, Alegion had left several hours ago for the fight taking place in the woods. Eerin ached to join him and bathe his sword in blood, both human and lighter fae, but his duty had kept him tied to the city until now. Wards had to be strengthened and new ones set. Since he, as leader, was closest to the darkness flowing through the woods, his energy was needed during the crafting of such spells and enchantments. Now, though, his city was as safe as he and his mages could make it.

He pushed through the final set of doors and into the main chamber of the halls. A full room met his gaze, and he blocked out the metallic smell of blood and entrails. Miri was nowhere in sight. He strode deeper into the cavernous room, ignoring all the eyes on him. He was here for one reason and one reason only. All he knew was that he wouldn't be denied this, his only succor during his long day of duty and toil.

A golden-haired healer-in-training rushed toward him, wiping her hands on the apron she wore. "My lord, are you in need of assistance?"

"Where is Lady Miri?"

Her brow cleared, and she glanced around the room. "She might be in the storeroom, as she's in charge of replenishing supplies."

He nodded curtly. "I thank you. I'll leave you to your duties now."

She bowed and then strode briskly away to an awaiting patient. He set his sights on another set of doors, the ones that led to the healers' offices and the storeroom.

Anticipation and the waning hour pushed him down the hallway. His skin tingled, and he swore he sensed her near. As he neared the storeroom, voices floated out the open doorway. He slowed. Was that Eamandian? Maybe he was helping Miri or, at least, would know where she was.

He drifted closer, hearing a female's voice that sounded suspiciously like Miri's, though the words were indistinct. Most rooms in the healing wards had dampening spells cast on them so that even Taelin hearing couldn't pick out normally spoken words from a distance. He stopped when the occupants inside were in his line of sight.

Miri. The breath he'd been keeping hostage slowly released itself from his lungs.

Her back was turned toward the front of the storeroom. Eamadian was indeed with her. Neither of them noticed him.

Eerin opened his mouth to announce his presence, but the healer's next words gave Eerin pause. "You should rest. We have matters better under control now."

She shook her head, a few stray locks falling loose from her chignon. "I'm fine. I know my limits."

Eamandian scoffed. "Do you? I'd say otherwise. You're pale and drawn and all but drooping with weariness."

As if her body wanted to lend credence to Eamandian's word, Miri swayed. Eerin wanted to rush forward, but something held him immobile as the healer's hands shot out to steady her. Jealousy kindled in his gut. Eamandian seemed very familiar with Miri. He'd noticed it before but had shrugged it off. After all, everyone knew Eamandian adored Innara. But now, to see this...

"You need to rest, Miri. Think of the child."

Child? What child? Eve was likely safely ensconced with her usual childminders or Calieth. His previous moment of jealousy drifted away as if it'd never existed.

"I guess I am tired." She turned slightly so that he saw her profile. "This pregnancy has a way of wearing me down."

Shock froze Eerin's mind. Only one word kept flashing and blaring through his thoughts. *Pregnant? Pregnant!*

Eamandian patted her on the shoulder. "All pregnancies can do that, but since you carry a hybrid of human and fae blood, you're likely to find yourself more weary than usual."

Eerin swallowed the lump forming in his throat. She was carrying a child of mixed parentage, which meant...

The healer sighed and let his hand fall to his side. "I am needed in the main chamber, but go rest. I'll send Innara to you when she's free."

Miri nodded. "There's no need. I have to find Eerin. Those people in the woods..." Her voice cracked. "I need to know."

Eerin's heart clenched, even as his head spun. A wave of dizziness crashed over him. Of course, she'd worry about the humans in the forest. They were her people. *No,* they had been her people, but no longer. His people were hers now. She was his. She and...and their baby. Eve also.

"He might've already left for the fighting in the woods," Eamandian warned.

"That's what I'm afraid of." Her hand slid down to her stomach, which she caressed lovingly. "I've been trying to tell him for weeks now. I was so sure tonight was the night..."

"You should have let me or Innara tell him."

She gave a watery-sounding snort. "That he fathered a child when he'd saved my life and Eve's? He hated me, then. He still hates humans. Only now do I have hope that he won't instantly hate this child—and me."

The fear, dread, and truth in her tone pulled at him in a way he would've never believed possible. He couldn't even find the energy to be angry at her for keeping this secret for...for how long? His mind refused to comply and do the math. Oh, to be sure, he wasn't happy to be kept in the dark for so long. But more...he felt overwhelmed, panicked. A baby?

Eamandian responded to her, but the words faded into the buzzing that had overtaken Eerin's consciousness as they spoke on.

How far along was she? How long until he became a father? He had no reason to doubt this was his child. They didn't even know he was there.

His first time with Miri seemed an age ago, but a quick calculation revealed it'd only been two and a half months ago. The night that had signed his fate and his fatherhood.

He'd be no fit parent. Managing his people was hard enough. An innocent being who would be dependent on him? Oh, there were children aplenty in the city and surrounding hamlets within the forest, but he wasn't directly responsible for them. That fell to their parents and guardians.

And the child... How human would it be? Miri and Eve were no longer completely human, but neither were they completely Taelin. Would this child be similar, or even more Taelin in nature due to his genetics?

His mind swam with unanswered questions, and there was a war being waged in his woods at this very moment. He didn't have the time for this.

His feet itched to carry him back the way he'd come and pretend he'd never heard this conversation. But the truth, once heard, would never be dismissed so easily. Besides, he'd never been a coward. He was many things but not that.

He could only watch as both turned toward the door, where he was standing in plain view. They both froze. In some distant, disjointed part of Eerin's mind, he mused that it was fascinating that Eamandian hadn't noticed him before now. The healer's abilities, superior even among Taelin, were slipping.

Miri's face reflected shock, horror, fear, and longing. Longing for what? Him? His acceptance of her and their child? *All of that.* Right now, he wanted to assure her of that, wanted his mouth to form the words, but he just couldn't. His mind was still struggling to process all he'd learned. He wasn't sure if it ever would be able to.

"Eerin?" she said, stepping toward him slowly as if afraid he'd flee. He forced himself not to inch back.

"I have to go," he said lamely. "I'm needed in the woods."

Her brow furrowed. "But you just—"

Eamandian laid a hand on her arm and said quietly, "Let him go. He can't fully comprehend this latest news right now and is panicking. You can clearly see it in his eyes."

Miri stared at Eerin, her gaze searing through him. Then she nodded slowly. "Go do what you have to, but then we need to talk...about the pregnancy."

The walls swayed in closer, pressing in, threatening to suffocate him. Eerin cleared his throat. "Y...you have my word."

Before he completely lost every shred of composure, he spun on his heel to face the door. However, something stopped him before he could step over the threshold. Maybe it had been seeing her so lost and frightened. He didn't trust himself to do much in regards to her at the moment, but he couldn't leave like this.

He pulled back around and closed the distance between them. Reaching out with hands that shook far more than he approved of, he quickly grasped her arms. "This is not a rejection. I merely... Too much is going on, and I have no time for thought."

She smiled tremulously and blinked rapidly as if trying to hold back tears. "I know." She patted one of his hands. "Go do what you must."

Fearing if he didn't turn around now, he would never be able to, he pulled himself away from her and briskly walked from the room. Hurry was needed. He had expected to be in the forest by now.

Miri's faint voice carried down the hall after him, but he didn't stop. "Oh, damn, I forgot to ask Eerin about the humans, if my father might be with them."

Eamandian replied, but Eerin couldn't make out what he'd said. Good Spirit, her father could be among those heathens in his woods? He frowned. If so, that would complicate matters. She would never forgive him if he seriously hurt or injured the man. Surely, her father had more sense than to enter the Dark Forest?

This is Miri, though, beloved Miri. If possible, his mood darkened even further. Wouldn't he, himself, do much to get her back if she were taken? He raked a hand through his tied-back hair, not caring if he pulled some of it up, and cursed.

Whereas before he'd wanted nothing but to spill blood, all he desired now was to clean up the woods so he could return to Miri as quickly as he could. They had much to discuss. However, he couldn't dwell on that, not if he wanted to protect his realm and its people.

At least, Miri would be safe in the city. And if her father was out there, he would find him.

Stumble

Miri cursed again and scrubbed a hand over her face. Damn it, why hadn't she remembered to ask Eerin about the people in the forest?

Eamandian laid a hand on her shoulder and guided her toward the door. "He heard you before he was out of range, I think."

She froze and refused to budge. "But will it be enough?"

Silence met her query. Finally, Eamandian sighed. "That I cannot answer. If your father is out there, he may already be injured. I've heard reports that the lighter fae and humans are also being wounded."

"Why are they doing this?"

He cocked a brow at her. "You need to ask what your townspeople are here for?"

She flushed. "I guess I meant the lighter fae. Why help humans? It's not like they had anything to do with us before."

"They have their own agenda, one I wouldn't even try to ponder at. I'll leave that to our leader and his advisors and captains." He gave a delicate shudder. "I'm a healer for a reason." With a gentle push, he got her moving again, and they stepped out into the hallway. "Go to your rooms and rest. That is the official order of a master healer."

Exhaustion dragged at her feet, so she didn't protest. Rushing around for the last three and a half hours had depleted her energy. Her legs ached, as did her back. Even her mind felt fuzzy. The worry preying on her for Eerin and her father didn't help. Still, leaving a ward full of patients was no small thing. "After I rest, let me know if you need help."

"Go," he said firmly. "Innara is here." His gaze grew distant. "In fact, she needs my help. I've been gone too long."

Miri furrowed her brow. Was this the Taelin mind bond she'd heard talk of that formed between couples who'd been together for a long time or who were particularly suited to each other? She shrugged off her curiosity. There would be time to ask about it later.

They parted ways in the main chamber of the halls. The sun had all but set, and the only people out were guards and other Taelin who were going about their duties. Good. The thought of talk didn't please her at the moment.

She breathed in the evening air, trying to settle her frazzled nerves. Without the cooling enchantments that were placed on many buildings, heat and humidity pressed in on her. It wasn't doing a thing for her exhaustion, either. Her bed beckoned, but she doubted she would actually be able to sleep. Not with Eerin out in those woods with God knew who from her old town.

Her shoulders slumping, she strode slowly down a stone path that would lead her home.

Huh, home? Taerin was home, though. It was where both she and Eve belonged. Her hand slid over her stomach. No one was around at the moment, and this section of the sidewalk was dimly lit. Time had taught her that Taelin hearing might be sharp. However, their sight wasn't much better than a human's.

She paused, staring at the building on her left. Wasn't that the building that held the cells? Without much conscious thought, she drifted down another path, toward the crystal-lit, white stone building. Henry was still down in the cells. She hadn't had time to convince Eerin to do anything else with him.

More importantly, Henry hadn't told the Taelin guards much, nor had he relayed anything useful to her or Eerin.

She bit her bottom lip. What did he know of this attack? Had the lighter fae's involvement been preplanned? Was her father among those in the forest? A sprout of excitement unfurrowed in her chest. Surely, Henry might know *something*, and that something could be whether her father had planned to venture into the woods.

As she strode up to the door, she frowned. Where were the guards that had been there last time? Maybe they were needed at the town's walls? Anyway, there would be guards inside.

She pushed open the door and stepped inside. Silence met her in the antechamber. With a darting gaze, she took in her surroundings. Not a soul in sight. How odd. A twinge of unease trickled down her spine, but she dismissed it.

There was no cause for concern. A guard or two would certainly be standing watch near Henry's cell. The rest had apparently been needed elsewhere due to the attack. She straightened her shoulders. She had a mission to accomplish. Time to get it done.

As she made her way down the dark stairs, her foreboding grew. She chided herself. Her imagination was overactive. That was all. A sudden movement at the bottom of the landing caught her attention. A shadowy form was making its way up the stairs. The thud of its boots echoed in her ears, drowning out all else.

Her breath hitched, and her hand tightened on the railing. Every instinct screamed for her to whirl around and flee. Her feet, however, wouldn't listen to reason.

The person was now close enough for her to make out the distinctive silver cloak worn by all guards. The tension leaked out of her shoulders. The guard watching over Henry! Of course. What a silly goose she was being.

She cleared her throat, stifling a nervous laugh. "You're so quiet, you gave me a fright." She pressed on, not pausing to see if her attempt of humor had lightened the moment. "I'm here to see Henry. I trust he's awake."

The person halted, a step between them. The hood of the cloak concealed the guard's face. Odd that he should have it up. Though cooler due to the cells being underground, it wasn't chilly by any means.

"I'm quite awake, Miri."

She inhaled sharply as a spike of apprehension speared her heart. "Henry, what are you doing out of your cell? Where are the guards?"

He gave a bark of laughter and tossed back his hood. "Not that I don't appreciate your lover's genteel hospitality, but I'm afraid we must leave. The guards won't be bothering us." He fingered the high collar of his stolen cloak as he gave a gloating smile.

"Us?" For a second, she forgot how to breathe. Then sense reasserted itself, and she readied herself for a sprint up the stairs. Somehow, he's disposed of his remaining guards. Right now, she wasn't interested in asking him how.

"Why, of course," he said, surprise evident in his tone. "You're monstrous right now. Don't you want to seek a cure?"

She reared back slightly but then collected herself. So he thought she was so horrible now? "I don't think there is one." Her voice was frosty. She *knew* there was no cure. The process had nearly killed her. She couldn't live through it again, not even for the promise of all her humanity being restored.

"The lighter fae may know of one. How can you not try?"

He knew of the lighter fae? She glowered at him, her mind busy connecting all the pieces. "Trust me, quite easily. And your group of lighter fae is the same one attacking the forest as we speak?"

"*Ah*, they kept their promise." The smile in his voice was as clear as the one on his face.

That cemented her suspicions and kindled anger in her gut. More than one Taelin had died and several more hovered near death. "So you knew they were planning an attack along with our people and kindly didn't mention it. How long ago was this planned? Is my father among them?"

"So my townspeople are your people now? I thought you'd tossed in your lot with the tar fae. You're the lover of the tar leader and seem in no hurry to break your curse." Disgust laced his voice.

Her hands clenched at her sides. "They will always be my people, but since when are the lighter fae your friends? We barely even knew a thing about them mere months ago. When did you become bosom friends?"

"Since when did the tar fae become your bosom friends?" he shot back.

She angrily swept her hand over her face and down her body. "Given the way I look, I don't think I'll be accepted in human lands again."

"No,"—he agreed coldly—"that's why we have to try to save you."

What if she didn't want to be "saved?" Even if she could regain her old self, she wouldn't. Who knew what it'd do to her, Eve, and the baby? Her life was here now, for better or worse. Eerin was here. That was a huge part she couldn't discount.

She shook her head slowly. "Even if it means my death?"

"Surely you see death would be better than..." His normally good-looking features twisted into something ugly. "Well, being as you are."

Fury for the Taelin, for her, flared in her chest. They weren't monsters! Any pity she'd felt for Henry being stuck in the cells died a swift demise. The words were out before she could stop them. "I remember why I didn't want you courting me. You've always been a supercilious prig and overstep yourself constantly."

His face darkened as he flicked his hood back up. "You know nothing, least of all what you need or want." His hand shot out and latched onto her upper arm painfully. "Come, we've wasted enough time."

She twisted in his grasp to no avail, a spurt of anger and fear cascading through her. Damn it, why couldn't she get free? Eerin had said Taelin were a bit stronger than humans. So either she hadn't been gifted with that extra dose of strength or human males could still be stronger than female Taelin.

"Let me go. Now," she said through gritted teeth.

"Move." He pushed her, making her stumble backward into the upper step.

With a yelp, she careened sideways into the wall, knocking the breath from her body. Fortunately, she stayed upright.

She shakily pushed herself from the wall and glared at Henry, who hadn't even attempted to stop her near fall. Her hand itched to punch him, but she reined herself in. With the baby, she couldn't chance a fall. Getting off the stairs was paramount.

He grabbed her arm again. "Come on. We need to meet up with our party if we want to get out of these woods alive." He forced her around, keeping her arm bent behind her back.

With no other choice, she moved stiffly up the steps. Henry's presence hovered over her like a dark weight. His fingers bit into her skin and would surely leave bruises. Eerin would want his blood for this trespass, no doubt.

She took a deep, steadying breath. Eerin wasn't here to help her now. Somehow, she had to get loose. "This party is the lighter fae and townspeople?"

"What do you think?" he snapped as they stepped onto the first floor.

"Is my father among them?"

Silence met her query, so she halted in the anteroom, refusing to budge until he'd answered her. He pressed harder on her arm, wringing a wince from her. "Move. We don't have time for this."

"My father?" she asked again.

He growled low in his throat. "I thought you were smarter than this, Miri. To think that I actually considered making you my wife."

Thank the heavens he hadn't succeeded. "My father?"

"He may be."

She sighed at his caginess. It wasn't a denial, so it might mean that her father had planned to participate in the attack. Given that Henry had been locked up in Eerin's cells for the last few days, though, he couldn't know for certain if her father was in the woods. Damn it, she hoped he wasn't. But hope was a fickle thing. Pray that he was uninjured then. That thought made her feel no better. Her father was no warrior, and though he was reasonably fit for a scholarly librarian, he was advancing firmly into his middle-age years. If he could see her and Eve now, what would he think? Would he be as horrified as—

"That's all the answer you'll get. Now move. Don't think about calling out for help. I have a blade and won't hesitate to use it." As if to prove his words true, a prickle of something sharp bit into the back of her neck, causing her to flinch.

An ice-cold shiver trickled down her spine. Dear God, she had to get away from him, but for now, she was well and truly caught. His temper had always been somewhat uneven. Though she'd never truly feared him before, now was another thing entirely. Desperate people committed cruel, terrible acts. She sensed that sort of wildness in him as if the air was laden with it.

He prodded her forward none too gently. This time, she complied.

Forest on Fire

Eerin ducked a well-aimed stab at his throat from a lighter fae soldier and landed a slash to the assailant's arm. Around him, his warriors were locked in a similar battle.

By the Dark Woods, the humans and lighter fae just kept coming. He would actually feel helpless if he had more than a moment to spare on such useless sentiment.

Smoke clogged the air, and Eerin was sure he was in the hell that apparently so many humans believed in. Magical torches, courtesy of the lighter fae, had set some of the black-trunked trees ablaze and painted the surrounding woods in patches of shadow and light. Night was quickly approaching, so the darkness would soon be nearly all-consuming if it weren't for those trees. Though there were spells to aid one's sight in the dark, doing such magic while battling was no easy feat. Worse, the lighter fae had no such vision limitations in the dark, not with their cat's-eyed pupils.

Smoke tickled his nose and lungs. The noxious air, though, seemed to bother the humans the most. The lighter fae also were more affected than his people were. It appeared that the darkness flowing through his people's veins was good for something. Still, the enemy kept coming.

After spinning back around, he hacked at the enemy fae in front of him. He managed to land a killing blow but not before the male sliced his blade into the shoulder of Eerin's sword arm, right between two pieces of plate armor.

Eerin hissed in pain but otherwise ignored the bleeding wound. Cold resolve and anger drove him. There was room for nothing else. With a swift sweep of his gaze over the large clearing that surrounded them, he took stock of the battle. Most of his warriors were out here, though a few troops from other settlements in the woods were being called in. Hopefully, they wouldn't reach them too late.

On the periphery, the dark trees, both those that were on fire and those that were not, weakly whipped their branches at the lighter fae and humans. Some damnable spell the lighter fae had concocted was sapping the energy from the forest and keeping the interlopers safe from the woods and its denizens. *This is why the enemy was able to venture so far into the woods.* Somehow, someway, the lighter fae had found a way to best the forest.

Neither Eerin nor any of his soldiers could call upon the land and draw forth a burst of magic to aid them. And what they carried in their veins was being leached out by the desperate forest around them. The lighter fae was magically starving the woods. The only consolation was that the lighter fae couldn't use this kind of earth magic for themselves, as they weren't born and bred on it. Still, the situation was dire for the Taelin.

If only he could commune with The Spirit of the Forest to obtain some answers or insight. However, it wasn't answering his call, nor was he able to channel it beyond connecting with the plant and wildlife around him. Given that the trees and animals were in acute distress and he was fighting for his life and those of his people, merging his mind with theirs even for a second wasn't wise. Still, the cries of pain from the woods and its animals radiated through the strong bond that he shared with them and shredded at his heart and soul. It was a bond that he knew the other Taelin felt to a lesser degree, but it still affected them deeply. His people were in pain, too.

With icy rage so strong he should be quivering from it, he ran a lighter fae through. He didn't wait for the body to hit the ground before he did the same to a young human male aiming for his heart. The man gasped, looking down at the spreading stain over his chest before dropping his blade.

Eerin could almost feel sorry for the loss of such a young life. Almost.

A subtle sound slid into his consciousness. He froze and then dropped to the ground as a tiny, speeding projectile flew past him, hitting a tree only a few feet away. For a second, he lay there as the battle waged on around him.

He'd almost responded too late to the ball that had nearly implanted itself into his forehead—and likely would've killed him instantly. Only his hearing had saved him. If not for that, he would've returned to the earth, leaving Miri and their child alone.

His heart pounding, he rolled back into a standing position and found the rat who had fired the shot at him. With quick strides that still seemed far too slow—and pushing more than one unsuspecting or lighter fae out of the way—he set out toward the honorless coward who had not engaged him as a proper enemy should. He'd be happy to deliver a swift death to him.

Other worries plagued him, though. Now wasn't the first time he'd heard or seen one fired tonight, though they did seem in short supply. Where had the humans gotten such weapons? Most likely the lighter fae, damn them, as the Taelin themselves had dabbled in gunpowder and rudimentary guns before relegating them back on the shelf.

The man stared at him with wide eyes before biting the top of a small paper container. With shaking hands, he dumped the contents down the barrel of the weapon. Something shiny in his hand glinted from the unholy fires that had overtaken part of the forest. Then the metal ball disappeared down the muzzle.

By now, Eerin was almost upon him. As the male lifted the gun, Eerin bared his teeth in a vicious smile. Lightning quick, he grabbed the barrel with his free hand and yanked the gun away from the dumbfounded man. As Eerin raised the gun to bash the man over the head with it, he paused, eying the man closer. The human had brown hair with a fine dusting of gray. Nothing of his features or bearing spoke of him being Miri's father. Still, he was loath to permanently damage anyone who might be her sire.

"Are you Miri and Eve's father?" he demanded harshly.

The man's brow furrowed. "W-what?"

"Are you?" repeated Eerin. Were most humans stupid? His Miri and Eve were anything but. However, they were different, unique.

"No. No!" The man shook his head violently.

Eerin lifted the weapon, not caring to use his increasingly painful sword arm, and watched as the man crumpled to the ground under the force of the blunt hit. Was he alive or dead? Eerin didn't care, not as his forest burned around him.

He spun around slowly, taking in the carnage around him. His gaze landed on a man with salt-and-pepper dark-brown hair awkwardly wielding a sword. The human seemed determined to stay out of the way and wasn't fighting any of the Taelin at the moment. What drew his attention, however, was the man's piercing blue eyes. Even their almond shape was just like Miri's. And the man's face...it was a masculine version of Miri and Eve's.

Damn it to the Dark Woods, their father was here in the middle of this melee, but where else had he expected the man to be? From what Miri had said, he was a devoted father who adored his children.

A huge sigh gusted from Eerin even as he blocked the swung of another incompetent human swordsman. With his sights still on the father, Eerin knocked the legs out from under the thirties-something-looking man. Guessing a human's age was so hard.

Once that was done, he raced toward Miri's father. What had Miri said his name was? Well, whatever it was, the human was in trouble and was about to be cut down by one of Eerin's more novice soldiers.

Before the Taelin's sword could slice into the human's neck, Eerin intercepted the swing with his own blade. His shoulder protested, and he gritted his teeth to bite back the profanity that was burning on his tongue.

"Go," he ordered the young Taelin, who wisely chose to melt away into the battle around them.

The human male's eyes widened as he took in this apparent newest opponent. His throat bobbed as he swallowed, and his sword wavered before he brought it up higher. As if that would scare Eerin.

Eerin knocked it aside, and the blade fell from the man's hand. Scholar, indeed. The man couldn't even keep ahold of his weapon. It was a wonder he'd survived this long without serious injury. Other than a few bruises and shallow cuts, he appeared to be in good shape.

Stepping closer, Eerin grabbed the man, reeling him in toward him. The man gasped but then had the forethought to struggle and yank away. Even wounded, Eerin had more strength in one arm than the man had in two.

"Stop," Eerin said, his voice almost a hiss.

The man complied but raised his chin. The gesture was so reminiscent of Miri that Eerin had to bite back a smile. "You can kill us all, but we won't stop until Miri and Eve are back in their rightful place."

Eerin cocked his head to the side. "And who are they to you?" he asked cooly. He wanted to test the mettle of this man who called himself Miri and Eve's father. A warrior of weapons he was not, but his love claimed he was one with his words.

The man looked him boldly in the eyes. "They are my daughters, and I demand to see them before being put to death."

"How do you know they're alive?" That was something that had also bothered him. Why were the humans so sure that the girls still lived? Why risk their lives and an all-out war if they were already dead? Unless the humans merely fought for revenge, but somehow he doubted that. For hundreds of years, they'd been afraid of the forest, of his people. With good cause.

The man seemed to deflate before him. "I don't, but the lighter fae say they are."

Of course, the lighter fae. They were behind all this somehow.

Now, he only had to find out why.

That would come later, though. For now, he had to ensure the man was brought to safety. Then he had to see this battle to its end and the enemy vanquished. "They are alive and well, though not quite as you are used to."

The man perked up before his brow furrowed. "What do you mean?"

"That you will have to see for yourself." Eerin cast around for one of his men that could be spared to see the human into the city.

Seeing one nearby who had just disposed of his opponent, he beckoned him over. "See that this man is led to the city. Keep him alive and unharmed but watched at all times."

"Yes, Lord Eerin." The soldier's neutral voice betrayed none of the confusion in his eyes.

Though Eerin owed him no explanation, he said, "This is the father of Lady Miri and Lady Eve."

"*Ah,*" the Taelin said as if that explained it all. It probably did. Eerin's relationship with Miri wasn't a secret. Though there were some disgruntled whispers, most of the Taelin liked both sisters well enough.

Before he handed Miri's father over to the guard, he leaned in toward the human. "I'd have your name, human."

Miri's father had watched the whole exchange with the guard with growing confusion on his face. Now, he appeared utterly bewildered. "Anthony," he said slowly. "My name's Anthony."

Eerin nodded. "It's only right that I greet the grandfather of my unborn child."

Anthony's pupils blew wide, and then his eyes rolled back in his head as he crumpled forward, unconscious.

Only Eerin's quick reflexes saved him from a nasty fall. As he handed the man over to the dumbstruck guard who'd overheard everything, he said lightly, "I guess that news was too much."

Eerin just hoped Miri wouldn't want his hide for spilling her—no, their—secret without her knowledge. He did have his reasons, though. Besides wanting to shock his likely future father-in-law a bit, he also wanted to publicly claim the child and Miri in the unlikely case that he was felled during battle.

That, however, he'd do everything in his power to prevent. He not only had his people to live for but now also a mate and a child.

Mind Joining

Before the guard carrying Anthony could walk but a few steps, a powerful blast of energy and color exploded through the area, knocking Eerin and anyone near him off their feet. Flat on his back and his muscles screaming at the rough treatment of the past few hours, Eerin blinked slowly. His sight was temporarily blinded, damn it. He gritted his teeth as fury pounded in his veins.

Damn the light, magic bombs were in his forest. And by the smell of it, catching even more trees on fire. The lighter fae would pay for this. And so would Castin, who was one of the enemy's leaders and whom he'd seen somewhere in the melee. Frankly, that Castin hadn't challenged him in a fight yet was highly surprising and somewhat worrying.

What was the man planning? He had to find out. Anyway, he made a wide-open target like this. Most likely everybody around him was in the same condition, though. But others would come flooding in and if they were enemy troops...

He forced himself upright and muffled the groan that tried to sneak past his throat. Once he was fully on his feet, he stared around the field. More individuals were on the ground than standing. Though he'd like to check that all his warriors were alive, there simply wasn't time. He needed a plan. Now.

The form of Anthony and his guard snagged his attention. Without much conscious thought, he slowly drifted toward them. Bending down was surprisingly hard, not only because he was sore but also because he didn't want to discover whether Miri's father had been killed in the blast. A quick press on his fingers to both Anthony and the guard's necks revealed they both lived. For now. He'd be damned if that changed. If he weren't in the middle of a battlefield, he'd snort at the thought of him caring so much if a human lived or died.

As he stood, a dash of gold through the hazy air caught his eye. Castin. That particular shade of hair was unmistakable, which meant that the bastard was still alive, not that he expected anything else. The lighter fae leader was too crafty to go down easily. Since Castin had been on his feet, had he been the one to cast the bomb? Why endanger his own people needlessly, though? The man could be ruthless, but that streak wasn't turned against his own people without cause. Then again, why even chance war with Eerin's people?

Eerin tried to track Castin, but the smog was too thick. Damnation, if only he could find him before most of the others roused. However, Eerin didn't want to walk into a trap, either.

The fine hairs on the back of his neck stood on end. He felt as if he was being watched. In all probability, someone was spying on him.

Keeping a wary eye out, he hurried to an intact tree. Its trashing stopped as he neared. He laid a gentle hand on its greasy, gnarled trunk and murmured the ancient greeting. His people revered these trees and treated them with the proper respect. They, however, did not shy away from touching them when needed. The blood that these sentient lives bled onto their bark also flowed through the Taelin.

Once the tree's approval seeped into him, he asked for its assistance in seeing the forest through the shared mindscape of the trees. Its ready, urgent acceptance made him swallow. Not all trees were so amendable, so it clearly wanted to show him something of importance. Was there other lighter fae somewhere else in the forest, doing ever more damage?

This wasn't the ideal time or place for a mindjoining. The act always left him vulnerable and blind to the outside world around him. He had no choice, though, and would have to trust the tree to protect him.

Joining their minds was an easy, familiar process. Sliding his consciousness into that of the tree's and then into the shared web that connected the forest filled him with a rush of crackling energy, though it was weaker than it had ever been before. That energy would disappear when he broke the mindjoining, leaving him shaky and tired.

A panoramic view of the clearing came into focus. Every living thing, plant and animal, had a white glow when seen through the trees' eyes. That made it simpler to spy figures scurrying in the darkness.

Suddenly, the image shifted, speeding up, covering a distance quicker than Taelin feet could go. The tree's agitation continued to bleed through their link, which twisted his stomach into knots. Castin couldn't have gotten that far, but it didn't mean one of his troop members wasn't out there, causing havoc. However, he didn't feel any telltale flares of pain and rage from that part of the forest. In fact, this portion seemed in nearly full possession of its magic. That gave him a spark of hope. If they could lure the enemy over there...

The image slowed as if running out of steam. What he caught sight of through the trees' aid almost made his heart stop. He didn't see Castin. No, he saw something much worse and infinitely more frightening.

Miri in the hold of someone wearing a guard cloak, a knife much too close to her neck. For a moment, his mind spun hopelessly. By the darkness, had one of his guards betrayed him? He was dimly aware of his body shuddering in the outside world, but it felt like a phantom act compared to the horror ripping through his consciousness right now.

Suddenly, in the moving picture, a stray tree limb ripped the hood from the person's head. Eerin inhaled sharply.

Henry. That rat had her. He dared to press a blade close to her neck!

Eerin's fingers curled against the bark, digging in until splinters pierced his skin. Though the pain was muted due to the mindjoining, he winced at the same time as the tree did and sent a quiet apology to his leafy friend.

Thank the darkness, Miri didn't seem as if she was injured, but he didn't trust it to stay that way. It was clear where Henry propelled them. They were headed straight for the clearing, though they were at least twenty minutes away. Likely considerably longer due to their slow pace.

Eerin hungrily stared at her dimly outlined form. She held a small lantern that Henry was apparently forcing her to carry. It was just big enough to provide sufficient light to illuminate the immediate path in front of her but nothing more.

He'd seen all he needed to see. Eerin made to cut the link, but the tree pressed its consciousness heavier on him. Though it wasn't exactly words that he heard, he knew the tree was telling him to wait and watch.

The image that streamed through his mind revealed something that ripped a sharp smile from him. The portion of the forest revealed in the image was gloriously awake, and he *adored* what it was doing to Henry.

Limbs of all shapes and sizes toyed with Henry, trying to get him to release his hold on Miri. Hope spread through his chest. The forest—and the animals within it— recognized Miri as one of their own, one of Eerin's people, and wouldn't strike at her unless she landed the first blow. Henry, however, they viewed as a dangerous interloper and taunted him whenever they could.

The animals of the forest continually put their voices to the air and would appear at a distance to stare at Henry with jeweled, malicious eyes. Once the man stilled, forcing Miri to stop, the animals would melt back into the darkness.

As soon as Henry started walking, the finger-like limbs of trees and shrubs snatched at the man's cloak and unruly hair. Eerin felt the tree's apology that they couldn't attempt to trip the man or interfere in any other way due to the knife at Miri's neck.

If the rat fell, he could send the blade into her throat. That was a risk none of them could countenance. Given their ongoing actions, they were taking enough of a chance as it was. If only the Spirit would answer and provide guidance. She—for he was going to call it a "she"—had been quiet during this whole ordeal, leaving the woods frightened and Eerin resentful.

Damn it all, where was the so-called Guardian? She answered none of her people's calls when she was needed most. Usually, the Spirit interfered like an old, gossiping lady. Miri's entrance into his life, not to mention her Change, had likely been orchestrated by her, and yet she ignored them all now in their time of need?

He calmed himself. His anger wouldn't save Miri. Only keeping a rational head could do that.

However, the forest's machinations slowed Henry down. Eerin wanted Miri nowhere near the fighting. That the human knew where to go was an indication that he'd known of the attack. Yet he hadn't breathed one word of it.

Fiery anger, just like the magicked flames that were searing his forest, coursed through his mind. Revenge. Honor. Then the healing of the woods. The mantra was so consuming he wasn't sure if it was coming from him or his woods.

He had been under too long. The link, with the aid of the trees, broke with a snap, and he gasped as he came back fully into his body. He sagged forward against the oily, slick surface of the tree. The sound and smell of battle filled the air again.

With a slight jolt, he took in the mangled forms of humans and lighter fae about him, which told him not only had attacks been made upon him while he was vulnerable but that whatever spell that had kept the enemy relatively safe from the trees was weakening. The land was also gaining back access to its magic, which in turn meant the Taelin would soon be able to call upon that power. That likely meant one thing—the lighter fae spellcasters who'd performed the spell were either seriously injured or dead. For several powerful spellcasters would've been needed for a spell of this magnitude.

Eerin had been too soft, not wanting to harm anyone Miri had cared about. That was an oversight he'd take care of. Henry soon wouldn't be able to pose a threat ever again. Fortune, though fickle it may be, seemed to be on Eerin's side for the moment. *Let's keep it that way.*

Another plus... Anthony and the guard were nowhere in sight. With any luck, they were on their way to the city.

He leaned into the welcoming embrace of the tree, letting the oily substance soak into his clothes, into his skin. He was weak, but the tree was becoming stronger by the second and would give him what he needed. Each moment, more energy filtered into Eerin's veins. The Taelin, with a tree's permission, could take from it what it willed. This one was willing to give him much. Even now, echoes of the screaming forest rang in Eerin's ears, louder than ever due to his contact with the tree.

With a gritty determination and a sense of renewed strength, he pushed away from his black-trunked ally. He had a soon-to-be wife to save, along with his woods and people.

After dispatching a few enemies, he gathered his closest able-bodied soldiers along with two captains. They also confirmed his findings of the weakening spell. Though Eerin preferred to leave orders with Alegion, the man wasn't anywhere to be seen. The fighting had once again spilled out of the clearing, so his absence wasn't necessarily an indication of his friend being injured or dead. At least that was what he told himself.

But any of his captains were more than up to the task of leading their men. He leveled brisk looks on Captains Calin and Kalumen. "Marshal all nearby forces and strike at the enemy before they can regroup. As the trees free themselves, they may be able to lend us the strength and energy we need. Commune with them as needed."

Both captains nodded, and Calin replied, "It shall be done, my lord."

Eerin took in his surroundings once more. Many of his warriors were drawing an infusion of magic from the land and trees. As power blasted from the palms of his soldiers, the enemy soared through the air and into waiting cages made of live branches. The hisses, growls, and other sounds of the forest creatures that also rounded up the enemy sang in his ears, as did the creaking of the land as it opened up into pits to capture the fleeing interlopers. Assured everything was now under control, Eerin spun around and commanded two high-ranking guards to follow him with torches.

Without sparing a moment more, he set out into the forest with the two males by his side. The bite of his fingernails cutting into his palms pierced his consciousness, but he brushed aside the pain. He had far more important things to contemplate, like tracking a rat and saving his burgeoning family.

Leafy Escapades

"What...what was that?" asked Henry, his voice wild. His hold on her arm tightened, and she could picture the blade near her neck wavering in his alarm.

She rolled her eyes. It wasn't as if he could see her. She was slightly in front of him, after all. "As I've already told you, it's one of the creatures of the forest. There are many dangerous ones roaming this forest."

For some reason, unlike with her first foray into the forest, she wasn't afraid of the feral animals they might meet. Oddly enough, several had already appeared several meters away from them, only to disappear once Henry seemed suitably spooked. In fact, it almost appeared as if they did it on purpose but dared not venture too close.

"Well, then, what are you waiting for? Get moving." A shudder ran through his arm. "The quicker we're out of this damned forest, the better."

"I'm going as fast as I can."

Her eyes throbbed as she continued her perusal to locate anything that might trip her. If Henry fell flat on his face, she wouldn't care one whit as long as he didn't stab her with that blade. However, she couldn't risk either of them taking a fall. Not with her being pregnant. The lantern he'd made her carry only shone a foot or two in front of her. Now, her eyes ached from overuse and strain.

Henry had also been adamant that they remain on this path. Of course, she'd tried to "accidentally" lead them off it, but he'd quickly squashed that notion. The side of her neck still smarted where the tip of the knife had dug into the skin. There was a slight cold, damp feeling that told her he'd drawn blood. She, however, wouldn't give him the pleasure of acknowledging it.

She'd love to return the favor with a much larger slice, but he had one of her arms locked securely through his and that damn blade at her throat. For the moment, there was nothing to do but "behave" and do as he willed. She pressed her lips together, staring resolutely at the ground ahead of her. Being this helpless wasn't high on her list of priorities. Though she was still frightened, she also had a good dose of anger pushing her onward. Henry would pay for this if it was the last thing she did.

"Can't you go any faster?" Henry asked curtly.

She winced. Taerin hearing was definitely better, and she didn't even think she had a full dose of it. "Please don't speak in my ear. It sounds as if you're screaming."

"What are you talking about? I wasn't screaming. Merely asking quietly."

She'd be damned if she told him about her hearing. If he didn't know, she might be able to use it against him somehow. She doubted he'd heard the sounds of far-off battle like she had. Those noises were getting ever closer with each step. Smoke was also in the air and tickling her nose. Was Henry aware of what hell he might be leading them into? Probably, and she was his insurance for getting out alive if the Taelin caught them.

Her stomach twisted at that thought. She had to get away before they reached the battle, but Eerin was likely there, as were others who would be able to help her. Well, as long as her former people didn't shoot her on sight once they noticed her Change. That also discounted the lighter fae, who were apparently masterminds behind this attack. How would they react to a human-Taelin hybrid? These were all worries she had no answer to.

After letting the silence stretch between them as long as she dared, she answered. "With this small lantern, no. It's already hard enough to remain on the path. I don't want us tripping, and you plunging that knife into my neck."

He grunted. "Just keep moving."

She took in a deep, steadying breath. The smell of something metallic was in the air, along with the natural scents of the forest. By now, they were in the black part of the forest, where the trees bore that oily residue that she somehow knew was behind her Change. Of course, Innara had told her the same thing.

However, *feeling* it was totally different. The blood in her veins had been humming most peculiarly ever since they'd entered this portion of the woods. It wasn't painful. In fact, an infusion of energy coursed through her that had nothing to do with the horror of her current situation.

She hadn't been this deep into the forest since all those months ago when she first entered it. So this sensation was new, foreign. Disconcerting. Icy fingers of apprehension slid up her spine. Worse, she swore the trees were whispering, weeping. What kind of nonsense was that? Except...except...her whole life for the last several months had been defined by the supposedly impossible. Whispering trees didn't seem so unlikely now.

A *boom* reverberated through the forest.

"What was that?"

She feigned nonchalance with difficulty. "Your guess is as good as mine. Maybe it's your lighter friends." An unfortunate play on words. Given the smell on the air now, the enemy was lighting the trees on fire. If so, the trees had something to weep about, and so did the Taelin who revered these woods.

More worry bubbled up in her gut. Though she mourned the loss of life—any life—she didn't relish the idea of walking through a burning forest. Behind her, Henry sniffed loudly. "Do you smell that?"

"The smoke? I think your friends brought a means of fire with them."

"Lord Castin promised a diversion," Henry said, his voice contemplative.

"Castin?" she snatched onto that unfamiliar yet fae-sounding name. And diversion? What else was being planned? It surely meant nothing good for the Taelin.

"One of the lighter fae leaders." He paused and then asked snidely. "Doesn't your noble lover tell you anything?"

She ignored his slight. "Diversion for what?"

"Like I'd tell you. How stupid do you think me?"

Did she answer that? He was leading them toward a deadly battle. That didn't sound as if it were the brightest idea. Henry had no fighting skills that she knew of. She had none, either, unless she could frighten the human faction with her appearance. That would likely only get her killed, though.

"Why don't you tell me the reason for all of this, and then I'll answer that question?" she said, gesturing around the forest.

His fingers bit into her arm. "You corrupted whore, you better watch your mouth. I should've mounted you months ago when I had the chance. Now, you're ruined and beyond use."

She couldn't keep her huff of disbelief and revulsion locked away. "I didn't let you touch me, then. I wouldn't let you now, either, even if you were so inclined."

He snarled and shoved her forward. Her foot slipped against some moss, and she stumbled forward. Henry's hold on her arm broke. Her free hand landed against one of the slick black trees, and she caught herself before she could fall.

A jolt shivered through her palm and up into her arm, and the black leaves above her rustled noisily. Something brushed against her mind. Something foreign that spoke to the new blood pumping through her veins. More of that strange energy filled her. T-the tree's essence? Was that what she was feeling?

She stared at her hand, visible in the sparse light of the lamp she'd somehow kept clutch of, her skin so white against the blackness. Except for her veins. They were a perfect match for the tree.

She closed her eyes, and a vision inserted itself into her consciousness. Her breath stilled. Eerin in the forest, going away from the battle, coming toward her. Two guards were at his side. The tree seemed to whisper, a vast, hoarse voice filled with the creaking of thousands of branches, *Help is on the way.*

Relief and fear settled deep into her chest.

The urge to gape was strong, but she didn't have the time. Too much rested on this evening, on her and Eerin surviving. She pulled away and turned toward Henry, who only stood a foot from her. "Don't push me again."

He sneered. "Or what? Your lover isn't here to save you. For all your changes, you appear as weak as ever."

God, what had she ever seen in him? "Funny you say that. You're the one who has to wield a knife to show your 'strength.'"

"You know the expression, 'might makes right?' Well, I have the might right now."

He reached out to grab her arm. Suddenly, a long, thick limb dropped down between them, crashing onto his forearm with a *crack*. Henry gave a pain-filled shout, dropping the knife in his other hand, and ripped his arm back to clutch at it. All color drained from his face, and he stared at the hanging branch with wild eyes. He stood rooted in place as if afraid to move or breathe.

The whispering of the trees grew louder, and she knew that the falling of the branch had been no accident. She inched back toward the trunk. Best not to get in the way of whatever plans it had. Though she was still a newcomer to this realm, she wasn't stupid.

A moment later, the limb snaked around him as if it were a rope. He screamed as leaves wound over his mouth and curled over his cheeks in some parody of a lover's caress.

With a lurch, it hefted him off the ground, leaving his feet dangling several feet in the air. She gaped at the sight and couldn't but help remember a similar time she'd been caught up in a tree like that. However, this tree looked a touch angrier.

All its boughs were stooped and quivering as with rage. She crept back another inch and bumped into the tree. This time, she did gasp from what she picked up from it.

It was angry, furious, at what was being done to its forest, to its denizens, to its ensorcelled brothers and sisters. And it held the human it cradled in its branches at great fault. Even she, as tender-hearted as she could be, couldn't dredge up much sympathy for Henry. His muffled screams and pleading eyes didn't move her. Probably because she knew he'd take her prisoner and maybe even use that knife if he were free again.

She laid a hand on the oily bark, silently sending a thought of thankfulness to it. Whether it worked or not, she didn't have a clue. At least, not until a feeling of acceptance not her own suffused her mind. Something brushed against her shoe. She glanced down and jumped a good few inches off the ground. There, right by her foot, was Henry's stolen knife, and it'd been delivered by none other than her rescuer tree.

With a shaking hand, she snatched it from the leafy tendril that held it loosely. If the tree wanted her to have the blade, then take it she would. Though she really didn't know how to properly wield the damn thing.

After one last look at the bound Henry, she turned away. If the tree had his death planned, she didn't want to stick around for that. Even after what he'd done...she couldn't watch that. She wanted to heal people, not witness fruitless pain.

But where should she go? Back to the city? Eerin was coming for her, so maybe that wouldn't be wise. The creaking of the tree and a high-pitched whine from Henry, followed by some mysterious popping sounds, caused her to clutch the knife tighter. She needed to move now. Her own peace of mind wouldn't let her do otherwise.

She'd walk just far enough so she couldn't see, even if she could still hear, what was happening behind her. Getting any closer to the battle wouldn't be wise. Hopefully, that would be enough. It had to be.

The Lighter Fae

Miri faltered to a stop after a few minutes. This was as good a place to stop as any. The sounds of battle were a bit closer but still seemed far enough away to offer her some safety. The tree and Henry...she'd done her best to block out. Now, she didn't hear anything from that direction. A cringe slid up her spine when she thought what that might mean.

She stared around at the pitch-blackness engulfing her. Her hands shook, her nerves making her jittery and twisting her stomach into coiled knots. How she wished she were back in the city. Though the forest wasn't as frightening as it had been before, she didn't feel at ease. She couldn't go forward nor could she go back. She was hemmed in by danger and squeamishness, and she hated that feeling.

The snapping of a twig made her lurch forward a step. She clutched the knife tighter before sense reasserted itself. The noise was likely from one of the trees shifting slightly or from an animal foresting for food. Nothing to be concerned about. No, nothing at all.

Still, tension lay across her shoulders like a cloak and wouldn't be shrugged off so easily. She spun in a slow circle, the light from the lantern revealing nothing. As she released a shaky breath, she prayed Eerin would arrive soon.

A hand fell on her shoulder. She jumped, a half-formed scream ripping from her throat. Another hand slipped across her mouth. Her heart thundered in her ears. Was...was that Eerin?

"Well, who do we have here?"

Oh, God, not Eerin. And not a voice she was familiar with from her town.

"No screaming now, not if you know what's good for you."

Strong hands turned her around, one remaining banded around her arm. Light from her lantern fell on the form that now loomed in front of her.

A fae male stood but a foot from her. That wasn't what stole her breath, though. No, it was the fact that this fae wasn't Taelin. Her stomach sank. This was one of the enemy fae, and she'd all but walked into him.

There was no doubt he was fae. He had the same pointed ears and almost otherworldly beauty, but that is where all similarities ended.

This male was bronze-skinned with no trace of the black veins that marked the Taelin. The pupils of his eyes were slitted like a cat's, and he bore hair as bright as gold. Funny that this lighter fae seemed darker in countenance than the Taelin. Were the other lighter fae similar in this regard? Most importantly, were they darker in deed, too, than the so-called tar fae?

He appeared to regard her curiously. "So it's true. A human who's undergone the Change."

There was a tone of cold fascination in his voice that caused her to shiver. It was as if he didn't see her as human but as some...some *experiment*. She licked her dry lips. "W-who are you?"

"I'd say your worst nightmare, but that would be so cliche."

Was that an attempt at humor? If so, he wasn't funny. "Let me go, and go back to your people. You're a trespasser in these woods."

He smirked. "So were you at one time." His hand tightening around her arm, he started to drag her forward.

"What are you doing?" She tried to pull away, but he was too strong. So she did the next best thing. She swung the lantern at his face. The metal item nearly made contact with his nose before his palm knocked it away and out of her hand with a loud *crack*.

He yanked her closer. "Don't be unpleasant. You'll make our trip most disagreeable."

"Trip?" Her voice came out squeaky with fear.

"You're going to be the welcome guest of the lighter fae. We're *very* curious about your Change."

The lump forming in her throat almost made her gag. She had to keep him here, keep him talking. Eerin was on his way and would take care of her would-be captor. If this fae got her out of the forest, she had a feeling she'd never return alive.

"Then you should've talked to Lord Eerin like civilized beings instead of attacking their people and forest."

"*Ooh*, so protective already?"

She narrowed her eyes. "The Taelin kept me alive when they could've killed me. That deserves a certain amount of loyalty."

"Yet it was them and their forest that afflicted you with these." He traced one of the veins snaking down her neck with a light finger.

She knocked the appendage away, unease icing her spine. He still held her in place with just one hand. "Don't."

"What? I've heard you've become quite close to Lord Eerin. Do I not warrant the same treatment?"

How did he know so much about her and the Taelin? "No, you don't. You're planning to kidnap me. Besides, I don't even know who you are."

He gave her a wolfish grin, revealing the slightly pointed teeth that the Taelin also had. "Feisty. I'm Lord Castin, by the way. I can see why Eerin likes you, even though you're from human stock and he hates humans. However, I bet you make a nice, little pet to warm his bed during the Taelin's process of monitoring your Change."

Monitoring her? "What do you mean?"

"Oh, come on. You think the Taelin aren't interested in your Change when you're the only human to survive it? It gives them valuable insight into their affliction."

The only ones who monitored her at all were Innara and Eamandian. Of course, they were curious about the effects her

Change wrought on her, but there wasn't anything nefarious in their treatment of her or Eve. "They might be interested in the effects of my Change. However, I'm always treated as a person and never as a specimen, as you're inferring. As for them being afflicted, there's nothing wrong with them. If it ever was an affliction, it is no longer."

He chuckled without humor. "Oh, you poor misguided changeling, what utter nonsense have they been filling your head with? They're corrupted, an abomination, in every way."

"Because they're different than you?"

Castin shook his head as if she didn't understand and forced her into a march.

She tried to drag her feet as much as she could. Though she couldn't root herself into place, she could walk as slowly as possible. Besides, without the lantern, she was nearly blind. The lighter fae who held her didn't seem to have the same problem, and then she remembered his cat-shaped pupils. He could likely see better in the dark than a human could and maybe even better than the Taelin. Innara said Taelin eyesight was only a bit better than a human's.

She glanced at the dark shapes of the trees. They weren't helping her or hindering the lighter fae in any way, so these particular trees must still be ensorcelled. At least they seemed able to keep the path smooth for her. It was a small mercy, one she'd gladly take as she didn't have much else going for her.

Come, Miri. Stay positive, and don't let him take you far. Keep him talking. "What do you really have against the Taelin? From what I can tell, they largely keep to themselves, only venturing out to trade with other groups. Who are they hurting?"

"As I've said, they're not natural. And they have the potential to corrupt others. They can turn whomever they will."

More like the forest could. She didn't think the Taelin could do any such thing without the consent and help of the Spirit of the Woods. She pretended to stumble over a tree root, taking a moment to "catch" herself and pause. Then she glanced at him. "If you're that concerned, why are you here where you can be turned?"

"Clumsy changeling," he muttered under his breath as he dragged her forward and onto another path that veered to the right. "My warriors and I aren't afraid of the Taelin. If they think to spread their hold to the humans, they are deluded."

She scoffed. "I've heard no such thing in my time here."

"Do you think they would tell you such a thing? They're not completely without sense, though it seems you are."

They were getting closer to the fighting, the sounds ever closer. However, they seemed to be taking a route that might skirt around the area rather than directly into it. She didn't know whether to be relieved or more terrified than before. She wouldn't show a smidgeon of fear in front of this pig, though.

She pretended to gasp and rub her side with her free hand. "Please, may we slow down? My Change has left me weak and easily tired."

Castin shoved her forward. "We can't afford to lose any more time. Move."

Damn it, Eerin, hurry up. She brushed the back of her hand against the trunk of a tree. She didn't know what she was expecting, but it certainly wasn't the message that streamed through her mind in a blaze of resolve not her own and froze her solid to the ground.

The trees...they were awakening slowly from their bespelled, sluggish stupor. In the meantime, they were more than happy to lend some of their magic. Suddenly, a jolt of foreign power flowed into her body, causing every nerve in her body to tingle. The sheer immensity of it ripped a gasp from her.

The world around her sharpened painfully until she swore it was nearly daylight in the Dark Forest. She could make out every leaf, every insect, that came within her sight. She could even see the puff of the lighter fae's breath as he exhaled. Everything was shaded in glitters of white.

"What is it now?" her captor asked, his tone laced with impatience.

Miri turned to him with a coldly brilliant smile, untold power and energy surging through her. "Nothing. I'm merely feeling quite recharged all of a sudden."

Castin's eyes widened, and he stumbled back a step.

The Spirit and Miri

Eerin raced along the dark trail, the whispering of the wakening trees telling him he was near. That Castin was, too. His two warriors followed close behind, torches still lit. His heart hammered swiftly against his ribcage, his feet pounding out the same quick tempo on the ground. A small magic light bounced ahead of him. He hated to use the energy, but he couldn't afford to slow down nor did he want his hands burdened down with a torch.

Though he tried to impose calm on his thoughts, his mind was consumed with thoughts of Miri. Oh, gods, had Castin already found her? Had Henry injured her in any way? The trees had given conflicting news. Their whispers were confused, as they were just coming out of the spell that had held them immobile.

He had to find Miri unharmed. If he didn't... No, it didn't bear thinking upon. She would be fine. Safe. There was no other circumstance he'd entertain.

A muffled cry ripped through his mind. *Miri!* By the Spirit, it'd come from ahead, from around the bend. Pushing his body harder, he sprinted toward the curve. Fear and adrenaline fueled him. He barreled around the bend and stumbled to a halt.

His mouth fell open, and he couldn't find the power to close it. Miri stood there, unharmed, thank the darkness. But that wasn't what caused his astonishment. No, it was what she was doing and to whom.

She had Castin hoisted up by the throat. With one hand. Her eyes glowed with a black light, and power, familiar power, leaked off her in waves.

By all that was unholy, she was somehow channeling the magic of the forest. The mighty strength of the Spirit flowed through her. Though the Spirit was in everything in the forest, it had now condensed within Miri. It permeated the crackling air around her, making the hair on the nape of his neck stand on end.

His guards made to draw their swords, but he held up a staying hand and shook his head. This was a precarious situation that would be best handled alone. With a wave of his hand, he dismissed them. Though they hesitated for a moment, they soon melted back into the forest.

He took a slow, wary step toward Miri. Such power was always better approached cautiously. Anxiety clawed at his gut. The sooner Miri was back to normal the better. Even if she weren't carrying his child, the strain on her body and mind would be immense. Mindjoining was exhausting, and this was far beyond that.

He shifted his eyes to Castin, who was still alive. He was held aloft by the scruff of his bunched-up undertunic, where Miri's grip squeezed it tightly around his neck. That had to hurt, but Eerin didn't have an ounce of sympathy to spare for the lighter fae leader who'd brought death and destruction to his woods. Castin's usually golden-tanned face was turning red, and his eyes bugged out.

Still, Eerin's hand clenched on his sword grip, indecision weighing on him like a shroud.

"Miri," he said, his voice gentle.

Her head turned toward him. Eyes, as wild and black as the forest, speared into him. "The lord of the Taelin. Come for our lady and to vanquish our foe?"

The deep, creaky voice that came from her lips caused a chill to speed down his spine. It was as ancient-sounding and fathomless as the forest. No hint of Miri lurked within that voice, which was concerning. That the Spirit called her *our lady* backed up his suppositions that Miri and he had been thrown together on purpose. The conception of their baby had been the result, but he'd never regret Miri coming into his life, nor their child.

He wet his dry lips. "I've come for Miri, yes, and the enemy is being routed by our soldiers. They will be caught before they can leave this forest."

A sound of pleasure rumbled in Miri's chest. "Good. They should be quashed like the bugs they are. We are in pain, and we demand recompense."

"Justice will be served. Please release Miri."

Her gaze flicked back to Castin. "Not until this one pays his due."

As much as he wanted Castin dead, he didn't want Miri's hands to carry out that sentence. She was a person of kindness and a budding healer. If she took anybody's life, it would shake her profoundly, more so because Castin, though he deserved death, was powerless against her at the moment. That she had no control over her actions at the time would matter little to her.

And that was only if she made it out of this alive. Her skin was growing paler, while the streaks of black under her skin glowed in the darkness. The power was too much for her body. He could see it in the ragged breaths she took that seemed independent of the Spirit's voice. Could see it in the fine trembling that had taken hold of her muscles.

With a calmness he didn't feel, he slid his sword from its sheath. "If you release him, I'll dispose of him. Please release Mir now. This is too much on her body."

Her head snapped toward him. "You think to tell me what to do?"

He wanted to scream *yes*, but he couldn't be that reckless. At least not yet. "Nay, but *I know* you are behind Miri being here, behind the evening that began our relationship. You need to release her before irreparable damage is done to her. You've entrusted much to the Taelin, made us your people. Let us continue that honor."

Considering eyes assessed him. "The forest is counting on *you*. Don't make us regret that."

He met the Spirit's gaze evenly, for he could do nothing else. "My people rely on me. They rely on this forest. Neither is a responsibility I take lightly. However, if I am to be the Taelin leader, Miri must remain unharmed." His ultimatum rested between, heavy and clear. He meant every word, too.

The Spirit's voice arose in his mind. "*Hmmm. We rely on each other. You don't know how true those words are. And yet, if left to your own devices, you and the Taelin would've failed our forest. Never forget the seeking of new blood. We need it to live, and so do you. You will remain the leader of the Taelin. I will it.*"

He ignored that last demand and instead concentrated on what she had uttered before it. Seeking of new blood? Could she mean... Half-formed thoughts and theories roared through his mind. Like the long-ago realization of the dwindling birthrate of the Taelin, which had always been shrugged away due to the nature of their nearly endless lives. When one lasted for millennia, what need was there for large families? Then memories of Miri, of the siren's call of her sweet blood, crashed over him.

Though most Taelin tried to suppress it, blood called to them in some of their more passionate moments. There were even those who experienced it during their battle lust. Ever since the Taelin had taken up residence in The Dark Woods, these urges were said to exist when their passions were roused. But with Miri's blood...its intoxicating properties that he'd only tasted once but still hungered for... He'd experienced nothing like it before.

A slow, sharp smile spread over Miri's mouth, and a chill slid down his spine. That smile was nothing like Miri's usual warm grin, but this wasn't Miri. No, it was merely the shell of her body. Hatred at that fact, and hatred of the Spirit at that moment, bloomed hard and fast in his chest.

"I see the dawning of your understanding," the Spirit said. "The Taelin take from the forest, and the forest takes from the Taelin. We give to Taelin, and the Taelin also give to us. Our sap is within your veins, and your blood is within our roots. But we both slowly grow weakened as isolated as we are from all others. We need renewal, and we will have it one way or another."

She stared at him for a long moment before fixing her attention back on Castin. "This body weakens."

Eerin's chest tightened because he didn't know if she referred to Miri's body or Castin's.

"One thing first," the Spirit murmured. She lowered the lighter fae onto his feet, where he slid to his knees, gasping for air and clutching at his throat. Her hands clamped around his head. "I would know what's in his mind."

Castin's face twisted in apparent agony, and his mouth opened in a soundless scream. Miri's trembling increased. Eerin wanted to grab her, to support her, but he knew he'd either be pushed away by the power coursing through her or make matters worse.

Eerin clenched his hands. "Release her immediately," he said, his voice thundering around them as he drew magic from the earth.

Miri's hands suddenly fell to her side. Her eyes closed before they slowly fluttered open. He sucked in a sharp breath. Her eyes…they were blue again and so confused looking. She swayed, one hand coming up to press against her forehead. He shot forward and caught her before she could crumple to the ground.

While crouched, Eerin swept his frantic gaze over her. She was breathing, but it seemed much too rapid. Gathering her securely into his arms, he stood up. He needed to get her back to the city and Eamandian. That crusty healer always knew what to do.

After he took a few quick steps, he froze. Castin! He whirled around. Castin wasn't there, and Eerin couldn't spy him through the trees. By the darkness' bollocks, the lighter fae had escaped. He couldn't be far, though. If the forest didn't stop Castin's flight, Eerin could send some guards after him. He just...

Eerin glanced down at Miri, who seemed more palish-gray than ever. That cemented his decision, and he set off toward the city at a brisk jog. Castin either would be caught, or he wouldn't. Right now, Eerin had to see to the welfare of his soon-to-be mate and the child she carried.

***

Eerin watched with hungry eyes as Miri's lashes fluttered against her pale gray cheeks. He leaned down closer, hoping to catch a glimpse of any other telling movement, no matter how small.

"Miri, child, wake up," Anthony said. He stood on the other side, clutching his daughter's hand. The man wore a bandage around his head, but other than that, he seemed no worse for the wear.

Eerin had to admit a grudging respect for the man. Other than being momentarily—and understandably—nonplussed by his daughters' Change, Anthony had accepted the truth in nearly the next breath. To him, they were still his children, not some freakish creatures to be repudiated and feared. Eve had been ecstatic at her reunion with her father. However, Miri's...illness, damn the Spirit, was weighing heavily on all of them. It said it wanted new blood but then turned around and nearly destroyed Miri and their child?

Next to Eerin, Innara clapped her hands in delight. "I think she might be coming around!"

Eamandian snorted. "About time. I don't know what she's been waiting for." The healer's brisk voice contained a note of relief that was telling. "I'd expected her to rouse an hour ago."

Eerin let his eyes slide closed. Heady relief poured like a much-needed balm over his frazzled nerves. For nearly two days, he'd prayed for Miri to awaken or to gift him with just one coherent word. Minutes ago, when she first squeezed his hand back, he'd shot out of his seat. The squeeze of her hand against his had been one of the sweetest things Eerin had ever felt.

He was hovering over her still. Would hover here forever if he had to. Though he felt wrung out and exhausted, he couldn't leave her side. He had already had to leave more than once since returning with her to the city. Though he trusted Alegion, who was acting as second-in-command, he couldn't abandon all responsibility to his people in their time of confusion and pain. More than one family had lost a loved one.

What was his grief compared to theirs? Miri still lived and the pregnancy still held, though several times Eamandian had believed they might lose the baby or even Miri herself. However, Miri's condition had taken a positive turn several hours ago, and now Eamandian was sure they would both pull through. Even now, tears welled in his eyes, but unlike last time, he didn't let them fall.

"Everyone back," barked Eamandian. "The poor girl doesn't need to come to consciousness with practically the whole city looming over her."

Eerin didn't open his eyes, though he sensed Innara, Anthony, Calieth, and a few other attendants inching back. "I'm not moving."

Eamandian huffed out a sigh. "Didn't expect you to. After all, no one is insane enough to try to remove you from her side."

"See it stays that way." Eerin flicked his eyes open, though they wanted to remain closed, and pinned the healer with a glower.

Eamandian and he had nearly come to blows several times over his continued presence at Miri's side. Eerin could eat and sleep later. Miri and his people came first. His own comfort scraped in last. Eamandian had only backed off when Eerin reminded him that Eamandian would be no different if Innara were in Miri's place. That had shut up the crusty bastard. Normally, Eerin would've taken delight in witnessing the healer's mouth snap closed. However, he couldn't find a flicker of satisfaction at the time. He doubted he ever would, not when it concerned the health of Miri and their child.

He glanced down at his beloved Miri. Now, it seemed as if his wait would be over in the next few minutes. It had to be. She had to awaken.

Rousing Miri

Miri was floating lazily, barely moving a muscle. In fact, she wasn't sure she even had a body, though she had the vague sensation of one. All she knew was that she could stay in this cocoon of darkness forever.

Suddenly, she froze. Someone was calling to her, beckoning her to come to them. Whoever it was sounded so far away. She kicked herself around, trying to place where the voice was coming from.

There! From above.

She could feel her frown. Since she'd awoken in this warm darkness, she'd avoided going too far up, where the surface awaited her. Somehow, she knew pain lurked up there. The tide—she didn't know if that was the right word for it—around her was warm and comforting.

Still, she found herself slowly swimming upward toward that horizon of light. It blinded her, and she glanced back at the darkness below her. But the insistent voice wouldn't let her rest. With a silent sigh, she forced herself upward once more. The closer she got, the brighter the light seared her eyes and threatened to split her head in two.

Right when she was going to give up and sink back down, a hand grabbed onto hers. Suddenly, voices and words became semi-understandable.

"—is working!"

"Get out of my way!"

"She's squeezing—" a masculine voice murmured excitedly.

That voice. It struck a deep, intimate chord within her.

"Miri, wake up!"

These voices. She knew them, didn't she? Why couldn't she recall the names of their owners, though?

A moan reached her ears, as did a pounding in her head that she suddenly became aware of. She gritted her teeth. That moan came again. Was someone sick?

"Medicine. Hand me the medicine."

A name broke into her consciousness. Eamandian? Who was he treating? Hands lifted up her body, which suddenly felt very real and very painful. Pain sliced through her head. She groaned. A horrible reality dawned. Oh God, that moaning was coming from her.

Something was pressed to her lips, and something cold trickled into her mouth. The urge to sputter choked her, and she coughed.

"Easy, easy."

She finally managed to swallow a few drops of the liquid without feeling as if she were drowning. Her throat now burned and tickled. However, after a few blessed seconds, or maybe minutes, that pain faded away with her headache. All the while those voices murmured around her, but she largely tuned them out.

Finally, once she could think coherently, she took a few deep breaths. Instantly, the unique smells of the halls of healing wreathed her nose.

What had happened to land her in here, though she couldn't quite remember what *here* was beyond it being a healing hall?

She scrunched her brow. If only she could remember. A hand tightened around hers. Instinctively, she tightened her grip, too. It felt natural, as if she'd been holding this person's hand all her life.

One name had come to her. Eamandian. Yes, Eamandian, that was it. He was here, and he wasn't...human. He was Taelin. And so...so was Eerin.

Eerin! Memories crashed through her mind, threatening to sweep her under a maelstrom of emotion. The forest. Henry. The sound of fighting nearby. And then... With a gasp, she forced her eyes open.

Blinding light pierced her right down to her eye sockets and sent an accompanying spiking throb through her temples. Disorientation slammed into her. "Too bright," she rasped.

The sound of a curtain being pulled shut had her taking in a deep breath and cautiously opening her eyes again. Her sight took several moments to come into focus. Even then, it was blurry, and an aura surrounded the first thing her gaze fell on. Eerin's face was haloed in a bright glittering white, yet she could still make out his features. How beautiful! It was as if little fairy lights crowded around him.

He appeared blessedly whole and unharmed from the battle.

His mouth moved, and a couple of seconds passed until her mind could process his words. "Miri, thank the Darkness you're awake. How are you feeling?"

She blinked. The haze around his face abated but didn't disappear. How was she feeling? "Out of it."

It was hard to talk. Her vocal cords felt rusty with age and her mind filled with cotton candy. Cotton candy...how she adored it and ... She frowned. No, that was not what she should be focusing on.

So what should she be?

Eerin, yes. Eerin and...the baby! She yanked her hand down to her stomach, only noticing then that Eerin's hand was still clasped around hers. "The baby?"

"The baby is well," he said roughly, stroking her cheek with the fingers of his free hand.

Tears of thanks sprang to her eyes. "You sure?" She didn't have the energy to form more than a few words.

He nodded. "Eamandian assures us all is well."

"Us?"

He hesitated and glanced at Eamandian, who was standing next to him and also bore an almost similarly bright aura. Eamandian merely lifted a brow at Eerin, who sighed and said, "Innara and me. But do you not feel your other hand being held?"

She stared at him owlishly. Other hand? Slowly, she flexed that other hand and found, indeed, it wasn't so free. She slowly tracked her gaze to the left side of the bed where— *"Father?"*

He patted her arm gently with his free hand. "Yes, I'm here now."

"How?" She drank in his beloved face, which also was ringed by that strange aura, though it was slightly dimmer than in the others. This was something to worry about later, though. Her reunion with her father was much more important. All she could do was stare as if he might disappear if she looked away. Maybe he would. Just like a mirage.

But he was a tired-looking mirage, then. His red-rimmed blue eyes spoke of a few sleepless nights. How long had she been out?

Eamandian pushed himself in front of Eerin. "Enough with the talk, people. Let's not overwhelm the girl. She needs a thorough examination and rest, not to be gawked at. No one listened the first time, but you all must leave. *Now.*"

Apparently seeing her pale at the mention of an exam, the healer shook his head. "This is just a standard precautionary measure I'd do with anyone under my care. Your child is fine."

"I'm not going anywhere," Eerin said, his mouth settling into a grim line.

"That's Miri's decision, *estinfanyo ritan.*"

Estinfanyo ritan. Lover boy.

Miri's lips twitched into a smile. Some things never changed, like the banter between the healer and Eerin. She'd be amused if she weren't feeling so overwhelmed, just like Eamandian had said. Her throat tightened. Good heavens, she adored them all so much! Her child still thrived and her father was here...and this all was nearly too much for her overflowing heart.

"Eerin can stay," Miri said, rubbing the back of her thumb over Eerin's hand.

Calieth and others headed toward the door. Her father bent down and kissed her forehead. "Rest. We'll talk later."

She didn't want to see him go so soon, but no one bossed Eamandian around in his own healing halls. Well, except for Eerin. She gave her father a wan smile. "Come back today."

"I will. I might even bring Eve if that is fine with your healer. Though on second thought, though, we have a lot to catch up on." His gaze swept over her and settled on her stomach for a moment. "I hear I'm to be a grandfather."

Heat sped up her neck and into her cheeks. She'd been too surprised about seeing her father and had forgotten about being unwed and pregnant. Now, however, it was hitting her full force. Not that she was truly ashamed, but still... This was her father! And her Change. Oh heavens, how could she have let that slip her mind? She must've looked like a freak to him. Still, he held her hand, touching her of his own free will, and she didn't detect any disgust.

"Yes," she said, her voice cracking.

He chuckled. "Don't look so alarmed at what I might think about the babe. I've already raked your young beau over the coals for it."

Young? Did he have any clue how old Eerin was?

A clouded expression crossed his face before it drifted away, and he smiled. "Truly, that you and Eve are both alive is more than I could've hoped for."

"But we've changed."

"You have, but that's something to which we can adjust." He bent down and kissed her forehead. "I'll be back later."

She watched him stroll for the door, her heart fuller than before.

***

Eamandian pushed his mobile instrument tray away. "I'm done here. Both mother and baby are looking well." He sent a look to Eerin. "Let's keep it that way."

Though Eerin huffed a bit at Eamandian's last words, she noted the easing of Eerin's tense shoulders. Miri let out a slow breath she hadn't realized she'd been holding. Though the healer had assured her that everything would likely be fine, finding out the examination had revealed nothing concerning was a relief. She really needed to mention the glowy aura thing, though.

She opened her mouth to speak, but Eerin beat her to it. "Good. You can leave now."

Eamandian held up a hand. "Not so fast, *estinfanyo ritan*. You may be leader of the Taelin, but I'm the leader of these halls. I will leave the two of you alone, but you *must* let her rest soon."

Her *estinfanyo ritan* nodded, a scowl darkening his features. "I understood the first time you mentioned it...twenty minutes ago."

Miri couldn't keep in her spate of laughter. "You're both hilarious, and I don't even think that you mean to be." Tiredness and apparently nearly dying left her tongue loose.

Both Taelin males stared at her, their brows raised high. Another chuckle escaped her. Somehow, she knew they were sniping at each other to release pent-up stress.

Eamandian bent at the waist, giving her a small bow. "Glad we could provide some entertainment."

"You certainly make a scene everywhere you go," Eerin said snidely to the healer.

Eamandian aimed a cool look at him. "You're one to talk, my lord."

"I'm powerful and handsome, so naturally I draw attention everywhere I go."

The healer snorted and turned away, pushing his cart with him. "Personally, I think the surly personality has something to do with it."

A smirk curved Eerin's mouth. "You would know, wouldn't you?"

"I might," Eamandian said with a toss of his head that sent his braided hair over one shoulder, and out the nearest door he went.

She shook her head gingerly, easing upward against the pillows. That cotton-candy feeling still lingered in her head, and she didn't desire a spinning room around her. At least her mouth no longer felt as if it were coated in sand, thanks to the surprisingly good medicinal tea Eamandian had given her. "You two are something else."

He slipped an arm around her shoulders and lifted her upright easily. "You shouldn't sit up for too long."

Miri groaned. Of course, overprotectiveness would have to be part and parcel of his personality. "If I have to lie down for another second, I'll cry. My muscles ache from staying in one position for too long."

He sat down on the bed abruptly and pulled her gently toward him. "The pain isn't just from lying abed for a few days." His jaw tightened. "What the Spirit did...it was nearly too much for you. That's in large part why you ache so much."

"You blame the forest," she said softly, settling into his side.

"The Spirit," he corrected. "It gambled with your life. That's something I can't overlook."

She snuggled deeper into him, a shiver coursing down her spine at the hazy recollection of the Spirit taking over her body. "What can you do about it?" She wasn't exactly pleased with the entity, either, but there seemed little they could do about it.

Except Eerin *was* tempted to do something... No, why was she even thinking this? She couldn't possibly know his answer before he said it. Pure craziness.

"Other than give up my position and leave the forest? Nothing."

Her breath caught in her throat as he repeated the words she'd just heard echoing in her head. "You wouldn't do that," she said weakly. Maybe she was still a bit more befuddled than she thought?

He slanted a look down at her. "I'd do much for you and our child."

She tried to get her mind working again, to stay on track. "Could we even survive outside the forest? I don't just mean surviving attacks from ignorant people." She frowned. Knowledge that she shouldn't have arose to the front of her mind. "To be cut off from the forest permanently means certain death to a Taelin."

"Not many have tried, but given none have come back, you are most certainly right. How—" He shook his head. "The Spirit has left that knowledge planted in your mind."

"I think so." Was this a good time to mention the other gift that the Spirit had left behind?

"What is it?" he asked, his tone laced with worry.

Damn it, he was too perceptive. "Though my remembrance is hazy at best, my eyesight was...changed when the Spirit overtook me. It still...isn't normal."

A strange look passed over his face as if he knew exactly what she might be talking about. "How has it changed?"

"Everything has a white glittering glow about it."

He sighed, which she swore she could feel right down to her bones. "I fear that might be a leftover effect of the Spirit's hold on your body. We Taelin can mindjoin with the trees and animals of this forest, and our...eyesight, for lack of a better word, takes on this quality, too."

"Will it go away?"

"When we mindjoin and break the connection, it leaves right away. Yours...was a bit different."

"You mean the Spirit took over my body." She bit her lower lip, not liking where her mind was going. "I was like a puppet."

He shivered against her and, instead of denying her assertion, said, "I'll never forget the moment I found you and realized what was happening. I never feared the Spirit until that second."

She frowned at the note she picked up in his voice. Then, as if she could sense his thoughts, the reason for it came into clear view. "It pains you," she said softly. "Not to trust the Spirit like you used to."

He jerked against her. "Can you read me so easily?"

Unease wound through her. "Not usually to this degree, though I've gotten better at it over the weeks we've been together. Now, for the last several minutes, it's as if I can sense what you're thinking at times." She paused, furrowing her brow at him. "Is this another effect of the Spirit?"

"I don't think so. At least not in totality. I'm...also sensing errant thoughts and emotions from you when they aren't shielded."

"Shielded?"

"If you shield, you can block others from hearing your thoughts and keep their thoughts and emotions from your mind. It's something that can be taught, and normally, I'm quite adept at keeping myself shielded. However..."

"Yes?" She leaned her head back on his shoulder so she could easily look up at him. Was he shielding himself now? She wasn't picking up anything now except for what she could glean from his body language.

"Part of it is that I'm emotionally and physically drained, so my shielding isn't what it should be. The other factor is...I believe we share the beginnings of a mindjoining."

"Isn't that what you do with trees and animals when you connect with their consciousness?"

"Yes, but among the Taelin, it often signifies a developing bond between a couple, unless the individual is unusually gifted in the arts of mindjoining. Even then, if such a gifted person can't control it around a certain person, that's telling."

Her mind swam with a plethora of questions. Tackle the easiest first. "Are you gifted?"

He shrugged one shoulder. "I have some affinity for it."

She'd take that as a yes. "So what does that mean for us?" This bond he'd mention?

He tensed. "It means we're compatible and have spent enough time together for our minds to start joining together...without our knowledge."

"Oh." She wasn't sure how she felt about that. *I like my mind being my own, thank you very much.* Suddenly, the white sheet covering her lower half was quite interesting, and she picked at it with a restless hand.

"As I said, we can shield," he said, his tone wary.

Her hand paused. "That usually works?"

"Most of the time unless you're emotionally distressed or physically injured." He hesitated. "Since you were human-born, though, I'm not sure how that will affect your ability to shield. If you can't, I'm strong enough to do it for both of us, unless, again, I'm injured or emotionally compromised."

Like they were both at the moment. Well, that was something. "And this mindjoining will allow us to communicate wordlessly?" She'd seen Innara and Eamandian do it but hadn't understood the mechanics of it at the time. She still didn't. It was so far outside her previous scope of what consisted of a "normal" human life.

"Yes, if we so desire." He tilted her chin up with two fingers. His serious eyes stared at her from under a furrowed brow. "Does this upset you?"

Her responses were causing him to panic, which she didn't want. "No, it's just a shock. I'm feeling overwhelmed by...everything right now."

Some of the tension melted from his body. "A lot has happened to you in a short amount of time."

"Yes, Eve and I losing the ability to return home, the Change, the baby—" She broke off as it hit her that Eerin had been blindsided by a lot, too. "The baby." It was her turn to regard him warily. "You found out about my pregnancy right before you left for the battle and suffered from your own shock."

His face remained impassive for a second and then he audibly swallowed. "It was a shock. At the time, I couldn't process the news properly, not when I was going out to fight for our forest."

Our forest. He viewed it as theirs, not just his. "And now?"

His hand slowly slipped low over her belly. "I've had time to come to terms with the news. I want this child. I want you."

Her throat grew as parched as a desert while her heart seemed to expand another two sizes. "You do?"

He nodded. "After you fainted in the woods, I feared losing you both. I couldn't even truly become upset that I seemed to be the last to know about the child. Though, there were a few times I wondered why you hadn't told me." When she opened her mouth, he held up a hand. "I'm wise enough to realize why you didn't and that you had tried to tell me on several occasions." He grinned wryly. "Innara also talked to me and set me straight about a few things."

Miri made a note to thank his cousin. "Thank the Dark Woods for Innara."

"Indeed."

She turned slightly toward him, as she was getting a crick in her neck from gazing up at him. "So we're having a baby and we're in a relationship? A committed one?"

She held her breath as she waited for his answer. The question had been a hard one to voice, but she had to know if they were at the same place when it came to their expectations.

A puzzled frown turned his lips downward. "Haven't we been in one for the last couple of weeks?"

"I think so?" Then she snorted softly at the absurdity of their conversation. They both had been ridiculous. "But we never discussed what we were to each other, and I was scared to try to press you for more, even if that 'more' was just a definition of what our relationship encompassed."

His mouth twitched into a smile. "It seems we have to work on our communication skills."

Eerin's hands came up to cup her face. He opened himself up enough to her that it stole her breath away. She didn't know what he was planning to do. Only that his intent was strong and life-changing.

Apparently seeing her reaction, he smirked slightly. "As to leave you in no further doubt as to the state of our relationship, will you do the honor of wedding me and joining our minds together fully, Miri?"

The Question

Astonishment froze her muscles, even her very breath. She gawked at him until she found one word she could utter shakily. "M-married? Joining our minds together fully?"

His fingers ghosted over her cheeks. "Yes, and since you are human-born, I know you're used to your mental privacy. You can be as shielded as you like. Even within the bonds of marriage, our minds will be our own when we desire them to be. This holds true for most Taelin couples. Most don't want to share their minds twenty-four hours a day."

She pulled back slightly, and his hands fell to her shoulders. Part of her wanted to fling herself at him, but another portion... "But how is fully joining our minds different from what we're experiencing right now? Or what Innara and Eamandian experience?"

"Not that much different other than the mindjoining link will become permanent."

"How?"

His gaze dipped down to her neck, and his tongue darted out over his lips before he glanced back up. "By the exchange of blood."

"Our blood?"

"Who else's?" he said with a touch of fond exasperation.

Instances of their lovemaking rose up sharply in her mind. "That almost biting you do...that's how we would exchange blood?"

"Yes, precisely."

Desire pooled low in her stomach. The idea of what he proposed wasn't as huge of a drawback as it should've been. And she'd be married to him, which was what she wanted but hadn't allowed herself to hope for in more than a passing thought. "I...yes."

"Yes?" he echoed, almost as if he were afraid he'd misunderstood her.

"*Yes!*"

"You're completely sure?" he asked, appearing adorably unsure.

"Yes!"

She wasn't sure who moved first, but their mouths met in a tender yet increasingly fiery kiss. Each swipe of his tongue sent her higher until he drew back with a groan. "You're still recovering. We can't let ourselves go too far yet."

She couldn't stop her pout, but tiredness was taking its hold. "You're right. Still, I want to get better right away."

He chuckled, shifting on the bed and pulling her sideways onto his lap. "Keep resting and listening to Eamandian. You should be back on your feet in no time, thank the Dark Woods," he added with a heated expression glowing in his eyes. "I want to wed as soon as possible if that's acceptable to you."

"In a few months' time?"

"A few weeks."

She blinked. "That's fast, but I guess I have no complaints. My father is here. It'd be nice if he could see us wed." She paused as a terrible idea hit. "He'll be allowed to stay until then, right?"

"Of course. He refuses to go, and the forest seems to accept him." His brow furrowed. "There are a few other people from your town that the forest approves of."

"You sound a bit worried." Some small measure of unease leaked from him, too.

His hand slid into her hair, where he slowly massaged her scalp. "The Spirit said something I've been puzzling out about how both the Taelin and the woods need new blood."

Since she'd closed her eyes in bliss, it took more than a few seconds to figure out where his train of thought was headed. When she did, her eyelids flew open, and she gaped at him. "You think these people are the 'new blood?'" What would that mean to her father?

"I don't know, but it's possible. It's not just a handful of men residing within the borders of Taelin lands, either."

"It's not?"

He shook his head. "A few young ladies from your old town snuck in after the enemy force, apparently wanting to see what their fathers and their beaus were up to. The forest rounded them up but didn't hurt them."

"What?" Already, she was groaning inside, and not just from the notion of her family and friends being "new blood," whatever that meant. There were some downright harridans and mischief-makers in her old town. A couple of possible culprits came to mind easily. Taerin would never be peaceful while these young women were kept here. If they were indeed here, that was. But she'd worry about that later.

"Do you know what the Spirit meant by 'new blood?'" Several different meanings ricocheted through her head, some slightly more palatable than others.

He smirked. "Though I'd like to think that she meant them as a sacrifice to the woods, I don't think that was what she was angling for."

She smacked his arm weakly. "My people aren't living sacrifices."

"Some were," he stated quietly. "Henry was one of them. The forest deemed him a serious threat and addressed that threat accordingly."

She flinched, her last memories of Henry flowing back. She hadn't had much time to think about him since then. Though his treachery was undeniable, the kind of death he'd suffered...

"Your heart is soft."

She nodded. There was no point in denying it. "Yeah, too soft."

"Nay, if anything, mine is too hard. You are the perfect counterbalance for me. A staying hand, if you will. We won't always agree, but your words will give me pause and make me consider all sides."

His words were a warm blanket over her soul. "I like the sound of that." Some of that fuzzy feeling faded. "What happened to the others not deemed a serious threat but also not accepted by the woods? Or were there not any?"

"They are in our holding cells and will be kept there until their individual motivations are uncovered." A mirthless smile twisted his lips. "We have ways to ascertain their truthfulness that range from painless and relatively non-invasive to those that are brutal on the mind and soul."

Miri shivered at the dark note his voice had taken on, but she didn't say anything. The measures he enacted to protect the Taelin and the woods would sometimes be harsh by necessity.

Eerin continued on, one hand ghosting up and down her spine. "If the humans trespassed and attacked us out of concern for you and Eve, most will be allowed to return to their town. However, if they were here for something more sinister, then a sentence will be placed upon them. The heaviness of said sentence will hinge on their motivations and if their actions resulted in any Taelin deaths or large-scale desecration of the woods."

"How about those who were here for Eve and me, but they might've also hurt the forest or one of the Taelin warriors?"

"We have Taelin trained in the mind arts who will ascertain if the human in question acted in self-defense or malice. What's revealed will be taken into account."

"Fair enough." It was more than she could've hoped for several months ago. Eerin being willing to spare a human life? That would've been an insane expectation when they first met. He was changing, whether he'd admit it or not.

She couldn't just concentrate on the people from her old town, either. "Did your warriors suffer many losses?" Her heart lurched at the thought of some of her new friends being injured or worse.

"There were a few casualties but far more on the human and lighter fae side."

Her stomach dropped at his words. So she might've lost people not only from the human side but also from the Taelin, too.

As another thought intruded, she grabbed his arm. "Lord Castin and the lighter fae? Did he and the others manage to escape, or was the forest able to detain them or...dispose of them?"

His features twisted into a scowl. "Some escaped with the aid of their stronger magic, Castin being one of them."

A shiver coursed up her spine. "He was creepy, creepier than even you were at the beginning."

A sound huffed from him. "I don't know whether to be offended or flattered."

She patted his chest and then smothered a yawn. "I don't find you that creepy anymore."

"I'm so glad to hear that."

His dry tone got a giggle out of her. Then she sobered. "Lord Castin seemed very interested in my Change. I think he and his people wanted to study me or Eve."

"Yes, we did extract that from the lighter fae in our custody."

Extract? She didn't want to know.

Eerin snorted. "They fear we have control over the process of the Change and are perfecting it. In all our long years in this forest, we haven't been able to harness it with any reliability."

Her eyes closed, exhaustion covering her like a blanket. "But they don't believe that."

"Of course not. They think we've been keeping the process from them."

"Do you think they want to harness it themselves?" she asked, leaning her head against his shoulder.

"That seems likely, but none of the lighter fae caught were of a rank to know anything more in-depth."

"None?" She felt her brows climb high.

"Those of higher rank either escaped or were killed by us or the woods."

"That seems convenient for the leaders of the lighter fae."

"Indeed."

She turned her face into his shoulder, tiredness pulling her in deeper. "Do you think Lord Castin will try something again?"

"If he does, he won't succeed. We'll be prepared if there's a next time."

"I trust you to keep us safe."

The hand on her back stilled. "By 'us,' you mean our people?"

She hummed a bit. "That, but I meant Eve, me, and the baby."

His lips were suddenly pressed to the top of her head. "Sleep. There's time aplenty to talk later."

He lay back on the bed and adjusted her until she rested securely against him. Then a light blanket was spread over her. A small smile pulled at her lips, and she sighed happily.

His solid body felt heavenly against her softer one, and his arms were a harbor she never wanted to be without. With that last thought in her mind, she tumbled into sleep's embrace.

Wedded

Innara eyed Miri critically. "A dash more rosy grayness to your cheeks, and you'll be perfect."

"You claimed that a few 'dashes' ago," Miri said with a good-natured laugh, shifting in her chair and obediently turning her face toward Innara again.

Though Miri was chatting and joking with the ladies surrounding her, nerves churned her stomach. She was about to wed the Taelin she loved. Not a huge deal, right? Only the whole town was gathered outside the tent where she and her attendants were primping in. Well, not just the whole town. Taelin from a few far-flung settlements within the forest had also arrived for the momentous occasion.

Calieth adjusted the circlet of glittering, translucent fairy flowers on Miri's head. "The petals on these bring out the blue of your gown."

"They do, don't they?" Miri smoothed a hand over the fabric covering her knees. "I still can't believe these flowers are pollinated by faeries. I haven't seen one yet!"

Calieth cocked her head to one side, taking in her handiwork. "They're shy creatures and will show themselves to you when they're ready, which I think will be very soon. That they offered up some of their precious flowers speaks highly of their regard for you and Eerin."

"Well, of course, they think well of Eerin. He's their leader."

Calieth and Innara traded a look and burst out laughing. "Only one of their own can rule the faeries," another attendant added.

"So there's a faerie leader?"

Innara dabbed something fragrant on Miri's wrist. "They have a queen who's the cutest little thing. She has the loveliest wings that are rose-colored at the base and then fades into violet. However, she had quite sharp teeth. They all do."

Miri blinked. "What is it with all you fae creatures and sharp teeth?"

"Taelin teeth aren't that sharp, are they?" asked Morgan, one of the young ladies still being kept in Taerin. She'd been one of Miri's friends and had taken Miri's Change with barely a bat of an eye. It'd seemed natural to select her as one of the wedding attendants, of which she had seven. Miri narrowed her eyes, focusing on her friend. The glow around Morgan was particularly vibrant today, white with pale-blue glitters. Interesting.

In the last few weeks, her little "gift" from the Spirit hadn't abated. If anything, it was deepening, giving each living thing its own distinctive aura. But she was also getting used to tuning out that "extra" sight when she didn't want to be bothered by it. Several of Taerin's mages had been most helpful in that regard.

Miri aimed a smile at Morgan. "Sharp enough when they're going for your neck."

Morgan shook her head, sending her auburn curls bouncing, while she arranged a bouquet of flowers. "Like a vampire?"

Chuckles from the Taelin women sounded around the tent. "Maybe one day you'll find out," Miri said.

" I don't know about that. If this forest ever lets me leave, I plan to be an old maid back in our Knocton."

Calieth pouted. "That's so boring. You need a beau!"

Morgan's eyes flared wide in seeming panic. "*Ah*, that's okay. You keep your beaus to yourself. Males are more trouble than they're worth."

Miri frowned. So Morgan was still nursing her broken heart or, at least, her bruised pride. When she'd found her betrothed, Ben, in bed with another woman six months ago, she'd been devastated. Especially when she had just given said betrothed with her virginity.

Morgan's bitterness had continued to grow, though, which was concerning. Miri worried for her friend and cursed Ben yet again.

Why hadn't she punched the ass when she'd had the chance? At least, she'd gotten to tell his family, who *adored* Morgan, of his misdeeds. The last she'd heard, they were still quite upset with him, especially since he'd married the other woman not long after Morgan discovered the affair.

Maybe it was a good thing Morgan was stuck here for a while until they figured out what the forest wanted with her and the others. Eerin said he'd try to return them to Knocton after the wedding, but he didn't know how successful the endeavor would be if the forest was opposed to it. And right now, the forest wasn't telling him much.

"Hello, may I come in?" Miri's father called from outside the tent.

Miri glanced around. Everyone was dressed, so it seemed safe enough. "Yes, come in."

Her father slipped past the loose flap. When his gaze fell upon her, his eyes brightened. "My dear, you look lovely. Never has there been a more beautiful bride."

A pleased flush heated her face. She stood up, crossing over to her father. "You're looking quite handsome."

He was resplendent in a silver Taelin tunic embroidered in a silvery blue thread that caught the light. Matching gray pants and black boots rounded out the outfit. Even the salt-and-pepper effect of his hair echoed the mood of his clothes.

With a grin, he gave her a gentle hug. "*Psshaw*. Nothing can outshine you on this day."

She squeezed him back. "Thank you."

"If only your mother could see you." A sudden gleam sparkled in his eyes, and he blinked rapidly. "You've turned into a wonderful young lady...soon to be leader."

Miri grimaced and released him. "I'm still not used to that last part, but I really do love the Taelin. They're as much my people as the people of Knocton are."

"You're up to any challenge."

They chatted for a bit longer, and Miri didn't miss the looks that one or two of the Taelin maidens were giving her father. She smothered a smile. It was no different in Knocton. He was a handsome man and had weathered the middle years of his life with grace.

Any lady would be fortunate to land her father as a husband, but so far, he'd been disinclined toward any female companionship. He'd loved his wife, her and Eve's mother, fiercely. Still, she'd bet her last herb that he had lady friends with whom he took pleasure. He had charm aplenty when he wanted, and good looks to sway most heads. He wasn't rich by any means, but neither was he poor.

Truthfully, the man needed a wife since neither she nor Eve could return permanently to Knocton. And with her getting married and Eve growing up... Well, she'd see what she could do.

After a few minutes had passed, another voice spoke from outside. "It is time for the ceremony to begin."

Miri released a slow breath. "I'm ready."

Soon, with her father by her side, she was walking over a delicate bridge. The ceremony was taking place on a small raised island, which was clearly visible from the shore. The head mage, Lady Muriel, stood by the arbor that had been decorated in faerie flowers and would perform the marriage rites.

As soon as Miri's feet stepped onto the island, Eerin stepped out from behind the arbor. Her breath caught in her throat. He was dressed in a blue that matched her gown. His long hair flowed free over his shoulders, not tied back into a braided ponytail for once. His tunic could've graced a king. He sure wore it like one. And those leggings... She swallowed thickly. They clung to the strong muscles in his legs. Both she and Eerin had been so busy for the last few weeks, they hadn't seen that much of each other and had fallen into bed, exhausted, each night. They hadn't indulged in each other since the battle with the lighter fae.

At first, she'd been healing, and then there were the preparations for the wedding and all the usual day-to-day activities to oversee. The townspeople that were still in Taerin had taken up quite a bit of Miri's time as well.

Now, however... She had huge plans for their wedding night, where they would privately perform the true marriage rite, the exchange of blood that would connect them even more deeply.

Eerin glided forward and took her hand in his. Everyone else ceased to exist as he guided them to the arbor.

Lady Muriel came to stand before them and started to speak, but Miri only half-heard what was being said. She managed to reply at the appropriate times. Eerin was leaving himself wide open to her, and he was suffering from the same problem, the same delightful disorientation.

The ceremony passed by in a blur for both of them, and her father joked they were halfway married. He wasn't so far off the mark.

There was feasting and dancing as soon as they arrived back on the shore, but neither she nor Eerin wanted to stay for long. They talked with guests, humored and danced with Eve, and smiled until they thought their faces would break. After they consumed the barest of morsels, they escaped to their bedchamber during a rare lull.

They paused on the threshold. The room was aglow from carefully placed lights, flowers, and other luminous things she couldn't even guess at right now. All she knew was that it was beautiful.

"Not as beautiful as you," he whispered next to her ear, apparently picking up on her loud thought. Tonight, neither had any control over their mind-sharing.

She shivered at the heat that coated his voice. "You know what would be beautiful?" she asked huskily.

"What?" he asked with a catch in his voice.

"You and me, naked. In the bed. On the floor."

He gave a groan of pure need and pulled her to him. "You're a wise woman."

She waggled her brows at him. "And totally healed."

Without another word, he scooped her up and carried her to the bed. Their clothes were discarded in record time. She pressed him down onto the mattress and nuzzled his neck. "Who goes first?"

"I don't think it matters."

A bout of nerves took up residence in her stomach. "You go first."

He framed her face and captured her lips in a searing kiss. After he released her, he deposited her onto her side. "Let me ease you into the rite."

His thumbs feathered over her throat, sending her desire up a notch. He bent his head and nipped gently at the curve of her shoulder. His mind touched hers, amplifying the need coursing through her veins. Or was it through his?

Suddenly, the smooth bite of sharp teeth pierced her skin, and she moaned. What he was doing didn't hurt. Whatever inherent magic he possessed stopped any hurtful sting. Though she could feel the sensation of teeth, it only aroused. Both her desire and his mingled in her mind, in the pit of her stomach. The lick of his tongue over sensitized skin shuddered through her. Her hips bucked against his as they mimicked the motions of lovemaking.

She wasn't sure how long his part of the rite lasted, but all too soon, he was lifting his head. Seeing him lick his lips was one of the most erotic things she could've ever imagined.

He lay on his back and spread his arms out to the side as if offering himself to her. "I await you, my lady."

She crawled over him, nerves twisting in her stomach. What if she hurt him? Her teeth weren't that sharp. Not like Taelin teeth.

"I'll be fine," he said softly. "Take a bite of me wherever you want. Whenever you want."

Okay, that was definitely sexy. She nosed her way down his neck, taking in the intoxicating scent of him. Hers. It was all hers. As she was his. She settled for roughly the same spot where he'd taken his "bite."

As she gently licked him first, he quivered under her. His erection was now impossibly long and thick, pressing against her thigh. She set her teeth to his skin and slowly applied increasing pressure. After she detected no wince, she pressed harder. Just when she feared she wouldn't be able to break the skin, a warm, slightly salty taste filled her mouth. It wasn't as bitterly metallic as she'd feared it would be. In fact, the sensation of it hitting her tongue caused lust to shoot like liquid fire through her veins. His mind flooded into hers. Or maybe her mind flooded into his. She couldn't really tell where one began and the other one ended. Not at this moment.

His words came sharp and clear to her as if he were saying them out loud, though he sounded as drunk as she felt. *And we...we l-likely won't be able to separate ourselves until we join o-our bodies and t-thus settle our minds.*

Belatedly remembering how he'd swiped his tongue over the wound, she did the same. Moaning reached her ears, and she froze as she realized the sound was coming from both their mouths. After a few more swipes, she lifted her head, feeling as if she'd drunk two more bottles of the finest wine.

They both stared cross-eyed at each other before they chuckled lowly. Soon, however, all hilarity left them as they joined their bodies, and their minds joyously followed along.

Afterward, they collapsed into a sweaty heap on the bed. Miri stroked a finger over his chest. "I can still feel you, but now I feel more like myself, though the sensation is still a bit overwhelming."

He sighed into her hair. "It'll abate in the next few days as we learn how to handle the bond. That's why all people undergoing a marital mindjoining are granted a week's leave from all duties."

She grinned. "I can think of a lot of things to do during that time." She projected an image of what she wanted to try next.

His brows climbed, and then a delighted smile crossed his face. "Well, we better get to work, then."

###

ABOUT THE AUTHOR

Lisa Kumar is a wife, mother, and romance writer who grew up in small-town Indiana. She now resides in the suburbs of Chicago with her husband and son, who are used to sharing her attention with her not-so-trusty computer. When not spinning tales of romance and fantasy, she can be found with her nose buried in a book, or more accurately, her e-reader. Her scholastic background is in psychology, which enabled her to get low-paying jobs in the human services sector. She's now writing full-time.

To learn more about Lisa and her books, visit https://linktr.ee/LisaKumar

Once there, you'll find links to Lisa's newsletter and Readers' Group.

Bound to the Elvin Prince
Mists of Eria, Book One

College student Cal Warner spends a good portion of her time trying to keep people from thinking she's crazy. She just wants to finish college and live a normal life. Whatever that is. But her carefully constructed reality is turned upside down when she discovers that Relian, the seductive elvin prince who has been starring in her sensuous fantasies, isn't merely a myth. Now she's bound to an elf and stuck in a magical land where no one, least of all Relian, is willing to spill any answers about the truth of her arrival.

Relian has lived a life that hasn't changed in millennia, and he likes it that way. As Prince of the Erian people, he has his conscripted duties. And a human woman, even one as desirable as Cal, does not fit into them. But as the enemy darkindred knock on the borders and the magic of his people fades, he might just have to find room. The only other hurdle? He has to make her fall in love with him so she'll tie her life to his—forever.

Excerpt

Relian led them down a steep ravine, one side dwarfed by a small cliff face. After hopping from his mount, he lifted her down from hers. He grabbed her hand and pulled her to the looming stone. Laying his free hand on a thick tree trunk that rested in front of the rock face, he murmured in Elvish again. Then he repeated the same procedure on the gray stone. Neither spell seemed to do anything. What was he doing? Their pursuers were sure to find them, even with the cover the branches provided.

As if to back up her thoughts, cursing voices carried on the wind. Relian stiffened but didn't move. Just as Cal was about to pull on his arm, the tree suddenly bent to the side. A faint orange-colored outline of a door glowed against the gray stone.

Cal blinked to make sure her eyes weren't deceiving her. Relian placed his hand against the makeshift door and pressed.

With a groaning sound, the rock moved, revealing a shadowy corridor lit by floating blue lights.

"Come," Relian said, pushing her toward the door.

Cal hesitated, her feet digging into the ground.

He sighed impatiently and pointed to the entrance. "Safe." Then he gestured toward the canopy of trees where the angry voices floated ever closer. "Not safe. Now go."

Closing her eyes, Cal plunged into the opening. No lightning struck her down. She opened her eyes. No bogeyman charged toward her, either. Relian said something to the horses, and they neighed, shaking their heads. Then he stepped in beside her and shut the door with a handle she now only noticed. "The horses?" she asked. Though fear stilled clawed at her, she didn't want the horses to be hurt.

"They go back to palace. Will be fine."

She nodded, easily following his short, simple sentences after a few seconds of thought. Relian reached for her, and a flash of something red on his arm caught her attention. Squinting, she saw there was a gash in his sleeve, with a matching slice to his skin that still had blood welling from it.

She gasped and lightly touched the area below the wound. The damp fabric was tacky from the blood. Not used to touching such things, she had to stifle a shudder. "You're hurt."

He shrugged, not seeming fazed at all. "A mere flesh wound from arrow. Nothing at all. Will take care of later."

That was a mere flesh wound? She'd be rigid with pain if she sported that slice. But he was a warrior for a reason and had probably dealt with much worse. Which was a thought she didn't want to dwell on because when she did, an invisible fist squeezed her heart.

https://books2read.com/rl/Lisa-Kumar-Books

Bound to the Dark Elf
Mists of Eria, Book Three

Liar, murderer, traitor...these are all names Eamon has been called, and he wears them with pride. Depending on which side one falls, those titles are only too true. But it's all part of his orchestrated manipulations. Up until the day he was banished from the fae land of Eria, he had schemed for millennia to protect his people, even resorting to murder. As punishment, the Erian king exiled him on Earth to live amongst the lowliest creatures of all—humans. Yet one frustrating and captivating woman shakes his ingrained beliefs to the core.

Newly minted physical therapist Caralyn Alberts has been drawing images of a handsome, otherworldly stranger for as long as she can remember. She's chalked it up as a fluke occurrence of life. But when she finds the arrogant Eamon sprawled out on the ice at a local park, her life becomes just as slippery and dangerous as the hauntingly familiar elf. Enemies, friends, and unwilling partners inundate them from all sides.

When Eamon's treacherous past makes a reappearance, they'll have to trust each other in order to keep their hearts—and their very lives—intact.

This series will be a crossover with The Faerin series. Kaiden and Ashlee from Crashing into You, which is the first Faerin book, appear in this story

Excerpt

His gaze alighted on something that backed up his drive for sex, and he froze. Skimpily clad statue-like forms stood in the display windows of one of the stores. Never before had he seen such undergarments — or had the pleasure of removing them from a warm and willing female. Could he...

Raking an assessing glance over Caralyn, he nodded. Yes, she'd look quite fabulous in that intimate wear. And he'd get to unwrap her like one of Santa's presents.

Caralyn stiffened, her expression morphing into one of horror. "Don't even think about it."

"Too late," he said cheerfully. He finally had a clear mission—one he'd take delight in fulfilling.

She backed away from him, holding her hands up to ward him off. Eamon chuckled and grabbed her wrist, pulling her toward the store.

***

Caralyn yanked against his hold. "Let me go, you creep." She furtively glanced around to make sure no one was watching them.

He paid her no heed. Since she was leery of making a scene, she gave up her ineffectual struggles but walked as slowly as she could.

Damn him, he had her cornered. The smug grin he threw back at her showed he knew it, too. And she had to go along with it. She'd seen the way he'd glowered at Santa and his merry elves. He'd looked as if he were about to hurtle himself at them like a bowling ball, so she definitely wouldn't trust him now if some bystander or security person became involved.

Maybe it hadn't been wise to enjoy poking fun at him so much. She'd forgotten he would make her pay for it—and it appeared her IOU had come due.

Eamon led her into Whispers, and it seemed every pair of feminine eyes snapped to them. The women's gazes slid right over her and lingered on Eamon in a way that turned her blood into liquid fire. Didn't they see he was with her? Never mind that they weren't really together — when a man entered an intimates store with a woman, the expectation was that he was in a relationship with said woman.

Though it pained her to admit it, Eamon had a model-perfect face and an air that commanded attention, even when he was dressed in sweats. So she couldn't totally fault the women, but she didn't have to like it. She— *Wait.* She wasn't jealous, was she? No way. Sure, his attention was flattering at times because he was superbly good looking. But her worry merely stemmed from wanting to get him out of her apartment as quickly as possible. She didn't need him involved with someone who might only further mess up things.

But her reasons didn't quite hold up. First, if he did meet a woman who he was interested in, Eamon could move in with her. Second, his prejudice would probably stop him from having any kind of relationship with a woman besides a one-night stand.

Eamon drew her over to a rack of lacy bras and matching panties. After inspecting them, he picked up an ivory-colored set that had delicate blue snowflakes and held the pair up to her. She shied away, an embarrassed flush working its way over her face. Oh, God, he was visually measuring her.

Once they were back in her car, she'd kill him. Happily with a smile on her face.

Eamon chuckled and addressed the sales associate who was sauntering up to them. "My girlfriend is so shy. Isn't it adorable?"

The tall blonde nodded, barely glancing in Caralyn's direction. "She's beyond adorable." Her tone left no doubt that she meant Caralyn was cute like a puppy, not a sexy woman.

"Do you need any help?" the lady asked Eamon, looking at him through her lashes. She gave him an obvious once-over, and she paused as she took in his sweat pants. A slight frown formed between her brows, but when she returned her examination to his face, it cleared instantly. A star-struck gleam entered her eyes that seemed to mirror every woman's there.

Caralyn wanted to smite the harlot into next year, but Eamon merely smiled charmingly at the woman and shook his head. "Not at all, thank you."

After his polite yet pointed rebuff, the sales associate's lissome body stiffened. "Have a good day," she said woodenly.

A traitorous relief stormed through Caralyn. Though he'd put her in this position, at least he wasn't going to flirt with other women in front of her. For some reason, that was a comforting thought she really didn't want to explore.

Eamon closed the space between them, shaking the set in front of her face. "Dearest, I think you'd look stunning in these. And it's your size if I'm not mistaken?"

She blinked and then blinked again. Was she dreaming? He'd called her dearest. Though she knew he was only doing it for the benefit of their audience, she never thought he'd go that far.

Before she knew what she was doing, she'd reached out a hesitant hand so she could glance at the tags. "Yes."

How'd he known? Had he really been with so many ladies that he could guess their proportions? Or had he snooped through her unmentionables? Both were a disturbing thought, though for totally different reasons.

He cast a wicked smile her way. "Wonderful. We'll take these, then, and enjoy them tonight."

Heaven help her, but heat coursed through her body at his words. She shifted to disband the sensation and kept quiet. He wasn't making this easy. At all.

Apparently not satisfied with her level of mortification yet, he said, "I'll love unwrapping you like a present."

Her face flamed even brighter, and she grabbed his arm. "Let's go get your clothes." Her voice came out plea-ridden.

"After we make our purchase here. We don't want to return home without these." He raised the bra and panties higher, probably to show the whole store, the ass.

She snatched them from him, glaring and mouthing *I hate you*.

He merely waggled his brows at her, so she stalked toward the registers. Of course, he followed like a burr stuck on her butt.

Once they vacated the store, she shoved the sack at him. "Here, I believe you wanted these."

"I'm afraid they're not my size."

A groan of frustration ripped from her throat. "We need to get your clothes before I change my mind and you leave empty-handed. It'd be no more than you'd deserve."

"I love it when you talk dirty."

She rolled her eyes skyward and plowed on ahead of him.

https://books2read.com/rl/Lisa-Kumar-Books

The Fae Lord's Companion
The New Earth Chronicles, Book One

Six years ago, a fae raid stole away Lina's parents. Since then, she's managed to scrape together a decent life with her grandparents. But that happy, simple life is shattered the day the arrogant Sidhe lord who took her parents returns...and claims her as his mistress. Though she vows to never stop plotting for her freedom, she can't deny the otherworldly pull between them.

Lina. The human that the fae lord Gabreon couldn't forget. Though something in her spirit had sparked his cold soul, Gabreon knows too well the heartache attachments can bring. When he sees Lina again, he can no longer ignore the longing she ignites in him. Though claiming her goes against everything he was brought up to believe, he takes her as his companion. During the day, she holds herself away from him. At night, however, she flares to life in his arms.

As a human revolution ferments, his growing relationship with Lina becomes even more perilous as enemies seek to use her against him. Will he be able to earn her forgiveness and love? Or will they both perish before either has a chance to achieve what they so long for—Gabreon his redemption and Lina a sense of freedom?

https://books2read.com/rl/Lisa-Kumar-Books

Printed in Great Britain
by Amazon